A GOOD DAY TO DIE

A GOOD DAY TO DIE

a novel by
DEL BARTON

1980
DOUBLEDAY & COMPANY, INC.
GARDEN CITY, NEW YORK

ISBN: 0-385-15667-7
Library of Congress Catalog Card Number 79-7794

*To those who lost their
world and are no more—
and
to those of us who must
now exist in two worlds—
our hearts in the world of
our fathers and our feet
in the world of our conquerors.*

FOREWORD

This story is true.

Every person mentioned within these pages lived—and I have portrayed the way they lived as accurately as I can (after nearly twenty years of extensive research and countless hours of listening). I make no claims to absolute accuracy in all details.

This book is history, but I classify it as a historical novel because history demands documentation and the history of this period was recorded by the white man.

I classify it as historical because I believe that even the experts will agree that the events of my story did occur.

I classify it as a novel because the white man recognizes no truth that is not documented and redocumented.

I say it is true because this is the story of an Indian, and it was told to me by persons whose veracity was impeccable and whose memories were unfailing.

Most of this story was told to me by Gray Wolf himself. The remainder was told to me by several of those who knew him and shared many of his experiences.

This book is first and foremost a tragedy played out in the mountains, plains and deserts of a vast country writhing in the labor pains of a new nation, heralded by the trumpets of a cavalry charge, the bellow of "Wagons ho!" and the spat of rifle fire.

It is a romance, kindled in the tinder of mistrust and fanned by the futility of vengeance.

It is a biography of a man endowed with all the virtues of his race and possessing a sense of duty, discipline and unimpeachable integrity.

It is a history of a man who was the product of a people in

their death throes, caused by a corruption called "civilization"; a man trained from childhood to play the part of a prince—without a principality.

It is a narrative of a people who were dispensable because they were an obstruction in a stream of insatiable greed and the hunger of haunted dreamers.

It is the story of a people—my people—who once were, and are no more!

Del Barton

A GOOD DAY TO DIE

1

Crying Boy had not moved a muscle for many hours. He sat with his thin haunches resting lightly on the backs of his shabby moccasins. His bony hands were clasped lightly over knees that doubled up to just under his chin. His gaze was fixed on a point in the dim distance at the far side of the basin.

He had held this position since early dawn. Now the sun had set and the crimson western sky gave its deceptive light to the land below. It was near the end of the day, and Crying Boy was near the end of his endurance. He prayed fervently for the sight of a moving speck that would tell of the arrival of the warriors. If they did not appear soon he would have to end his vigil—if not because of darkness, then surely because his aching muscles would refuse to take this punishment longer. He would have to change his position or fall over the rim of the cliff.

Thinking about it, he decided to fall rather than relinquish the honor he felt he must have obtained this day. Crying Boy was sure that the people had noted his great fortitude. He could not, would not, endure a failure by moving before absolute darkness or the arrival of the warrior band. Every muscle in his body cried out for the relief of movement. Crying Boy sat on.

He had looked upon fourteen summers, and he still carried his cradle name. It was humiliating. It was more torment than this daylong vigil that he had imposed upon himself to draw attention to the fact that he was no longer a boy. To have fourteen summers upon his head and not yet a man's place was almost more than he could endure. He was a man without the distinction of manhood.

The fact that there were other boys, some even older than he, who had to endure the same situation was of no comfort. It did not ease his pain in the least. Crying Boy's misery wanted and tolerated no company. It was personal and it was mighty. Each time he had pleaded with the elders to be allowed to perform his *hanblecheyapi*,[1] they had shaken their heads and refused. Crying Boy knew why. There was only one reason—the reason was *Wasicun*.[2]

Crying Boy had never seen a *Wasicun*, although he had heard about them all of his life. Whenever two warriors met, the talk always turned to *Wasicun*. Everything in life was regulated by *Wasicun*. All the old ways and the old customs were modified because of *Wasicun*. Boys were forced to remain boys, performing the small duties of boyhood long after they should have been apprenticed to warriors, all because of *Wasicun*. Crying Boy had never seen one of them, but he hated them.

When he had been very small and had cried in rage against something that had not suited him, thus earning the despised name he now bore, his grandmother had threatened to leave him where *Wasicun* could get him. Crying Boy had known that this was the worst thing that could happen to a boy. He knew that they ate little boys and in fact preferred boys to any other kind of meat. He had heard the women whisper, especially after some gross disobedience, how the *Wasicun* roasted little boys over slow fires, and how the pitiful cries gave them great pleasure. When he had been small he had believed those stories and they had frightened him. Now that he was a man, he believed those stories and they angered him. In fact, his anger was so great that he had long ago abandoned the pleasant games of boyhood and devoted most of his time to practice with his bow, his lance, his slingshot, knife and tomahawk. He practiced riding, too, but he was never allowed out of the valley.

Crying Boy longed to leave the valley. He yearned to see the rest of the great world. He ached to be allowed to continue stalking a deer when it went over the rim of the mountain. But it

[1] A dream that gave a boy his name and the status of manhood.
[2] White man.

was forbidden. *Wasicun* prowled the mountains and roamed the plains and forests. No boy of the village was allowed to leave the valley alone. No boy had enjoyed such permission for as long as Crying Boy could remember. They were forced to remain boys long after the time when they should have been riding with the warriors, learning firsthand the arts of warfare. These days a boy had to await the notice of some warrior who would plead his cause at council and ask for him as an apprentice, and a boy could sometimes wait a long time. It was difficult to get a warrior to notice one's accomplishments and even more difficult to move a warrior's heart.

The very thought of such injustice made Crying Boy clench his teeth and a tiny muscle twitched in his cheek. The small violation of his self-imposed ordeal angered him more and he forced his mind to the discipline of concentrating on each muscle in his body until it relaxed into easy alertness. He had done this at least a hundred times this day and he determined not to allow his thoughts to betray him again. It was useless. Bitter thoughts kept haunting him. He knew that the cause was fatigue, but he would not allow himself the luxury of giving up.

My belly dislikes its emptiness, he thought as the aroma of roasting meat wafted past his eager nose.

But I won't think of being hungry now. Today I will prove I have taught my whole body obedience. It may not earn me a name, but it will prove I can endure much. Maybe when they ride out again I will be riding beside them. I will not be waiting for them to come back, standing in line to take a bridle rope.

The thought gave strength to his weary legs and his mind slackened its intensity of concentration to wander over his various accomplishments. He could not think of any single thing he had neglected. He could place an arrow as true and as deep as many of the warriors. Naturally, he had never been allowed to compete against a warrior, or even a brave, but he had watched their matches and he could equal the skill of many.

They knew it, too, for the warriors always watched the boys compete, but not one of them had ever said the words he had worked so hard to hear. No one, in fact, except Curly Fox had ever spoken about his ability at all. And Curly Fox's opinions did not matter in the least. Oh, Crying Boy had been happy to listen when Curly Fox would boast of his best friend's skill, but Curly Fox was scarcely older than himself. Besides that, he was lazy. He didn't care whether or not he ever became a warrior. Curly Fox spent his time playing games or his flute and was never concerned in the least that every boy in the village bested him in shooting, riding and wrestling. Curly Fox simply was not ambitious. He was lucky when he was able to draw a bow strongly enough to bring down a small deer. He was more than lucky when he could draw one true enough to use but one arrow. So Curly Fox's boasting did not count, despite the pleasure it gave Crying Boy to hear someone laud his abilities. No, he decided, there was no fault to be found with his archery.

He calculated each phase of his riding ability. He could mount his pony from a standstill, from either side or the rear, and have the animal in a dead run in three jumps. He could guide him without even the jaw rope. He could slip to, hang by one leg and place an arrow by shooting under the pony's neck. He could dismount lightly and not lose his footing even before the pony slackened his pace. No, there was no fault to be found with his riding.

Crying Boy reviewed his accomplishments objectively and critically. He could recite not only the legends of the Dakota, but also those of his mother's people, the Seneca, and make no error. He could throw a knife the width of the stream and sink the blade deeply in a pine. He had lain with a woman—in fact, done so four different times now—and, if Sparrow Woman was to be believed, it had taken at least three cups of herb tea to prevent her from going into retirement for at least nine months. Sparrow Woman had told this to Crying Boy's mother, so it must be true. Both women had giggled and looked at him sideways, but, even though he had been greatly pleased, he had given no indication that he had heard their talk. But they knew he had heard. They had meant that he should and it had helped acknowledge his manhood. But women's acknowledgment was not a warrior's acknowledgment.

Why, he thought, I could probably sire any number of sons right now if it was permitted for me to marry.

But such a thing was not permitted. No man less than a proven warrior could think of marrying, but Crying Boy was not interested in that restriction. He was not interested in women, except for Sparrow Woman's lodge, now and then.

Thoughts of the misery and the delight he had known in that place sent a tingling through his loins and the pleasure lured him into reflections on the times he had visited there.

The first time when his father had taken him, he had been terribly shy and a little afraid. But Sparrow Woman knew her work. She was a widow who had refused to take another husband, and so tutored the boys of the village in the basic arts of manliness. She had been gentle and patient that first time and she had guided him in the ways a man must be toward a woman. He had left her lodge with a feeling of acute embarrassment and no little disappointment. The anticipation had far exceeded the reality, and he had been unable to appreciate what the older boys had seen in it. But they had reassured him.

"We all felt the same the first time," they had said. "Don't think about it. Next time it will be better."

And they had been right. It had been better and the last time he had gone he had not wanted to leave. Sparrow Woman was patient and she had allowed him to stay for just a little longer than before, but she was also firm and warned against excesses. He decided that tonight as soon as full darkness set in and his ordeal was over he would go to her lodge. He didn't feel that she would be inclined to deny him all the time he wanted after the feat he had done today. Maybe, he thought, he might stay the whole night. Maybe.

His buttocks hardened and pulled upward in a convulsive gesture.

Across the basin there seemed to be a slight movement among the gray shadows. All thoughts of Sparrow Woman's lodge disappeared and alertness drew his eyes into narrow slits. He watched. The tiny movement separated from the shadow and became a thin line. It moved slowly out onto the basin floor, pointing directly toward where he sat.

Crying Boy stood up. His legs trembled under him. He raised numb arms skyward. Faces around the cook fires turned to look at his tall, thin silhouette against the darkening sky. Over the valley there rang the long, low welcome wail of the Dakota and far down on the floor of the basin an old and weathered warrior heard the faint echo and smiled.

The moon rose high over the tip of the old, scarred pine on the eastern rim of the valley. Fires were burning and cook pots steamed unsampled in the cold, clear air of the mountain. Not a child was in his blanket. Only babes in cradleboards slept. An air of quiet suspense and composed excitement gripped even those so young that a full belly, a warm bed and frolic with playmates seemed to be the whole of life. The usual squeals of childish laughter and the confusion of tumbling young bodies darting around the cook fires were stilled. Only an occasional muffled giggle slipped between small fingers pressed against irrepressible merriment, to be met with a soft but firm "hist." The village awaited the return of its warriors.

Waning Moon and Small Owl stood side by side, each pulling a protective blanket over the evidence of their expectancy. They were foster sisters and they waited. Willow Twig stood a little apart from the rest of the girls her own age. Her marriage had been delayed by this absence that was now over, and she watched the trail that disappeared over the edge of the west rim. Old Crooning Woman stood, bent and gnarled, her sightless eyes blinking rapidly, her mouth slightly open as if to catch some sound her ears might miss. And all along the trail the boys sat, squatting on their heels, ready to leap at the sign of the first horse, each anxious to be handed the rope of an esteemed warrior's pony. They did not speak. They knew that soon they would see their fathers, their brothers and their uncles—or they would be told that they must never speak a certain name again.

Crooning Woman turned her head ever so slightly. Everyone noticed the small movement. They depended upon Crooning

Woman, with her sightless eyes and aged ears, to see and hear sooner than anyone else. The moonlight softened the old, wrinkled face and illuminated the toothless smile that started at the edge of her puckered lips.

"Huh," she grunted softly.

The waiting village was graven in listening. The soft plod of unshod hooves sounded—and over the edge of the rim came the first rider.

Red Cloud, chief of his clan, sat his horse proudly, silhouetted against the twilight of the early evening. He pulled the laboring pony to a standstill and looked into the upturned faces, hating his role as chief. He wondered why it had been his desire to be a leader, and what it was that had led him to this moment. He wished that he could stay where he sat, keeping the line of warriors behind him and the sight of riderless ponies away from the eyes that looked back at him hopefully, expectantly, trustfully.

He saw Small Owl and pushed his glance past her—not too quickly, not too slowly. His heart hurt within him. Small Owl was very dear. There too was Willow Twig, and among the other women her mother, Yellow Bird. They too were dear to the chief of this band of Teton Dakota. But were they not all dear to him? Was it not easier to be a simple warrior? It would have been preferable to Red Cloud to have had his own pony riderless than to look into these faces he loved so well. Had he been a *Wasicun* the great chief would have cursed profoundly, if only to himself. But the Dakota tongue knew no profanity and there was no verbal relief for the heartache that possessed him. There was no relief for the weight of these days when it was impossible to observe the decencies of either life or death.

His band here in the remote valley, instead of being of one family as was the age-old custom, was peopled by members of many clans and many families. And his fallen warriors, instead of being brought back to be placed on proper platforms raised to the sky, were now buried under a distant layer of earth where *Wasicun* vandals would not be likely to come upon their places of sleeping and desecrate their slumber. This was a time when the beauty of life was sometimes difficult to disentangle from the bitter visitation of disaster that had befallen the people with the coming of the *Wasicun*. And there was no relief that one could foretell. The white plague came on and on in ever-increasing force and frequency.

Red Cloud raised his face in haughty obduracy and sprang lightly from his horse.

Behind him, one by one, they rode up into the valley. Directly behind Red Cloud rode old Bending Bow, too aged to ride the warpath, but too wise, too cunning and too experienced to be allowed the luxury of his woman's fire when warriors were so badly needed. Demonstrating his agility, the old man swung a leg over the pony's withers and leaped vigorously to the ground. At the sound, Crooning Woman grinned a great, toothless smile. Her sightless eyes glowed.

"Old fool! Acting like a young buck! He'll break a leg one of these days," she muttered.

She turned and trotted off toward her cook fire, needing no hand to guide her.

One by one they came over the rim and at each appearance another woman's face would change its quiet expectancy to happy softness, and she too would hurry away toward the cluster of lodges and fires.

The men walked slowly in single file after their chief, their weariness showing through the stiffness of their backs and the high elevation of their chins. Red Cloud went to stand before his own lodge. He folded his arms across his massive chest and stood, eyes looking deep into the nothingness of despair.

A rider appeared, heeling his own mount, one arm back, pulling on the lead rope of a riderless pony. Small Owl clutched her blanket closer. Waning Moon reached out a gentle hand, but Small Owl's chin raised and she pulled away. The moonlight reflected the glitter that suddenly appeared in her lovely dark eyes. She turned toward the winking fires, but her feet had lost their lightness.

One by one they came. Twenty-eight riders—and four riderless ponies. The warriors gathered before Red Cloud. The women returned to their fires, holding their children about them. Small

Owl stood alone. Willow Twig moved very close to her mother, doubly bereaved. Both her lover's and her father's pony had been riderless. Waning Moon's eyes were fixed in bright gladness on the back of a very young warrior standing in the semicircle before the chief.

Red Cloud's voice came, deep and resolute.

"Hear me, my people," he said. "We rode from our camp to meet with those who invade our land and our men fought bravely. But hear me and hear me well! We did not win! We are few and they are as many as the grasses of the plains. They carry fire sticks that make death as far as the eye can see. We would like to tell you that your men have driven away our enemies. But we cannot tell you this. We did not win. There are many of them who have gone to their fathers, but we cannot boast of this. When we would send one on the cloud trail there would be another and yet another to take the same place. We did not win! We did not drive them from our lands, so we cannot say to our women, you need not be afraid anymore. But our men fought bravely and hard and we have returned tired and our spirits are weary, for we have not returned victorious. When we left you five sunups ago we were three times the fingers of our hands and two more. We have returned to you with four fingers missing. Now hear these names for the last time, and from this moment let no Dakota speak them again lest a loved one be disturbed and restless in his new land."

Red Cloud raised his arms skyward.

"Lame Dog," he shouted, "you fought bravely and well until there was more need of you where you now live. Blue Feather! You counted coup before any of us and more often until the warriors in the Cloud Land knew they could not do without you. Young Stag! You took four of the enemy with you and no doubt even now are making them wish they were not there. Big Horse! You smiled as you left us. Your arrows stopped more than one."

Red Cloud lowered his arms and looked directly at the people.

"Let us eat and rest to renew ourselves in the love of our families so that we may gain strength of body and wisdom of mind to avenge those lodges that are lonely this night."

The men turned to talk together as they moved toward their own fires. Women stirred kettles and chucked wood into flames. Boys wrestled one another and girls giggled. The quiet of the village was broken by the sounds of life and living. Activity stirred the dust in front of all but four of the lodges. The fires in front of three of these were deserted and the flaps were dropped. But Small Owl did not move. She stood alone, looking fixedly at the tip of the old pine.

Morning Dew's action belied concentration on her work. She had turned resolutely away from the stricken look in Small Owl's face and given her whole attention to her own husband, who had returned grievously wounded. She had appraised the ugly bandaging that had obviously been applied hastily by another warrior and had returned to her fire to replace the stewing meat with a kettle of water and strong healing herbs. Red Hawk had given no indication that his wound troubled him, but Morning Dew knew her husband well and she had known that he had suffered greatly when he had leaped lightly to the ground. She worked, not listening to Red Cloud's words. She knew them without hearing them and it seemed that if she did not hear the chief call out the name of one of the departed warriors she would not yet have to feel the pain of the loss of another one of her sons. Her hands were quick preparing the herbs for the kettle. Secretly she felt that a speedier balm to her sorrow would be screams of despair and anger at life, which had already robbed her of five of her six sons. But she did not dare publicly to lament her loss. Pride in herself and her own people restrained any action that might bring shame to her husband. She had lived long enough among these stern Dakota to know how severely they frowned on intimate maternal relationships.

Had she been a woman given to rebellion, Morning Dew would have balked at living here among her distant cousins. She was a Seneca woman, reared in gentleness toward her family and her husband, and obedient to a love that was too great to ask a man like Red Hawk to live among her people, who were scattered to the four winds or confined to government agencies. The Senecas as a people and the Iroquois as a nation were no more. When she had married she had relinquished the custom of having her husband become a member of her clan, and she had come with him to live with his people, who were still free. And if at times the Dakota way seemed stern and rigid she never indicated it. She held her head proudly over the penalty of her love for her man, and she had relinquished her sons to other women to be reared and trained and loved until they had become warriors. And then she had relinquished them one by one to death, without an outward cry of the anguish she felt.

She fed her fire with steady hands and allowed her eyes to seek out the figure of her last and youngest.

Crying Boy was standing at the edge of the group of warriors. He was listening with all of his attention to Red Cloud's words. Morning Dew's heart gave a shudder of sorrow. How eager this last of her sons was to become a warrior. She thought of this day and how he had sat on the edge of the rim refusing to move a muscle—proving himself. And tonight there were more warriors missing from the band that was already lacking men. In spite of all her prayers, Crying Boy was going to enter his apprenticeship before another sun would set. She knew in her heart that it would be so and she knew too that each time the warriors left this valley, she would suffer as she had always suffered, until their return.

Crying Boy was moving away from the circle. She saw him looking toward where Small Owl stood, stiff and straight beside her dying fire. She could read the boy's thoughts. He was thinking of the ancient custom that allowed a brother to take the widow for his own to protect.

No! No! Morning Dew tried to force her own thoughts into the boy's mind. You are far too young. You cannot hope to snatch manhood from boyhood.

He was so headstrong. He was so impatient. How many times she had heard him beg to start his apprenticeship. How many times her own heart had pleaded silently for refusal. She watched him across the campground and knew she could keep him safe no longer.

He was walking now, trying desperately to keep from running

toward Small Owl's lodge. Would Small Owl accept him? Somehow Morning Dew knew that she would in spite of his youth, in spite of his inexperience, in spite of any disfavor it might incur. Was Crying Boy not the brother of the gallant Blue Feather? Was he not the playmate of Small Owl's childhood? Was this boy not the best answer to the child-bride's agony? Morning Dew knew that between them Small Owl and Crying Boy would defy their elders and win their cause because of an ancient custom that had not been followed for a long time. Morning Dew saw him approach Crooning Woman, who had also started toward the stricken girl. She saw the old woman shake her head. She saw Crying Boy talking earnestly. Then, together, the boy and the old woman walked to the girl, who had not yet even seen them approaching.

Red Hawk groaned a little as he eased himself to the pile of skins spread in front of his sleeping couch. His pain made him oblivious to everything but the poultice and the herb tea Morning Dew had ready. He sat back and closed his eyes as she tenderly removed the filthy piece of rawhide and washed the torn flesh. After it was cleansed and poulticed he sipped the strong tea she held to his lips. He was very sleepy.

"Where is my son that he does not come and greet his father?" he asked.

"He has gone to Small Owl," she answered, keeping her eyes down.

"What is this?" Red Hawk was plainly startled.

"He has gone to Small Owl," she said again. "I think he will be staying in her lodge tonight."

Red Hawk struggled to sit up. Gently she pushed him back.

"Is he so soon a man?" Red Hawk dropped back, too exhausted to protest.

Was he indeed? Morning Dew thought of the restless nature of her youngest. She thought of the long hours he had spent in practicing with his weapons. She thought of how he held his gangling body and how he walked, clenching his fists to make his arm muscles bulge to look bigger than they were. She thought of the look in his eyes when the warriors rode without him. She thought of the times he had pleaded to be noticed, and she thought of her love for him—a baby who was a baby no more.

"He is now a man," she murmured gently.

Crooning Woman hobbled about her fire and hummed the tuneless little song that had given her her name so many snows ago that she had lost count. She tilted her head, birdlike, as Bending Bow came to the fire.

"Huh," she grunted softly, "and how long is it since you have eaten your fill?"

"As long as I have not looked into your lovely face," he replied.

He touched her arm gently. Her sightless eyes looked straight at him and then turned questioningly toward the quiet area of Small Owl's lodge. Bending Bow understood his woman well.

"All right, little bird," he sighed. "Ask her if you will. I think maybe I am not yet too old to provide for one or two more."

Crooning Woman darted across the stretch of hard-packed earth. A hand reached out and touched her arm. She stopped.

"Thank you, Grandmother." Crying Boy pushed his voice down to its deepest tones. "I would eat at my sister's fire tonight if she will hand me meat. Will you speak for me?"

"Crying Boy!" The old woman's voice cracked in astonishment. "Has your mind taken a walk? You are not yet even a brave."

"I am not yet a brave, but that is not my fault. I am a man and I am my brother's brother. It is my right."

"What is your right is only your right when you are man enough to make it your right." Crooning Woman's voice was full of disapproval.

"I am man enough." Crying Boy was stubborn. "I make it my right."

"You know the penalty if you fail?" Crooning Woman wrung her hands with agitation.

"I know the penalty. Speak for me, Grandmother."

"Ah-h-h." Crooning Woman bobbed her head. She seemed to be considering. "Times change. When I was a girl no boy dared assume the duties of manhood without proper preparation."

"When you were a girl, Grandmother, a man was not kept a boy after he was ready," Crying Boy said. "This is my right. It is the law."

"It is an old law."

"A law is a law, old or new. The elders have said this many times."

"Yes, yes." Crooning Woman clasped and unclasped her hands. "And I do not think it will make the people happy if I consent to speak for you. But it is true, a man is a man when he does a man's duties," her voice turned sharp, "and carries them out."

"I will carry them out, Grandmother. I will not fail."

"I do not believe you will." The old woman made up her mind. .

She seemed to consider only a moment more, then reached out and took Crying Boy's hand. They turned and walked to Small Owl.

"You are welcome to my fire, child," Crooning Woman said gently. "But Crying Boy has asked me to speak for him. You do not have relatives to help you. I will be your relative. But this boy has asked by the old law. I advise you against it, but I ask for him."

Small Owl had been unable to comprehend her abrupt bereavement. The sight of her husband's riderless pony had propelled her shocked mind into stoic seclusion. Only her heart thudded spiritless messages of anguish.

Little more than a child, she had been married less than a year to a man she not only loved, but idolized with all the passion of adolescence; her husband had been to her a tangible god who had sanctified her existence in a way she both understood and cherished.

She was Cheyenne, orphaned before her memory, rescued by the Dakota from a massacre and brought back to this valley, where she had lived her life in the lodge of adoptive parents. Although she had never lacked the profuse devotion lavished upon her foster sisters and brother, she had endured a vague and mysterious yearning for a more kindred alliance. Her marriage to Blue Feather, one of the most handsome and accomplished young braves in the village, had satisfied that yearning. Her spirit had radiated her enchantment with her destiny. She had been a happy bride and she had been a happier wife. He too had been well content with his choice and they had been the most popular pair in the village. He had only recently earned his status of warrior and this had been his first real raid.

Youth had flowed too strongly in them to harbor thoughts other than the wonder and beauty of life. They had gaily anticipated all the promise of their days. Their world had been a blossom-strewn arena and life a great wrestling match in which he was undisputed champion and she his proud and appreciative audience. Their love and pride in each other had been a constant source of delight to everyone. Theirs had been a marriage that had brought smiles of approval from the settled and sighs of envy from the young.

In spite of her youth, Small Owl had tended tirelessly to her duties. Her lodge was always spotless, her skins a perfection of softness and her cooking passably palatable. Her beadwork was a model of loveliness in design and her husband had displayed the finest regalia in the camp. She had taken intense pride in fashioning finery to enhance his natural charms. Mercifully she would never know that it had been the exquisite medallion which he had been loath to remove from his neck that had been the irresistible target for the keen-eyed recruit behind a broken barrel.

It had never occurred to her, or to him, that a capricious fate could ever prove him mortal and claim him.

Small Owl stood beside her lonely fire, unable to understand that it had been done. Some of the enormity of her situation seeped through her imprisoned emotions when that gentle Medusa, Crooning Woman, spoke the words that voiced her widowhood. She knew that the old woman was being kind and that her offer to share her fire meant that the old woman was asking her, Small Owl, to become old Bending Bow's second wife. A shudder went through her and panic pushed her heritage into revolt. Mutely she screamed out the name of her beloved. She possessed a childish inability to refrain from her act of sacrilege. Selfishly she clung to her priority on his being. Silently she screamed out again and again, Blue Feather! Blue Feather! Help me! Do not leave me! And from out of the limbo of his lifelessness he came and took her hand. A faint, quavering smile played around the corners of her lips and she was hearing Crooning Woman's voice saying that Crying Boy was asking to take his brother's place. She felt Blue Feather press her hand in approval. She opened her eyes and her voice was faint but firm.

"The meat is ready," she said.

The pressure on her hand was more firm. She looked down. Crying Boy was holding her fingers in his cold palm. He loosened his hold with a self-conscious gesture and let her hand drop.

"My heart is glad," he said, gulping over the words.

Small Owl ladled some of the steaming stew into a bowl. She kept her eyes averted. Crying Boy wished she would at least look at him and at the same time was pathetically grateful that she did not. He had felt so sure of himself. He had been elated when Small Owl had accepted him. He had never before in his life felt so proud, but he had tried not to show it. He had tried to walk about the fire casually as other warriors were doing at their fires. He had succeeded only in feeling self-conscious and very, very foolish. The inspiration to grab at this opportunity at manhood had carried him to the heights of exaltation. The reality of his success appalled him. He decided that he should sit down. He could feel the stares of neighbors and he was no longer sure that they were admiring stares. He felt as if they might be looking straight into his heart and seeing that it was acting in a very strange manner. It felt as it did when he ran very fast for a very long time. There was also a disquieting feeling rising in his belly.

Directly in front of the lodge flap was a fold of skins. It was the place of honor where the man of the lodge sat for his supper.

Crying Boy looked at it. He was the man of this lodge now. He took a faltering step toward it and the uncertain feeling in his belly turned into a vicious cramp. For a fraction of a second he was certain that he saw his brother, Blue Feather, sitting there where he had sat so many times. Crying Boy almost staggered the few steps to the side where he had always sat when he visited at his brother's lodge. He dropped to the earth. He did not see the small smile of satisfaction that hovered in Small Owl's eyes. She came to him as if it were perfectly normal for him to be sitting on the bare earth. She held out the bowl of stew. He took it from her and his hands were shaking. She pretended not to notice. He was grateful to her for the courtesy.

I must not allow myself to feel like this, he thought. A man does not act like a child. I thought I saw something and it made me afraid. Men are not afraid. Only boys are afraid and I am no longer a boy. I am a man—a man with his own woman. I did not see my brother's ghost. There is no reason for it. I have done an honorable thing in taking his widow so that his child will not be a stranger to his father's people.

He caught his thoughts quickly. He must not allow himself to think of his brother. He must think on what Red Cloud would be likely to do as soon as he learned that Crying Boy was sitting at a dead warrior's fire. If he did nothing tonight, then everything would be all right. Once he had spent a night in Small Owl's lodge there was no changing the fact that he was her husband. And a husband was expected to provide for his family. No one could deny him the right to ride with hunting parties at least. And a hunting party was almost always a war party. There were too many *Wasicun* to avoid it. Maybe Red Cloud would be too weary and too preoccupied with his own thoughts to notice before it was too late. He wished he might forgo the formalities of supper and go now into the lodge. With the thought of spending the night as the man of the lodge, the cramps coiled again in his belly. He became conscious that Small Owl was looking at him. He had been holding the bowl and had not eaten. It was the last thing he felt like doing in spite of the emptiness of his belly, which had fasted the entire day, but it was impossible for him to say so. His throat gripped his voice into silence. There was nothing to do but eat. He dipped his fingers into the bowl and shoveled a great chunk of meat into his mouth. It was burning hot. The impulse to spit it out was almost overwhelming, but he already felt a complete fool. He hung onto the chunk. It was too big to swallow and too hot to chew. It burned. His eyes filled with tears of pain and rage. He held them wide to keep the humiliating flood from showing.

Small Owl turned her face away from his shame. When he could, he chewed carefully and concentrated on the food to keep himself from feeling more of a fool. When he emptied the bowl, Small Owl promptly filled it again. He was utterly unable to refuse it. He continued to eat. When he had emptied it a second time, she refused to notice and his gratitude was great. And then he was angry at the gratitude. His emotions were getting completely out of hand. Things were not going at all the way he had visualized them. Instead of feeling truly a man, he was feeling more and more like a boy. Instead of feeling like a savior to her, he was feeling more and more like a child she was pampering.

Nearly everyone had left the supper fires, and flaps were being lowered for the night. Crying Boy found that he was no longer anxious to enter the lodge. He almost hoped to see Red Cloud coming across the campground. But there was no one in sight. He had eaten far too much. His belly was by now in actual revolt. He was afraid to move. If he was going to be sick here for all to see, he knew that he would walk out of the village, over the mountain, and let the first *Wasicun* who came along kill him mercifully.

Small Owl went inside. He could hear her feeding sticks into the small lodge fire. He wondered again what she might be thinking. She had not said a word to him since she had offered him meat. He wondered if she too was sorry, especially since he had made such a spectacle of himself with the meat. He tried to think of something that would be proper to say to her, but his thoughts refused to walk a straight line through the mountains of his emotions. Vaguely he felt that he must be experiencing fear.

The meat in his belly climbed the ladder of his throat and spat sour accusations into his teeth.

He remembered another time and another fear. He and Curly Fox had sneaked away to the bank of the creek. Curly Fox had had a pinch of his father's tobacco and they had rolled it in leaves and were smoking. They had tried to outdo each other by drawing the smoke deep into their lungs as they had seen the elders do. Neither of them would admit—then or ever—the results they had both been feeling. They had been startled and relieved, in spite of their alarm, when Curly Fox's second father had spoken very close to them.

"What is this?" he demanded harshly. "Are you now men who have learned to pray that you dare sit here and blow smoke to the four winds?"

They had known that they were doing wrong, but somehow the discovery of their sin had magnified the transgression. For many days after the incident both boys had been very careful of their behavior. They had both expected some terrible punishment from some unexpected quarter at every moment. Who knew what thing they had prayed for by blowing the sacred smoke indiscriminately. It had been a bad time for them, and Crying Boy remembered how his belly had cramped and been unhappy with food at that time. When many days had passed without disaster after the smoking incident, Crying Boy had gradually begun to feel better. He had then been convinced that the angelic behavior he and Curly Fox had practiced had somehow given them a reprieve. Then, just when they had decided that everything was all right after all, the storm came. The lightning had been terrible and since the thunder and the lightning were spirit brothers to Crying Boy, he knew they were angry. They had struck the old pine on the mountain and started a fire in the forest that drove away all the small game the boys had been allowed to hunt. For the rest of that summer there had not been so much as a squirrel at which to aim an arrow. And Curly Fox and he had known that they were to blame. Curly Fox's second father had nodded his head wisely at them and said, "See what happens when young ones do not heed good advice from their elders?"

And they had felt miserable for a long time because not only they had no game to hunt, but neither did any of the other boys who were innocent of wrong.

Crying Boy wondered what kind of misery this act tonight might bring upon the village. He recalled the threat in Crooning Woman's voice when she had warned him. He wished now that he had heeded advice and been content to remain a boy until the proper time. But it was done and there was no way to undo it. He, Crying Boy, had a wife and she was inside the lodge waiting for him. This was no sport of short duration in Sparrow Woman's lodge. This was real. He was glad that Small Owl's condition meant that he would sleep on his own couch for a long time to come. He did not know how he would ever face being a real husband. Why was his belly acting so badly? He could understand why it had done it when he had smoked. That had been a bad thing. But this thing he was doing was a thing of honor. Were honor and virtue then so much like crime and guilt? Certainly they seemed to have the same effect on the belly.

A small voice spoke in his ear.

"Your sleeping couch is ready."

He jumped. He shook all over. His heart pounded and his hands grew cold and wet. His mouth went dry and his tongue refused to moisten his lips. The most difficult thing he had ever done was to get to his feet. Although he did not know it then, Crying Boy would never again in all his lifetime feel so acutely the despair of heroism.

"I do not understand how it is I even spoke for him."

Crooning Woman lowered the flap of her lodge with a snap. "That boy has no more than fourteen summers on his head. He has never even been on a hunting party. If it wasn't for Small Owl's condition it might be different."

Bending Bow settled back against the sleeping couch and stretched his legs to the fire. His toes wriggled comfortably inside his moccasins, saluting the warmth.

"No one ever expected the boy to take his brother's wife," Crooning Woman snapped. "It isn't as if no one offered her anything else. I was there. Crying Boy didn't have to say a word. I don't think he was thinking so much of doing an honorable thing as he was thinking of a way to make the council apprentice him. I would have been glad to have her in this lodge. You need warmth in your old age."

"Hist such foolish talk, woman," he scolded mildly. "What would I want with a young wife? Have I ever desired another woman but you? And as for that, when did you ever leave me energy for another wife?" Bending Bow grinned wickedly.

"Huh," she agreed, delighted at his words. "You speak truth. I have always been a selfish woman, but I have been frolicsome, haven't I? But selfish or no, you should never have listened to me. A man of your standing should have had several wives. It hasn't been right for you.

"Besides"—and now it was her turn to grin wickedly—"if you had insisted, I could have always kept them busy kneading buffalo hides while I kneaded yours."

She cackled her glee. When he did not reply she continued. "I've wanted you to take another wife for a long time now and you know it. But you have always said no. So it is your own fault if you have to turn to the fire now for your warmth."

"Yes, yes. You have been willing and even anxious for me to take another woman since I have lost my appetite and my ability," he answered shrewdly. "But, I tell you truly I am well content that Small Owl has a young buck to share her blanket. It will make her forget her sorrow that much quicker."

"Huh," she agreed.

"I am a content man," he said.

"My heart is happy to hear you say this." Crooning Woman felt for his shoulder and, finding it, settled down by his side. "But," she said, "I should have seen to it that you had sons to go on the warpath in your place so you could sit by the fire as you have earned."

"I have had my sons," he said, "and it is no fault of yours that

I do not have them now. It is the times that have denied me that comfort, not you, little bird."

"I still think the young people are forced into too much too soon," she said. "Just think on it—Crying Boy—what a name for a father!"

"He will get his name in time." The old man moved to rearrange his aching bones. "Everyone in the village knows where that boy is sleeping tonight. He has assumed the responsibilities of a man and he has done it in an honorable way. It won't go unrewarded. Red Cloud will not deny him."

"Ha," she said triumphantly. "That is it! If Red Cloud allows Crying Boy to take on manhood without proper initiation there are others, even older than he, who can and will demand the same privilege. And, Red Cloud will have to grant it in all justice. You have said it to me many times, that the mountains and the plains are full of *Wasicun* who want nothing more than to kill us all. You have said many times it is unwise to allow an inexperienced boy outside the valley."

"I have said this," he answered, "and it is true. I am more than glad that it is Red Cloud who is chief of this clan and must make these decisions. I feel it much better for my peace of mind to sit here by this fire and listen to you chatter like a jay. But remember this, woman, while you are criticizing Crying Boy, I was very little older myself when you opened your blanket to me."

"And you remember, old man," she retorted sharply, "you were an exceptional man. And it was quite a different thing. It was a good many moons before you were forced to sleep in your own blankets. I was a bride and I spent no little effort in pleasing you with your choice. I was a good bride, wasn't I?"

Her voice was wistful with remembering. He laughed and pulled her gently to him. He tugged at the grizzled braid that hung over her shrunken breast.

"You were a fine bride, little bird. You were a fine bride. But those were the good times when a man could take a bride and spend his nights enjoying the blankets. These are times when a man must spend most of his energies stalking meat. Those were

times when meat was plentiful and there was little fear of the
Hungry Moon. These are times when the nights are for sleeping
with the ears awake. These are the days when men are as scarce
as game and they become more scarce all the time. The young
ones must grow quickly to fill the empty places. They must face
things we never knew when we first shared the blanket. Crying
Boy is a man and tonight he is proving it. All we can do is wish
him well and be proud that our people sire such sons. I think
maybe the reason you fret overmuch is because you are getting
lazy and want a young woman that you can order about to do
your work for you."

"You speak in fun," she said. "Wasn't your meat ready for
you? Do I not have a full bag of herbs always in my lodge?"

"True, true," he answered and pulled her head back to rest on
his shoulder.

"You are a good wife and I want no other. You do all the
things a good wife does for a man—and you do them better.
These young ones could learn much from you. But I cannot help
but wonder what kind of witch's work it is that keeps you so
young and beautiful while I grow old and ache in my bones."

Crooning Woman giggled like a girl and nestled closer. Bending Bow smiled knowingly into the fire and the flames winked
back and snapped merrily. He pulled a long draw on his pipe
and sent a great billow out to mingle with the wood smoke. The
two wisps intertwined and spiraled upward in a conspiracy of
contentment.

The soft slap of the flap dropping behind him sounded louder
than thunder in the chaos of Crying Boy's mind. He saw, and yet
did not see, Falling Leaf, the "Old One" of the lodge. She sat
hunched beside the fire. She did not look up. She was not a
blood relative. She had been chosen by Small Owl and Blue
Feather when they had been married, since no Dakota lodge was
complete without a "grandmother." Because she was not a blood
relative, Falling Leaf was free to mourn openly and she stayed
inside the lodge, her pipe cold in her hands, her eyes closed
against the reality of the day.

If she had heard what had taken place outside the lodge she gave no indication. She followed the rigid rules for Old Ones: she respected her place and gave no advice until asked. No one had asked for advice, so she sat by the fire and rocked her body gently to and fro, mouthing mute lamentations.

Crying Boy was conscious of Small Owl standing beside the fire. He could not bring himself to look at her. He had known her all his life. She was but one summer his senior and as babies they had been playmates. Small Owl had been adopted into the lodge of Waning Moon's mother and her cradleboard had been placed beside that of Crying Boy as their mothers had worked at the household duties. It had been Small Owl who had smiled at him when he had been fretful over the confining straps.

Later, when they were small children, she had raced with him and Curly Fox and it had been she who had many times pulled him back to his feet when his legs had failed to keep pace with his body. As they had grown and he had become the larger, it had been her whom he had taken to see the nestlings he found or the fox cubs in the cave up on the hill. They had splashed together in the stream, rolled and played and laughed and fought —nude, joyous and free. But always, if they fought each other, each was quick to come to the defense of the other in the event of another child's aggression. They had been brother and sister. Only the event of her maidenhood had finally separated them. At first he had resented it greatly, but as his own adolescence had approached, his thoughts had turned to other things. He had grown to miss her only when he had wanted a confidante.

When she married his older brother it had delighted Crying Boy. That union had once again opened the door of their friendship. Had she married any other brave she would have been lost to Crying Boy forever, but the kinship of the marriage she chose created the opportunity for free access to her lodge and her confidence. He could no longer take her on the long walks they had enjoyed as small children, for she was now a woman, with the dignity of womanhood, but he could relate his own adventures to her. And he had carried wood for her and often had brought small delicacies such as watercress or mushrooms and even the sweet tree gum, when he could find it. Such attention had always pleased her and it had pleased Blue Feather. More and more he had taken to confiding in her the dreams and the ambitions that filled his mind, and she had always understood and encouraged him. She had been as fond of him as he was of her. And now she was a stranger.

Inside the lodge she had removed the blanket and her pregnancy stood out before her like a barrier that embarrassed him. He was no stranger to life, birth and death, for they were natural things that he had been acquainted with all of his life, so he could not find a reason for his embarrassment. Perhaps her swollen belly was a rebuke to his inexperience and his premature assumption of the role of husband and father.

At this moment he knew that he should have waited and begun his manhood in the proper way. He wished fervently that there was some way to turn time backward and reconsider his impetuousness. He stood there, grim and silent, and made a vow to himself that never again would he act on impulse. He had forgotten that he had made the same vow many times before. He was completely incapable of realizing that he would make it many times more. He did not know himself at all. He was totally unaware of his own nature.

Crying Boy had been born impulsive. He had come into the world a full two months before the end of the proper time in his mother's womb. He had refused to be hindered by his precocious act and had been lusty with life the moment his lungs had filled with air. He had turned from his mother's breast and grabbed for meat before he had grown a tooth; he had literally kicked his way out of the confines of his cradleboard and had stood on his short, uncertain legs before they would hold his weight. He had climbed to the back of a pony before his legs were long enough to clasp the withers. He had howled for a bow before his pudgy fingers could hold a slingshot, and now he had taken a wife before he had become a brave. He was going to become a father before he had been a bridegroom.

He had choked on the meat and had rolled in the dust; he had been tossed from the pony's back. He had burned his arm with the bowstring, and had skinned his knuckles pounding out his rage against the bark of the pine tree. But each of these things he had finally conquered with only his own scars to show for his mad rush into life. Before him was a vastly different problem. Any scars to be gained from this rash act would be shared by another; the thought was frightening. He knew he should say something to her, but he did not know the words.

Small Owl looked at the boy standing there in his misery and bewilderment. Her intuition told her that this was probably the most delicate moment in his existence. She felt that she must find a way to allow him to save face and find the courage to carry out what he had started. Her heart told her that his ego was suffering and near to death with the doubts that bore in on him. She clasped her hands together with her effort. It was good that she knew him so well.

"Are you sorry that you came to me?" she asked and then rushed on before he had time to answer. "You are the kind of man who always does the honorable thing in spite of his own feelings. I suppose I should have given you time to consider before I accepted you so quickly. But you see, I was afraid. I felt so alone until you came. I did not stop to think that it is only natural for a man to want his first wife to be a woman of his own choosing and not an obligation."

Crying Boy raised his head in wonderment.

"Is that what you think?" he asked.

"It is what I fear," she said. "You are very quiet and thoughtful. I think maybe there is another girl you prefer for your first woman. I think maybe you are wishing you did not have to do this. It is a very old custom and no one will shake his head because you do not follow it. I know how much you want to become a great warrior and I will not blame you if you change your mind about me. It will take a great deal of your time hunting for us"—she touched her belly delicately—"and I do not want to be a burden to you. A woman does not like to feel that she has hindered a man."

A feeling of the old friendship and intimacy was beginning to return to Crying Boy. His belly settled down and some of the elation he had felt at first began to push away the fears inside him. She spoke again.

"You are a man"—she seemed to stress the word "man" just a little—"who is destined for great honors for yourself and our people. I have always been proud of you and I was relieved when you came to my fire. I have great respect for Bending Bow and I love Crooning Woman like a mother, but I could not think of being a wife to him."

"I hoped that you would not." Crying Boy felt almost like his old self. He found that he was able to talk freely and frankly once more. "Bending Bow is a great warrior, but he is much too old to be a husband to you."

"Blue Feather would not like me to go to Crooning Woman's lodge," she said.

Crying Boy drew back in dismay.

"Hist!" he said sharply. "Do not speak that name."

"I shall speak that name." Small Owl was showing a side of her nature that Crying Boy had never before seen. "A thought is the same as a word," she continued, "and I have already in my thoughts called his name. I did it when you and Crooning Woman came to the fire. And Blue Feather does not mind being called back from the Cloud Land for me. I know he does not. He is here and he will help us both."

Crying Boy felt real alarm.

"You must stop talking like this," he cried. "It is a forbidden thing."

"I know it is forbidden," she said sweetly, "but I am not afraid. I tell you that he does not mind."

"Perhaps not." Crying Boy wished she would stop. "But he is not the only one. The others will punish us and maybe all of our people for this."

He was really frightened now. If the people ever found out what Small Owl was doing, they would drive her from the village. No one but the very special and very wise had the right to recall anyone from the spirit world without risking disaster for everyone.

"Blue Feather will not allow anyone here or in the Cloud Land to harm us." Small Owl was confident.

"Please—hist," he pleaded. "Keep your voice down. Suppose someone outside should hear you?"

"No one will hear us." Quietly and very naturally she had implicated him in this gross indiscretion. "You saw him. I know you saw him. He is here and he will protect us."

Crying Boy shuddered. She spoke the truth. Indeed he had seen the ghost of his brother sitting in his place by the cook fire. He looked at Small Owl helplessly. How had she managed to get him involved in this violation? How, he wondered, could anyone so gentle and so obedient as she had always seemed be so sacrilegious? He knew he should immediately start a purification, but he was afraid that if he did there would be too much interest in the events taking place in this lodge, and already there was more interest than he cared to think about after this kind of talk.

"I won't talk anymore about this tonight." Small Owl was watching him closely. "But you will see. Nothing but good will ever come to us."

He was relieved that she was going to stop the words that were sure to bring them disaster. He turned to look at Falling Leaf. He wondered what the Old One would do about this. She still sat rocking back and forth, mumbling her incantations, and did not appear to have heard anything that had been said. Crying Boy knew that appearances were no indication of reality. Falling Leaf had heard, and words once said and heard were words that could not be changed.

"We had better go to bed," Small Owl said. "Much will happen tomorrow."

Crying Boy agreed more wholeheartedly than he could voice. Much would probably happen tomorrow that even he had not anticipated. He knew that he would never be able to sleep, but he would consent to anything at this moment that would stop her words and give him time to think the thoughts he would surely have to think. This entire day had been crooked enough without this last—and the worst—of all wrong happenings. And besides all of this, he was going to have to share the lodge with a ghost! He wished fervently that he had not seen what he had seen. Perhaps if he had not, he would be able to fool himself into thinking that she had been excused for her act of folly. But it was no use. The ghost of Blue Feather was even now occupying the sleeping couch. Crying Boy staggered to the side of the fire, careful not to cross between it and the couch. He collapsed to the hard earth of the floor. His knife dug into his backside. He pulled it to one side but did not remove it. Neither did he take off his moccasins. He knew he would never sleep. He heard Small Owl preparing for her bed. He was no longer embarrassed. The destructive uncertainty of his own self had been replaced by his concern for another. He wondered how he would ever solve this problem. He knew what he should do. He should get off this floor and leave this lodge. But he knew he had no intention of leaving. He was impulsive. He was rash and he was unruly, but he was no coward. Whatever awful fate awaited Small Owl, it awaited him too. He must find a way to deal with it—somehow—somehow. He sighed deeply and never knew when sheer exhaustion closed his eyes and confusion and anxiety drifted into peaceful boyish slumber.

Falling Leaf opened her eyes. She had been waiting for the regular breathing that told her the boy had fallen asleep. Painfully the old woman got to her feet. Small Owl turned on her couch to look at her with anxious eyes. Neither woman spoke. Falling Leaf hobbled over to the empty pallet and carefully removed the top robe. She walked around the fire and laid it gently over the sleeping boy. She straightened her bent back and looked at the girl. Their eyes met and mutual understanding and approval passed between them. The old woman shuffled to her own blankets beside the entrance. She heaved her ancient bones down and pulled the blanket over her head. Ghost or no ghost, she was not going to leave these two innocents. They were going to need her. She had seen too many terrible things in her lifetime to run now from the mere specter of a magnanimous man whom she had loved as a son. No, these two innocents were going to need her if they kept on with such idiocy as she had heard this night. Her eyes closed and she slept.

Out in the night the moon sailed serenely across the sky, un-concerned with the multitude of tragedies beneath it. Only curi-ous little beams probed among the shadows of the sleeping lodges to seek out a deeper shade. Red Cloud, chief of the Tetons, indomitable warrior of the Dakota, stood in the night and wept for his people. In agony he pleaded with an oblivious god. Only the winds heard and moaned softly in the treetops.

Crying Boy opened his eyes. His awakening was instan-taneous. There was none of his usual meanderings in the trance world between sleep and sensibility. This morning, fantasies of adolescence seemed pale beside reality that jolted his mind and muscle into vivid awareness. He lay perfectly still and contem-plated the curious sensation that crept slowly up his spine and chilled his body. It was very dark and very still.

Outside, night had sheathed the moon and recalled the stars to declare the deep, black armistice between yesterday and tomor-row. The depleted world was in the deep, deep sleep that comes just before awakening. The wind, purged of its distress, lay down to rest before the dictates of a new day. Frost settled into the grasses. No creature moved or murmured, save one. On a pine-covered pinnacle toward the land of the rising sun a restless lobo howled his frustration for the night's failures and his defiance of tomorrow's destiny.

Crying Boy heard the savage challenge. He felt an awesome kinship with the gaunt, gray ghost of the forest. He pulled his robe closer and remembered that he had fallen asleep un-covered. He pondered for a moment before he realized who had placed the blanket over him. He was comforted. His chill began to abate. To feel the approval of an Old One was reassuring. Those matriarchs were well known for their sternness and dedi-cation to propriety.

The wolf howled again. It was a good omen, he decided, and promptly went back to sleep.

The rising sun sparkled on a heavy frost. It was Harvest Moon, and high in the sky a flight of wild geese honked their way toward the land of constant sun. They called out the warning that North Wind was breaking camp and packing snow and ice for his trip southward. A gray squirrel paused briefly to glance upward and chatter before scurrying off in a frenzy of harvesting. Wild bees buzzed around late flowers to swab out the last bit of precious pollen. A jay scolded angrily when he found no piñons under his favorite tree. He flew in furious indignation to the edge of the clearing, and from that vantage point hurled insults on those below. It infuriated him when they paid no heed. They ignored his most acid remarks and opinions, and went about polluting the morning air with pungent smoke and the sickening smell of charred flesh. The jay gave up his tirade and flew off in disgust to locate some source of food that might have escaped the sharp eye and greedy claw of the Dakota.

An old crow, searching in vain in the berry patch by the river, agreed with the jay and added his croaking comments before he, too, flapped off to a more productive field.

The area around the Dakota camp had been stripped bare by busy fingers that allowed no morsel of waste. Not a chokecherry, not a wild plum or a grape, remained on tree or vine. Even the ground under the trees was clean. Only the gray squirrel did not complain. He had no patience with those who did not provide for the Hungry Moon. His motto was "the speediest harvester profits most." He understood the Dakota and enjoyed being their neighbor.

Crying Boy stepped out into the chill morning. He straightened to his full height and stretched his arms to the rising sun to sing his morning song. The breakfast fire was crackling and the smell of roasting meat tantalized his forgetful belly. He was hungry in spite of last night's discomfort and lingering tensions.

Small Owl tended her fire, her blanket forming a cowl to hide her face from the world. It was her only outward sign of mourning. Old One sat by the fire, her hunched figure shrouded except for one hand clutching her pipe, which still awaited a live coal to warm its bowl.

Crying Boy finished his morning song and folded his arms across his chest, imitating the warriors. He looked around the camp. In front of their lodge, Willow Twig and her mother, Yellow Bird, worked completely shrouded. Curly Fox stood beside them, grave with dignity. His father's failure to return home had left him with the responsibility of his mother and sister, and he did not have Crying Boy's ambition or bold confidence to bolster him. The boys looked at each other across the circle, each feeling acutely his own raw transition.

Long ago they had, as many other small boys do, pledged brotherhood in a very solemn rite, complete with blood oaths and secret ceremony. It had meant much to them at the time, but as they had grown older their natures had come between them. Curly Fox had been happy, carefree and content. Crying Boy had been ambitious, impulsive and impatient. Curly Fox had played and loafed about the village, avoiding every possible duty and piloting most of the madcap mischief that plagued the women and pleased the girls. Crying Boy had prowled, practiced, rehearsed and plagued the warriors.

This morning the boys stood and looked at each other in mutual bereavement for their boyhood. Their eyes met and their friendship surged forward; each was eager to sustain the other. Brotherhood was silently repledged across a strip of hard-packed earth, and reality stripped the pledge of any mystic ritual.

It was late morning before Red Cloud emerged from his lodge. His face bore no sign of his sleepless night or his morning of deep meditation. It was as calm and constant as the face of the mountain.

A crier ran from lodge to lodge, calling for council. It was time for Crying Boy and Curly Fox to leave the village. This council concerned them. There was the task of selecting tutors for each of them and it was only courtesy for them to be far from the sound of any silence that might follow the request for volunteers.

By mute, though mutual, agreement they walked toward each other and met in the center of the campground. More than one inflexible face softened and more than one piercing eye twinkled with fond and sympathetic amusement as the boys walked stiffly out of camp. Their self-consciousness walked with them, as pride and apprehension kept step.

They took the favorite trail of their boyhood, each intent on guarding his own misgivings. Long habit forced Crying Boy to the lead where the trail narrowed. He fell into a languid trot and Curly Fox followed, content. Habit, too, led them to the well-beaten trail at the far end of the valley where they turned off to the secret place where they had first pledged their brotherhood. There, beside the pool formed by long-departed beaver, they threw themselves down on a carpet of moss that covered the ground under the giant arms of an ancient pine. Here they would await the sound of the drums, which would announce that a decision had been reached and they could return home.

For a time, neither of them spoke. Each of them pondered his problem in his own way. Then Curly Fox rolled over to his back and pulled his flute from his loin strap. He placed it to his lips and the plaintive notes of his music told the pathos he could not voice. The low, mournful wail wept for his father, who was no more; it beseeched for his friend and it despaired for himself.

Crying Boy was annoyed. He had no talent for making music and less for listening. He would have liked to have been able to snatch the reed from his friend's lips and break it to bits. He chafed at the necessity for always showing courtesy to others. The flute had been one of the prime causes for their separation. Crying Boy had always had the uneasy feeling that Curly Fox's fondness for the thing indicated some weakness that was almost effeminate. And Crying Boy had small regard for anyone other than a warrior. His own ambition was to belong one day to one of the *akicita*,[3] and those lodges contained no "woman-men." The haunting sob of the reed filled him with loathing. He wished his brother-friend might be more meticulous in his habits.

The music wavered and broke on a high, quavering pitch of despair. Curly Fox threw the flute from him. It landed with a small thud at the base of the tree. He flopped over to his belly and buried his face into the moss. His arms curled protectively around his head. Crying Boy watched and waited. He waited for

[3] Dog Soldier Societies.

a long time and Curly Fox gave no indication of changing his position.

"Are you afraid?"

Crying Boy could keep still no longer.

"I am afraid."

Curly Fox's voice was muffled. Crying Boy hoped it was because of the moss. He did not want to admit that his brother-friend was crying like a child. No man cried.

Curly Fox sat up very abruptly. He was very, very angry. His eyes were red and his face was wet.

"All right, I am crying!" he shouted.

He sniffed in the very unlovely manner of a child who needs to blow his nose.

"You think I am a woman," he accused. "Maybe I am. I never wanted to be a warrior. I have always wanted to be a medicine man."

His voice trailed off and his lips trembled. Crying Boy said nothing. He did not know what to say. He contemplated the water of the pool. It would not do to shame his friend more by looking on his undisciplined face.

"I am not like you," Curly Fox continued. "I never have been like you. I do not want to kill anything, especially people. The only reason I could never pull a bow was because my arm did not want to kill. I never want to kill—not even a *Wasicun*."

Crying Boy felt a flush of shame. It did not seem possible that a Dakota boy would be saying such things. The position of medicine man was highly respected, but no man followed the holy road without dictation from the *maiyun*[4] during a *hanble-cheyapi*, and neither he nor Curly Fox had as yet been allowed to cry for a vision. How anyone could prefer being a medicine man to being a warrior was more than Crying Boy could understand.

"You do not have to be my brother-friend any longer," Curly Fox said. "I will understand. I release you from your pledge."

"I do not want release," Crying Boy said. "We will remain

4 Spirits.

brothers." And he was unable to define to himself why he did not take this opportunity to free himself from an alliance that was sure to bring nothing but dissatisfaction.

"You will not be sorry. I will be a warrior and I will be a good one. You will not have to take care of me. You will see that this will be true."

Curly Fox's face lost some of its woebegone expression and he almost smiled.

"There is only one thing. I do not know who is going to want to tutor me."

He pulled a fistful of moss and crumpled it in his hand. He threw it into the water and watched it eddy about before it sank slowly down until all but the very ends protruded.

"As for that," Crying Boy said, "I do not know who will tutor me either. I only hope it is not Lame Deer."

"Lame Deer is one of the best warriors. I cannot see why you say this." Curly Fox was surprised.

"It is because he is always saying everyone should learn the *Wasicun* tongue. It is just because he can speak it himself and wants to show how much he knows."

"Maybe he is right when he says it would be a good thing to know," Curly Fox mused.

"When I get close enough to a *Wasicun* I will not be talking to him." Crying Boy's voice was grim. "I do not want to waste my time learning to speak to a man I intend to kill before there will be time for talk."

"I hope you get who you want." Curly Fox was very sincere. "I will be glad to get anyone. But when we are warriors I will always follow you. You will be a big man some day."

"You will be a big man, too." Crying Boy hoped he was speaking truth.

"No, I will never be a big man." Curly Fox smiled sadly. "I do not even want to be a big man. I will follow you and I will kill our enemies, but I will not like it. I do not think killing people is a good thing."

"The *Wasicun* are not people," Crying Boy said. "They are savages, and we must kill them all."

Curly Fox shook his head. "We will never kill them all. I think one day they will kill all of the Dakota and there will be no people, only *Wasicun* in our land."

"You talk crazy words," Crying Boy cried out. "This will never be. We will kill them. I feel it."

"Feel it then," Curly Fox said, shrugging his shoulders, "and one day we will see which is to be."

"Is this what makes you afraid?" Crying Boy asked.

"I am not afraid in the way you think it," Curly Fox said. "I am afraid only of myself."

Crying Boy looked at his companion and wondered if he would ever understand this strange brother-friend of his. He decided that he would not, and changed the course of their talk.

"I wonder what takes the council so long?" he asked.

"I told you they would have a hard time to find one who will want to tutor me." Curly Fox grinned. "Let's start back along the water so when we hear the drums we will not be so far away."

Crying Boy was happy to follow the suggestion. He had heard quite enough of Curly Fox's wisdom for the day. It made him uneasy.

Above the pool, the stream was narrow and swift for a distance. Great rocks lay along the banks, scattered at random by myriads of spring torrents. Crying Boy, forgetting for a while that he was now a man, jumped from rock to rock pitting his agility against the chance of an icy plunge. Curly Fox walked quietly along the bank. Where the creek widened, the rocks were farther apart and Crying Boy made precarious leap after leap. Each jump took him farther from his friend. Finally he was faced with an open expanse of rushing water. The only rock within distance lay against the far bank. It was a long leap away. He called over his shoulder to Curly Fox.

"Watch me!" he called.

He heard Curly Fox cry out. There was alarm in his voice, but his words were lost in the rumble of the rushing water. Crying Boy smiled to himself. Curly Fox was a coward. He poised his body and measured the distance. He leaped.

The tip of one toe caught the edge of the rock and he felt the sharp edge rip the flesh off his shin as his leg slipped down into the water. He landed hard on the other knee and his hands. His breath caught at the surging pain in his leg. Numbness crept up his arms into his shoulders. Painfully he drew the injured leg up under him.

Crouched on his hands and knees, he felt another sensation. It had nothing to do with the pain or the numbness. It was the prickling sense of acute danger. It ran up his spine and raised the small hairs on the nape of his neck. Slowly, deliberately, with every nerve and muscle coiling, he raised his head and looked straight into a pair of eyes—eyes that looked back unflinchingly, treacherous and venomous as those of a rattler. But they were not the eyes of a snake. These eyes were blue—as blue as a cloudless sky reflected in an icy pool.

2

By the white man's calendar it was the year 1859. By Dakota reckoning it was a good time to die.

A Dakota did not number the years. His life was not burdened with that which had no reason, and there was no reason for counting years. A man was born without being consulted. He lived a short time or a long time, wholly determined by a power other than his own. A man was not old until his years became a burden. He was not young after he was able to carry his own honor and dignity. A time was either a good time or a bad time. A good time was to be recalled with pleasure. A bad time was best forgotten. This was a time to die. It was a time to die because the Dakota could find no alternative. He had seen his lands expropriated and he had moved back into the hills. He had seen the buffalo killed and left to rot while Dakota bellies were empty. He saw his water being polluted, his forests burned, his game killed or driven away. He endured having his villages pillaged, his women violated and his people enslaved. He met charlatans with courtesy and was called a fool. He fought back and was called a savage. He welcomed a stranger and was robbed. He defended what was his own, and was looked upon as less than human.

Dakota dignity was trampled in the dung of alien greed. Dakota ideals were pulverized to dust upon which the white man spat. And on and on they came, pouring over the plains, screaming, cursing, racing even into the hills and badlands to claw into the earth for the yellow stuff they cherished more than their women, more than their children, more than their lives, and even more than the thing they called "salvation."

The Dakota could not live any longer with dignity—but he could die with dignity. It had been a hard decision, for Dakota hospitality was tenacious. Dakota courtesy was revered, and the Dakota code of conduct toward others was rigid. But more than these, Dakota dignity was imperious.

So an academy of animosity became an added institution in Dakota life. Youth was inoculated against the white plague of the plains. Credence in white man's word was mocked in the councils, and hatred was bred into the breasts of Dakota babies.

It was a time to die.

Nothing Crying Boy had ever heard, nothing he had ever seen, nothing he had ever been told, had prepared him for this moment. The face that looked into his was not the face of a man. It was not the face of any animal he had ever seen or heard about. It was a tangled mat of filthy red hair with malignant eyes and fetid breath. Crying Boy had never envisioned such an apparition. But the dull gleam of the metal that was inching through the brush, halfway between face and ground, gave tangibility to the delusion. Crying Boy had never seen a *Wasicun*, but he had seen a death stick, and this one was slowly, cautiously being brought to bear directly between his eyes.

Spontaneously the boy lunged, aiming a flying tackle just below the death-dealing barrel. There was a grunt of surprise. The man tried to step backward, but his legs were shackled in relentless Dakota sinew. He crashed backward into the undergrowth. The gun flew from his hand. Half-stunned by the unexpected onslaught, the white man felt the release of his legs. He rolled, but was caught in the tangle of vines and brush. In an effort to untangle himself, he gave up reaching for the gun and somersaulted with a splash into the racing water. Crying Boy was on top of him almost as soon as he went under. He tried desperately to hold the white man down, but his strength did not match that of the woodsman. He came up sputtering and flung the boy aside. Crying Boy scrambled to get his feet under him. He slipped on the slimy rocks and fell heavily against the bank.

The knife the white man had pulled from his belt sang past Crying Boy's ear and fell into the brush beyond.

Completely unarmed, with soggy clothing hindering his every movement, the white man made a clumsy rush for the bank. He clawed at the earth, only to fall back as the water swept his feet from under him. Tumbling over and over, he was swept downstream.

Curly Fox had stood on the opposite bank, palsied by the deadly drama he had been witnessing.

"The village!" Crying Boy screamed at him over the rush of the water and swept his arm to emphasize his gasping words.

Curly Fox, struggling with loyalties he could not rank, was relieved from his burden of decision. Without more hesitation, he darted away into the undergrowth in the direction of the village.

In a frenzied leap, Crying Boy sprang to the bank. At his feet lay a rock. Without pausing he caught it up in his hand and slipped into the cover of the scrub. Stealthily he crept to a spot close to the long rifle, which lay where it had fallen. The white man would go downstream for a while, but he would come back for that precious piece of property. And, if he did not come back for it, Crying Boy could think of nothing for which he would rather risk his life. He looked at the scarred and ancient piece and found it beautiful. It fascinated him. To own it was to be a man. So great was his eagerness to touch the prize that he trembled and a small branch across his face quivered. The movement sobered him. He felt sure that the white man was somewhere near, and such an indiscretion could cost his life. He reprimanded himself and settled back to wait.

He wondered how long it would take Curly Fox to alert the village. One *Wasicun* meant many *Wasicun,* and this *Wasicun* was closer to the village than any had ever been.

Crying Boy called silently to the spirits to speed Curly Fox before the council drums might sound. He hoped that the urgency of the situation exonerated his unauthorized plea.

His leg ached, but he dared not shift his position to relieve it. There was no sound except the sound of the water and a slight rustle of leaves. He knew the *Wasicun* must be close, for no bird cheeped although it was almost sunset, the time when their twitterings should be loud. It worried him that he could detect no sound. From all he had heard, the *Wasicun* was supposed to be clumsy and noisy when he traveled. But there was not so much as the snap of a twig, nor an unaccountable rustle of a dry leaf. Only the silence of the birds told of the enemy's presence. Crying Boy began to feel the tension of his situation. He felt exposed. He wished he had taken more care in his concealment. Suppose the *Wasicun* had circled him and was behind him? He wanted to turn his head and look, but he did not dare. He looked to the right and to the left as far as his eyes would travel without turning his head even a fraction. He felt the sudden need to relieve himself, and once the need was acknowledged it grew acutely. He gritted his teeth to ward off the humiliating demand. It seemed that every crisis in his life brought about this inglorious necessity.

A twig a few feet away moved where no breeze blew. Crying Boy's mind and body crystallized into intent suspension. The twig moved again and a pair of blue eyes appeared to search every tree, every leaf, every stalk of grass and bit of brush. Crying Boy felt a quiver of excitement. The cold, hostile gaze raked over his hiding place. Crying Boy did not breathe. The gaze swept on. Carefully, silently as any warrior, the *Wasicun* stepped out. He saw his gun. Anxious as he seemed to be to have it in his hands, he did not hurry. Step by step, he moved toward it. When it lay directly before him and almost under his feet, he still searched the foliage. Crying Boy did not dare look up. Slowly, deliberately, the man looked in every direction. Then he stooped and reached for the weapon.

Crying Boy exploded to his feet. He swung the rock up with him and there was a dull thud. The man sank to the ground. There was an ugly flow of blood from the gash the rock had made in his forehead. It gushed out to form a pool on the leaves. Crying Boy pulled the gun from under the body.

"Whose gun is this, *Wasicun?*" he snarled. "Who is the warrior here?"

There was no answer from the inert form at his feet. Triumphantly the boy raised the weapon. He was filled with exhilaration. He opened his mouth to voice the wild Dakota war cry, but it never came. Humiliation clapped its rude hand over the victorious shout. The whisper of the wind could not conceal the small, dribbling sound of water trickling down on dry leaves.

The sun sank behind the trees and the sky blushed crimson.

The camp was in an uproar. Children raced about, chasing each other, screaming with the mad excitement of peripheral participation. Dogs barked and raced with them. Women laughed and called back and forth to each other gaily. Cook fires burned hot. Kettles steamed and meat spit fat into the live coals. Young boys jostled each other and shuffled when they looked at their compatriots of yesterday.

Crying Boy and Curly Fox stood side by side, apart from everyone else, too proud and too awed with that pride to speak, even to each other. Girls tossed their hair, smirked and cast sidelong glances in their direction. Members of the council sat in their exclusive circle awaiting Red Cloud. They smoked and joked with each other. Young warriors not members of the council stood or lounged in groups of twos or threes. There was a festive air over the camp.

Small Owl and the other women who had spent the day before shrouded in blankets worked with heads and faces open to the world. It would have been discourteous to the honored ones to seclude themselves in the selfishness of mourning. No melancholy note should mar the joy of triumph. Smiles superceded their sorrow, and laughter said their requiems.

It had been a watchful and sleepless night for everyone. At dusk Curly Fox had raced into camp breathlessly to gasp out the story of what was happening at the river. The council had long since concluded its discussions, but had remained to smoke and talk and deliberately delay announcing decisions. Having to wait sometimes strengthened composure in the young, and it had been their opinion that one of the boys under discussion was badly in need of some strengthening in that quarter.

When Curly Fox had burst into camp with his incredible story, a sort of precise pandemonium had erupted. Warriors had darted in four directions to cover all sides of the camp. They had formed three separate circles, one outside the other, about the camp. Others had taken to the trail with Red Cloud leading them. Only a few stayed within the camp itself. The women had hurriedly packed bundles. There was no hysteria, no sentimental indecision of selection among their belongings. Bundles were light with bare necessities. Children, without command, gathered to stand close to their own lodges. No orders were given. No orders were needed. Every member of the clan outside the cradleboard knew his position and took it. Within minutes the camp was ready to make a stand or flee, as necessity might dictate.

The moon had been casting shadows before Crying Boy had staggered into camp. He had been dirty, bloody and jubilant. On his back he had carried the long gun. He had pulled a makeshift travois to which his captive had been securely bound with vines. People gathered about him and pressed close. They had moved aside only enough to make a path down which he had dragged his prize. Eager hands waited to assist him, but he had ignored them with weary hauteur. He had limped his way to his own lodge, where Small Owl and Falling Leaf waited. He had seen the pride in their eyes and it had given him strength. He had held the shaft of the travois out to Small Owl.

"I have brought you a slave, woman," he said.

She had taken the shaft from him and had thanked him and looked proudly around at the people. Falling Leaf had hobbled around to where she could look closely at the captive. She had prodded him with her walking stick.

"Ha!" she had cried out loud so everyone could hear. "See this?"

And she had drawn attention to the matted blood on the man's head. She had been very proud and she had been sure no one missed noting the size of the bound man. She had tugged at the bonds Crying Boy had tied around him and had cackled boastfully over them. She had urged others to see their excellence for themselves. She had wrinkled her nose in comic abhorrence when she had leaned over the prostrate figure.

"This will take a lot of water to make it fit to be near people," she had said and had been gratified by the ripple of laughter. She had pressed the people to come close and see what a fine thing Crying Boy had done.

Small Owl had taken Crying Boy's arm and pulled him into their lodge, leaving the others to examine the *Wasicun* that had been conquered by one of their own.

At sunrise the warriors had returned. There had been no evidence of other *Wasicun* in the territory. Red Cloud had been smiling and he had called the people around him.

"When the sun is straight up we will make a feast," he had said, "and the drums of honor will beat."

Now the sun was straight up and Crying Boy and Curly Fox stood awaiting the sound of the drums.

Crying Boy was clad in the new breechclout that Small Owl had stayed up the night to finish. She had bandaged his leg in her finest white doeskin. His black braids gleamed and his skin glowed bronze from the sweat bath he had taken for purification. He was impressive in spite of his youth, Small Owl thought, regretting the lack of time that had kept her from sewing new moccasins for this great occasion. But the gun that was slung from his shoulder drew attention away from the shabby footgear. She had cleaned the weapon thoroughly, scouring away the *Wasicun*'s ownership before oiling it and the strap with clean bear grease. It gleamed nicely and Crying Boy wore it proudly.

Curly Fox lacked only the rifle to rival his friend in finery. His breechclout was also new and so were his moccasins. He was equally clean and shining and his hair was as carefully braided, with strands so equal they looked as if the very hairs had been counted.

They waited in their scrubbed glory for the drums—those long-awaited drums—that would beat out the beautiful chant: "Now you are a man—now you are a man—now you are a man!"

The wild staccato of the drums tripled in tempo. By now the

beat was a blur of rhythm. Only No Water, Red Paint and Touch-the-Cloud were left in the stamping, whirling dance. Their bodies glistened with sweat. It ran in small streams down their faces. It oozed from their backs and legs. It soaked their breechclouts and moccasins. They had been dancing for a long time. One by one the others had surrendered to weakened legs and laboring lungs. They lolled on the ground, vanquished, but delighted even in defeat. They gambled recklessly on the outcome of what had become a contest. It was a gay day. No somber shadow clouded the laughter. No bitter morsel soured the feast. The Dakota were celebrating.

Crying Boy and Curly Fox had told the events of the past two days so that all could hear everything that had happened to them. From all of these things the holy men would find some sign that would decide the names that would replace those of Crying Boy and Curly Fox. The holy ones still pondered in the seclusion of their special lodge. Outside, the festivities flourished.

Crying Boy was not happy. He had slept a dreamless night through, and exhaustion had smothered his mind from the meditation he had intended to occupy his thoughts. He had not been conscious of anything until the lone lobo had again awakened him in the early hours. So he had solved nothing and Small Owl's transgression still lay heavily upon his heart. He could take small joy in his honors this day. He could not bring himself to look toward the place where she sat, serene and docile. He could not look toward his mother's place either. He was afraid of the pride that he knew was reflected in her face. He felt sure that his lack of action in rectifying the wrong he had committed by hiding Small Owl's violation was in the nature of a lie, and a lie was repugnant to Crying Boy. It was a cowardly thing in which he had never indulged, and it was smarting him more than his torn leg. He wanted recognition and he wanted honors, but he wanted them untainted. He wanted them with the blessings of the people—all of the people—those in Cloud Land as well as those of the village. But Crying Boy felt sure the *maiyun* did not look upon him with much favor since he had not found the time to find a way to nullify what had been done. They would, without doubt, reveal to the holy men some name that would reflect his negligence if not actual dishonor. And he so much wanted a strong name, a name that would carve awe into the black hearts of the pale barbarian. He wanted such a name almost more than he wanted life, and it was too late. His childish inability to stay awake and meditate until he found the solution had betrayed him. He dreaded the moment when the holy men would come out of their lodge.

Red Paint faltered in his stamping rhythm. He sat down very suddenly. He folded his arms across his heaving belly and laughed weakly. No Water dropped beside him. The drums stopped and Touch-the-Cloud was cheered loudly as champion. He joined the other two on the ground. They all laughed and laughed. They slapped each other weakly on the back and praised each other loquaciously. Bets were paid off with both the winners and the losers in high good humor. Everybody was happy—everybody except Crying Boy.

The holy men came out of their lodge. Silence met and followed them. This was the moment! Black Elk and Pine came to the council circle. They sat down facing the way of the rising sun and Big Bull, who knew all the laws of life and earth, stood between them. Warriors came from all directions to sit in a circle with the women behind them. Black Elk lit the pipe and handed it to Big Bull, who raised it with his two hands, first to the sky, then to the earth and then to the four winds, one after the other. He called to the All Powerful to come and join his children. He called to the four winds to come and bring within their embrace all who were brothers to the Dakota. Crying Boy and Curly Fox felt very solemn. This was the most holy moment of their lives, and Crying Boy closed his eyes in weary acceptance of what was surely to come.

Big Bull finished his songs and lowered the pipe. He sat down and placed the pipe to his lips. He drew deeply and puffed a great cloud of the smoke toward the two boys who sat within the circle facing him. Slowly, reverently, the pipe was passed from hand to hand. Each man drew once and puffed his smoke toward the boys. Crying Boy forced all things but repentance from his mind. Under his breath he sang his own song as the smoke wafted its purification of prayer around him.

"Great Father, I meant no harm. I meant only to protect her because she is a woman who is not as strong as a man. I will take a punishment on myself and bring honor to a weak name if it will make you forget what she did."

He sang it over and over and tried hard not to add the thought that insisted on being thought: But I want a strong name.

The pipe had gone all around the circle. Crying Boy was startled to hear his name being called.

"The one who has been known as Crying Boy!"

Quickly he rose to his feet. His heart thudded in his breast. He looked at Big Bull with eyes that were hot and dry. For once the ever-welling fountain of tears that he had battled all of his life was dry.

"Truly," he thought, "this is a miracle."

"You are of few summers," Big Bull said, "but you have brought honor upon yourself and your people. You have met with an enemy and you counted coup. You brought this enemy into your camp, alive! You wear his fire stick across your shoulders. You are a man and are surely favored by the spirits. You heard the voice of Lobo after you conquered your enemy. Lobo is then your brother. This is good. And this then is your name. Warriors and women, people of the Dakota, the boy who was Crying Boy is no more. Before us is the man, known to his people from where the sun now stands, as Gray Wolf!"

Big Bull stooped and picked up a single eagle feather from the medicine bundle. He fastened it in the left braid of the new brave's hair. It hung, tip down, over his shoulder.

"Gray Wolf," Big Bull said, "wear this feather of victory proudly to let all people know you are brave and you have counted coup. Walk always in the way of honor, my son, and may your shadow walk many trails before it wearies."

Gray Wolf! Gray Wolf! Gray Wolf! He said the name over and over in his mind. He had wanted a strong name and he had a strong name. It was as strong as any man ever had. He recalled the sound of the voice of Lobo in the two dawns before and his spine tingled with pleasure. The feather in his hair stirred in the breeze and it took all his powers of discipline not to glance sideways to admire it.

Thank you! Thank you! Thank you! he said in his mind. And he was very close to tears again. He looked down at the ground and hoped the people would not think it strange that he could not smile.

"The one known as Curly Fox!" Big Bull was calling.

Gray Wolf stepped back. He did not want to detract from the glory that was to come to his little friend. Curly Fox came forward. He looked small and frail. His expression was one of quiet dignity, touched with a strange melancholy. Gray Wolf remembered the talk by the river. He wished he could hope for a strong name for his friend, but it was useless. No one looking at him could ever think of him as a warrior. Curly Fox was simply Curly Fox, generous and gentle as a woman and almost timid here before the council.

"You too have but few summers," Big Bull addressed the boy, "but you too acted in the manner of a man, even without the benefit of a *hanblecheyapi* to guide you. You have given proof of your bravery and your generous nature by racing through a place of possible danger to give warning to your people. You came with the swiftness of a pony when you did not know but what *Wasicun* lurked hidden, ready to kill you. This is the act of a man who is not afraid, even if he is a little foolish in judgment. So there is honor upon your head, for bravery is or it is not. Judgment comes with living. People of the Dakota, the boy who was known as Curly Fox is now no more. A new brave stands with us. We welcome him. He is known as Crazy Horse."

3

"Scrub!"

Falling Leaf screamed and threatened the naked, hairy giant with her stick. She danced up and down in her frenzy and the crowd roared with laughter.

They sat in the cold of the morning, enjoying more fun than they had known for a long time.

"Scrub!" she screamed, and she threw another handful of moss toward him. It landed in the water at his feet. His legs and body were fish-belly white and he stood in the icy water that came only to his ankles. He crossed his arms over his hairy chest and ignored the crowd of people watching him. He gazed into the distance, as tranquil as a heron.

"He smells like a polecat," Falling Leaf addressed the gathering. "He knows no more about water than a polecat. What do you say?" She turned to speak to Small Owl, who sat wrapped in her blanket. "Shall we call him Polecat?"

"It seems to fit." Small Owl smiled faintly. She looked up into the strange face of the man and spoke directly to him.

"Why don't you want to bathe yourself? We only want you to be clean. Did you never take a bath before?"

"It is no use speaking to him." Falling Leaf snorted contemptuously. "He doesn't know a word we say."

"Maybe the blow on his head made his mind go for a walk," Small Owl thought aloud.

"Huh!" Falling Leaf said. "His mind is right where it belongs. He watches all of us too carefully when he thinks no one notices."

"Maybe he has been touched by the spirits." Small Owl felt protective toward her possession.

"The only thing he has been touched by was Gray Wolf's rock." Falling Leaf enjoyed the ripple of laughter that followed.

"Should you speak to him in his own tongue?" Gray Wolf turned to Lame Deer, who was now, in spite of all his prayers against it, his tutor.

"Maybe it would be good to let him know someone here can speak his words," Lame Deer mused. "But then maybe it would be just as well not to yet. He is tricky. Remember the other day when you pointed the rifle at him and he turned away from you in that way? He knew you did not know how to make the gun speak again. He did it to make you a fool. Maybe you should make him a fool instead. Why don't you use an arrow?"

Gray Wolf looked at Lame Deer admiringly. He wished he had thought of this himself. At the time the gun had seemed the more frightening of the two, but Lame Deer was right: after that first time he had not been able to make it speak again. And, he did not know how to do it. Others had said he needed to have some of the little hard berries that were like arrows to a bow. And there were no more of the berries to be had. He had searched long and carefully, trying to find the one he had shot, but he had been unable to find it anywhere. The *Wasicun* had watched all of this and there had been a gleam in his eye that Gray Wolf had not liked. He had stayed away from the *Wasicun* until today, when he had come with some of the others to watch the women trying to make him wash.

"Stand back," he shouted to the people. "Since this polecat is good for nothing else, we will use him for a target."

Deliberately watching the *Wasicun* with the side of his eye, Gray Wolf strung his bow and fitted an arrow. The *Wasicun* did not even turn to look.

"We must not kill him," Gray Wolf said. "Only take a little hide. The one who takes the smallest piece is winner."

He pulled back the string and the arrow sang through the air. It went past the man to land on the other side of the pool, but there was a small trickle of blood running down the man's neck from the tip of one ear, which was gone. The crowd yelped with joy. Lame Deer fitted an arrow and took careful aim. The other ear was minus the tip of the lobe.

"Let me! Let me!" It came from all sides as bows were strung and arrows pulled from quivers.

"No! No!" Small Owl ran to Gray Wolf. "You gave him to me and I do not want him hurt."

"We are not hurting him." Gray Wolf smiled down at her. "See, he hardly even bleeds."

"It hurts him," Small Owl pleaded. "I do not want you to do this. He is mine and I have the right."

"True," Gray Wolf agreed. "You have the right and anyway I grow tired of such small sport. Take him. He is yours. But this I will say. He will not get another blanket to ruin. He will sleep cold unless he washes the stink from his hide."

Small Owl went to the edge of the pool and motioned. She reached out and took the giant's arm and pulled him with her. His white skin was a sickly blue and gooseflesh covered him. It was a very cold morning.

The crowd fell back to open a path for her and her strange captive. As they came to where Gray Wolf was standing the man paused.

"You skinny little son of a bitch," he said in a flat, toneless voice. "One day I will have the pleasure of hanging your balls on a brier."

He went on, following Small Owl, who pulled at his arm.

"What did he say?" Gray Wolf turned to Lame Deer, who was grinning from ear to ear.

"Ha!" Lame Deer was obviously much amused. "Haven't I told you it is a good thing to know their words?"

"You have told me." Gray Wolf did not share his teacher's amusement. "What did he say?"

"If I tell you, will you then learn?" Lame Deer was bargaining when Gray Wolf did not feel in the mood to bargain.

"Maybe I will and maybe I will not," he said. "I have not yet made up my mind."

"Well, I shall tell you anyway." Lame Deer grinned again and translated the *Wasicun's* words faithfully.

Gray Wolf's eyes widened. His mouth dropped open and then snapped shut with a click of his teeth.

"I have made up my mind! I will start learning that tongue now."

Lame Deer's grin turned to a smile of satisfaction. He turned to follow the rigid back of one very angry Dakota who strode away muttering under his breath.

A snarling wind blew in. It brought an abrupt end to autumn's pleasant haze. It whipped the last leaves from the trees and left denuded limbs glazed with ice. Day after day thick scudding clouds swindled the sun of warmth and light. Water holes and ponds froze over. The piercing wind tore at the lodge skins and chilled impotent flames until the water gourds froze beside the fires.

The Dakota huddled in their blankets and stirred only to feed wood into the flames and meat into their mouths. The lone lobo of autumn was joined by his pack and they howled dismally. And each night they came in closer to the camp. The world cowered before the storm. Bears sought windfalls. Squirrels nestled in hollow trees and the deer stumbled toward warmer winds. Only the lobos defied the elements. Only Gray Wolf stepped out of his lodge.

Each day he wrestled the winds to Lame Deer's lodge to labor over alien accents. His passion to learn kept him warm and the *Wasicun* in his lodge fed the fires of that passion. Gray Wolf knew that behind those serene blue eyes and that placid face the man was laughing at him. Hatred he understood; enmity he acknowledged; revenge he honored; retaliation he expected; but ridicule . . . ! Ah yes, Gray Wolf would learn the *Wasicun's* tongue. He would learn their ways. He would learn everything there was to know about them.

The wind shook the lodgepoles and the men drew their blankets closer about them.

"I will never be able to bend my tongue around these words."

Gray Wolf felt discouraged. For weeks he had struggled to learn to speak the *Wasicun* language, and nothing he had ever attempted had seemed as difficult. He was glad when Crazy Horse had decided that he, too, would learn. He and Touch-the-Cloud had joined the classes early, and although none of them felt they had made any progress, they had learned almost as much English as many of the unlearned settlers who came to their country.

"I like this word 'son-of-a-bitch'!" Gray Wolf said.

"It is a mean word," Lame Deer said, "and it is said when a man feels mean."

"It is a good thing to have a mean word to say when you feel mean," Gray Wolf persisted. "The Dakota should have such a word."

"I do not feel the need of a mean word when I feel that way," Touch-the-Cloud remarked. "A knife or an arrow is better."

"I want it for Polecat," Gray Wolf said. "One day I am going to do to him what he said he would do to me."

"I would like to be there." Lame Deer smiled. "But we are not learning. Say again the words I have told you."

"Go!" Gray Wolf pronounced.

"Not go! Come."

Lame Deer and Gray Wolf leaped to their feet. Touch-the-Cloud and Crazy Horse crouched. Polecat stood looking down at them. Amusement was thinly veiled in his cold blue eyes. They had heard no sound of his approach. They had felt no breath of air stir when he had slipped into the lodge. He stood there, almost smiling at their discomfort, arms folded Dakota-fashion over his chest.

"What are you doing here?" Lame Deer's knife gleamed in his hand. Gray Wolf saw the gleam and realized with chagrin that he had not reacted with the alertness of the seasoned warrior. He dropped his hand to his own knife, but he did not draw.

"Maybe I didn't speak clearly," Polecat said. Then in perfect Dakota dialect he said, "I thought I heard English being spoken. Forgive me!" He inclined his head, taunting them with exaggerated courtesy.

"You speak our tongue?" Gray Wolf yanked the knife free

from his belt. He half raised it. His eyes glittered with the fury that shook him from his moccasins straight up into the hair on the back of his neck.

"Certainly I speak your tongue." Polecat seemed oblivious to the threatening knife. "Don't you speak mine?"

His tone and his words were insulting to the point of utter contempt. Had he not been inside a Dakota lodge he would have died instantly. It was obvious that the tongue was not all he understood about his captors.

"Forgive me," he said again, "but we are wasting time. Falling Leaf sent me. I believe . . ."—he turned to look directly at Gray Wolf—"I believe you are about to become a father."

Small Owl's eyes met his and there was a distinct interval before any light of recognition dawned in them. She smiled faintly and then slipped back into her trance of agony. Her fingers plucked restlessly at the blanket about her. She gasped deeply and her lips writhed as though she would scream, but it was entirely inaudible. She pushed herself back and forth, accompanying the effort with alternate apologetic smiles and clenched teeth.

Gray Wolf looked at her, and his eyes dilated with fright. He had never seen her like this. He had never seen any woman like this. He had never before seen a woman in labor, and he had never associated childbirth with pain. He did not now associate her pain with the birth.

"What is wrong?" he asked Falling Leaf, who knelt by the fire trying to blow the coals to more energy.

"What do you suppose is wrong?" the Old One snapped sharply. Then, as she turned and looked at his strained face, her words softened. "It is the child," she said gently. "They do not come into the world easily. They cause the mother pain to bring them, and they cause the mother pain most of their lives. And they cause her pain when they leave the world. But a man does not know these things. This is not the concern of men. We need wood. We must make this place warmer. And we need your mother. Go get her and then get wood and stay out of here."

Gray Wolf stood gaping at Small Owl as she paced. Falling Leaf looked from the boy to the girl. She shook her head. "Get wood!" She spoke sharply and her tone startled him. He bolted out into the gale. Women were already hurrying toward the lodge. Lame Deer had called them.

"Wood!" Gray Wolf's fumbling emotions focused upon this familiar requirement. Many times he had joined in just such a frenzied task. Heretofore it had been a frolic—a rompish toil, done with much laughter and jovial innuendos. He wondered if those other mothers had endured pain and if those other fathers had felt as he did at this moment. He tried to recall their behavior, but memory was blurred in his confusion. Small Owl was dying. He knew she was dying and he felt that he was to blame. Finally the punishment for her unorthodox behavior had come. Break a law and you must pay the consequence! It was the unbending rule. Small Owl was going to die and so was the child he had come to look upon as his own.

Toward morning the wind gradually ceased to howl. It left in its wake the stillness of intense cold. Lodgepoles groaned. Limbs snapped from the trees. Ponds and streams became solid blocks of ice. Gritty snow slithered over the ground, hissing in the stiff grasses.

Gray Wolf, chastened by forces he had not been able to control, shivered in his blanket. The air was painful to breathe. He, Crazy Horse, Lame Deer, Touch-the-Cloud and Polecat shared Bending Bow's fire. They rested their foreheads on their knees to breathe the warmer air from the fire, captured by their bodies.

The women had taken over the lodge where Small Owl struggled. They had sent the men away after the wood had been piled high outside the lodge flap. And it grew colder.

"She will die." Gray Wolf voiced again the torment he had nursed all through the long night.

"It always seems so when they bring a life," Bending Bow spoke soothingly, "but they seldom do. These are things only women really understand. One moment you are certain they are going to die and then the next they are smiling and forgetful when the small one is in their arms." Gray Wolf wished he could believe.

"Do you really believe live wood makes a hotter fire?" Lame Deer spoke to Polecat.

"I know it does," Polecat answered.

"It is probably because its spirit is still in it. I hope we did not offend the God of Life by burning it." Crazy Horse was troubled.

"How can you offend God by burning wood?" Polecat asked.

"Wood when it is alive is alive," Crazy Horse explained as if it mattered what a white man understood. "I am not sure that to burn it is a good thing."

"Without it Small Owl would die." Polecat sounded angry. "Would you let her die rather than offend some god?"

"What is life?" Crazy Horse looked at the white man. "It is a thing the Great Spirit gives or takes, and it is nothing. But when a man offends, that is another thing."

"You sure are funny about how you offend," Polecat remarked.

Gray Wolf felt his anger rising. Why was Crazy Horse polite to this creature? He wished the man had tried to escape when they had been gathering wood. No one would have bothered to stop him. But there was no doubt that he was wise enough to know that he could not survive a day in this weather. He had worked as diligently as any, but he had convinced them to take live wood to burn for greater warmth. Gray Wolf felt that this was another unforgivable transgression that he had allowed simply because it concerned Small Owl. How was it, he thought, that a man began to get himself in trouble as soon as a woman became part of his life? If only this world was as simple as it had been such a short time ago when he was still a boy—but it was useless to think on such things.

A wolf howled with startling clarity. He was very near and bold in his hunger. Bending Bow raised his head.

"Lobo smells the birth," he said. "He has not eaten for many days. His hunger makes him desperate. We must stand guard."

"I will go." Lame Deer rose.

"No! It is my duty." Gray Wolf threw his blanket from him.

"It is everyone's duty." Bending Bow spoke gently but firmly. "We must take turns. It is too cold to stay outside for too long."

"You shall be first, then." Lame Deer sat back down and pulled his blanket close about him.

"I will go with you." Polecat stood up and looked at Gray Wolf. Gray Wolf stared at the white man disdainfully. Polecat stared back.

"I am your slave," he said. "It is my duty."

Gray Wolf continued to stare. He had not expected a *Wasicun* to ever admit he was a slave.

"Some white men," Polecat said, "can be trusted. Some even have as much honor as a Dakota."

Gray Wolf did not reply. He spun around and reached for his bow.

"The gun is the only weapon against a wolf," Polecat said. "I know how to make it speak again even if Gray Wolf does not. I will take it." He smiled in the insulting way he had of doing. "That is, if Gray Wolf is not afraid to be out in the dark with it in my hands."

"Afraid!" Gray Wolf sneered. "Bring it, since you are apparently afraid to be without it. But how do you use it without the berries which give it voice? We keep Lobo back with firebrands. Lobo is my brother."

Polecat reached for the gun. Crazy Horse was at his side instantly.

"It would be well for the *Wasicun* to be careful," he warned gently, but there was a cold look in his eyes that no one had ever seen before. Polecat fingered the empty gun. He looked down into the little brave's face and blew his breath between his teeth when he saw the look of the black eyes. He nodded his head and went out into the cold.

"There is something in that one," he muttered to himself, "that I will take care not to rouse."

Inside, Crazy Horse sat down. Bending Bow watched him and then tamped a bit of tobacco in his pipe. He inched closer to the fire to reach for a live coal and a chuckle rumbled deep in his throat.

No Dakota could remember when the people had not felt empty bellies by the time of the Hungry Moon. But the winter when Gray Wolf became a man surpassed all others. Everyone blamed the *Wasicun*. They had cut live trees to burn the night Small Owl's woman child had been born, and Nature had been angry.

The fury of the first storm was only the beginning. The extreme cold passed after two days and a fitful wind arose. It flounced around the lodges, swirling smoke and scuffing at the flaps. It sighed and veered, finally to die. Then the sky darkened and lowered to cling to the very tops of the trees. It started to snow.

At first it came gently, then furiously, and it filled the air. For six days it obscured the world. Layer upon layer covered the ground. It smothered the pond and buried the stream. It piled into a fluffy quagmire high around the lodge and imprisoned the people. Each lodge became an isolated universe smothered in the chest-high drift. To find wood meant floundering and groping in ceaseless labor.

Polecat tried in vain to get them to use green wood again, but they had listened to him once and Nature was already angry enough. Even the wild creatures lost their will to move. There was no track, nor trail, nor any imprint on the surface of the great white earth around them save their own.

Days followed days, each as dim as a twilight. The leaden overcast banished time, and days merged into weeks. Then one night the wind began to whisper outside the lodges. Soon it began to whine and then it rose to a screaming gale. The mists were swept away and the stars glittered in icy brilliance. The temperature dropped and a brittle dawn opened its door to a sun that rose in a blinding glare. It held no warmth for the Dakota. It sparkled and glittered at them with fanatic menace. And the world was a grim sheath of ice.

To walk was a feat. To find wood was a major exploration. To lift it from the belligerent earth was a combat. It had to be hacked loose from the ground. And the cold pursued their every move relentlessly. Any attempt to hunt was unthinkable. The cache of food dwindled with alarming rapidity. Spring was far away and starvation snarled louder than the gaunt, gray wolves that stalked the village.

They knew the day was swiftly approaching when there would be no more food. By common and unspoken consent, the older ones took very little of the thin, watery broth that the women brewed for a meal. As they grew more hungry they accepted less and smiled more and ladled their portions into young mouths that gulped in eager ignorance—and they prayed to retain enough strength to draw bow should the game reappear or nature relent—and for strength to fight off the impatient jaws that slavered outside the lodges.

To conserve wood and provide mutual protection, they huddled together. Gray Wolf brought Bending Bow and Crooning Woman to share Small Owl's lodge. It was crowded with six bodies, but six breaths and the tiny fire kept the lodge almost warm. Bending Bow weakened without solid food. He was unable to wallow through the snow or fight off the wolves. He stayed inside the lodge, where he kept careful control of the supply of wood. He sharpened axes and mended moccasins cut by the sharp ice. Falling Leaf kept the fire burning and rationed the remaining food into the kettle that she kept hot and brewing. Crooning Woman sang soothingly and renewed flagging spirits with her cheerful unconcern for the hard times that were with them. Small Owl had been unable to leave her couch since the birth of the weakened woman child, who became weaker each day. Falling Leaf spooned hot soup into her pale lips frequently, and she took more than her share in an effort to activate the decreasing supply of milk in her thin breasts. She held her child close to her body in an effort to lend warmth to the reluctant life. But it was evident that the child was starving. She slept fitfully and a small, racking cough came from her tiny mouth.

Morning Dew battled her way to the bedside each day until the threat of the wolves forced her to stay inside her own lodge. Willow Twig and Crazy Horse came frequently and brought precious morsels from their own lean pot. Waning Moon, her own time near, waddled her way with small offerings before the depth of the snow halted her lumbering gait. And Red Cloud, gaunt with hunger, brought a half-frozen jay he had stoned from a tree. It made a strong, unsavory stew, but it strengthened Small Owl in spite of its unpleasant flavor. And the wolves howled and pressed against the lodges in the nights.

Gray Wolf and Polecat grimly applied themselves to the task of finding wood. It was getting very scarce and they foraged farther and farther from camp, breaking their laborious way through the crusted snow. It was an agonizing progress, for they too were getting weak. They were obliged to rest often. They took turns breaking the trail. A fragile truce had been called between them, and they labored side by side, seldom speaking.

One bitterly cold day, they were struggling along when Gray Wolf spotted the windfall.

"Look." He pointed to the great stub of a tree that stood above the snow. It had been blackened by some long-forgotten fire and the main trunk and branches lay on the ground. The half-exposed limbs were a tangle of dead vines under a great mound of snow. It promised a bountiful treasure and they stumbled as they rushed toward it. Gray Wolf clawed up the slant of snow to reach the dry limbs above. He stopped suddenly and his eyes widened with excited anticipation. He raised his arm to stop Polecat, who had climbed behind him. He leaned down to examine the snow carefully. He sniffed.

"What is it?" Polecat was bewildered.

"A bear!" Gray Wolf breathed reverently.

"Are you sure?" Polecat was trying to claw his way up.

Gray Wolf pointed. In a small indentation of the crusted snow was a dark hole. The edges dropped inward and from it came a faint, pungent scent.

"Are you certain there's a bear in there?"

Gray Wolf chuckled.

"You stand back and learn," he said.

He braced his feet and swung his ax against the stub of the tree. It was as hard as stone and the ax bounced off, but the stump shuddered under the blow. He swung again and again.

Any doubt there might have been in Polecat's mind came to an abrupt end. There was a heaving of the snow. Gray Wolf yelled. The snow became a geyser, and the bear reared up on his hind legs. An infuriated roar came from his gaping mouth. His great forepaws swiped out toward the vandal who had wrecked his winter peace. Gray Wolf lost his footing and sprawled flat on his back. The great beast shook the shower of snow from his coat and swung his shaggy head back and forth. He dropped on all fours and lunged toward the prostrate form. Polecat sprang forward. Spinning and swinging from his heels, he brought his ax in a powerful, sweeping arc. The blade sank with a sickening thud into the bear's skull. The monster lurched and sagged. His legs sprawled and he sank wearily into the snow. Gray Wolf sat up. He gaped at the bear and at Polecat's feverish face. A wide grin split his lips and he yowled with a wild, joyful whoop. He reached out his hand. Polecat leaped forward to grasp it and fell headlong. Gray Wolf clapped him across the shoulders and they rolled and laughed together, forgetting in the spectacular light of this great miracle that one was *Wasicun* and the other Dakota.

Gray Wolf rolled to his feet. He shrugged his shoulders. He squirmed with elation. He slapped his thigh and clicked his tongue between his teeth. He kicked at one great forepaw and grinned.

"Pretty good! Pretty good! Huh?" He said it in English. His eyes were shining. Polecat laughed aloud.

"Pretty good!" he agreed.

He stood up and brushed the snow from his soiled buckskins. He came to stand beside the bear. His ax, still buried deep in the skull, drew his attention. He reached down and grasped the handle. Gray Wolf saw the movement and raised his arm.

"No!" he cried in alarm, but it was too late.

A gush of blood spurted out to spray the man's leggings and stain the snow. Gray Wolf clapped his hand to his forehead in dismay.

"You fool!" he moaned. "You big fool!"

"You got to bleed this critter," Polecat protested. "I don't care if you people do eat blood and guts. I ain't going to do it and I got a share in this bear."

Gray Wolf looked sick. He sat down in the snow. His elation was gone. He looked at the *Wasicun* in disgust. The amity between them was finished.

"You are more than a fool!" he said. "How do you think we will get this back to camp now?"

"Drag him," Polecat said.

"You drag him." Gray Wolf sneered. "You drag him through a whole pack of wolves that have already smelled the blood."

Polecat's mouth dropped open. He looked as sick as Gray Wolf felt.

"My sainted virgin aunt! I never thought of that." He dropped his face into his hands.

"You are right. I am a fool. Shoot me. I deserve it."

"No," Gray Wolf said grimly, "I won't shoot you. I may need you to feed to my hungry brothers while I get this bear back to camp."

"You'd do it, too." Polecat looked up. "By God, you'd do it and I wouldn't blame you. We'd better do something fast."

"We need help," Gray Wolf said.

He jumped to his feet.

"We don't have much time. Get up there and throw down some dry wood—fast! We will send for help. Make a fire to keep back the wolves." Gray Wolf was working feverishly.

He formed a small pile of the sticks. He selected two and with his knife cut a slit into the side of one. He stood the other upright and started to twirl. Out of the corner of his eye he saw a movement. It was a big, gray, slinking form.

"Get me wood," he called out. "Lobo is here!"

The wolves gathered fast. They hesitated and circled, uncertain but determined. Gray Wolf spun the stick. It grew hot and a tiny spiral of smoke curled up. The splinters were too large to catch. Sweat started out on his forehead. The wolves moved closer. They were mad with hunger and the smell of the fresh blood would soon overrule their caution. One great, gaunt beast edged closer. The palms of Gray Wolf's hands burned and yet the splinters did not catch. He half saw the wolf crouch. He did not raise his eyes. The brute gave a sudden yelp and drew back.

Polecat stood, another stick raised ready to fling. He had scored a bull's-eye on one tender snout. He was ready to try again. The lobo was slapping at his nose with a front paw.

"Fer Christ's sake, will you get that fire going?" Polecat was almost moaning. He hurled another stick into the cluster of animals.

If only he had something fine and dry, Gray Wolf thought. Why wouldn't the fire start? Why was it so stubborn when he needed it so badly? He had to get this meat back to the village. He was a man. He must act like a man. A man can think. Why couldn't he think? For the sake of Small Owl—for the sake of the warrior he had replaced—for the sake of the brother he had allowed to be betrayed in the Cloud Land—for the sake of Blue Feather—Feather—feather!

Deftly he dropped the spinning stick and grabbed at the eagle feather in his hair—the feather he wore so proudly. He flicked its tip into the charred smolder and with a mighty effort to control his breath he blew gently. It sent an acrid stink into his nostrils. He blew again, gently, gently. A tiny flame started. Daintily he laid a small splinter on the flame. He blew gently.

Polecat was yelling. The wolves were snarling and snapping. Sticks were flying. He blew gently. The splinter caught. Carefully he selected another and laid it on top of the tiny fire. Meticulously, carefully, he built, without regard to the grunts and floundering around and directly over him. He nursed the flame as if it were the only thing in the world to hold his attention.

"You slab-sided, overgrown coyotes!" Polecat was yelling. "Git back, you damned varmint. I'll mash your heads, ya scurvy, mangy sons-o-bitches—"

Gray Wolf grinned. If mean-mouthing lobos was a way to hold them off, he was glad Polecat had a full vocabulary. *Wasicun* were funny.

The fire started to blaze. The dry wood caught and flared. He continued to feed it. Sticks were flying and Polecat was cursing worse than ever. The fire grew into a real blaze. The wolves drew back.

"Take this." Gray Wolf held up a burning branch. "It works

better than son-of-a-bitch." His eyes twinkled. The situation was coming under control.

"We still need help." Polecat did not yet feel like grinning.

"We will get help, soon now," Gray Wolf answered, and he shook his head at the ignorance the *Wasicun* sometimes displayed.

"How?" Polecat wanted to know. "It's too far from camp to call."

"This smoke will make the call for us," Gray Wolf explained. "Do you think the people will not wonder why we burn wood out here?"

Polecat did not miss the faint sarcasm, nor the fact that he had asked a stupid question.

They had to wait a very short time. Warriors came from all directions, warily at first, until they saw the reason for the fire, and then swiftly, leaping inside the protective ring of fire and grabbing brands to drive back the hungry wolves.

Red Cloud bent down to nudge the bear with his hands. He nodded and clucked his satisfaction at the feel of the layers of fat.

"Good. Good!" He included Polecat in his approval.

It was a long, hard journey back to camp with the wolves stalking their heels, and Polecat could not understand why they were still reluctant to kill the beasts.

"A brother may be a brother," he said, "but when he tries to take the food from your mouth—"

"Maybe," Gray Wolf explained, "that's what makes you *Wasicun* and me Indian."

"Maybe!" Polecat was not impressed.

Winter tired of its tirade. It swept its storms eastward and the clouds drew back to open the sky once more. A friendlier sun wilted the snowbanks into slushy puddles that filled the hollows. It ripped the frigid gag from the voice of the river and the waters danced free in the topaz days. The game returned and the lobos departed. Laughter was heard again from the lodges.

Bending Bow and Crooning Woman returned to their own lodge and each morning they found wood and meat outside the flap. Red Cloud's face grew less gaunt and stern. Red Hawk and Morning Dew visited the lodge of their daughter-in-law, and the woman child clung to a fragile life. They called her Snow Maid, and fed her herb tea and sang songs. Waning Moon gave birth to a lusty boy and her husband strutted and gave lavish gifts to all. Willow Twig grew more listless and suffered a starvation that meat did not ease. Crazy Horse regarded his sister with misgivings and petitioned his mother, who only shook her head and sighed, her own dejection thinly veiled. And the name of Polecat ceased to be.

They had feasted swinishly on the bear. They had feasted and laughed and sung many songs. They had derided the winter, scoffed at the cold, and forgotten their misgivings. Gray Wolf had wallowed in the fraternity of seasoned hunters and the *akicita*, who praised him and glutted themselves. He had lolled back against a willow backrest and smiled benignly upon the *Wasicun*.

"What do your people call you?" he had asked.

"My name is MacLaughlin," he had answered, and Gray Wolf had flung up a hand that held a gnawed rib and called out in a loud voice.

"Hear this!" he had shouted. "The *Wasicun* is known as 'Macklin' to his own people. He is too great a hunter to be called by a woman-given name. Do you not agree? There has been enough of Polecat. No?"

"*Henala! Henala!* Enough! He has been called this enough. We agree!"

The approval was voiced in the rush of goodwill and bulging bellies. And the name of "Polecat" was laid on the embers of the forgotten.

And the winter passed and the warm winds came and the new green leaves began to show on the trees, and Snow Maid clung to life. Small Owl returned to her cook fires, and Gray Wolf rode with the warriors who took to the plains below in search of food and trespassers. And beside his brother-friend rode the reluctant brave who bore the colorless name of Crazy Horse. And in far distant places the pale-faced menace was looking away from Dakota land toward a place called Harpers Ferry.

4

"Look!"

Small Owl nodded her head toward the small figure squatting at the edge of the bluff.

The women turned to look. Their fingers continued to pluck at the ripe red berries. They laughed together.

"What is it?" Crooning Woman was peevish these days and she snapped her words.

"It's Rabbit," Small Owl explained. "He's sitting out on the edge, where he has been since the rising sun. He is trying to attract attention like Gray Wolf did so long ago."

"So long ago?" Morning Dew laughed. "You sound like an old woman recalling her years."

"It was a long time ago," Small Owl said. "Snow Maid is no longer a baby."

"And high time she had a brother!" Crooning Woman reminded.

"Remember the time," Waning Moon hurried to change the subject, "when Gray Wolf and Macklin got the bear?"

"I remember," Small Owl said. "How angry Macklin was at all of us because we ate it so fast. He was sure we would starve before that time was over."

"He was afraid for his own belly." Crooning Woman was not pleased with anything this morning.

"He was afraid for us all." Small Owl's voice was firm. "Macklin has been very good for us. He has taught us much."

"Much we could have done as well without."

"He cannot help being a *Wasicun*." Small Owl wanted to drop this conversation, but she could not allow the last word to be against the man she had come to regard with a mixture of awe and approval, guardianship and gratitude.

Back during that awful winter when Snow Maid had been born Macklin had won the heart of Small Owl. The child would have died but for him. When she had struggled for breath, the medicine men had come and then gone, declaring her too weak for the world. Macklin had taken the tiny body into his arms. He had pulled the suffocating mucus from her throat with his fingers, and with his own mouth he had forced air into her fragile lungs until she had been able to breathe her own breath once more. And Small Owl had turned her face away from the disapproval his act had brought from all sides.

The women had understood, for they were women and knew that the pangs of motherhood could overrule the laws of fitness. And they tolerated Small Owl's possessive protectiveness of the *Wasicun*—all except Crooning Woman, whose wisdom went beyond the grief of relinquishing a child.

"A rattlesnake cannot help being a rattlesnake," Crooning Woman said now. "But one does not take it into the lodge."

"Gray Wolf pulled his fangs," Morning Dew ventured gently.

"Maybe so and again maybe not so," Crooning Woman scoffed. "It is not a wise person that mistakes a dozing puma for a sleeping kitten."

"Well, he will be gone soon anyway," Morning Dew soothed.

"I wonder what he will do?" Waning Moon said. "Do you suppose he will find his own woman and children after all this time?"

"He will find them." Small Owl felt confident. "I wish you were coming with us."

"I wish it too." Waning Moon's eyes glowed. "I have always wanted to see places that are far away."

"Well, I have not wanted to see them. But that makes very little difference." Yellow Bird entered the conversation for the first time. "I would prefer to stay right here where we can live decently."

"Nonsense!" Crooning Woman snapped. "You could stay here

if you really wanted to. You are going just because you still treat Willow Twig like a child instead of a woman."

"I do not." Yellow Bird was ready for a quarrel. "She has never been the same since—" She trailed off, not having the courage to bring up the time when Willow Twig's beloved had not come home.

"Of course she has never been the same," Crooning Woman said. "You have not let her be the same. You yourself should have married again a long time ago—"

"It is very easy for you to tell us all what we should do." Yellow Bird was angry.

"There is no need for a quarrel," Morning Dew said. "The men will be back soon and we still have a lot of berries to pick."

"I have to empty my basket." Yellow Bird wanted an excuse to break away. She left the patch and went to the cluster of willow baskets set in the clearing. She emptied a few of the berries into her own basket and the rest into Crooning Woman's container. She winked at the women and they all smiled in their conspiracy.

"Your basket is almost full, Crooning Woman," she called.

"Certainly it is!" the old woman snapped. "If you picked more and talked less, yours would be almost full too." Her deft fingers plucked a handful of the ripe fruit. The rustle of buckskin against the bushes hid the sound of the berries that dropped to the ground instead of into the fold of doeskin at her waist.

"You are right," Yellow Bird answered. "But even then I would not be able to keep up with you."

"Huh!" The old woman snorted, but it was evident that she was mollified by the compliment.

Rabbit sat on his haunches and watched the plains below. His legs ached. His back ached. His belly felt the awful emptiness of a growing boy's belly that had been denied. He wished fervently that he had not decided to use Gray Wolf's method of attracting attention. It had seemed easy when he had thought about it. Now it seemed the hardest way of all. Rabbit wanted very much to have Gray Wolf take him as an apprentice. He admired Gray Wolf more than any other warrior he had ever seen. He wished he could move but he remembered—he who cheats, cheats only himself. He did not move. He sat and watched the trail below.

Out at the edge of the shadow of the far rim he saw them. He untangled his cramped legs and rose unsteadily.

I did it! he thought. I did it! And some of his exaltation sounded in the welcome cry that echoed over the plain below.

Down in the valley, Gray Wolf turned to grin at Crazy Horse.

"Would you like to make a bet that it is not Rabbit?" he asked.

"I would lose." Crazy Horse laughed. "It is Rabbit! That boy is so much like you it relieves my mind to know he was sired before you found interest in womanhood."

Everyone laughed and Gray Wolf laughed hardest of all. They were trail-weary, but the hunt had been successful and there had been no sign of the *Wasicun* in all the country they had covered. It was as if they had disappeared from the earth. It was said that they were killing each other at a most satisfactory rate somewhere back across the father of waters. The Dakota had been delighted to hear this, and they had listened to everyone who had brought news of the battles and the deaths brought about by people who, it was said, were neither *Wasicun* nor Indian.

Neither Gray Wolf nor Crazy Horse resembled the boys who had trembled into their manhood. Crazy Horse was still quiet, reserved and melancholy, but he was lithe and sinewy, plain and colorless. No feather or bead adorned his person. A long scar, the token of his first encounter with an enemy, was etched across his face. He wore it with morose dignity. No one, not even Gray Wolf, who should have remembered, guessed the tragic price his soul had paid for distinguishing himself less than a year after the puberty rites. Crazy Horse rarely spoke in public—never in council. Yet no warrior, young or old, was more cunning, more tenacious, more loyal or more discerning. Crazy Horse was respected and he was reticent. Men sought his thoughts and it frightened him. He was loved and it humbled him.

Gray Wolf was strikingly handsome, a fact of which he was pleasantly aware. He stood head and shoulders over all of his comrades. He was powerfully built and his aristocratic head, gift of his mother's forefathers, poised majestically on his broad, bronze shoulders. He was slim of waist and long of leg. He had the grace and speed of a cat, the smile of an Adonis and the eye of an eagle. He wore two feathers now, entwined in his glossy braids. He was bedecked in beadwork. He was the kind of man who made women forget their pledges and their men condone the lapses. Gray Wolf was moral and proud of it. He was a formidable adversary and delighted in it. His courage was boundless and it pleased him. The brother he had replaced had been a knight among his people. Gray Wolf was a prince.

The past years had been good years for the Dakota. Secession, states' rights, Confederacy and Emancipation Proclamation were not Dakota words. Manassas, Antietam, Gettysburg, Spotsylvania and Atlanta were not Dakota villages. Douglas, Grant, Lee, Lincoln and Sherman were not Dakota names. Only the faint echo of cannon sounded in the Dakota hills, and those echoes brought joy, not tears. The *Wasicun* had finally proved to be as deranged as the Dakota had always known him to be. Fortunately he was garroting his own kind with his madness. The smell of death and the stink of hate was smothering the arrogant tyrant, and the Dakota was well satisfied. They settled more and more into the old ways.

There had been a few skirmishes with the Gros Ventre and the Crow—just enough to provide opportunities for counting coup and practicing strategy. Those encounters were met with anticipation. Little blood was shed in such adventures, for there was no particular honor to be gained in taking life. None of the deadly endeavor used against the *Wasicun* accompanied these meets.

Both Gray Wolf and Crazy Horse recalled, when they chose— which was seldom—the first battle that had marked them as warriors. Gray Wolf remembered the glory he had gained that day. Crazy Horse remembered the blood he had shed.

It had been an unexpected fight—a wagon train lumbering across the plain, the buffalo scattering, Red Cloud's face hardening at the sight. Gray Wolf had plunged his horse forward, his mouth wide with the battle scream that came so naturally—"It's a good day to die!"—rushing from somewhere inside his throat, Crazy Horse close behind, silent, determined.

The emigrants had been surprised. It was evident that their leader was raw in the ways of the wilderness. The war screams of the charge had hardly ceased to echo before it had been finished.

Gray Wolf had ridden hard upon a burly man working desperately over flint and powder. The lance had been raised. It had been thrust. A look of astonishment had crossed the bearded face and a puzzled sorrow had filled the eyes. Slowly he had sunk to the ground, reproaching his killer with his weariness. Gray Wolf had killed for the first time. The sounds of the battle had faded. He had wheeled his horse and raced away. Deep in the undergrowth, weak from retching, he had staggered upon Crazy Horse, clinging to a tree, hawking his vomit.

They had sat together after a while, ashamed of their sickness and sick with their shame. When they finally gained the courage to rejoin the band, no one had appeared to notice their absence. They had been offered food and praise. Gray Wolf had accepted one with relish and the other gingerly. Crazy Horse had rejected both—but so unobtrusively that not even his queasy ally had noticed. They never spoke of that time. Gray Wolf's squeamishness had callused. For Crazy Horse it was a burden buried deep in his melancholy.

Summer had come to tame the wilderness once again and each living thing responded to the warm, life-giving sun. The thickets buzzed and droned, rustled and chattered with the lives of bees and birds, mice and moles. The deer had shed their shaggy coats for summer slickness and spotted fawns mimicked their mothers' dainty caution. Wild ducks piloted their fluffy fleets in and out of the reeds at the ends of the ponds, and fat, irrepressible bear cubs tumbled and rolled and poked inquisitive noses under windfalls and into holes. Birds gave furious concern to coaxing fledglings into flight and frequent thundershowers kept the earth moist. The air was sweet with the aroma of pine and cedar. It dulled memories of the past snow, which had been so like that of more than five snows ago. It dulled the memories of all creatures except Small Owl. To her the bitterness of the cold and the thinness of the soup remained a vivid fear and a stark threat.

Snow Maid had barely survived the mild seasons that had followed the terrible time of her birth. And when the stinging cold penetrated to frost the breath inside the lodges the child always collapsed into spasms of burning fevers and chattering chills. Racking coughs always shook her frail body and it seemed as if each winter would be the last of her wan existence. And the more frail the child became, the more viciously Small Owl fought for her life.

"What this child needs," Macklin had said to her one night when it seemed as if the child would not survive the darkness of another dawn, "is to be taken to Arizona."

"Where is that place?" Small Owl had asked and she had listened when the *Wasicun* had told her. From that time on Small Owl had decided that somehow she would take Snow Maid to this land of constant sun, and she had pleaded with Gray Wolf.

"I must think on this," he had said, hating to deny her even while he approved of her action not one bit more than did the others. He was troubled by her insistence that the child be kept alive. It was never wise to interfere with nature, and nature had long since set her stamp of disapproval upon the child.

In a civilization that could tolerate no deformity, no insalubrity, no imbecility and no depravity, this delicate child was a constant source of concern. But reverence for independence, self-determination and responsibility held that concern from interference. No word of dissent had been uttered, but Gray Wolf was acutely conscious of the bleak disapproval that hovered over Small Owl and the *Wasicun* slave. And as heartily as the people disapproved Small Owl's action, just as heartily did they approve of Gray Wolf, and he felt that they pitied him for his predicament. It was that which finally became intolerable to him and shaped his decision.

"Before the cold moons I will take you to your own people," he said to Small Owl. "That is nearer the land of constant sun. From that place I will have to decide if we will go farther."

And Small Owl was happy. The gladness shone in her eyes. Falling Leaf, hearing his words, had risen painfully from her place beside the entrance of the lodge. She had gone inside and when she had come out her few belongings were wrapped in her blanket. Without a word she had hobbled to the center of the campground and sat down, her shawl covering her face. Gray Wolf had hung his head in shame. Small Owl had pretended she did not even see the old woman. The entire village saw, but Falling Leaf sat alone. Out of respect for the warrior no hand had been held out to the Old One as long as the light of day would reveal the act. But when the next dawn had come the campground had been empty and Falling Leaf had been beside another breakfast fire, spooning broth into another small mouth. And word of Gray Wolf's promise to his woman was told from fire to fire.

Crazy Horse had come to stand beside Gray Wolf and he had said, "When do we ride?"

"My oldest sister is married to an Apache," Crazy Horse had said, more to have something to say than anything else, for everyone knew about Crazy Horse's oldest sister, and how she lived like a *Wasicun* woman, with an Apache for a husband.

"I have long wanted to see her. I will ride with my brother and so will my youngest sister and my mother."

Gray Wolf had been filled with happiness. He had invited Crazy Horse to eat with him while they discussed the trip. Then Bending Bow came with Crooning Woman by his side.

"It is a fine morning," Bending Bow had said, and Gray Wolf had replied that it was indeed a fine morning. And then Bending Bow had said that he had heard his young friend was planning a journey to the land of the constant sun.

"Will you eat with us?" Gray Wolf had said, hardly daring to believe that Bending Bow was going to approve. "We have plenty, Grandfather."

And Bending Bow had smiled and said, "Yes, I would like to eat with you and so would my woman."

And they had sat down at Gray Wolf's fire, and everyone had watched, and everyone had seen when Crooning Woman patted

Small Owl's hand and then gone inside the lodge with her after they had eaten.

Bending Bow sat back after he had finished and lit his pipe. He had smoked for a long time before he had spoken. "This is a long way you think of traveling. I went that way once when I was a young man. I remember the trails. But the land of the constant sun is not over-friendly. The Apache people are not over-fond of visitors and strangers."

"I have heard this," Gray Wolf had said, "but I have spoken and so we go. Crazy Horse and his sister and his mother go with us."

"I would go too," the old man had said, puffing his pipe.

"I would be honored to have my grandfather go with us." Gray Wolf had not kept the eagerness from his voice. He had learned since his boyhood that being a man did not keep emotion from the soul and there was no disgrace in showing it.

"It appears to my eyes that your woman is in need of an Old One in her lodge." Bending Bow continued to smoke, looking away over the hills to make it seem that there was no disgrace in the lack. "And Crooning Woman has long been fond of Small Owl as a mother is fond of a daughter. She has waited long for the opportunity to sit beside the entrance of this lodge. She would be happy if she was made welcome. I, too, would be glad to have a place in a young man's lodge so he could go on the warpath for me in my old age."

Gray Wolf had been almost reduced to tears. To have these Old Ones so honor him was a happiness he had never expected.

So the lodge of Bending Bow and Crooning Woman had been dismantled and they had moved into Small Owl's lodge, and with the move disapproval dissolved in the people's eyes. And Falling Leaf sat in another lodge and nursed regret that she had made such a hasty decision.

Rabbit dogged Gray Wolf's heels. He followed the warrior everywhere he went and listened to plans for the coming journey. His great, black eyes were mute with misery and Gray Wolf was not even aware of him. It was Crazy Horse who finally brought it to his attention. He drew Gray Wolf aside and said, "Rabbit wants to go with us. He will die if you do not pay attention to him. I think he might even do worse and try to get me to take him as apprentice if you do not take note."

"Rabbit?" Gray Wolf had laughed. "Why, he is but a boy yet."

"Ah yes," Crazy Horse agreed, "and was it so long ago you forget when the same was said of you?"

"Yes, it was long ago, wasn't it?" Gray Wolf remembered with warmness in his heart. "And do not worry, I will notice him even if he could do worse than be apprenticed to Crazy Horse."

"No," Crazy Horse said. "I do not want an apprentice. I have enough difficulty in disciplining myself."

Later, on his way to the sweat bath, Gray Wolf turned quickly. Rabbit was at his heels.

"Rabbit!" he said sternly.

"I am here." The boy was eager.

"Why are you following me?"

"Because my feet will not go in another direction." The boy was almost trembling.

Gray Wolf stood and looked down into the boy's face with inflexible stiffness. The boy quaked before the gaze. He was in terror of being rejected and humiliated, but he stood returning the gaze without lowering his pleading eyes.

"If they will not go in any other direction," Gray Wolf growled, "it comes to my mind they might as well be useful. Take care of my weapons while I take my bath."

The light of a rising sun came into Rabbit's homely features and his grin split his face into a thousand joys. He squared his shoulders and darted his eyes sideways to see the looks of envy on the faces of his former playmates. He grabbed the weapons and strode off, trying to match his stride to that of the giant warrior.

Red Cloud watched the excitement with a troubled eye. Oh, to be young again and full of the precious promise of life! There had been a time when enthusiasm had burned within him like a pure, bright flame, but the unspeakable agony of his years had dimmed that light and cooled the warmth. And why? Because of the mortal shame of subjection to the brutal force of hostility, ignorance and greed. Because some benighted sharecropper's son sought to swap the bigotry of his betters for an empire of his own. Because some vagabond rustic envisioned a liege's crest to embroider his homespun. Because "they" hurled themselves westward, recklessly, impatiently, bruising, tearing and wounding the land. They ground their brogans not only into the breast of Nature but into the hearts of the Dakota, the Cheyenne, the Kiowa and the Apache, just as they had done to the Seneca, the Huron, the Cherokee and the Mohawk a hundred years before.

They had turned back and had been absent for a while, and there were those who believed that the *Wasicun* were gone forever, but Red Cloud was not one of those. He felt their presence, their eyes and their intentions. He knew they would be back. They would be back as soon as they settled their own affairs. The peace his people had recently known was but a recess in the annihilation that was yet to come. His spirit had spoken thus and Red Cloud had listened.

Bending Bow came across the campground. His rheumatic bowlegs rolled his body from side to side like a great, lumbering bear.

"Well, my brother," he said to Red Cloud, "we ride with the morning sun."

"So you leave," Red Cloud said. "We have not been parted since first I became your apprentice, so long ago it now seems like a dream."

"This is so"—Bending Bow nodded—"and I sorrow that we now part. But when the young ones become reckless, the old ones must go along to lay a hand on their foolishness."

"This is true," Red Cloud said. "But I would wish it had been another who had done it. I am glad for Gray Wolf, however, that it is your hand, for it has always been a gentle one. I should know. I have felt it many times, and there has never been a sting in it."

Bending Bow smiled.

"Let us smoke together a last time, my son," he said, and they sat down and lit their pipes. No other words were spoken. They smoked in silence. Among the trees the cool shadows deepened and the evening light glowed, intimate and familiar. The noises of the camp muted to the gentle hum of twilight. Still they sat and smoked in profound dignity. Emotion too deep for utterance, too poignant for parting, delayed their retiring.

The evening star was dancing in the sky before Bending Bow tapped the ash from his pipe. He labored to his feet and Red Cloud stood beside him. They reached out, each to place their hands on the other's shoulders. They looked deep into each other's eyes. They stood for a moment, two strong men, fused by their love for each other. The darkness surrounded them. Their arms fell away.

Bending Bow turned and walked away. Red Cloud watched him go.

The holy one's voice quavered as he sang.

> *Wind from Fire Mountain!*
> *Wind from the Sleeping Sun!*
> *Wind of Midnight Rainbow!*
> *Wind from the Warm Spring Run!*
> *Listen to your brother.*
> *Listen to his word:*
> *Hark, and hear your brother pleading.*
> *Sing to him that you have heard.*
> *Go you with our sons and daughters*
> *To the land of warmer fires.*
> *Whisper in their hearts each wakening*
> *All the teachings of their sires.*
> *Let no anger, fear or failure*
> *Turn them from the path of honor.*
> *Let no sorrow, hate or envy*
> *Turn their tongues away from candor.*
> *If one day, their eyes grow lonely*
> *For the faces of their people*
> *Guide their hearts back to their homeland*

Where we always wait to greet them.
Go you with them, East Wind! West Wind!
North Wind, South Wind, with them ride.
Go you with them. Keep their shadows
Always walking by their side.

He lowered his arms. His song was done. Gray Wolf sprang to the back of his pony. He looked around into the faces that looked up at him. His eyes lingered long on the face of Morning Dew and clung to Red Hawk's eyes. Then he clucked softly. His mount moved. He turned his face away and did not look back. The sound of travois grating over stones started. He held his head high and fixed his eyes on the trail toward the south.

It was not the trail the hunting parties used. This one led down through the valley, past the place where Macklin had been captured, into a narrow gap where steep, tree-covered sides rose like a canyon. Here the trail dropped rapidly and the brook ran smoothly, swiftly over slick rock. The ride along here was labored, and it took time. It was late in the day before they came to the place where the stream boiled free into a green glade inhabited by giant cottonwoods and overhung on all sides by great, gray rocks.

Gray Wolf would have preferred to go farther, but the women and the horses needed rest. The women were unaccustomed to travel and the horses were weary with the strain of miles of rock and precarious footing. He curbed his impatience and called to make camp. The women responded with the gay chatter and happy laughter of a picnic. They unpacked the travois and gathered wood for fires. Bending Bow stretched his legs and eased his back up to the trunk of a tree. He lit his pipe, leaned his head back against the bark and closed his eyes. He puffed contentedly. Macklin and Rabbit helped the women with the wood. A small travel lodge was raised for Crooning Woman's comfort. The others would sleep under the stars. They were all like children. Snow Maid looked for pretty pebbles along the edge of the brook and Crooning Woman followed the sound of the child's footsteps.

Gray Wolf strode away to the grassy summit that overlooked the trail ahead. Below him yawned a valley, narrow and long, that lost itself in the distance. The hills were split by many of these valleys, ruled over by crags, rugged with a nameless wildness that was akin to the untamed beat of his own heart. His dark, piercing glance fixed on the trail below. His naked shoulders rested at ease. There he watched as the hours passed. The happy sounds behind him faded and he was conscious only of the hope and joy inside him, the love of promised adventure and the challenge of the future. He was glad Small Owl had brought all of this about. He let his thoughts wander and they drifted back over the years of his unfolding manhood. He thought of his long and strange relationship with Small Owl. Something deep in his heart vibrated. He loved her. He loved her and he wished he could have been in love with her. He was not. And she was not in love with him. No magic spark of physical magnetism had ever ignited between them. His love and hers was molded of firmer substance—and yet he craved, not spiritually but physically, not always but often—to know the gossamer enchantment of infatuation.

He had seen first one and then another of his friends, half crazed with the excitement of desire and the dismal fear of rejection. He had derided their idiocy, exhibited his own tranquillity and wrestled mightily with envy. He had wondered more than once if romance had been omitted from his being. He had secretly eyed every maiden in the village, but not one had worn the aura of mystery for him. Since there was never a secret in a Dakota camp, everyone was well aware of his brother existence, and he had come in for his share of shy, sidelong invitations, but none had ever slackened his step toward Small Owl's fire and sisterly devotion.

He wondered if somewhere out in that vast beyond there was a doe-eyed girl who would kindle a flame within him. He hoped it would be so.

He felt, rather than saw Crazy Horse come to squat a few feet away. He made no sound in his approach and he sat near, but not close. No one, not even Small Owl, could rouse such warmth as did this small, melancholy man who was his brother.

The sun moved on until it tipped the peaks with rose and purple. Twilight moved in and painted the shadows under the trees a deep blue. Only then did the two men turn, half reluctantly, toward the campfire that beckoned them back from their dreaming.

Darkness had settled by the time the meat was broiled. The women had spitted it on sharp sticks and turned it over the hot coals. They all sat about the fire and ate with relish. As the fire burned down to a ruddy glow, the night moved in. Crooning Woman grunted and groaned into the protection of her small lodge. Bending Bow rolled his blanket across the opening. The others spread blankets on the grass to rest, if not to sleep. A cool breeze came down from the peaks, and the stream sang its own mysterious chant in a silky monotone. The stars shone brightly, and under the cliffs shadows brooded. The wail of coyotes far in the distance sounded wild, haunting and poignant. Sleep did not close Gray Wolf's eyes to the star-studded ceiling of the valley, nor did it tranquilize his spirit against the magic of the night. He lay still and wide awake. There was the soft pad of a moccasined foot and Crazy Horse loomed dark and silent over him. He paused only a moment before he slipped away into the night. Gray Wolf folded back his blanket and rose to follow.

They climbed again to the place where they had spent the quiet hours before sunset. They settled down side by side.

"Do you remember the day we smoked and got caught?"

Gray Wolf could not see his friend's face, but he heard the smile in his voice.

"I remember," he said.

"I do not think we would get caught tonight," Crazy Horse said.

"No," Gray Wolf agreed. "I do not believe we would."

A soft glow showed in the darkness. It brightened and caught the gleam in Crazy Horse's eyes. The sweet smell of tobacco mingled with the night air.

"You are still a sly little fox." Gray Wolf chuckled. "How did you get that live coal up here without my seeing it?"

"In a handful of green leaves." Crazy Horse almost giggled. "It sure got hot in my hand, too."

Out here on the trail he seemed to have recaptured some of the shy humor of his boyhood. He pulled deeply on the pipe and blew a cloud of smoke skyward. He passed the bowl to Gray Wolf.

"I could not sleep," he said.

"Nor I," Gray Wolf answered.

"I feel like speaking to my brother."

"I feel like listening."

They passed the pipe back and forth. Gray Wolf waited, respectfully silent, for his brother-friend to speak. The night held many hours and there was time. Finally Crazy Horse spoke.

"I think maybe when we come back my mother Yellow Bird will marry my second father."

"I also think she will do this," Gray Wolf agreed. "I am only surprised she has not done so before."

"It has been because of Willow Twig," Crazy Horse said, "and I think Willow Twig will not be coming back with us."

"You think then she will stay in that place with strangers?" Gray Wolf could not believe that Willow Twig would consider such a thing.

"I think she will stay." Crazy Horse sounded sorrowful, but he said no more.

"If she stays and your mother marries again," Gray Wolf ventured, "then you will have no lodge. Will you lodge with the akicita?"

"You know the akicita would not have me." Crazy Horse did not sound as if he cared. "I will lodge in my own lodge."

Gray Wolf knew he was leading up to the point of this midnight conversation.

"How so?" he asked.

"I intend to take a wife." Crazy Horse expelled the words like a guilty confession.

"A wife!" Gray Wolf had never noticed his friend's interest in any woman. "Who?" he asked.

"It is Dawn." Crazy Horse breathed the name.

"Dawn?" Gray Wolf felt stupid repeating his friend's words, but he was too surprised to think of anything appropriate.

"Yes. Dawn!" Crazy Horse puffed the pipe with vast satisfaction. "I have loved her since she was a child, and when we return I shall take my best ponies to her father's lodge."

"Then you will be anxious to return very quickly."

Crazy Horse was thoughtful for a moment.

"No," he said, "Dawn is still very young. There is plenty of time."

"Has she promised to wait for you?" Gray Wolf asked. "Aren't you afraid someone else might find favor with her while you are away?"

"We have never spoken words since she has become a woman," Crazy Horse said. "She is a good girl and obedient to her womanhood. But I have asked her with my eyes and she has promised with hers."

"I am glad." Gray Wolf touched his friend's arm lightly. The glow from the pipe again caught the gleam of happiness that had driven the melancholy from the small warrior's eyes. They smoked until the tobacco was burned out. They had no coal to light another pipe so they sat and listened to the voices of the wilderness and felt the wonderful goodness of life.

It was gray dawn before they slipped silently back to their blankets, where Crazy Horse fell instantly into a sleep that brought dreams of a sweet face that kept fading from his sight. Gray Wolf dreamed of a nameless horror that escaped his memory the moment he awoke, but hung onto the fringes of his mind to haunt him with uneasy dread.

Southward they traveled, and then before them lay the great, endless plain. The holiday atmosphere changed. They moved deliberately, stealthily and as swiftly as possible.

The stealth irritated Gray Wolf. It gave him a sense of unjustifiable guilt for simply being. Alone, or with a band of warriors, he would have ridden openly, defiantly, and woe to the creature who would have dared challenge his passing. But he was not alone. He did not have a band of warriors. He was the leader of his own *tiyospaye*[5] and it was small. So he skulked when he would have chosen to stalk boldly and his mind concentrated on memorizing every feature of the vast plain.

He ordered fires only when the smoke would mingle with the haze of early dawn and late dusk. He kept the march in arroyos and gulches, despite the rocks that were destructive to the travois. He constantly watched the skyline and permitted no one to silhouette himself against the horizon.

The past years had been fairly peaceful, almost without incident, as far as the Dakota were concerned. But visitors had brought news of the battles fought by the Cheyenne, the Comanche, the Arapaho and the Apache. The Cheyenne were supposed to be at peace now. White Antelope, whose village was their destination, had been with them this past summer, and he had assured Gray Wolf that a firm treaty had been made between the *Wasicun* and Black Kettle. But Gray Wolf was wary of treaties, and in spite of them, in spite of warnings and battles, wagon trains still ventured through Indian territory. Gray Wolf would take no chances with the women and the child. And a sullen resentment filled his heart that it had to be so. He became terse and demanding, and the women looked at him puzzled and a little fearful. Bending Bow looked at him with satisfaction and approval.

Gray Wolf was uneasy over Macklin, too. He watched the *Wasicun* closely and noted the ill-concealed impatience that was growing in the man. He had lived with the red-bearded giant for the past five years. He had learned to speak his tongue. But he did not feel that he knew him. He had come to have a certain respect for him and had given reason for that respect to be returned, but Macklin was still a *Wasicun* with *Wasicun*'s nature. And Gray Wolf could not bring himself to trust that nature. He hoped that he had not made an error in promising the man his freedom when they arrived at the Cheyenne village. Macklin had told them that his home lay within a few hours' ride from the village, and White Antelope had said the same. It was at a place

5 Band.

they called Fort Lyon. Gray Wolf had believed White Antelope when he said there was peace between them and the soldiers at the Fort. He had believed with his mind, but his spirit remained uneasy. Forts meant Long Knives and Long Knives meant trouble sooner or later.

Gray Wolf wanted very much to walk among the *Wasicun*. He wanted very much to see one of their villages. He wanted to see for himself some of the things he had heard and his reason had told him that he might do so. But the farther he traveled the less his spirit listened to that reason. He wished he knew why he felt this way. But there did not seem to be any answer. Macklin grew impatient, but that was a natural thing. The *Wasicun* was never good at concealing his feelings, and Gray Wolf tried to think how he would feel himself if he was going home after so long. Still he could not trust Macklin, and the passing days that seemed to bring no end to the rolling, treeless plain did nothing to add to his cheer. The sun burned very hot and only the child seemed to thrive in it. Crooning Woman was finding the journey extremely wearisome, but she did not complain. Gray Wolf ordered her to ride the travois. Yellow Bird did complain. She grew sore and stiff from the many hours on foot, and more sore and stiff from more hours on the back of the horse. Willow Twig and Small Owl, after the first few days, had become accustomed to the strain and caused no worry over their ability to keep up. And the days passed into days, each like the other, and still the plain seemed endless.

In the Cheyenne village, Black Kettle had been to a place called Denver where he and his friend Major Wykoop had talked to the white chief governor. The pipe had been smoked and a good peace had been made. The white chief had promised soldier protection as long as the Cheyenne kept the peace, and the Cheyenne, to show that they meant to keep their word, had turned in most of their long guns. They kept only enough to use for hunting, and if there were those who had questioned the wisdom of that action, there were others who, for the first time in many years, felt secure. They lived a happy, carefree life with plenty of food and pleasant days on the banks of Sand Creek. And they watched the trail northward for the visitors from Dakota country.

Early in the beginning of the change of seasons Gray Wolf saw the smoke of Cheyenne fires. The journey was done. He smiled and his mind cast aside the dark thoughts and doubts it had carried along the trail.

The Cheyenne saw them, and White Antelope rode out to meet them. In the village there were welcome calls, for Cheyenne hospitality was lavish and Small Owl was a Cheyenne woman coming home for the first time since she was a child. Fine lodges of good buffalo hide were ready for their comfort, and kettles steamed with an abundance of food. The air was filled with the good smell of roasting meat.

Crooning Woman rolled off the travois and sat on the ground. She groaned and held out her little hands.

"Somebody help me up," she said, "while I make a vow not to travel anymore where my feet will not carry me."

There was a deep-toned laugh from a young Cheyenne warrior who came to her and took her hands in his. Gently he pulled her to her feet.

"Those pretty little feet should carry a pretty little thing like you anywhere you would want to go, Grandmother," he said.

Crooning Woman tilted her head.

"Don't we have a pretty tongue!" she said. "You must be in love to have such pretty words in your mouth."

"Oh, I am," he cried. "The very moment I saw you I was no longer a lonely man."

She giggled appreciatively.

"Old Man!" she called to Bending Bow. "You had better come or someone will almost certainly get into the wrong lodge tonight."

Bending Bow came and took her arm. He smiled at the warrior.

"It's always like this," he said. "Everywhere I go men try to take her from me."

The Cheyenne smiled back.

"Since she is already taken," he said, sighing with exaggerated emphasis, "I suppose I must bear my loneliness a little longer. But my heart is sad because of it. Welcome to our village. I am called Roman Nose."

"Such nice people," Crooning Woman murmured wearily as Bending Bow led her to the lodge that had been erected for them. She sank down on the couch. "I can't help but wonder how I shall ever make the trip back home. I do not seem to take to travel very much. My feet do not want to stay with my heart anymore."

"It's all right," he said to her, pulling a blanket over her. "Don't worry about it. It will be a good while before we go back and you can rest."

He looked down at her fondly. Already she was asleep. It was the first time in his memory that Crooning Woman had slept while the sun was in the sky.

Are we getting so old? he thought, peering closely at the old and wrinkled face. But he saw none of the lines that marked her features. He saw only the fresh, smooth cheek of the girl he had taken for a wife and the gentleness of first love was still in his fingers as he touched the braids that had somehow turned from glossy black to silver.

Gray Wolf stood on the small rise behind the village and looked down over the expanse of lodges blanched by overexposure to decades of weather. The predawn air was sweet and clear and bracing. The slight stir of the wind mingled the aromas of smoke and sage. The fire of the dawn kindled in the east and burst into a flaming sun that warmed his body and suffused his being with a vibrant benevolence. He breathed deeply. His chest expanded in a mighty effort to nourish the exuberance that was being born inside him. He felt intoxicated with a sensation of growing and expanding in size and stature until he towered over all the tawdry deficiencies of humanness.

Wonderingly he lifted his face. He felt the firmament brush his cheek. He raised his arms and found infinity at his fingertips.

Fervently he chanted his morning song, awed with his own being and with his unity with the universe.

He could not understand what had happened to him. Always he had striven for this oneness with life, and always before it had eluded him. What was here in this land that brought it about? He did not know, but he knew that some great and special thing had happened. It was an elation with life, and he wanted to share this wonderful experience with Small Owl. And he wanted to find someone who could explain it to him and tell him what it meant. His eagerness to share his experience goaded his feet into a pace that his dignity refused to follow. With great deliberation he walked down the rise toward the lodges. His eagerness grew. He strode around the lodge where she knelt beside the fire. His elation faltered and deflated. Macklin was sitting across from her. He should have been gone. The light in Gray Wolf's eyes dulled and darkened. Why was the *Wasicun* still here? The wonderful feeling inside him turned sour and all the mistrust that had haunted him on the trail returned.

"You do not seem overeager to see your own people," he said as Macklin rose to greet him.

"I have been waiting for you," Macklin said. "Small Owl said you had gone to sing your morning song."

"I always sing my morning song in the morning," Gray Wolf said dryly. He did not feel hospitable toward this man. He wondered if the wonderful elation he had experienced had been because the *Wasicun* was no more in his lodge. It was as if for all this time it had been he and not the *Wasicun* who had been the slave. This morning he had tasted freedom such as he had not known since the days before his manhood. And now the beauty had turned sour and mean in his belly.

"I thought maybe you might like to ride in with me," Macklin said.

"Why would I like this?" Gray Wolf was mistrusting more and more.

"There is peace. There is no danger," Macklin said.

"I have not always walked in places where there was peace." Gray Wolf was suspicious that Macklin was baiting him.

"I did not imply you were afraid," Macklin said. "I would like to have you come to my home. I have been away a long time. I do not know if they are even there. I think they would believe I was your prisoner if they saw you."

"They will not believe this if you tell them?" Gray Wolf was puzzled. Could it be that the *Wasicun* did not trust the word of each other?

"You don't know my woman." Macklin shook his head. "I would like to have you come with me when I tell her that I have been away all these years because I could not come back."

"She will know this when you tell her!"

"No she won't. She will think I stayed away because I wanted to," Macklin answered. "I do not even know if she will be glad to see me."

"You think seeing you with the Dakota will make her glad?" Gray Wolf could not keep the irony from his words.

"I would be pleased if you would go with him." Small Owl spoke for the first time. "He has told me about his people and I understand. We are to blame for his being away and I would be pleased to have him welcomed back. It would make my heart glad to repay the debt we owe him."

Gray Wolf was angry. It was an anger at her as well as an anger at Macklin.

"It is time to eat," he growled and sat down, using the time of eating to think what he should do. Small Owl did not know his nature or she would never have asked this of him, and he wondered how this could be so. They had lived in the same lodge for a long time. There had been no marriage of their bodies, but he had been content, for he had honored her right to a vestal existence. He had never claimed any title to her person. But he had always felt that there had been a marriage of their hearts. That she would ask this thing of him made him realize that she did not place his desires above those of a *Wasicun*. He had pledged his spirit to her, and until this moment he had never questioned that she had done the same. He looked at her as he ate and saw that her face was serene. She did not even know that she had wounded him. She was a dry river, a sky without a sun, a night without stars. He had wedded himself to any empty lodge that held nothing but the look of a woman. She had no regard for him because she had no regard for anything but the ghost of the man who had sired the weakling child that had brought them all to this land that was not their land, and these people who were not their people.

The realization was bitter and it made his words bitter.

"I will do you a service and take your trembling slave to his home," he said to her. He rose from the fire and strode away to catch his horse. And, he thought to himself, when I come back I am going home and you can stay here with your relatives and your child and your empty heart. And I will forget you and live because I am alive and you are dead as you have been dead since the day I took you for my woman.

5

"You ain't goin' no place!"

Louise MacLaughlin punched at the glob of gray dough she was kneading. Flour sprayed up and clung to the coarse hair on her arms. Her uncomely features became more unlovely with her anger.

She was not a large woman, but heavy bones and large work-callused hands gave her the appearance of one. Her straight, sparse hair, gray at the temples, was drawn back into a hard, tight knot on the back of her head. Her worn calico dress was shabby and faded and shapeless. It was pulled in around her waist by apron strings that had long since wilted into twisted cords. Her colorless eyes blazed with wrath.

"They is times," she flared, "when I wish you was back wherever you come from—wherever that is. Blood always tells, my mother used to say, an' it's the truth. Your blood is tellin' on you. I told you before and I'll tell you agin. I ain't goin' to have you actin' like no whey-faced bitch while you are in this here house."

The girl stood poised and defiant. Her lower lip protruded in a pout. She was as lovely as the angry woman was plain. She was tall and willowy, with a mass of silver-blond hair that curled into tiny ringlets where it escaped from the bright red ribbon that held it loosely at the nape of her neck. Her skin was ivory white and it glowed with translucent loveliness that bespoke of careful protection from the sun. Her dress was as faded as the woman's calico, but it fit her without a wrinkle and followed every curve from the high prominent breasts to the tiny waist and down over the swell of full round hips. Her wide blue eyes were sullen.

"You can stand there and try to look like a lady, but it just don't go over when you act like a slut," the woman said, "and a slut is what you are, playin' up to a half-breed like Jack Smith."

"I ain't been playing up to no Jack Smith," the girl said.

"Don't you go tellin' me I don't know what I see with my own eyes," Louise MacLaughlin snapped. "I seen you, Melody Mac-Laughlin! I seen you, and I ain't never been more shamed in my whole life."

"I can't help it if he follows me around," the girl whined. "I never ask 'em to."

"Askin' with words ain't the only ways there is to ask!" She punched the dough with her fist. "I never was so mortified. I made up my mind right then and there you been up to the fort fer the last time. You're goin' t' act decent if I have to chain you up. You can jest make up your mind right now. Tonight you're goin' t' stay home. You ain't goin' t' no dance."

"I am too goin'," the girl flared. "I'm goin' and you can't stop me. You're jest mad because not even Paw could stand you, and you can't stand to have men like me. I'm a goin' to that dance." She stamped her foot and fled from the room. As she went the woman yelled after her.

"Jest you try it, miss, and you'll get the biggest comeuppance you ever got. An' take the red ribbon outta yer hair around here. You look enough of a floozy without that."

The house was L-shaped. On the longer side was the common room with the fireplace at the end. Rude cupboards and the table formed the kitchen. It was here that Louise MacLaughlin made her bread, cooked her meals, washed the clothes and directed the frustrated existence of her fatherless family. At the end of the room opposite the fireplace were two small rooms, one of which she had occupied since the day Big Tim MacLaughlin had brought her here as a bride. It was in that room that she had borne their son and it was in that room that she had learned (because her big red-headed fool of a husband talked in his sleep) about the Indian woman who had occupied it before her. She had faced him with his nocturnal mutterings and he had confessed, shamefaced and contrite, to the association, which even then had not been terminated.

Louise had been badly wounded. She had been so badly wounded that the only relief from her pain had been to hurt in return. She had locked him out of her room and developed an acid tongue that had become famous over the countryside.

At first Tim had begged her forgiveness, and she had meant to give in—in time. But before she realized it Tim had given up asking and started spending more and more time away from home and the sound of her voice. She had decided that he had taken up with his "squaw" again and she was merciless. Then Tim had taken to scouting for the Army and he had not even bothered to let her know when he would be coming or going. Finally, she had known that he came home only to see the boy, and to punish him for this she had started on a campaign to discredit the father in his son's eyes. Little Tim, too young to know what was happening, had responded to his mother's teachings and it was not long before he was so frightened by his father's appearance that he would run and hide when Big Tim came home. After that Big Tim had come seldom, only often enough to see that the woman and the boy were not in want. And so they had lived for a number of years.

Louise realized too late what she had done and did not know how to undo it. She had turned to religion and had derived a perverse pleasure from reading the passages of her Bible that had reference to adultery and whoring and penalties attached to such transgressions. She became an authority on all such verses and took great delight in quoting them. Every now and then she had periods of remorse and would do everything in her power to entice Big Tim back into their home and her bedroom. But Big Tim did not entice easily.

It had been during one of these periods of remorse that Tim had come back from a scouting trip carrying a baby girl whom he had named Melody. The troops had found the child, the lone survivor of a bloody massacre of a small wagon train. In the verve of her current remorse and affirmation to mend her ways, she had begged Tim to allow her to take the child as her own. Young Tim, she had said, was growing up, and with Big Tim gone so much she would be glad to raise the girl. Because no one else wanted the responsibility, Big Tim had agreed. And because she thought it would soften Big Tim's heart toward her, Louise had been delighted. But not for long. It had not softened Big Tim's heart. Instead he had become foolishly fond of the girl and the child had returned his devotion passionately. The only thing it had accomplished was to bring Big Tim home more and harden his hide against the lashings Louise continued to pour on him. His devotion to the little girl only added fuel to Louise's jealousy. The household had become divided, with Big Tim and the girl against Louise and young Tim. Even when she had become old enough to understand the plainly phrased descriptions of her father's faults, Melody had turned a deaf ear to her mother's accusations.

Then Big Tim had gone and he had not returned. For a long time Louise had not even inquired, but after the family became nearly destitute, she made discreet inquiries at the fort. It was then that she learned that Big Tim had not gone on a scouting expedition. No one knew where the big man could be. Months—a year—then two years went by and in the fort it was the consensus that Big Tim MacLaughlin had "got hisself kilt." Louise held the opinion that her husband had deserted her. She knew she had driven him to it and she had wept and prayed for his return. She had read her Bible and read the passages about forgiveness, after which she would read again the Scriptures that promised eternal damnation for his carnal soul.

And young Tim grew from a gangling boy into a strapping man, a physical replica of his father. And Louise, fearing that he might turn into the paths his father had traversed before him, made sure that his education was complete concerning whoring and its penalties.

Melody grew into a raving beauty, in spite of all Louise's efforts to keep her plain and unattractive. But Melody displayed tendencies that Louise imagined were so like Big Tim that she became suspicious, and in the long, lonely nights, she came to the conclusion that Big Tim had lied about the girl; that the girl was, in fact, Tim's own bastard that had been foisted upon his God-fearing and unsuspecting wife. And Louise came to hate the girl as passionately as she loved her son. Her sole comfort became the Bible and the boy.

When Jed Clooney, the sire of the trashy Clooney clan from south of the fort, came to the house with his half-wit daughter Sara Jane and demanded that young Tim marry the girl without delay, Louise MacLaughlin's entire world crumbled. Bitterly disillusioned, she relegated the young couple to the loft that had Melody's pallet, and gave the girl her son's bedroom. It was not through any hope or regard she had for Melody, but because she felt a bedroom was too good for the half-wit Sara Jane. Her days were nightmares with trying to run the homestead, keeping Melody away from the men who gravitated toward her like flies to honey, and enduring the presence of the detestable Sara Jane. Her nights were worse, for young Tim's brat, born a scant six months after the hasty marriage, screamed and squalled while his mother and father made unmistakable sounds that shook the floorboards of the loft and sent streams of dirt down on the kitchen table. Louise lay, night after night, grinding her teeth in rage as the thumping and wrestling went on over her head and her mind conjured up visions of what her "innocent" young son was doing. Day after day she worked herself into exhaustion, and alternated between pleading with the Lord to deliver Big Tim back to her safely and thanking the Lord that he be sizzling in hell if he was dead.

Outside she heard Melody scream. She clutched the lump of dough in hands that turned icy. Perspiration gathered on her forehead and upper lip, for Melody was screaming over and over, "Paw! Paw! Paw!"

Gray Wolf had turned away from Small Owl in a blind rage. It rode with him as he galloped his pony out of the Cheyenne village. It seethed and rankled, but now it was directed upon himself. It gave birth to a recklessness that was the only thing that would satisfy the biting passion. He was eager to invite some dire danger upon himself. He craved punishment. His thoughts raced with his pony.

He had started his life wrong. He had taken Small Owl to wife long before he had been ready for such a responsibility. The fact that he had cared for her successfully and carried out his undertakings properly could not and did not condone the act. He had lived in a fool's world. She had defied the universal laws, and he had lent his support to that transgression. He had known retribution would be forthcoming, and yet he had not turned away. He had set himself above the law. He had pitted himself against the sacred system, and not until this moment had he even realized that all along he had been paying the penalty. The penalty was just. He would not argue that. The fact that he had been unaware of its presence was another thing. He had been a fool and that was the source of the rage consuming him. That was the source of the invitation for peril toward his person. He was loathing himself and nursing a wounded ego. His being was bruised and the rage inside him was intolerable.

Tim MacLaughlin sensed the warrior's mood. He rode in wary silence, wondering what had brought it about. He tried to think back over the few words that had been spoken and could find nothing that would bring on the turmoil that was apparent in the man's manner.

He had enjoyed a peaceful existence among the Dakota because he had weighed and measured his every act during the whole time he had been with them. He would have taken a Dakota woman and stayed with them if Gray Wolf had been willing to relinquish his ownership and declare him free. But Gray Wolf had offered freedom only to return to his own. For the first time since the early days of his capture, Tim MacLaughlin actually feared for his life.

But Gray Wolf was not thinking about the white man. He was thinking only of himself and what had been and what was to be. He had never felt a complete assurance with Macklin, and his natural aversion to a *Wasicun* convinced him now that he was riding to his death. But he was not afraid. He was almost eager. He felt that all of his people must have known all of this time that Small Owl had stayed married to a man no longer of this world, and they must have pitied him for his ignorance. They had felt he had been cheated. He knew he had cheated himself.

It was too intolerable to endure, and rather than face it or them again, he would die. He rode in sullen silence. To live in disgrace was an awful thing. To die in disgrace was almost as bad. There was no balm for his suffering. He only hoped to end it quickly.

They topped a rise in the barren waste and far ahead lay the fort. They pulled their ponies up and sat to look. Macklin waved his hand and said, "That's the fort over there." He waved his hand in the other direction. "My house is over there. You can't see it because it is under those cottonwoods, tucked down in a little draw. It's protected from the winds there."

"Also out of sight," Gray Wolf remarked without interest.

"Also out of sight!" Macklin answered. And then, boldly trying to pull the warrior from his mood, he added, "Indians, you know."

Gray Wolf was not amused. He looked at Macklin coldly.

"Oh well." The white man sighed. "Might as well ride on. You don't have to come any farther if you don't want to. It was a fool thing to ask anyway."

"I will ride all the way." Gray Wolf sounded stubborn.

"Well, you won't be sorry." Macklin wanted to make conversation. "Wait until you see that girl of mine. Must be a woman by now and you never saw nothing like her. Got hair like pure sunshine."

Gray Wolf was irritated. "Hair like pure sunshine!" Why was it that the *Wasicun* felt he had to set the bait after the catch was already made? Hair like pure sunshine! But it was really of no consequence. After this he would have no more to do with *Wasicun*—or Dakota. If the *Wasicun* did not kill him, he would ride away to a solitude where he could nurse back to health the wound in his soul.

They rode under the trees. Macklin dismounted. Gray Wolf did not even bother to get down. He watched Macklin as he studied the cabin. Gray Wolf had seen settlers' cabins before— watched them burn—but he had never sat so openly and studied such a place. He felt naked and exposed. Some of the torment that had ridden with him dissolved under the instinct of caution.

"They are still here," Macklin said.

Just then the door of the cabin came open and a woman came running out. It was evident that at first she did not see them. The wind caught at her dress and whipped it out to billow behind her. She reached up with a small white hand to pull away the red ribbon that held her hair. Only then did she look up. She saw them and stopped, her hand suspended. Then she screamed. She screamed and started running toward them. Gray Wolf was stunned. Macklin had not lied. Never had Gray Wolf's eyes seen anything like the woman running toward them. She was unlike any creature he had ever seen. She was not mortal. Her hair was not like "pure sunshine," it was sunlight itself. It streamed out as she ran. She was the sun. She was the wind. She was a flower, blossoming in a pure day. She was the most beautiful creature he had ever seen, and she was throwing herself at Macklin, laughing, crying, screaming, "Paw! Paw! Paw!"

Gray Wolf stood against the wall, rigid as rock. His nerves were jumping. He felt raw and sore. A prickling repugnance tormented his spine. He felt acutely the need to leave this place. The thought slid through his mind without triggering any intent to obedience. He suffered.

The faces, pasty and hostile, the voices, rattling like hail on a lodge, the room, cluttered like a pack rat's nest, closed in around him. The smells of grease, dust, bread and urine mingled sickeningly in his nostrils. The smoke from the stove and from the lopsided flame of the lamp smarted his eyes. *Wasicun* smell was overpowering and it revolted his stomach.

"Goddammit!" Macklin was talking as if everyone was deaf. "Seems to me I could spend an hour after all this time without listenin' to this kind of yappin'."

He gulped greedily on the contents of the mug he had filled and refilled. His face was becoming flushed and his eyes held a strange light. The baby screamed and Macklin's woman screamed to be heard over the sound.

"What you expect? Comin' in here after all these years without so much as a by-yer-leave and bringin' that with you." She nodded her head toward where Gray Wolf was standing. "Here, you Sara Jane, come git this brat an' shut 'im up!"

"You be careful how you talk, woman," Macklin howled. "Gray Wolf knows what you're sayin'."

"I don't care what he knows," the woman snapped.

Sara Jane slouched across the room. She passed close by young Tim, who lounged against the mantle glaring at Gray Wolf. He took his narrow eyes away to grin at his slovenly wife. He reached out and pinched her fat bottom. She simpered and made a gesture so unmistakenly vulgar that Gray Wolf recoiled in shock. Young Tim threw back his head and laughed an obscene laugh. Gray Wolf wished he was out of this place. He did not know how he had come to be here. No, he thought, that is not truth. He did know. The instant he had beheld the golden woman they called Melody, he had ceased to care about anything except the sight of her filling his eyes. It was as simple as that. He was so sick and dizzy with enchantment, all his intrinsic suspicion and misgivings that clamored for attention succeeded only in plaguing his nerves. He could no more walk away from the sight of her than he could cease to breathe. There was no sense in what he was doing, but he was powerless to do otherwise. He was being a fool again, and even that did not seem to matter. He could smell the hatred coming from young Tim and his mother, but as long as he could look at the golden cascade of her hair and watch her slim young body move with the flowing grace of the wind on the grass of the plains, it was worth any risk.

She was, without question, the loveliest creature that had ever been born into the world, and it was impossible to believe that she had been sired by mortal man or born of mortal woman. She was a reed, swaying. Her low, sweet laughter was the music of a gentle brook. And her eyes!—her wonderful blue eyes that had come from the very sky. They had looked up into his, unclouded by suspicion, hate or fear. She had looked at him as a woman looks at a man whom she finds pleasing to her sight, and the impact of that look had driven all sense from his mind. It had left him a quaking idiot. He had been unable to do anything but fol-

low where she led. And she had led him inside this *Wasicun*
lodge. Gray Wolf wanted this woman—this thing of unearthly
beauty. He wanted her more than anything he had ever wanted.
He wondered what it would be like to touch her, and the
thought almost drove him crazy. He had a terrible urge to dash
across the room, sweep her up, and carry her away from this
stinking man-made cave where the ceiling bore down and the
cold, pinched-nosed face of Louise Macklin blazed hatred—for
him and for the golden girl who sat clinging to Macklin's hairy
hand.

The place was pure pandemonium. The baby was squalling
again. Macklin was roaring and waving his cup. His woman kept
screaming about a "squaw" and young Tim and his woman were
indulging in byplay that was shockingly embarrassing.

Gray Wolf felt as if he were drowning. He needed air. He
wished the girl would look at him just once more so that he
could see the beauty in her eyes. But she did not.

Sara Jane swooped the baby up and flung it over one hip. It
hung, head down, and surprisingly ceased its screaming. It cooed
and slobbered contentedly. The mother went back to stand beside her man, and young Tim reached out to finger her breast,
pinching at the nipple that pushed out the thin cloth of her
dress. She swayed back against him and her free hand dropped
to fondle him openly. Gray Wolf was ashamed with a shame that
made his belly queasy. Silently, he slid out of the door.

Outside it was a little better. The smells were less dense, but
even here manure, rank outhouse odors, and stagnant water
smells fouled the air. Gray Wolf could not understand the *Wasicun*'s affinity for building special houses for storing up his own
offal. Neither could he understand why the *Wasicun* stabled his
horses so close to his own lodge. The *Wasicun* were dirty people.
They were dirty in their persons and they were dirty in their
habits. He would do well to ride from here and not come back.
The *Wasicun* girl was beauty, but Gray Wolf had seen exquisite
beauty growing in swamps. Once removed from the mire of its
root, such beauty usually withered and died. It thrived only in
its own mire. He stepped lightly over the boards of the porch to

look in at the window. He could see the gleam of her hair in the lamplight. He leaned against one of the posts that held the roof and studied her loveliness.

No one inside had appeared to notice his departure. It was rather pleasant outside in a position where he could look openly at her. She turned, as if conscious of his eyes, and her look penetrated the darkness. There were things in that look that made him shake with a strange excitement. He felt a fever start in his veins. He remembered the actions of friends who had been enamored by a woman. He remembered the wish he had made in the mountain pass. This, then, was what he had longed for—this then was what he had missed all of his life. He was enamored by a woman—and the woman was a *Wasicun*—a woman whose people were enemies, who could never be anything but enemies. He tried to pull his eyes away, but hers held him. Macklin and his woman were so engrossed in their quarrel that they did not see. Young Tim and his wife were so engrossed in their titillation that they did not see. And Gray Wolf became so engrossed in her eyes that his instinct prodded him only a fraction before he felt the cold steel touch his spine.

"Move a hair and I'll blow your guts all over that wall!" The voice was as cold as the steel.

He did not move. Not since he was a baby had it been possible for such a thing to happen to him. He had not heard the approach of anyone and yet the cold barrel of a rifle was pressing hard against his back.

"Hello the house!" the man yelled behind him. The shouting inside came to an abrupt stop. There was a crash as Macklin shoved the chair from under him. He lunged to the door and flung it wide to reveal Gray Wolf, lounging still against the post, being prodded by the rifle.

"Who'n hell are you?" It was evident that Macklin was not talking to him.

"I'm Jack Smith," the man answered. "And I come up to find this redskin lookin' through your window."

They all came pushing out, craning to see.

"Well now," Louise snorted, "look who's callin' who a red-skin."

"Hi-ya, Jack." Young Tim was grinning as he looked at the rifle.

"Whoever you be," Macklin demanded, "put that damned gun down. This redskin, as you call him, is my friend and I can't say's I can say the same about you."

"This here is Jack Smith," Louise cut in. "He's a breed from over the fort and he's been chasing Melody, though I can't say's she's been runnin' very fast."

The gun dropped away from Gray Wolf's spine. He still did not move. Melody had moved over close behind him. He closed the rest of them out of his mind and saw only her. She was very small. Her head did not come as far up as his shoulder. She acted as if she was entirely unconscious of him, but Gray Wolf knew differently. She was as acutely aware of him as he was of her.

"Come on in, Jack," Young Tim was saying. "This here's my paw. Just back from up Dakota country."

He turned to go in and the women followed. Melody and Macklin held back.

"Don't pay no mind, Gray Wolf," he said. "People's a bit touchy but it don't mean nothin'. Come on back in."

Gray Wolf said nothing. Macklin shrugged his shoulders.

"It's okay if you don't want to. Don't blame you much. Sounds worse'n a pack of coyotes and smells worse'n a pigsty."

He turned away. The instant his back was to them Melody reached out with a little, white finger and traced a line down over the bulge of Gray Wolf's arm. Her lips drew back in a strange smile. Her tongue flicked out to moisten her lips. She raised her eyes slowly until they met his. Naked admiration turned the blue of them to black. Then she turned and ran after her father. The door slammed.

The trembling started somewhere deep inside him. It grew until he was shaking. He clung to the post for a moment before he ran blindly for his pony. He lashed the animal into a dead run. For a long time he rode and gradually the cold night air cooled his fever. Finally he stopped and slid to the ground. He moaned. He shuddered and could not tell if it was from agony or ecstasy.

Afterward Gray Wolf was not able to clearly recall the days that had passed like some terrible dream. There had been no sense to any of it. He was never able to comprehend exactly what had happened to him. He had become a stranger to his own. He seemed to have forgotten Small Owl and Bending Bow and even Crazy Horse. He had seldom taken food, for Macklin had not invited him to eat and he had never been in his own camp. He had slept under the stars because he had been unwilling to stray far from the MacLaughlin cabin, and his pride had not allowed him to reveal the fact by carrying an extra blanket.

If Tim MacLaughlin had ever believed the warrior had craved his companionship for his own sake, it had no relation to truth. Gray Wolf had clung to the white man's company to be near the woman with the sunlight hair and the promise in her eyes.

He went everywhere with MacLaughlin, enduring the menacing atmosphere of the fort itself and the contempt allotted the apostates who had become addicted to white man's whiskey. He had stood with those degenerates along the walls in order to watch the white people as they did their dances in astonishingly vulgar embraces. He had stood on the fringes of the crowds that always came to listen to their holy men, who promised them eternal damnation for their badness. And he was amazed that they did not seem to fear the terrible things promised, for he saw, because he was always watching, things between them of which even they did not seem aware. And he found existence among them almost intolerable—almost but not quite—for always in his mind he lived in the time when he would take the golden woman for his own and live in the luxury of clean air and the sweet silence of the hills.

He had been reared in the simplicity of honesty, with no knowledge of the wiles of a coquette or that his reaction to the fine art of Melody MacLaughlin's flirtation was a source of great delight to her. He had been as unconscious of her deception as she had been of his sincerity.

Right now he only wanted two things—a bath and a talk with Crazy Horse. But as he came to the camp he found that the snow was keeping everyone inside. He went to the sweat-bath lodge and there he stayed until every pore of his body ran rivulets. When he felt there was no more water in his body he raced for the shallow pool in the creek. He plunged in and the water was so icy it nearly paralyzed his every muscle. He splashed until he was numb and purified of the *Wasicun* stench that had ridden with him.

Small Owl brought new moccasins and a new breechclout and leggings. He wished he could answer the question in her eyes, but he could not. He wished he could tell her his appreciation for her anticipation of his needs, but he could not do that either. The anger she had inspired was gone, but he could not return to the easy familiarity that had been between them.

He slept the remainder of the day and the tension of his nerves eased. He waited until the night was well spent before he rolled out of his blankets and went to the lodge where Crazy Horse waited.

"I feel like talking," he said to his brother-friend.

"I feel like listening," Crazy Horse answered.

The snow had stopped falling. Everything was covered with white. A dog prowling around the outlying lodges cowered when they approached, stuck its tail between its legs and slunk off. They moved quietly away from the village to the bend in the creek. There, where summer waters had cut deep into the earth to form a bank, they found a sheltered cave under the roots of a tree. They worked their way in and lay back on the soft earth. Crazy Horse pushed a blanket at Gray Wolf.

"I brought a pipe too," he said.

There was a silence between them for a long time.

"It was pretty bad?" Crazy Horse said at last.

"It was being lost and not knowing who you are," Gray Wolf groaned.

"You were lost for a good while," Crazy Horse said without accusation.

A good while! It had been an eternity. Haltingly at first, and then faster as the relief of laying down a burden came to him, Gray Wolf told his friend what he had endured.

It was the snow that had brought the end of it all. He had been freezing. He had risen with difficulty and then had to walk and stamp his feet to bring life back to his stiff muscles. A cold wind had been driving the snow hard. His pony had stood, dejected, against a small clump of brush, trying to shelter itself from the weather. The ground had been white in all directions. His feet had refused to warm, and he had turned up one foot to inspect the sole of his moccasin. He had been stunned to find it worn through. His entire foot had been exposed to the ground. He had inspected the rest of his person and even in the snow-filled dawn he had seen that he was a ragged and unkempt spectacle. His immaculate nature had revolted at his own appearance. His breechclout was all but gone. It hung from his hips loosely. He was almost as gaunt as when the Hungry Moon was in the sky. He was dirty as well and looked as unkempt as any of the miserable broken beings that hung around the army post fawning for favors. He had felt a rush of shame and the shame had cleared his mind. He had known what he had to do.

He had caught his pony and ridden immediately to the Mac-Laughlin cabin. He had arrived with the first light and just in time to see Melody going into the barn that housed the cow MacLaughlin had bought. He had counted himself lucky and had thought that the spirits must be with him. He had tethered his pony in the brush and gone after her. The snow had been falling thick and fast by then. Inside the barn it had been warm and pleasant after the cold. He had practiced what he had been going to say to her, for he had watched closely and had learned that *Wasicun* women spoke for themselves in these matters. But then the sight of her and the smile in her eyes had made him forget what he had been going to say. He had stood there like a tongueless idiot and then she had started talking.

"Well," she had said, "if it isn't my handsome warrior. How are you this morning, Chief?"

And he had still been unable to say what he had wanted to say.

"Does my Paw know you're out here?" she had asked. "I'll just bet he doesn't. Well, we don't care, do we? Paw told me to be careful around you. He said you could be dangerous. Are you dangerous, Gray Wolf? I like dangerous men."

She had dropped the pail in her hands and come up close to him, walking with the windblown way she had.

"Paw says," she had continued, "that you don't know about white women. Would you like to know about white women, Chief?"

She had been very close to him then and she had run her fingers lightly over his arm again as she had that first night. He had looked down into her eyes and his heart had beat so furiously that he had been unable to utter any sound.

"What is the matter, big warrior?" she had asked with a taunting sound in her voice. "Don't you want to kiss me? Don't you know how to kiss a woman? Want me to teach you?"

"No!" If it was possible to shout in a whisper he had done it. His voice had been thick and strange. He had not known what to think. He had believed that she was different from Sara Jane and her vulgar ways. He had intended to ask her to become his woman, but her actions were frightening and he had not known what to do. He had wanted her. He had wanted her as he had never wanted anything before in his life and he had wanted to ask. But the words had not come. When he had said "no" in that way, she had misunderstood. It had made her angry. She had pulled back and her face had not been beautiful for that moment.

"No!" She had echoed his word. "No! You are saying no to me! Well, if that isn't a switch. Why you stinking Indian. I am a white woman."

He had not liked that. It had sounded as if being white made her something special instead of being the only thing against her. He had even meant to tell her that he would overlook her color, but now he knew that would have been a mistake.

She had stepped back and she had looked at him—all the way from his head to his feet—and her look was no longer the look of a woman who found a man pleasing. It was the look of contempt that he had seen in the eyes of the others. She had put her hands on her hips and drawn her shoulders back so that her breasts had stood out against her dress. She had flattened her belly and swayed. And then, slowly and deliberately, without taking her eyes from his, she had unbuttoned her dress without the least pretense toward modesty. She had pulled it back to show the milky whiteness. He had grown hot and then cold, for somehow her nakedness was more than nakedness—it was obscene. She had moved her body in such a way that it had made his flesh crawl. She was, he knew then, truly a thing of beauty nourished in muck. The cold chills had dashed the fever from his veins and he wanted to get away from her. He would have as soon taken a bitch dog to mate.

He had charged for the door and stumbled over things he could not clearly see. With one great wave of his hand he had struck the doors open and almost fallen over young Tim Mac-Laughlin, who yelled after him as he ran for his horse. As he had ridden away he had heard Young Tim screaming at the girl.

"You slut! You nasty little slut. You dirty little bitch—makin' up to a filthy Indian. I heard every word—"

He had ridden as fast as the horse would carry him—back to camp and to reality. And now he was here, and now Crazy Horse knew all that had happened to him. It had been like being in another world. It had been like being someone else—someone he did not even know.

"It is a rare feeling a woman can start in a man," Crazy Horse said. "And it is a terrible thing when that woman is not a woman."

Gray Wolf felt good. It was over. Now he felt purified in mind as well as in body. He tried to recall the face of Melody Mac-Laughlin and the image was blurred in the eye of his mind. He saw only a vague remembrance of sun and sky and rippling water—and knew he could see those things all the rest of his days and they would not be tarnished with vulgarity and obscenity.

"It is time we took to the trail," Crazy Horse said.

"It is more than time." Gray Wolf voiced it joyously. He felt free and it was a good feeling. He felt alive and it was wonderful. They shoved at each other and laughed as they crawled out of the little earthen cave.

Then the laughter died in their throats. They stared at each other in shocked disbelief. The clear, cold morning echoed the blatant notes of a bugle—the voice of the Long Knife, the voice of the Pony Soldier—and the voice was sounding the spine-chilling notes of a cavalry charge.

6

"This cannot be!" Crazy Horse did not know he had whispered. The sounds of rifle fire denied his words.

As one they dropped to the ground. They snaked their way to the top of the little ridge. On the far side of the village the land was filled with Long Knives. They were as thick as needles on a pine tree. They were charging at a full gallop toward the men, women and children who came crowding out of the lodges.

A young brave was yanking at the rope on the pole over Black Kettle's lodge. He was trying to raise the red, white and blue cloth, gift of the governor of Colorado, pennant of the *Wasicun* pledge of protection.

The wind caught and unfurled the flag. It snapped in the breeze, but the sound was lost in the thunder of hooves and the spat of gunfire. Eyes that turned to look at it with confidence turned back toward the onrushing troops, realizing too late that its protection was a myth.

Gray Wolf saw the *Wasicun* holy man, Chivington, in the forefront. He remembered the fanatic hatred in the man's eyes and it was portrayed now in every tense line of his burly body as it bent over his horse's neck, urging the animal on. Gray Wolf remembered the words he had heard this man shout about the "vengeance of the Lord," and a cold chill came up his spine. Then he heard Chivington's voice shouting, "Kill them. Kill them all. Nits make lice."

And Gray Wolf knew that the "vengeance" was in reality the vengeance of Chivington.

"It is a mistake," Crazy Horse was muttering. "There is peace. It's a mistake."

"A mistake!" Gray Wolf's voice was bitter. "Does it look like a mistake?"

The charge came with a roar, shaking the ground. The people stood bewildered. One old woman came out of her lodge and watched the oncoming soldiers, fascinated, unbelieving. She staggered back, shot through the head, and she was dead before she hit the ground. Her falling body seemed to release the people from their trance of unbelief. They broke and ran. Calls of "Brave up, warriors," were heard from women lending encouragement to their men. Many who had not yet fully awakened from the sleep of the night came from their lodges to be cut down before comprehension of the fact that they were being attacked came to them. Warriors darted back into shot-riddled lodges to grab the few weapons they possessed. They made desperate attempts to herd the women and children toward the creek bed. Those who had guns made futile stands, trying to cover the retreat of their families. They were overwhelmed with withering fire and the horses of the cavalry rode over them almost unchecked.

Men, women and children, some half clothed, others naked from their beds, were running, trying to form some kind of organized retreat. And the soldiers came on, riding over the dead, the wounded and the fleeing people. It was past belief. It was like a horrible dream from which there was no awakening.

Crazy Horse stared, speechless, his black eyes big and round and as blank as a cat's. Cold as it was, sweat gathered and trickled down over the hard knots that swelled below his cheekbones. The noise was deafening.

He yelled something, but his words were lost in the din. Gray Wolf felt a prickling wave crawl up his legs and over his back and his belly. It was fear. He knew it. He had felt it before. He knew, too, that it would pass. It would pass as soon as he was in the midst of the action.

"Now!" Crazy Horse expelled the sound and the shout rose in his throat to swell into the screaming Dakota "war whoop."

"It's a good day to die!" he screamed and was on his feet running. Why did he have to do that? Gray Wolf wondered. Why draw attention to ourselves when we don't even have a bow. He pulled his knees up and was running too. Together they raced down the slope toward the village. Gray Wolf was astonished to hear his own scream tearing from his throat as he ran.

Bullets were hitting close to their feet. It had not seemed far when they had walked this way just before the dawn. Now it seemed that no matter how hard they ran the distance did not diminish. He recalled a dream he had had a long time ago. He had been running from something and regardless of how hard he had run he had not moved. What am I thinking about? This is no dream. This is reality. He wondered where Small Owl and the child were. He thought about Bending Bow and wondered who was taking care of old Crooning Woman. He hoped the women would not panic. They had never experienced anything like this. Don't panic. Don't panic, he pleaded, trying to send his thoughts to them. And then they were in it.

Gunpowder stung his nostrils. Soldiers, warriors, horses, women—they were all tangled up in fierce hand-to-hand struggle. The soldiers were leaning out of the saddles, using sabers, cutting down those who tried to haul them off their mounts. A woman ran past him holding up her hands; he saw the saber sweep and her hands fell from her upraised arms. A vomit of pure hatred stung his throat and he felt as powerful as a god. A horse loomed before him. He felt the heat of the bullet that somehow missed him and he sprang. He slapped both feet hard up against the horse, his hands gripped the booted leg and he heaved. The bluecoat came out of the saddle. The horse galloped away. They both hit the ground hard and rolled. The soldier's clenched fists still clutched his rifle. Gray Wolf leaped upon him. They wrestled and strained and then he had him on his back. He looked down into the bright blue eyes that stared back cold and hard. They panted and they pulled. The Long Knife was a worthy opponent. There was steel in his wiry sinew. A sudden twist and Gray Wolf was off balance. The gun barrel swung and rapped him hard across the nose. He was half stunned. He shook his head to clear his vision. Then the power of his rage came back. The long, thin hands gripped the weapon with relentless purpose and Gray Wolf knew the man was going to try and brain him with it. He grabbed and once again they grappled frantically, heedless of the pounding hooves around and over them. They were insensible to the blood and gore in which they rolled. The Long Knife's heavy clothing provided a good grip. Gray Wolf let go of the gun and, grabbing the cloth, he flipped his opponent. He jumped him and landed astraddle the heaving belly. He pulled his knife and got it against the buckle just over the man's navel. He eased back to let the point slide off the metal to the softness under it. Then he lunged forward, leaning with every ounce of his strength. The body arched up under him. It strained and it writhed. He turned the knife sideways with a vicious twist. He pulled back and jerked it out. The clenched fists relaxed and opened. The gun fell free. He kicked himself off the quivering belly and lunged for the gun. He felt no sympathy, no compassion, no regret. He felt only an exalted triumph. He wanted to get them all—get them just like this—just like this—

"Watch him!" Crazy Horse swung his toe to kick the knife from the already feeble fingers.

Gray Wolf gave his brother-friend a quick appreciative glance. Crazy Horse too had a gun. They turned to stand, back to back, using the weapons as clubs. They swung and they ducked. Then Gray Wolf felt the two quick jabs in his back that was the signal to move. He turned and they ran together for the scant protection of a wrecked lodge.

The dead were everywhere. They were lying in the grotesque, twisted way of violent death. He saw White Elk lying, crumpled on the ground, and knew that the old man was dead. He saw children, some dead, some crawling, dazed and bleeding, and still others just sitting with the vacant faces of terror.

They wanted to get to their own lodges and they tried, but there was a blockade of writhing annihilation between them and the places they had slept only a short time ago. A blue haze was gathering to hang around the tops of the lodges that were left standing. They dodged around a pile of wreckage and found Rabbit. His face was black with gunpowder. He was scared and

angry and screaming, and beating at the body of a dead soldier. Gray Wolf grabbed him by the arm. The boy did not seem
to recognize him for a moment, then he started shaking and dry
sobs caught at his breath. Gray Wolf jerked the boy and motioned for him to stay down. They crawled and ran. They darted
in and around lodges and bodies, but it as impossible to make
any headway. Long Knives were everywhere. They had to give
up trying to find their own people. They snatched up powder
horns and ammunition where it had been dropped. Rabbit saw
what they were doing and started collecting everything he could
find. Gray Wolf had to knock useless things from the boy's
hands. Dumbly Rabbit tried to imitate the warriors. He caught
up a knife and, clenching it, crouched close to the men.

They found Bending Bow crouched behind a lodge that had
been battered almost to the ground. Gray Wolf reached out to
touch the old shoulder.

"Come," he shouted, but the old man shook his head, his wal-
nut hands working the rifle like a maniac. His old face was wrinkled in agony.

"Crooning Woman?" Gray Wolf called.

The old man nodded his head toward the pile of rubble. She
sat, hunched down under a pile of skins. Her face was serene
and Gray Wolf fancied that he heard a tuneless little song coming from her lips.

"Go." Bending Bow waved them away. "We will join you
later."

He wanted to scream at the old man, but what was the use.
What was the use of anything. They were completely outnumbered. They had no horses, no weapons and no ammunition.
How could any man fight bare-handed against mounted Long
Knives who tried to pound you into the earth with the horses'
hooves? The dying were crying out as the horses galloped over
them. And the Long Knives were slashing with their swords and
clubbing with the rifle butts between the time of reloading.
Acrid clouds of gunpowder drifted over the blood-spattered
ground, the hundreds of broken bodies and the wrecked lodges.
People kept bunching up instead of scattering as they should.

A troop that had separated to run off the pony herd was cutting in from the side and Gray Wolf saw that they were about to be pinned in a cross fire. He leaned to jab at Crazy Horse. He leaned to the side to jab at Rabbit, but the boy was too far away. Gray Wolf felt a stab of rage. He leaped away to grab at the boy.

"Stay with us," he snarled, and did not care when he saw the frightened and bewildered look the boy gave him. Rabbit saw the way he backed up to Crazy Horse and understood, but he understood too well. He crowded in too close, blocking Gray Wolf's arm. It took more than one fight to train a warrior. Gray Wolf shoved the boy a little, afraid to take his eyes away from the soldiers closing in.

It was then that he saw her. He would know the shape of her anywhere. She was crumpled up in the pathway, a small, very still figure. He knew that she was dead. He should not have stopped, but he could not help it. He had been angry at those who had been trying to take their dead with them. He had felt that it endangered them all. And now he was unable to leave her. When he had stopped Rabbit had not. He bumped into him and some of the precious powder spilled. He jerked his arm away and dropped to a knee. Crazy Horse went down with him automatically, but he had to reach up and pull at Rabbit. The boy came down, clumsy, almost falling. The sound of his gun firing was lost in the shattering clamor that tore the morning apart.

Then he saw the child. She was naked. She was toddling up the path. She was crying, but only a little. She was looking for her mother. Gray Wolf tried to call to her, but his voice was lost. Somehow she looked smaller in her nakedness. Then she saw her mother and started toward her. The haze cleared a little and Gray Wolf saw the dust and snow kick up close to her feet. He looked around to see where the bullets came from. The wind whipped the haze farther and then he saw Macklin. He was sitting his horse between two soldiers who were aiming their rifles at the child. Seeing him was a shock. It delayed his own aim and just as he pulled the trigger smoke blew across between them.

He felt that he had missed and saw when the smoke cleared again that he had. What a fool he had been, using his load instead of getting out there and bringing the child back. Before he could leap to his feet she sank to the ground. She lay down almost gently. Vaguely he felt a pull at his belt. Angrily he shook off the hand. Reality seemed to slip away from him. He rose to his feet and stared. As if drawn by his gaze Macklin looked toward him. Their eyes met. He could feel the muscles of his face draw. A wild anguished scream tore out of his throat. Macklin heard it and paled.

Gray Wolf could see his former slave mouthing something, but he could not hear the words. He could not have heard them if Macklin had shouted. But Macklin had not shouted. He had barely whispered. Then a tangle of troopers came between them.

A flat, deadly caution drove everything from Gray Wolf's mind. They were dead. Small Owl and Snow Maid were dead. No one could hurt them now. He would leave their bodies. There was nothing else to be done. He had not thought much about whether he would live or die this day. He had never thought much about it one way or the other. But he thought about it now. Now he was going to live. He had a purpose—a purpose so defined that he did not even make a vow. The vow had been made for him.

A young boy came running toward them. He had no gun, no bow, no knife and no clothes. He was crying. Gray Wolf reached out and caught him. The boy fought, flaying his arms, sinking his teeth into the arm that held him. He was beyond all reason. Gray Wolf drew back his hand and slapped him hard across the face. It was something he had never done before in his life. His innate respect for the divinity in man was repelled by the act. But this boy was so crazed by fear that only an act more shocking than any he had yet seen could bring him back to any normalcy. It worked. He stopped struggling instantly, but his whole body shook with an uncontrollable palsy. Gray Wolf yanked him up and glared at him.

"Be a man!" he ordered.

The boy choked and gasped, but some of the shaking stopped.

They moved back again, this time in the direction of the creek. Gray Wolf tried to load and found the powder horn empty. He reached out and Rabbit slapped one in his hand. The boy was learning fast. He saw a rifle and grabbed it up. He pushed it into the naked boy's hands. He accepted another horn of powder from Rabbit's hoard and dropped the strap over the boy's head.

"Use them!" he ordered. The boy looked up at him blankly. "If you don't know how, learn!" he yelled in the boy's face. The boy jumped backward and started shaking again.

"Ay-e-e-e." Gray Wolf felt weary. The boy was as afraid of him as he was of the Long Knives and there was no time to comfort him.

They were at the edge of the village now. The creek bed was not far. It was filled with people. A warrior he could not recall having seen came crawling along dragging his leg. Someone ran out, trying to help. Over to one side a warrior with blood covering his face was wrestling with a Long Knife who was trying to scalp him. Gray Wolf threw his knife. He hated to part with it, but there was no help for it. The knife took the soldier in the throat and he staggered back. The warrior gave him a brief salute and backed away, edging toward them. He came into line, on the far side of the naked boy. Gray Wolf was glad to have him there. Maybe, he thought, we will make it. He could not see many bluecoats on the ground. Maybe there were more of them dead inside the village. He wanted to think there were, but knew it was wishful thinking. There were several riderless ponies around. A few warriors tried to capture them, but as soon as they were astride they were shot out of the saddles. The Long Knives were not going to allow anyone to get mounted. Crazy Horse signaled for a stop. Gray Wolf took a quick look. A woman sat on the ground, holding a baby to her breast. She was trying to force the nipple into the child's mouth. Blood ran from her back in a flood. Crazy Horse leaned over to touch the child. There was a hole in the back of the tiny head. They left them. They had to move around a young brave lying on his back, his eyes open, his lips working, singing his death song. No sound came from the froth that formed on his lips.

Some of the noise seemed to be diminishing. Some of the troopers seemed to have lost interest in the fighting. They were looting the lodges. Others were busy scalping, not bothering to distinguish between the dead and the living. Those who had survived to walk or run were down in the creek bed. From behind one of the lodges a Long Knife saw them. He fired and Gray Wolf heard the spat of the bullet. The warrior who had joined them staggered, but he did not fall. Gray Wolf started for the trooper, but Crazy Horse was ahead of him. The little warrior had fairly flown through the air. The force of his attack brought the man down. His arm flashed and Crazy Horse had used his knife to the hilt. Gray Wolf felt Rabbit jerk and knew he had fired at someone. Every time he fired the gun kicked the boy almost off his feet. Crazy Horse came back as fast as he had left. There was an extra knife in his girdle. He pulled it out and handed it to Gray Wolf. It felt good in the sheath.

They reached the creek and slithered down to the bed. Women there were working guns with the men. The fighting seemed much less in the village, but the soldiers were coming in on them here. Rifle fire cut into the banks. Some warrior up the line was trying to get the women and the children moving. There wasn't much cover, but a lot of smoke was drifting down and it gave some screen. It made Gray Wolf feel sick to see the way some of the old women tried to run, ragged and crouched like old crippled buffalo cows. But he had his own private frenzy and there was no help for their loss of dignity at a time such as this.

There was finally some kind of order. The men with weapons took a stand facing the troopers, holding them off so that the women and the children could get away. They retreated slowly, walking backward, stumbling over the dead and wounded.

It helped considerably being out here, facing the enemy, instead of being all mixed up with them, unable to shoot without the fear of shooting one of your own.

The embankment was fairly good protection from the rifle fire. Then there came a terrible, crashing roar that split the very air. Over to the side a mass of bodies was flung into the air. It rained blood, arms, pieces of flesh and gore. It was a paralyzing experience. Gray Wolf had heard about wagon guns, but this was the first time he had ever faced them. He felt like a raw apprentice, and his nerves jumped and twitched. Rifle fire was one thing. This was entirely another. He wanted to break and run. He did not know what kept him from it.

They fell back and the next shell fell into the creek bottom where they had just been. Sand, rocks and even the brush along the banks flew into the air in all directions. Rabbit and Naked Boy came running. They pressed so close that he had difficulty in moving. Why didn't they take off and go with the women? What did they think he could do for them?

A warrior beside them leaped into the air. His head snapped back and his body made a half turn before he fell, arms out, his black hair a blot against the snow. It was hard to see. It was hard to breathe. He reloaded and aimed for the hazy figure of a trooper. He felt a small satisfaction when he saw him leave the saddle. He hoped he had killed him, but the range was so long that he was afraid he had only inflicted a wound.

"Back! Back!" He heard the call thankfully.

It was a good thing. The shells were seeking them out again. Rabbit looked as if he would not be able to stand up much longer. Every time a shell fell he flung his arms up as if to ward them off. Well, Gray Wolf thought, I'm not doing much better myself.

There was a call to run. He got hold of Rabbit and half pushed him around to get him started. The naked boy was staggering. A curl of smoke was coming from his rifle barrel. He had learned to use it. Gray Wolf reached out and grabbed the boy around his skinny waist. He picked him up and ran. The boy kicked feebly to be put down. It was pretty humiliating, but he would never have been able to keep up. Maybe when this was all over, if it ever was, he could explain and restore the boy's dignity—if any of them had any dignity left.

They ran—just far enough to get out of range of the wagon guns—and stopped. They dug in. And so it went hour after hour. Dig in, fight, get bombarded, retreat—they gave five miles, inch

by inch, life by life. The creek bed was strewn with bodies. And
then it was nightfall.

He lay back to press his head against the earth and groan. Beside him Rabbit bent over and vomited. The retching sounded
crude and raw in the vacuum of stillness. Naked Boy stood, rifle
butt trailing in the dirt, the powder horn empty against his thin
ribs, and he shook. The madness in his eyes had changed to an
aged weariness.

The darkness was closing in and Gray Wolf wished he had a
drink, but the small pools in the creek were undrinkable. They
were red with the blood of those who lay in them. He tried to sit
up and found that his head would not follow his intentions. He
felt oddly as if he were dead himself and would never be able to
lift his head again. It was a strange sensation. He decided not to
struggle against it. In fact it was almost pleasant. He felt as if
he might lie here for a while and then he would be able to rise
and leave his body behind in the mass horror of this day. He
would be free to join those who had escaped from this mortal
madness. He would find Small Owl and Snow Maid and together
they would go to Blue Feather, who could not be far from this
carnage.

"Come with me!"

He heard the words, and with the belief that he heard the
voice of Blue Feather, he answered gladly, "I am coming." Then
dimly he realized that it was not his spirit brother who had
spoken. It was his brother-friend Crazy Horse, and he was urgent. He gripped Gray Wolf's shoulder so hard that it went
numb. He was surprised to find that Crazy Horse had that much
strength in his hands, and he was surprised to find that he could
think of such things.

"The moon will be up soon and we have to find them."

"Find them? Find who?" He did wish he could get his mind to
work properly. "Who is left to find?"

"I have to find my mother and Willow Twig—or I must find
their bodies. I cannot leave them dead or alive to those mad-
men."

Gray Wolf pulled himself up. He was relieved to find that his head would follow after all, but he wished it did not feel so dull. He pulled his legs up. An owl hooted plaintively. For some reason it struck him as very funny. He had difficulty to keep from laughing. The giggle in his throat horrified him. But it was funny —all the death, all the terrible day that had been, and an owl was hooting as if nothing had happened in this snow-covered creek bed. The owl hooted again.

The stars were coming out. He threw back his head to look up at them and to ease the tension in the back of his neck. He winked his eyes hard to clear them of the dizziness behind them. The million star-eyes winked back dispassionately. Their indifference jarred his mind into reality and when the owl hooted again he knew it for what it was. It took him a while to get his mouth wet enough to answer it. Crazy Horse seemed not to have heard.

Presently a slithering sound was followed by Bending Bow speaking softly.

"Help me with Crooning Woman. She is asleep with weariness and I cannot drag her any farther."

They went up over the bank and lifted her gently down. Bending Bow crawled after, too weary to stand.

"Is she dead?" Gray Wolf did not like to ask it.

"No," Bending Bow answered, "but it would be better if she was. The things we have seen this day!"

The old man sat and shook his head back and forth like a man in a dream.

"Did you see my mother or my sister?" Crazy Horse asked. The old man nodded first and then shook his head again.

"This morning," he said. "So long ago, this morning. They were going down the creek. They went into a little cave somewhere."

"The cave!" Crazy Horse was excited. "The cave where we were. They will be there. They will be all right. We have to go for them."

"Be careful," the old man warned. "The things they are

doing." The faraway and hopeless look on his face was clear even in the starlight.

The moon came up and they crawled. They did not know where the soldiers were and they did not dare take any chances. They were too beaten down to risk a fight. All they could do was hope to find the women and get back. They had left instructions for the others to wait only until the moon was straight up. If they had not returned by then they were to leave them. In the meantime they were to rest as much as possible so they could travel. Daylight would bring—no one knew what—after this day.

It was only five miles by the *Wasicun* calculation. It seemed more like a hundred. The voices from the village carried a long way. The soldiers were there. They had camped in the village itself among the bodies of the dead.

They slipped in close. If Yellow Bird or Willow Twig were there . . . They had to make sure.

It was Chivington. Gray Wolf knew him even in the uncertain light of the moon and the flickering light of the fire. He stood legs apart, his hands on his hips, in front of a warrior bound securely to a post. The fire burned at the warrior's feet and there was the sickening smell of charred flesh. Coarse jests and crude jeers were thrown at the hapless man. Elated by their triumph, the soldiers reveled in this added horror.

A fury beyond any he had ever known gripped Gray Wolf by the throat. Ay-e-e-e, was it possible that the things he had believed as a child were really true? Were these fiends cannibals, roasting a man for an evening meal? He knew he would never forget this grisly spectacle. He would remember it and when he felt the urge to feel anything other than hatred for any *Wasicun* he would see this night.

The warrior was staring into nothing; no sound came from his lips, which were strained back into a contemptuous smile. Gray Wolf lay and tried with all of his powers to reach mentally the suffering warrior.

"Send your soul away," he whispered into the night. "Do not let it feel your pain. Show these stinking *Wasicun* what a man is really like. One day, for you my brother, I will make some *Wasi-*

cun feel what you are being made to feel this night. Send your soul away, brother."

A small group of women and children were huddled together. They were prodded constantly by rifles to raise their eyes and witness the awful scene. Neither Yellow Bird nor Willow Twig was among them. Gray Wolf could hear the whistling of Crazy Horse's breath. They snaked back, sick.

They skirted the village and ran, crouched, to the creek bed on the far side of the bend. Noiselessly they approached the cave. Crazy Horse hooted softly. Yellow Bird came scrambling out.

"Where is Willow Twig?"

"I do not know. A child came by and she went after it. She has not come back. Soldiers came by and I could not follow."

"How long?" Crazy Horse was urgent.

"A little time—a long time! Who can tell how long any of this day has been?"

"Wait here. We will find her. We will come back. Stay in the cave."

They ran, still crouching, taking advantage of every twig, every bush, every rock. They ran, but they ran with caution, searching, expecting to find the worst. The worst was not as bad as what they did find.

She was standing, hanging on to the limb of a scrub tree to keep from falling down. She was naked and her skin was streaked with marks that looked as if she had been clawed by a cat. One breast was half torn from her body and a pool of blood coagulated around her feet. Her eyes were huge and no light of recognition came as she stared at them. Her lips moved and like some awful litany she chanted over and over what they had done to her. It was more than could be endured.

Crazy Horse reached out to touch her gently.

"Willow Twig, my sister," he whispered.

She did not respond. She did not cease or falter in her awful chant. Crazy Horse stepped back, sick disbelief in his eyes. A dry sob wrenched him. Then he stepped forward. His arm raised

—it fell! The chanting stopped. Recognition came back into her eyes. Faintly she smiled. Her lips moved.

"Thank you," she whispered.

Her body sagged. Crazy Horse gathered her into his arms as he threw the knife from him.

They carried her over the top of the rise and with their bare hands they dug her grave.

The snow had disappeared and in the shifting, wavering, quicksilver moonlight the earth looked tired and brown. Every sound was magnified in the windless chill and the people hurried, walking as lightly as they could, trying not to lay moccasin tracks too deeply. They scattered out into small groups to avoid making a broad trail, yet keeping close so that the few warriors could spread their thin protection around them.

It was a night of silence. Even the babies whimpered with less than the sound of a breath in their hunger and fright. And they all listened.

Every now and then a brave would drop behind to lay his ear close to the earth. When no throb of hoofbeat touched his ear he would hurry to catch up. His silence reassured them.

Roman Nose, who had the eyes of a buffalo, led them. It was not as it should be, but nothing in this day and night had been as it should be. The pathfinder lay behind them in the place where more than three hundred of their people lay with their faces turned up to the cold sky. So Roman Nose led, his warrior ears closed to the drum of vengeance until a later time. Behind him walked his nephew, carrying the sacred feathered headdress. Then came Black Kettle, carrying the pipe, and after him a few of the Old Men Chiefs who had been able to get away. Here and there someone clutched a sacred object, a medicine bundle, a scrap of blanket or a precious pot. But most of them walked with children, their own children and children who now had no mother or father of their own. And they all walked, quickly, silently—without meat in their bellies and without hope in their hearts.

Neither Gray Wolf nor Crazy Horse walked with them. They

had brought Yellow Bird and pushed her toward Bending Bow and Crooning Woman and Rabbit and Naked One, and they had spoken no word. Gray Wolf had motioned to Rabbit in such a way that the boy knew he was to take care of the group and then he had turned away and he and Crazy Horse had disappeared into the night. When they had done this the question in Yellow Bird's eyes turned to pain and her knees had gone weak. She had known then what had happened. It had to be endured.

Gray Wolf and Crazy Horse walked away to keep the deed that had been done from bringing misfortune on the others. And they all knew then that Crazy Horse had drawn blood on one of his own. And they knew too that it had been necessary to do so, and their hearts were bitter toward all who had a pale skin and belonged to the race the Cheyenne called *veho* and the Dakota called *Wasicun*. And the names were fitting.

When they had traveled far enough, Crazy Horse knelt down in the sand and unbraided his hair. He did it very slowly and very carefully. Then he took handfuls of dirt and broken grasses and rubbed it into his shining locks until the shine was gone and it hung loose and unkempt in a tangled mass. Gray Wolf did not turn his face away from this shame, for he would share it. It was a hard thing to be forced to choose between honor and that which seemed right—but it had to be endured.

When Crazy Horse stood up their eyes met briefly in naked brotherhood, understanding many things unsaid between them.

Instead of following toward the north where the people had gone, they turned their flintlike faces toward the south and the east.

The lights from the window looked like a small star pinned to the earth. They stood for a long time and listened and then they moved in—their feet as stealthy as stalking pumas.

Outside beside the porch Crazy Horse eased back into the deep shadows and pressed himself against the house. They could hear the rise and fall of the disagreement inside. Gray Wolf stepped as gently as his name-animal across the boards and not one creaked under his tread.

They were all there, even the baby, hanging head down on

Sara Jane's hip. MacLaughlin sat at the table, his head in his hands, a cup of the brown whiskey water before him. Young Tim lounged at the mantle and Louise was flinging her arms around in the agitation of what she was saying. The golden girl, the flower of his heart, sat beside MacLaughlin, her hand touching his knee. There was no one else—no soldier, no neighbor, no rifle laying near a hand.

You must feel sure, Gray Wolf thought, that no one with revenge in his heart lives this night. And the thought was bitter with the satisfaction he was beginning to feel. He motioned to Crazy Horse to bring the horses. The small warrior slipped away in the shadows and Gray Wolf stepped toward the door. Very gently he released the latch. He let the door drift open and stood drawn to his full height on the threshold. They did not look up until the cold air hit their faces.

"Don't move. For God's sake don't anyone move," MacLaughlin warned his family. He put his hands down on the table, his fingers spreading like stumpy turkey tails. He started to pull himself up out of the chair.

Young Tim started breathing hard in the way a cornered coward breathes when he decides to act, and Gray Wolf knew even before the man himself knew that he was going to jump. He charged like a frenzied bull buffalo, a wild noise in his throat. Gray Wolf scarcely turned. He snapped his knee upward into the man's crotch and young Tim slumped to the floor, his eyes bulging like a gigged frog. Gray Wolf sneered his contempt. He let his gaze travel slowly, deliberately, over the woman and the baby. He let it slide over Louise, who stood with her mouth agape from the last word of insult with which she had been flaying her luckless man. His eyes moved from her to settle on Melody. He studied her.

"No!" MacLaughlin whispered it. "You wouldn't kill a woman. You are a Dakota warrior. You would not disgrace yourself to kill a woman—"

His voice trailed off. It took Gray Wolf but one stride to reach her. He twisted his hand into the golden mass of her hair. He yanked her to her feet and pulled her back with him to the door.

He did not hurry. Slowly, deliberately, so that MacLaughlin would not miss any of the agony he must be feeling, he drew his knife.

"Don't kill me," she whispered. "Please don't kill me. Paw, don't let him kill me."

He wondered now how he ever could have desired her. She was disgusting in her fear. No Dakota woman would have spoken such words. A Dakota woman would have spat in his face—but she would never have pleaded for life.

He pulled her head back, watching MacLaughlin's eyes. He raised his arm. MacLaughlin paled and gasped. He brought the knife down with a quick, hard thrust. He knew by the way her body twitched that he had plunged directly to the heart. He was glad, for he had no wish to make her suffer. It was MacLaughlin who must know the pain. He pulled the knife free and waited the moment it took for complete insensibility to claim her. Then, he stepped back and with a deft twist of his wrist, he drew the knife across her scalp. He pulled it free and held it out, dripping with her blood, toward MacLaughlin.

"Put it with that of my woman when you show Indian scalps to your people," he hissed. "Do not cross my footsteps again in this life."

He snapped the gory thing by its golden strands and flung it. It slapped sickeningly across the *Wasicun's* ashen face.

7

Gray Wolf lay as motionless as the rocks. He watched Big Crow and the six warriors ride out of the ravine and charge. He watched the Long Knives as they scattered and ran for the fort. He smiled a little, knowing their relief when they gained the protection of the walls, and he smiled a little more when he heard the thin notes of the bugle. But his smile was without humor. It was a tight smile of satisfaction.

Big Crow was doing well. He was pulling his men back, slowly but not too slowly, defiant but not too defiant. In a moment the gates would swing wide and the Long Knives would come pouring out. Big Crow and the others would make a headlong dash—fast but not too fast—for the sand hills and then the Long Knives would come after them . . .

Gray Wolf's breathing became a little uneven. Every encounter was prefaced with tension. His stomach grew dull and empty. The pressure built up and the craving for action became almost unbearable. Action—furious action—was the only thing that eased the hate in his heart.

Sand Creek and its burden of blood, sorrow and shame had cost much. It had closed the road of honor. It had brought new ways of thinking. Always the people had lived by knowing the ways of things around them, and Sand Creek had shown them that it was time to know the ways of the *Wasicun*—the lip to smile when the mouth was bitter; the tongue to agree when the heart cried "no"; the pride to say "this will be" when it was for only as long as the eye could see. It was time to learn the ways of the *Wasicun* and it was time to live by those ways. Sand Creek had cost much. It would cost the *Wasicun* more.

The war pipe had been carried to the north. It had been carried to the south. It had been carried to the east and west and it had been smoked. Gray Wolf lay there on the crest with no more movement than the stone beside him and all around him lay Cheyenne, Arapaho, Dakota and Apache. The *Wasicun* would pay for Sand Creek.

It had been a bad time after the massacre. He and Crazy Horse, the darkness between them removed after he had slain a woman, walked together, following the survivors, guarding the back trail. They had ranged far to find horses for those who, because of their wounds or their age or sickness, had not been able to keep up. Here and there they had left stone chimneys standing in smoldering ruins, naked monuments to their bitterness. But it had been a poor revenge. Scattered settlers were not fit for warriors primed with fury.

The warriors ahead had been pretty thorough, so Gray Wolf and Crazy Horse had followed far out, where lonely settlers had not yet been warned to be cautious. And here and there they found a gun or two, a bullet mold, some caps or little kegs of powder, and these they always took, for the needs of their own were dire and the *Wasicun* with his power of numbers and his guns and his twisted tongue would furnish those needs.

Once, far to the east, they had come upon two girls and a small child. They were hungry and cold, with but one small blanket, which they kept wrapped around the child they carried in their arms. The warriors gave them food and a blanket and led them back to the trail and headed them in the right direction. And when the girls asked their names they told them to say always that it was the wolves who had fed them.

And when they came upon a woman sitting deep in a draw holding a newborn, grasping the little nose between her fingers, shutting off the breath until it seemed as if he would strangle and then loosening it until he started to cry again—teaching the new man-child that not even he could betray his people—they told her to stay and rest until they would return to her. They found an old horse, so saddle-marked it was assured he was gentle, and they brought it to her so she could ride and catch up.

And when she asked their names they told her to say only that the wolves had brought her the horse.

And when finally they had come up to the place where the people had camped they saw the head men around the fire. And they heard that even after what had happened Black Kettle was for the peace road. But Roman Nose and others, their blood hot against all whites, spoke against it.

"Many of our people have been left with their faces turned up to the cold sky," he had said, "and among them is our prophet, who was always a man of peace. This peace road gives us nothing but death—a shameful death without a chance to fight for our women and children. The only Indian not killed by the *veho* is the Indian not caught by the *veho*. I say take the war pipe and smoke it. I say send it to all the people to the north and to the south and to the east and the west and let all the people know what has happened to the Cheyenne on Sand Creek."

There had been many who had jumped to their feet and cried out in agreement.

"*Hou! Hou!* Let the *veho* feel our pain," they had said. And others, their anger flaming more fiercely, cried louder.

"*Hou! Hou!*"

So the pipe had gone out in the hands of the fastest runners and all the great chiefs had smoked, for their hearts had been sad for their brothers. And all the old grievances and old rivalries had been forgotten and they had pledged themselves to wipe out the hated whites from the country.

And neither they nor Gray Wolf nor Crazy Horse nor any man had envisioned that which was to come—a camp of thousands, sweeping a path over a hundred miles wide, north to the Powder River country. But Black Kettle, determined to keep his oath of peace, took with him a small band and went south to the Washita; they wished him well and gave the band guns and ammunition for game; and Gray Wolf had asked the chief to take Bending Bow and Crooning Woman with him. And they had gone because they were too old now, too saddened, too broken for hatred. But as for themselves—Gray Wolf and Crazy Horse lay here on a ridge and a fit enemy was thundering toward them

—straight into the ravine—where a hundred and more painted faces smiled with satisfaction.

It was difficult to understand how the Long Knives could be fooled by such an ancient trick. But they came at top speed. It was funny enough to make one laugh to see their faces when the sand spouted bonnets and lances from under their horses' feet. And it was funnier still to see how quickly they lost interest in fighting. They pulled their horses up so fast that the forelegs raked the air and, turning, they fled back the way they had come. Some never made the turn. Others rode frantically, trying to dodge lances and lead.

Before he could reload, Rabbit had his pony beside him and Gray Wolf sprang to the back. He rode furiously, his wild scream joining the others, his lance poised, hungry for the blue backs.

They left more than a dozen pair of blue-eyes with their faces turned up and followed the rest to the very gates of the stockade. Then they rode around the walls, yelling defiance, but the Long Knives behind the shelter hid themselves and sent lead singing like angry bees through the slits of the walls. No one was hurt, though, and after a while they turned to the settlement, which had been deserted while the fight had been going on. They looted the homes of the *Wasicun* as the Long Knives had looted the lodges of Sand Creek. They ripped blankets and clothing to shreds. They smashed the tables and chairs and cabinets and they used the pots and pans for rifle practice. They spoiled the food and polluted the water.

Someone found a box at the stage station and pried it open. It was full of the green paper the Long Knives got for killing people.

"Let us make fun with this," Crazy Horse said and held up a handful for all to see. "The Long Knife loves to have this paper. Take it out and feed it to the winds where they can see."

And everyone thought it would be a fine joke, and it was great fun. It eased some of the pain of the heart, even if only for a little while. But this was only the beginning. After this little fun there would be other little funs and other revenges—little revenges and big revenges.

"Destroy everything they own," Roman Nose said beside the night fire.

They divided into groups, each following his chosen leader, each taking a chosen trail. And they killed and they burned and they looted. They visited places the *Wasicun* called Julesburg, Beaver Creek, Lillian and Morrison and then went back to Julesburg while the Long Knives watched from behind their stockade. And they went to other places eastward and westward, northward and southward—to settled places and to remote homesteads. And neither raw wind nor freezing cold nor even sleet that pierced the skin with blades of ice could cool the fires of their hatred or temper their desire for revenge. And *Wasicun* men, women and children all up and down the trail they called the Overland Stage route paid for Sand Creek. And *Wasicun* men, women and children on wagon trains paid for Sand Creek— and yet the debt could not be balanced.

They forgot ambitions of honor and gallantry. They no longer counted the worth of the enemy. They hardened themselves against compassion for a fleeing figure or a whimpering fear. They pitted themselves against stinging wind, endless miles and countless hours on horseback. They ignored the ache of bone and the soreness of muscle. They lived to destroy, to kill, to annihilate. And Gray Wolf saw relentlessness replace the gentleness that had been in Crazy Horse's eyes, and did not know that his own had turned cold and stoic. They rode behind Roman Nose, the invincible Cheyenne, and denied themselves any thought of the glory of leadership, the comforts of a home, the warmth of a woman or the beauty of kinship. They lived and they rode side by side in stern, brooding silence and only the flowing blood of the *Wasicun* gave them moments of wild exultation—a shrieking joy that was no joy at all.

Winter passed, and the spring passed, and the summer came with bright steely days and yellow dust devils. And no one knew anything about a place called Appomattox Courthouse or a man named John Wilkes Booth. They only knew that the *Wasicun* were fewer in number, more hesitant in aggression. Rabbit became a man with the name of Iron Hail. Naked One replaced the new warrior as Gray Wolf's apprentice, and the name of Roman Nose struck terror in the hearts of the *Wasicun*.

Then the messenger came. He told Gray Wolf and Crazy Horse that Red Cloud lay, pierced through by an arrow from the bow of a stinking Crow. And they said farewell to Roman Nose and their Cheyenne brothers and rode the trail toward home.

There was a sound, a low, quivering gasp, that cut Gray Wolf like a blunt blade. He leaned forward in an unseen gesture of help and of helplessness. He stayed in that tense position until the racking quit, then he sank back.

Red Cloud's moment of tearless grief was passed. He spoke and his words came low and husky with the effort.

"My ears no longer hear the *Wasicun* who sings like a coyote in the night," he said. "My brothers may listen to his crafty song, but my ears no longer hear."

He turned his face away from them. His wasted hand raised feebly to wave a despondent dismissal. The warriors rose to slink out of the lodge. They gathered in a chastened group a little way away from the lodge. Gray Wolf turned from them and walked in another direction. His knees were stiff with anger.

A lowering sun painted the sky vermilion. A stir of wind swirled the smoke from smoldering cook fires and the voices of the people were mingled with the hum of insects and the dismal cries of hungry night hawks. It was the time of the day when one could rest and feel the beauty of the world. But tonight the vermilion sky and the sweet voices of the land did not bring him joy. He looked at the groups of warriors who sat stoically, their dark faces inscrutable and their eyes showing awareness of their inevitable destiny. Somewhere nearby a horse stomped and blew through his nose.

Spotted Tail and Tashunka Kopipapi had taken advantage of Red Cloud. While he had been incapacitated with his wound they had made a secret rendezvous with the whites and they had signed a treaty—a treaty guaranteeing the *Wasicun* safe passage through Dakota lands.

Red Cloud, when he learned of this, predicted that nothing but disaster could come from such a treaty, and Gray Wolf agreed with him wholeheartedly. Red Cloud had been amazed and bewildered by the betrayal, and from his bed he had refused absolutely and irrevocably to honor the paper. That Spotted Tail or Tashunka Kopipapi could have made such an agreement was beyond Gray Wolf's comprehension. That they could have sent word of their treacherous deed to Red Cloud when he lay so near to death was villainy of the worst sort. It had come to the point now where one could not even trust his own. Behind Gray Wolf's eyes was the flare of a powerful emotion. He loved Red Cloud as a strong man loves a strong father, and he loved his people as only an uncorrupted mortal can love his kindred. It was an unprecedented mood to resent a brother. It was a novel response to proscribe a tribesman. But something unbelievable was occurring within him. A dark certainty was forming in his mind. With cold fury he met the issue. He faced it, grim, bitter and fierce. The hatred that piloted his life could no longer blind him to truth—and the truth was that there were those of his own blood who were equal to any *Wasicun* in deception, in treachery, in villainy.

Gray Wolf's passionate soul revolted, but logic demanded that truth be given recognition. He walked away, struggling. Facing a truth such as this seemed a cardinally important task that was almost beyond his ability. He placed an iron grip on his temper and walked without joy in the world.

The ruby sunset faded into wan dusk. Gradually, from a source he could not define, he found strength to accept this appalling revelation. But the rippling sounds of the children's laughter, the good smells of roasting meat, the smiles of reunion could not make him feel that he was home again. He knew that the wistful anticipation that had ridden with him over the long miles to home had been but a dream. Home—and the wonderful elation of being home—was gone forever. And all the time that had passed since that long-ago day when he had ridden away came back to torture him. It came to make him shudder and sweat here in this place that he had thought was home. He turned slowly to walk back toward the cook fires and inside him lay a mixture of regrets—which was loneliness.

Red Cloud's wound healed. His tribesmen's treachery did not. The treaty festered in his heart and from his couch he talked bitterly against it.

"The *Wasicun* is a maggot eating into the soul of the Dakota," he said, "and like the maggot he multiplies before our very eyes and will devour us if we do not crush him out."

Later, when he could stand on his feet and sit on his pony, he fought savagely against it. He rode at the front of his turbulent warriors, who, for the first time, hunted down and killed the invaders.

The cold season came and went. The warm season came and passed and Red Cloud's warriors struck again and again until no emigrant, no wagon train, nor any troop ventured into Dakota territory without a strong escort.

Gray Wolf, growing more morose and taciturn each day, rode close behind his chief and by his side rode Crazy Horse, reckless and carrying the dangerous gleam that had lighted in his eye the day Dawn, her pain and regret plain to be seen, married No Water, a warrior whose hands were not stained with the blood of his own kinsman.

And although they rode side by side, their legs often touching at the shift of a horse or the press of battle, the brother-friends had, somewhere in the chaotic phenomena of their past two years, lost their ability to touch hearts.

When they had first returned home and Crazy Horse had watched as his beloved had married another his heart had broken. Despite the knowledge that Dakota tradition could tolerate no such conduct, he had persisted in dreaming dreams of his doe-eyed maid and her loss to him had been acid on his already lacerated heart. To Gray Wolf he had voiced his hurt and cursed the *Wasicun* for the crippling of his soul. And Gray Wolf, deep in the mire of his own complexity, had thoughtlessly added to his friend's grief.

"A thing that is done is done," he had said, voicing the inflexible Dakota logic that Crazy Horse's ears had no wish to hear. "Because conditions force a law to be broken," he added, "does not mend the law nor remove the penalty."

And Crazy Horse had walked away from him, bitter, hard and uncomforted, and married a maid whose family was less strict. It was a loveless match and Crazy Horse's eyes continued to follow Dawn with hungry longing. Black Shawl, his unwanted bride, pretended not to see, but No Water was not so decorous. He pretended nothing and as Crazy Horse's eyes followed Dawn, No Water's eyes followed Crazy Horse. He was suspicious and he was jealous, and he was disinclined to hide his churlishness.

When he caught Dawn and Crazy Horse in an illicit meeting, had his passion been less he would have killed the interloper. Fortunately Touch-the-Cloud had been near and when the shot No Water fired laid a furrow across Crazy Horse's face like a branding iron, Touch-the-Cloud had rushed in to wrestle the gun from the outraged husband's hands. He had prevented the greatest of all mistakes, but the unprecedented behavior of all three had split the harmony of the community.

Gray Wolf, steadfast in his loyalty to his brother-friend, elected to take the blame for all of it. He voiced his feelings of guilt for the events that had led to Sand Creek and thus to this state of affairs. But Crazy Horse, his face raw with the wound of his dishonor and his soul poisoned with his own transgression, had answered his friend shortly.

"You make water in a stream and blame yourself for the flood!" And Gray Wolf had drawn back, not understanding his friend nor the devastation of their world, or the mystery of people. He was baffled by his friend, who was friend to no one. And it developed that as they rode side by side in cold duty, they exchanged—without knowing it—their identities. And in the exchange they both grew, each in his own way—Crazy Horse, by the stress of his heart, to a cold, calculating, relentless warrior, whose only aspiration was death to the *Wasicun;* and Gray Wolf, by the struggle in his mind, which made him think, made him reason, to know he was unfitted for the leadership he had always craved. His courage, his ability and his gift to command had become blighted by his insight. His cunning and his hatred became tempered by questions. There was within him an unknown self, a defiant unquenchable self that was stirring, awakening and asking.

A messenger came to the village. Couriers from the *Wasicun* chief in Washington were in Fort Laramie. They wanted to talk to Red Cloud. They wanted to talk to him about another treaty— a treaty that he could honor.

Red Cloud deliberated for many days. He took many purifying sweat baths. He smoked many pipes and he spent many hours fasting and meditating. And one morning, sweet with the melody of birds and the ripple of water in the brook, he called the people before him.

"We go," he said, "and talk with these couriers. We go because I would not have them say that Red Cloud is a savage who wishes only to kill. I hold no hope that these couriers bring a more equitable treaty than those who came before them, but we will go and listen. I have dreamed a dream I do not like. I have seen a white eagle who comes to steal a road through our lands. So I think we go for nothing, but we will go."

Red Cloud had been only partly right. The meeting had solved nothing between the people and the *Wasicun* chief's commissioners, just as he had predicted. The council had, in fact, broken up in dramatic dissolution. But it had brought about something that even Red Cloud had never dared hope for—it had united the people as nothing, not even Sand Creek, had united them. It proved to all that Red Cloud was supreme in leadership. It proved that he was indeed counseled by the very spirits, for while the council was yet in session and all the chiefs were on the verge of signing the *Wasicun* paper, a column of troops had ridden in. Their leader had dismounted and the *Wasicun* commissioners had greeted him warmly.

Red Cloud had stared at this new arrival for a moment and

then he had leaped to his feet. He had pointed to the newcomer and to the shoulders of his coat, where the *Wasicun* wore the insignia of their medicine. There, for all to see, were the white eagles, fashioned from shining metal. The sunlight had glinted from them. Red Cloud had been as angry as it was possible for him to be and retain his dignity.

"We came to this place to talk peace," he told the *Wasicun*, "but White Eagle is not here for peace. I say he is here to steal the country of our fathers. I say he is here to build a road for the *Wasicun* through our lands. There is no more reason for empty words. My people will leave this place and we will fight the White Eagle."

The faces of the commissioners had reflected the truth of Red Cloud's words and there were none who did not see it.

Red Cloud leaped down from the platform where the council sat and walked away. He ordered the lodges struck and rode away. The other chiefs saw this and knew that Red Cloud had dreamed true and that once again the *Wasicun* had tried to make fools of them all. They rose one by one and also walked away.

The fact that the White Eagle immediately led his men straight to the Powder River country and started building a fort at the branch of the Piney showed everyone that Red Cloud was not a fool, nor did he merely guess. It was clear to all that he was in tune with the universal knowledge that revealed all things that were and were to come, and from all corners of the Dakota nation they came to stand by his side. Lodges were raised all up and down the Little Goose and Red Cloud's fire burned night and day. Together with the other war chiefs he forged a fighting force of more than four thousand fiery warriors, and together with the other chiefs he drafted a waking nightmare for invaders of Dakota territory.

Less than two days after he started construction on his fort, White Eagle was attacked. But only two soldiers were killed and only a few of their horses were stampeded before the warriors were recalled. Red Cloud did not want a full-scale movement against these soldiers.

"Dead men," he said, "are heroes. Do not make heroes of them. Let them sip of death. Let them taste of horror, but feed them no feast of glory."

The impetuous warriors resented such constraint, but obedience to leadership was as inherent as their horsemanship, and they executed Red Cloud's siege, keeping surveillance that never ceased.

They soon convinced the soldiers that they were faced with a foe who never slept, who never turned his face away. Should one of them stray even the smallest distance from the others, he was cut off and killed. If one of them exposed himself, even for a moment, night or day, he was laid low with a bullet or an arrow. Any detachment that set out without a powerful guard had to fight for its very existence. And a wood chopper or a herder who laid his rifle a trifle too far away to reach instantly never fingered it again. To cool the fever of their restraint, the warriors, when relieved from watch and surveillance, gathered into bands and ranged far to seek vengeance with withering assaults against wagon trains and travelers who ventured across their restless path. And of the more than four thousand pair of hot Dakota eyes, none were as hot with hatred as the glittering eyes of Crazy Horse. And as rapidly as his reputation for valor, tireless marauding and ruthless vendetta rose to zenith, just as rapidly did the blood lust of his brother-friend, Gray Wolf, cool and coagulate into disturbed and unhappy dissatisfaction.

Summer passed. Autumn passed, and the bitter cold of another winter brought dissension. The camp was no longer a small village. There were over fifteen thousand mouths in need of meat and the age-old custom of seeking sheltered sites where game was plentiful was hard to disregard. Many of the chiefs wanted to rush the fort, massacre the soldiers and burn the place. But Red Cloud was adamant.

"Massacre them," he said, "and two will come to avenge every one who was killed. The only way for us to rid ourselves of the *Wasicun* forever is to make life so miserable for them that they cannot endure it. And it is now that we must show them how it will be. If we wait there will be too many of them and they will change our way of life just as they have changed the lives of our cousins, the Iroquois. They will take away our land and they will tell us where we can live. They will kill the game and tell us how we will live. They will take our children and raise them in the ways of the *Wasicun* and there will be no more Dakota.

"Always we have not had the *Wasicun*," Red Cloud argued. "The *Wasicun* stays—we stay!" And he stood firm.

Still there was disagreement.

"There is no glory for men in this kind of fighting," they said.

"We do not fight for glory. We fight for the land of our fathers. We fight for our homes. We fight for our children," he answered them.

And Red Cloud kept to his grim purpose. A few who disagreed, like Black Shield, left with their followers, but they were so few that their departure was scarcely noted. Those who stayed kept the circle of agony around the fort and stalked wagon trains, gold seekers and settlers who had hoped to slip through Dakota country under the protection of winter.

For over a full round of the seasons, Gray Wolf lived and fought the never-ending battle against the *Wasicun* and against the breakdown of all he had held honorable. His loneliness and despair grew, for Crazy Horse was no longer his confidant and constant companion.

Crazy Horse had gone crazy indeed. He had become so lax in his morals that it seemed he was almost a *Wasicun* himself. He even indulged in affairs with two or three of the women from other clans and did so without seeming to care for the outcome to either the women or himself. Only his unblemished reputation as a warrior kept him from being exiled from his people. Gray Wolf could no longer talk to him, for his disapproval of such behavior was impossible to hide and it was impossible for him to condone Crazy Horse's actions.

Crazy Horse led a group of warriors who delighted in hunting *Wasicun*, and when such hunting proved insufficient to quench the thirst of their reckless furies, they spent their time with joyless, mirthless games of gambling, dancing and carousing that became rougher and more brutish each day.

The elders viewed these developments with consternation and made feeble efforts to curb the rowdyism, telling each other that it was but the spontaneous outbreak of too much youth confined within too small an area. But Gray Wolf and all the other younger men were wiser in this respect than the fathers to whom they had always looked for wisdom. They knew this recklessness for what it was. It was disillusionment and the acceptance of defeat. They knew that their world had come to an end and they saw, with the discerning eyes of youth, the bleak, cold and hopeless future.

Gray Wolf dreamed terrible dreams of a million feet, tramping over Dakota ground, carrying a special class of men bent upon creating a world of their own—a violent, cruel and bleak class of men, cheating for a grain of dust, killing for a yellow pebble, snarling over a handful of earth, bringing with them countless senseless tasks, thousands of diseases of the body and—the annihilation of the Dakota. It was so vast that he was overwhelmed, and it seemed to him that this was the shape and the outline of all of his future years. His confidence and his hope seemed lost forever. Hideous doubts and dark confusion tormented his soul.

The burning idealism and tranquil faith of his youth were gone. A shadow had come across his sun, and friendship and companionship were covered by the same shadow.

Unable to voice their disillusionment and disappointment in their fathers, who had allowed this inglorious existence to come about—unable even to admit that all the joy and beauty had left their lives—Crazy Horse and the other warriors covered their tormented, furied and lacerated honor with cynicism and frenzied brawling. And Crazy Horse brawled more and killed quicker than any other warrior of the Dakota, and did not seem to care that his brother-friend walked in loneliness, still convinced of the integrity and honesty behind the tormented fury he now displayed. The mature characteristics of the brother-friends collided in estrangement.

Despite his cunning, his insight and his gift to command, Gray Wolf lost his followers because he would not degenerate to butchery, he would not participate in brawling. They left him, to travel on a trail where he refused to walk. It galled him to find himself despised because he would not, could not abandon old standards that he had been taught from childhood.

Endless talk of ways to exterminate the *Wasicun* to preserve the old ways disgusted him, for already the old ways had been abandoned. Honor was sacrificed for achievement, courage for attainment and justice for dispatch. Bravery was replaced by sneaking trickery, and self-respect by swaggering braggadocio. Gray Wolf felt that he walked among the already dead, for he would not accept this as life.

With this terrible awakening of his soul he knew that he must somehow rise out of the ashes of this futility and make a life of his own. Where—he did not know. How—he did not know. He only knew that he could not waste his years in this inglorious living. He had had enough of violence, cruelty and senseless, unrewarding bitterness to crust his heart forever. He had had enough of buffalo hunters, gold seekers, wagon trains and soldiers. That was endurable. But he had had enough of brawling, bragging, sneering warriors who were Dakota—and that was not endurable. He had had enough of running and enough of staying. He had had enough of pitting his brain and his sinew against the never-ceasing flood of wretched, foul-smelling creatures that squirmed and wriggled across the prairie like oscillating caterpillars. He had had enough of standing fast to Dakota custom while his friends and kinsmen shook loose in a frenzy of forgetting.

Death came to all men and Gray Wolf was not afraid of death. Death was all that he intended to give to the *Wasicun*. Dishonor came only to him who would allow it. Honor he would not relinquish, not even to keep the fellowship of his own. Thinking such thoughts, he sought out Red Cloud and asked to be allowed to speak his heart.

Red Cloud listened and for a long time after Gray Wolf had ceased to speak, sat in silence. He sat for so long that Gray Wolf grew uneasy with fear that he had offended his chief. Finally, with great weariness, Red Cloud spoke.

"My son," he said. "My beloved son. I hear you. I know that

our people are walking down the path of degradation. It is inevitable. Do you think I love this dwelling upon lust for blood and lust for rampant living? I do not. But I must do it, for if out of these lusts I can see even one of our young men walk again with a sense of beauty and a compassion for life, then I can endure it. This day you have given me hope when my hope was almost gone. My son, I see your heart—and seeing it has warmed my own."

And again the Teton chief lapsed into silence. He seemed to have forgotten the young warrior who sat before him asking for a solution when there was no solution, despising sympathy when there was nothing to offer but sympathy. Red Cloud sighed.

"Come again in two suns and sit by my fire," he said. "I will think on this and when I have thought, we will talk again." And he wondered what there would be after all the thinking he could think that would change anything.

Disappointment showed sharply on Gray Wolf's face. He made an impatient gesture. Red Cloud raised his head and the intensity of his gaze reminded the young man that while certain liberties were permitted, there was but one chief.

Gray Wolf rose and stalked out into a starless night.

Gray Wolf came out of the warrior lodge as the dawn opened its blue eye of clean sky. Irritable with his perverse reproval of warriors who still slept soundly in their blankets, he faced the east and struggled to clear his mind of censure.

He heard a few voices here and there singing morning prayers, and he chafed at his inability to concentrate on his own conscience. He was keenly aware that his harsh criticism of the growing laxity in propriety had become almost rabid and was beginning to lend the taint of self-righteousness to his own deportment.

"Wakan Tanka, hear me!"

His voice sounded louder than proper dignity required because of his efforts to quell the ugly condemnation in his heart. In spite of his firm convictions, his own attitude made him as derelict as the worst offender who caroused in the night and slept through the rising sun. What was he to do? He lowered his voice and finished his morning song on a note of futility.

He walked slowly back toward the cook fires, without appetite, without anticipation. He felt impatient with the day that stretched ahead. The sun rose bright and glittering and it had turned cold. He wished that his band had been scheduled for patrol today, but they were not. There were too many warriors for too small a job, and nothing, not even hunting, was allowed to take them away from the camp, where they must be ready in case they were needed. Gray Wolf hated this kind of day. Sick as he was with this entire existence, he wished for action—any kind of action. And toward the middle of the day he got his wish.

The faint notes of the fort bugle sounded the now familiar "Boots and Saddles." It was a clarion call for warriors as well as for the soldiers it summoned, for it meant that the soldiers were in need of reinforcements—and if soldiers needed reinforcements there was the possibility that the warriors could use more help.

With one quick, smooth motion, Gray Wolf shrugged into his shirt and out of his lodge moccasins. He pulled his leggings on and stepped into his outside footwear. He swept up his ready weapons and was outside waiting when Naked One came riding by at a gallop, dragging the wild, prancing pony Gray Wolf rode in battle. He leaped astride before the boy could bring his own mount to a halt. They galloped away, the powdery snow boiling around the pounding hooves.

Gray Wolf's fighting band was a mixed one, and Dakota, Cheyenne and Arapaho came in from all directions to join him in the headlong dash toward the ridge. Below the brink they pulled up. Gray Wolf slipped to the ground and went to peer over the edge. Below, the gates of the fort swung wide and a column of the bluecoats rode out. Gray Wolf's eyes narrowed in the glare made by the sun on the snow.

"*Hou!*" It was Big Nose, a powerful and reliable Cheyenne.

"Fetterman!" Gray Wolf said.

"*Hou,*" Big Nose repeated.

"Maybe today is the day he is going to ride through the whole nation," Gray Wolf speculated, deriding the boastful words Fetterman had spoken.

"Maybe so!" Big Nose grinned, his eyes dancing with his glee.

They remounted and galloped to circle the narrow valley to the ridge behind them. Crazy Horse was there, directing positions for the ambush. Down the valley beyond a jut, American Horse kept a tight circle riding around a wood train that had formed into a stronghold from which soldiers kept up a constant stream of rifle fire.

Crazy Horse greeted Gray Wolf with an upraised hand. He flashed a smile of delight.

"*Hou!*" he called.

"*Hou!*" Gray Wolf answered, grinning back. It was at moments like this that the old brother-friend relationship was good again and the joy of it lifted the gloom from both of their hearts.

Gray Wolf ran an appreciative eye over the field, where warriors were rapidly vanishing from sight.

"It's a good day to die," Crazy Horse said.

"It's a good day to die," Gray Wolf agreed.

Crazy Horse held up his two hands with his ten fingers spread wide. He looked at Gray Wolf. Gray Wolf nodded. A thumb was lowered. Crazy Horse looked at Big Nose. Big Nose nodded. A finger crooked. Ten times Crazy Horse looked at a warrior and waited for his nod. Then his fist was closed and he called out.

"It's a good day to die."

"It's a good day to die," ten voices called sharply in reply.

Gray Wolf led them out. They whirled their ponies and galloped across the valley. They were partway up the slope when the troops from the fort appeared at the top. Gray Wolf reared his pony as if taken by surprise. The other warriors pulled their mounts around and caused them to bump into each other, as if they too were in a state of confusion. They could see that there was some hesitation above them. Big Nose became frantic with the fear that they would not pursue. He whipped his pony and rode forward recklessly. He dashed back and forth in front of the astonished line. Then rifles began to spit, but the big Cheyenne was not touched. He laughed in the soldiers' faces and rode back, taunting them with derision that no man could mistake. It was too much for the impetuous Fetterman. Triumph was already in his voice as he shouted the order to charge.

Never had a trick of decoys worked so perfectly. The ten warriors rode just out of rifle range and drew the troopers on and on until they were completely within the circle of hidden warriors. Then the decoys rode apart and crisscrossed, the signal to close in.

A wild whoop from nearly a thousand gloating throats seemed to paralyze the soldiers. The dismay showed in their faces when the earth so suddenly gave birth to so many warriors, who converged to make them a small island of struggling futility.

Arrows rained upon them and in a matter of minutes the rifles were silenced in hand-to-hand fighting. Lances clashed against rifle butts and war clubs descended with powerful intensity.

Only a few of the warriors even found the opportunity to raise a lance before the fighting was finished. More troopers were seen topping the ridge, apparently coming to the aid of the comrades who already lay with their faces turned up, past caring about aid.

There was no opportunity to deceive this new company, and no amount of taunting could entice them to repeat Fetterman's folly.

It was turning colder and a sharp wind presaged the blizzard that was surely on its way. Crazy Horse signaled for retreat. They rode away and did not even look back to watch the cautious troopers descending the hill toward the rapidly stiffening bodies of their late comrades.

That night the camp was an uproar of blatant celebration. The warriors whooped with glee as they told and retold how Fetterman the braggart had blown out his own brains when Spotted Colt, a mere boy, had brandished a little head-knocker—the only weapon the boy possessed when he had leaped into the fray.

They celebrated far into the night and initiated Spotted Colt into warriorhood without consent of the elders or regard to tradition. Then they got the boy drunk with the contents of a flask someone had taken from one of the soldiers. It was a wild revelry in which Gray Wolf took no joy.

It turned bitter cold and a howling blizzard began, increasing in velocity hour by hour. Toward morning, a half-frozen messenger rode in to report to Red Cloud that the scout at the fort had ridden out on the soldier chief's own horse.

It could mean only one thing. The soldiers were afraid. They were sending for help.

The warriors wanted to ride out and bring the scout back to the camp and have some fun with him, but Red Cloud shook his head.

"No!" he said. "A man who is brave enough to ride in such freezing cold deserves to be left alone to get through if he can. But he will not. Fort Laramie is the only place he can go, and it is many days' ride even in fine weather. He will die on the trail, but he must be left to die doing his duty."

Morning came and the snow was drifted up to the very top of the stockade. It would be easy to walk up and into the fort, but again Red Cloud said "no" and it took all of his powers to restrain the warriors.

"Let them suffer," he said. "They expect we will do this. They expect to face death every moment. Let them feel this, but do not give it to them."

And the restraint was maddening.

Gray Wolf went to talk again with Red Cloud. The old man received him graciously and he talked long and seriously. He talked about the old days and the old ways. He talked long about these new times and the things these new times demanded of a man. He talked as a father talks to a son, but in the end he confessed he knew of no way to ease Gray Wolf's pain. But the talk did ease some of the burden of Gray Wolf's mind. He went away loving the old chief more. He had not found the solution he sought, but he did find a certain serenity in his thoughts.

Tashunka Kopipapi, the traitor of the treaty, was jealous of Red Cloud. He had been sullen and mean in his actions ever since he had been proven a fool by Red Cloud's superior wisdom. He became outspoken against Red Cloud during the long winter, and a few of the less integral listened to his words. In the spring, after the passing of the severe cold and the heavy snows, he left the camp and a few discontents followed him. He went again to the *Wasicun* and made overtures for peace with them. But as he had already proven, he was not a shrewd man. He asked for ammunition and the *Wasicun* laughed in his face. He returned to the camp, chagrined and ashamed, and Red Cloud revealed the greatness of his spirit when he made no mention of this transgression and acted as if he had not noticed Tashunka Kopipapi's absence. Gray Wolf marveled at the patience of his chief and again his mind eased its tension of discontent.

Spring and summer brought no change in camp life, but gradually Gray Wolf came to accept it with more grace. They harassed the fort, allowing the soldiers no rest, no peace, and it became evident to Gray Wolf that Red Cloud's method was working well. The soldiers showed plainly that their nerves were strained to the breaking point. Wood was scarce now and the wood details had to travel a long way to bring it to the stockade. It was Crazy Horse's delight to torment these details, and it was on one such raid that it happened.

The detail was small that day. There were hardly more soldiers than there were fingers on the hands. They formed their wagons into the usual corral position. Crazy Horse led the band to the rise of land overlooking the detachment. When he was ready, he whirled his blanket over his head in the signal to attack and they rode down, yelling "It's a good day to die."

Everybody was eager to be first. After the first volley there was always the pause while the soldiers reloaded and there was never any glory to be gained from killing a man with an empty gun. It was easy to get within jumping distance of the wagons before the second volley came. It was the finest experience to make the leap just as the soldier fired the second time.

There were hundreds of warriors, all eager to count coup, and they massed together in their eagerness. The first volley came and then a strange thing happened. There was no pause in the firing. A steady stream of lead poured from behind the wagons.

It dropped warriors and horses in a melee of death. From every angle it came.

They split and rode around the wagons, but to no avail. It was the most bewildering thing Gray Wolf had ever seen. It made the hair on the nape of his neck rise. Guns do not shoot without reloading—but these guns were doing it. The spirits had joined the soldiers for some unexplainable reason and it was spirit guns they were facing. Gray Wolf did not like this. He had no intention of fighting spirits. He intended to turn his pony and ride away from this fight.

Three bullets hit him—all at the same time—and he knew no more except the sweet darkness of deep peace.

8

He returned from his already-forgotten walk in the land of shadows and saw Falling Leaf sitting by the fire. He knew he had been away for a long time and he tried to think what it was that had taken him away. It was very hard to separate real things from imagined ones.

Falling Leaf brought some liquid in a gourd and held it to his lips. He drank of the hot, fragrant herb tea and his belly recoiled. Falling Leaf forced the gourd to his lips.

"Drink," she said. "You need it to mend."

He took a few swallows and fell back, exhausted. He was appalled by the weakness that swept over him. He meant to ask Falling Leaf how it was that she was here. He meant to ask her where Small Owl was. He meant to ask her if he had been having dreams. But he fell asleep before the words would come to his lips.

He awoke again and there was the Holy One standing over him, chanting the song of healing, and there was a strong smell of something he did not like coming to his nostrils. He meant to ask them to take the smell away, but he fell asleep before the words could be said.

He was a long time mending. The whole summer passed and he lay in the lodge that Falling Leaf had raised to house him in his weakness. When he was able he did not return to the warrior lodge. He was aware of the mild derision and the waggish puns his unorthodox action generated. But his unsullied reputation prevented the stigma of outright derision.

He found a certain solace in the quiet orderliness of this lodge.

It was a thing he had greatly missed but had relinquished rather than take another wife.

He had worried over his inability to become interested in any of the girls in camp, and there had certainly been scores from which to choose. He had continued his monastic existence and sometimes wondered if he had become impotent. He no longer even felt any desire to find a woman that might stir his blood. He was content with the sterile ministrations of old Falling Leaf. As his wounds mended he entertained his warrior friends in quiet contentment and gradually they ceased to marvel at his odd preferences, accepting them as being his way of shaking off old traditions.

After the disaster that had led to Gray Wolf's wounds, many of the warriors lost faith in Red Cloud's leadership. They left the camp by the hundreds, their fear of the spirit guns making them certain that Red Cloud was no longer in tune with the universe. But Red Cloud still clung to his purpose: to force evacuation of the fort.

It was still another spring before his tenacity was rewarded, and then it came very unexpectedly.

They had surrounded the fort for so long without any satisfactory results that it had almost become a way of life and not many even hoped for anything more. They knew nothing of the consternation they had created in far-off Washington, where their destiny was to be decided. So it was with surprise and very little faith that they received another message that a new commission was at Fort Laramie asking for a council.

Red Cloud, ever ready for peace if peace could come without relinquishing Dakota lands and Dakota rights, went to the council with no more faith than he had gone to the last. But this council was different. To the amazement and delight of the whole nation, the commission agreed to abandon the fort and close the Bozeman Trail over Dakota lands. They asked, however, that in return the Dakotas refuse aid to the Cheyenne, who were having their troubles with the iron trail being built across Cheyenne lands toward the south.

To Gray Wolf's consternation, Red Cloud agreed. It was the

first time Gray Wolf had disagreed with his chief. The Cheyenne had given aid to the Dakota. It did not seem right to deny aid to friends who had given aid. But Red Cloud was tired and he knew the dissension his long siege had caused. He feared that if he did not sign this treaty his hold over his people would dissolve into more, and less successful, battles for Dakota rights.

The treaty ceded all of the Powder River country, including the Black Hills, to the Dakota, to be their land for as long as the sun would shine. What more could be asked than this? Red Cloud was ready to sign, but still he did not trust the wily *Wasicun*. He gave his word that he would sign as soon as the last soldier was recalled from Dakota lands. No one, not even Red Cloud, really thought they would do it. But one bright day the flag over the fort was hauled down and the people gathered to watch as the soldiers mounted their horses and rode away. After more than two years it was over.

Before the troopers were out of sight, they rode down and set their torches to the fort. They danced with their glee as the great billow of smoke rose to the sky. Gray Wolf watched silently. It was a great victory for the Dakota. He should have been happy, but he was not. He kept hearing the words of the treaty—refrain from aiding the Cheyenne . . .

In the many months it had taken for him to heal from his wounds he had spent much of the time in thinking. And those thoughts had brought a great plan to his mind. He had dreamed of all the tribes of all the nations uniting, much as they had done after Sand Creek, to make their power felt and make it known that the tribes would tolerate no more *Wasicun* aggression. He had dreamed of a great wave of warriors driving the *Wasicun* back across the Father of Waters and he had dreamed of a return to life as it was meant to be lived—full of beauty and honor.

To him the fact that the *Wasicun* had placed this condition in their treaty proved that they, too, envisioned just such a union— and that they feared it. It seemed to Gray Wolf that Red Cloud had failed even as he had won, and his disappointment in his chief was great.

While the Dakota had been fighting, the Cheyenne had been

fighting too. In their own land scores of mighty warriors had fallen before the scores of reckless, sweating, cursing laborers who spiked the iron trail that brought the belching, roaring demon that brought more laborers, adventurers, buffalo hunters, gold seekers and soldiers. And all along the trail they made roaring, stinking camps where they fought Cheyenne and fought among themselves.

Many a Cheyenne warrior had gone to sleep the long sleep, and Gray Wolf's friend Roman Nose had been one of these. No, he thought, the Cheyenne war is not a thing apart from the Dakota war. It is one and the same and this treaty is one that makes the Dakota a coward and a deserter. Gray Wolf could take no joy in the peace that had come to the Powder River country. The victory was an empty thing, but not even Crazy Horse would agree with him.

So with the coming of the Harvest Moon, Gray Wolf knew he could not honor his chief's treaty. He took his horse and his blanket and said good-bye to his mother and his father and to Falling Leaf, and he rode away from his home, alone and lonely. And he could not say good-bye to his brother-friend Crazy Horse, who was now the greatest of all Dakota warriors.

He knew where he was going. Bending Bow and Crooning Woman were still in Black Kettle's village. He would go there first while he thought about what he was going to do. Almost at once he was beset with doubts over his decision to exile himself from his own people. But there had been no other choice. When a man could not agree with his chief there was no other course, and he had not been able to agree. He had not been able to agree and had not yet learned to compromise. So he rode south with a heavy and lonely heart.

He seldom sought company and seldom accepted the hospitality offered along the devious trail he took to avoid contact with the settlements which had sprung up all over the plains. Once in a while, when his loneliness became too much for him to endure, he would stop at some friendly Cheyenne camp to join in a sing and listen to the news, but winter was at his heels and he never tarried long.

It was very cold the morning he tied his horse in front of Crooning Woman's lodge. The old couple were pathetically happy to see him. They too were lonely for their kinsmen, and they listened avidly to all he had to tell them. Bending Bow shook his head in sympathy when he heard why Gray Wolf had come.

"It is a bad thing to be cut off from your own," he said. "We have known this loneliness for a long time now, but we are too old to travel alone. But you are young, and even though a man must do what he feels is right, you must think more on this. This is a time when men must choose—and sometimes the choice is between two wrongs. Red Cloud had to make such a choice and he chose that which was least wrong."

"No man should have to do this," Gray Wolf said.

"No man should," Bending Bow agreed, "but this is the way it is. The *Wasicun* have made it so."

"If they have made it so then there is more reason for banding together and fighting them until all the nations are left in peace."

"If we did this there would be no more nations to live in peace." Bending Bow shook his head. "All our people would be lying with their faces turned up. The *Wasicun* are too many and the land is too big. Each nation must make what peace it can or no nation will survive."

"Maybe it is better then that we do not survive now than not to survive later." Gray Wolf's words were bitter.

"It is a thing," Bending Bow answered, "that each man must decide for himself. Maybe when you have not looked upon the faces of your own kinsmen for a few moons then you will know it is better to live with an honor laid aside than with all of life laid aside."

"I will never believe this." Gray Wolf was determined.

"When these snows are gone I would like to go back to my own country and see my kinsmen," Crooning Woman said. "Think on these things until the snows are gone, Gray Wolf, and

maybe when the new green leaves come you will feel like taking
Old Man and me back to our own people."

"I will think on it," Gray Wolf agreed, unable to disappoint
the old woman and relieved within himself that his decision was
not yet absolute. They were right in their wisdom, and a long,
lazy winter stretched ahead in which to decide what he had
thought had already been decided. His loneliness lifted, and
through the day and the night and far into the morning hours
they talked and laughed and kept the fire burning. The time
passed quickly and at last they rolled into their blankets and
were asleep before the fire turned to ashes.

And as they slept the falling snow covered the sounds of
creaking leather and the plod of shod hooves. The night hid the
inflexible features of a boy general as he crept to the top of a low
hill and strained his eyes through the darkness toward the camp,
etched against the winter white, and no ear except the ears of
the soldiers heard the whispered orders, and no person except
the *Wasicun* bluecoats felt the cold of the night and the cold of
the steel that was turned in the direction of the lodges.

To the soldiers it was a poor rendition of the opening bars of
"Gary Owen," attempted by lips that froze to instruments.

To Gray Wolf it was a raucous shriek of a hundred haunted
demons that jerked him out of his sleep. He sprang from his
blanket to the center of the lodge. Bending Bow was at his
elbow. They stood motionless, dazed by the strident clamor. The
sound staggered to a ragged end. There was a silence that lasted
only the length of a breath and then the chilling notes of
"Charge" unfurled like a banner of death.

Gray Wolf dropped to the floor of the lodge. He pulled Bending Bow with him. He snaked to his blanket to grab his knife
and his gun from where he had placed them when he had gone
to sleep. The rattle of gunfire and the pounding of hooves mixed
with the coarse shouts of men riding to kill.

Over the steadily mounting din Gray Wolf heard Black Kettle
shout.

"Hay-ay! Hay-ay! Warriors, do not run. Stand and fight—"

They were brave words, but Black Kettle was dead before he

could shout more and his wife lay beside him, her blood staining the white of the snow.

I am dreaming a bad dream, Gray Wolf thought. This is a dream of Sand Creek, because being with Bending Bow and Crooning Woman has brought this bad remembrance to my mind.

But he knew he was not dreaming. Men, women and children were running out into the freezing weather, naked from their beds. Bending Bow snatched up his lance and before the shout could form in Gray Wolf's throat to stop him, the old man ran out and fell in a hail of lead. Crooning Woman cried out her pain as the old man went down, her loving heart seeing the thing that was hidden from her eyes. Holding her frail hands before her, she stumbled out toward Bending Bow's sprawled figure.

"Wait for me, my husband," she cried. "Look back from where you are going and wait for me."

Gray Wolf caught her and pulled her back.

"Let me go," she pleaded. "Let me go with my husband."

And he let her go, influenced by forces over which he had no control. And she died. She died where she had always lived, by the side of the man who had been her love, her eyes, her life—that was no more.

An acute pain tore at Gray Wolf's throat and he stood looking down at them, heedless of the bullets flying around him. And then his horror broke into fury. Peace? Peace with these monsters?

He whirled to face the score of horses thundering down on him. A volley of bullets answered his own fire. He was not hit. He darted to one side and tripped over a man lying face down. A horse came charging at him. He flung his knife at the rider and missed. He rolled to his feet, bringing the dead warrior's knife with him. Soldiers were sweeping past him on both sides. He slashed out at legs, at saddle girths, at anything and everything within reach of the flashing blade.

A bullet from somewhere toppled a trooper out of his saddle and the rifle flew from his hands. Gray Wolf caught it up and he knew that in his hands was one of the "spirit" guns that had once frightened him. He laughed with savage glee and stood working it, scarcely bothering to take aim.

The soldiers swept through the village. They pivoted their mounts to come back, chopping down those who had not fallen in the first onslaught. Warriors were striking out with lances and even coupsticks. They used their few old-fashioned rifles as clubs and here and there a spirit gun fell into a lucky hand. But they were no match for the soldiers, who were slaughtering them like so many buffalo. Gray Wolf saw the people heading for the river and he leaped after them. The icy water numbed his legs. The jagged ice tore at his skin and once again water was running red with Indian blood. Then the soldiers turned away, but as they went they fired the lodges and drove some of the women and children into their wagons, and they left behind some of their own, who followed the women and children down the river, shooting them down as they floundered in the water. Gray Wolf sprang after them. Little Rock, a subchief, emerged from behind a cloud of smoke. He saw Gray Wolf and signaled. They ran for a point between the women and the soldiers. Another warrior joined them. They dropped behind a mound and there they made a stand. In the first volley Little Rock was hit. He rolled back, his gun dropping from his fingers. Just at the moment when it seemed it was to be the last in Gray Wolf's earthly life, warriors from another village rode in behind the troopers. The bluecoats were surrounded. They formed a tight circle and fought back to back, but within moments they were all dead but one. He threw up his hands and came with them outstretched. One of the warriors went toward him. As he came up the soldier snatched his long knife from the case on his belt and plunged it into the warrior's belly. Dozens of arrows sang and dozens of rifles spat. The soldier fell dead and the warrior's friends stripped the body and hacked it in their fury.

It was all over. Another thing just like Sand Creek. Bodies everywhere, blood on the snow—and this was peace!

Gray Wolf walked back to the smoldering village on legs that were stiff with cold and shock. He went to the place where

Bending Bow and Crooning Woman lay. Their bodies were already stiff in frozen sleep. Laboriously he fashioned a travois from the ruined lodgepoles and placed them on it. He caught a horse that stood head down in dejected weariness and hitched the poles. He led the horse out, away from the scene. He did not look back. He did not feel the bitter wind biting into his flesh.

During the days that followed he battled the bitter cold and sleet, searching for a fitting tomb in that winter-locked land, alone, without food or warmth. The travois carrying the beloved corpses bounced gruesomely over the icy rocks and frozen clods, and each jolt begat a curse upon the white race. Shifting passions tormented his heart and burned his soul until nothing was left but the cold ashes of a calm and deadly hate.

He never remembered, or tried to remember, when or where he found the cave where he placed them. He carried their frozen bodies tenderly and placed them in the dry darkness. He laid them side by side as they had laid in life asleep, and he covered them with the only blanket he possessed.

He rolled rocks over the open face of their tomb and stood for a moment with bitter eyes that promised payment for the debt of their dying. Then he turned his face away, and did not look back as he rode the stumbling horse down into a valley that seemed to have no end.

He followed the valley for a long way. He lost track of time and he knew nothing of the country in which he wandered. He rested the horse when it could go no farther. He slept cold, with only a tiny fire to keep him from freezing. He ate only when some small animal crossed his path and made him remember that food was necessary. He traveled farther and farther into unknown lands and his trail always led toward the south.

One night at dusk as he was searching a place to camp he smelled the smell of meat cooking. He slipped off his pony and crept to the top of the rise in front of him. Down on the other side of the slope was a camp. It was the cluttered camp of *Wasicun* gold seekers. He watched for a long time. He did not ponder in his mind as to what he should do. He knew what he was going to do.

He waited for night and for the flare of their fire to die into ashes. Then he crept down the slope. It was brief and it was merciful for the victims, for they never knew when they died in their blankets. He sought out those things that he could use from the debris of the camp. The rest he destroyed, and when the sun came up in the morning Gray Wolf no longer traveled without food or without blankets. He was rich with plunder and rich with satisfaction. He spat on the bodies that lay sprawled in the grotesque shapes of death and left them where they lay—carrion for the scavengers of the land, warning to other *Wasicun* who might come to seek the yellow metal—notification to all the land that Gray Wolf, the Dakota, had passed this way.

He rode on, and once in a while he met others who were riding to or away from a place where the *Wasicun* camped. Sometimes he would join those others and ride with them for a while, but then he would weary of their company and he would go again his own lonely way.

He stalked unwary travelers with the only joy he now knew, and when he would strike there would be more pale faces looking up into the sky with empty eyes. But no matter how many he left to the mercy of the elements and the wild creatures, he knew no satisfaction. With each passing season he grew more lonely and more hungry for the blood of those he hated. Often he thought of his own people and often he contemplated turning back toward the north, but his feet would not obey the longings of his heart. He knew that he was past his ability ever to make peace with a *Wasicun.* One day he would die, probably at the hand of a *Wasicun,* but he would never live by that hand. And so he wandered and hunted and more often than not it was the *Wasicun* that he stalked. No traveler, no lonely homestead was left unscathed. Five complete turns of the seasons went by and one day he lay and studied the desert long and carefully. He had never seen a place like this before him. He had come out of the deep, red-walled split of the great gorge where he had slept the night before and here was this land lying before him for miles and miles, each mile looking exactly like all the other miles.

It was a morning with no rosy glow in the east. Mists hung

like a curtain and the shadows persisted as if nature was loath to brighten the monotonous and melancholy prairie of dry and sandy reaches.

Silence hung like a mantle, and no track or trail was visible in all the expanse that stretched out before and all around him to reach and merge into a distant haze.

It was an awesome sight and he was not prepared for it. Here no rippling wave of buffalo grass, no rain-washed sculptured rock, nor any patch of oak or fringe of cedar softened the scene. There was an unreality to this desolate wilderness that tried to fetter him with fear. It lay exposed, naked, deceitful of its distances, begrudging of its life-giving waters, and jealous of its solitude.

The loneliness of the barrens brought a wave of homesickness, and reluctantly, with no alternative, his thoughts turned back to dwell on those who were forever gone from this world, who were no more. He laid his face in the sand and gave himself up to the grief he had not expressed except in blood, since that awful morning when he had heard for the first time the blaring notes of the Seventh Cavalry bugles on the banks of the icy Washita. And the grief racked his body and brought great sobs that tore from his throat. He wept as a strong man weeps at his helplessness in the face of his own despair. And while he lay with the water from his eyes wetting the sand, the sun bolted into the sky, white hot, and burned away the shadows. It revealed the scant and tortured brush and the wind-swept erosion, but no living or moving thing. In the white heat of this infinity, he lay and let his grief drain from him. When it was gone he lay weak and spent.

He stayed yet another day in the shelter of the rock. And then, with the rising of the next sun, he went out to descend into the trackless waste.

9

The mustang manifested more than his usual testy temperament. He jerked and pulled at the halter rope. He shied and pranced. Gray Wolf felt a tingling at the base of his skull where the delicate nape hair, educated to the proximity of a scalping knife, bristled a warning. Yet nothing, as far as he could see, moved. The sun beat down relentlessly. Even the scant brush sprouting from red mounds of sand did not cast a shadow. There was no sound to be heard.

For three days he had ridden in the blistering desolation, coming to dread sunrises that brought almost unbearable torture. The only living things he had seen were jewel-like lizards, odd little rodents, great long-eared rabbits, and lean, voracious coyotes. He had begun to feel as dry and burned out as the land around him. And there seemed no end. His water was low and he longed for a drink of the cold, sweet water of the Powder River country. But there was no water, except the scant cup of hot, foul liquid left in his waterskin.

He had not drunk since early morning, having given most of the unquenching moisture to the mustang. He began to feel that if he did not find an end to this desolation soon, he would no longer have to ponder the ways of life.

Toward the south, a weird, saffron shadow appeared. It rose from out of the red, dry earth and swept upward with incredible swiftness. It changed from saffron to a dull red. It became a great, menacing wall sweeping toward him. The air that had been so hot and still stirred and the sand began to move with a soft hissing sound. The wind started, first in small puffs and then in growing gusts. The seeping sand began to whirl along the ground, rising in some places high into the air in spinning yellow columns. As the wind increased in force, sand and dust began to sting his body.

The mustang's eyes rolled wildly. Gray Wolf looked for some bit of brush, some mound of sand that might afford a little shelter, but there was none. The shadow spread from horizon to horizon, swallowing up the desert as it swept toward him. It was terrifying. Sand and small stones began to pelt him like angry wasps. The mustang began to pitch, swaying his head in terror. Gray Wolf dismounted and wound the halter rope around his arm. He was afraid that the frenzied animal would bolt and leave him afoot in this wasteland.

As the storm bore down upon him, the sun dimmed to hang like an eerie red disk in an obscure sky. Dust and sand clogged his nose and he was forced to breathe through his mouth. The dry sting of alkali crusted his teeth and smarted his eyes. The wind rose to a gale.

The mustang snorted and tried to pull away. Gray Wolf pulled the tossing head down, forcing the velvet nostrils against his bare shoulder, and thus they stood in the weird gloom that surrounded them, man and beast, heads bowed, backs hunched against the vicious wind.

When it seemed as if his burning lungs could endure no more, the gale shrieked by and suddenly the air was clear of dust and sand. In its stead a raw downsweep of wind sucked black clouds down toward the earth. The sun was blotted out. A low roar swelled into rolling thunder. Lightning jabbed downward spitefully, and Gray Wolf began to shiver in the sudden chill. He fumbled, trying to pull his blanket roll from the pony's rump and maintain his grip on the halter rope. He got the blanket around his shoulders just as huge drops of water began to splash down. A dazzling flash of lightning flared, followed by a clap of thunder that sounded as if the very sky were being ripped from end to end. The air was filled with a sulfurous stink. The mustang reared and pulled him nearly off his feet. It took all his strength to hold the animal down. Rather than chance losing him he let the blanket drop and flung himself to the pitching back. He could feel the quiver of terrified flesh under his knees.

A torrent of rain struck him in a driving sheet, and the mustang bolted. He let the frightened creature run a little before turning him in a circle. He could not afford to get too far from the blanket that now lay sodden in the sand.

Almost as suddenly as it had come, the rain ceased. The black clouds rolled on as if fearful of being late at some predestined destruction. The blue sky appeared and a rainbow, vivid and magnificent, arched the sky. Gray Wolf pulled the pony to a halt and sat in rapt amazement.

Once again the sun appeared with all its intensity. It felt warm on his back and there was already a dry fragrance in the air, even while the sand beneath the mustang's hooves was wet.

He found the blanket and wrung precious drops of water from it into the waterskin.

A colorless little bird flitted from bush to bush, uttering a sweet, plaintive whistle, and far in the distance the clear air showed a hazy ring that was a plateau and the end of the desert.

But yet another caustic day was to pass in faltering torture, and the sun hung low in the western sky before Gray Wolf led his spent pony into the shadow of a ragged, broken wall. It stood straight up from the desert floor, sculptured by wind and time, gullied and cut by erosion, ridged and chiseled by the ages. It glowered out at the desert, which had failed to extort its toll from this puny intruder, and grudgingly lent its shadow to shelter the dejected warrior and his beaten pony.

Gray Wolf dropped to the ground. The pony stood, head down, all mettle and fire gone from him. Gray Wolf looked at the wretched animal through red and blistered eyes.

"This," he thought, "is the first time I have ever ridden a horse into the ground." He wondered if it would not be merciful to use one of his precious bullets to end the creature's misery.

Cautiously he shook the waterskin. There was barely enough of the hot rancid stuff to wet his parched lips. He knew he should feel some sort of concern for his situation and yet he could not. What lay beyond this unfriendly bluff he did not know. Where he might find water in this waterless land he did not know. His situation was acute and yet he was too filled with some calm, powerful feeling of elated wonder at his survival to feel any real, deep concern.

He shook the waterskin again and at the sound of the soft slosh the moisture glands in his jaws ached with a futile attempt to eject saliva into his arid mouth. The mustang heard the sound too and rolled his eyes pleadingly.

Gray Wolf raised himself and found the movement painful. He staggered over to the wretched beast. He took the hot, dry muzzle in his hand and, untying the waterskin, poured a few precious drops on the leathery lips. They quivered eagerly. He held the muzzle tighter. He could not afford to lose even one precious drop. With great care he guided the water into the animal's mouth. The flask emptied, and had his own throat not pained with longing, he would have laughed to see a half-wild mustang sucking at the skin like a hungry colt at its mother's teat.

It was a weird and confused night that followed. He had been reduced by heat and thirst to little more than half his weight; his feet became stumbling, weighted drags. With staggering obstinacy, he hunted the somber shadows for a break in the wall.

The moon rose, a thin, silver sliver that cast a pale, greenish light. It added a last unreality to the sand, the cacti and the rocks and to life itself. There was no sound save the dull thudding of his own laboring heart and the plod of the dejected pony's hooves as he followed, more like a faithful dog than a wild and spirited mustang.

Many times during these hours Gray Wolf felt that his torture must surely find an end in oblivion, but he refused to embrace such a welcome release. There had to be water and he knew he would find it before another sun rose to scorch the land.

He did not know when it was that the mustang took the lead. He was dimly aware that he was following the sound of what seemed to be a quickening pace. And then the night was gone. A golden-red light lined the rocks and bluffs. The morning light revealed the wide, deep wash that yawned before him. The mustang turned sharply and headed up the wash. And then there was the water.

It was a tiny, shallow pool, white-edged with alkali, bitter and warm, but it was water. Gray Wolf fell under the mustang's hooves and lay, his burning face and cracked lips in the water. The mustang nuzzled his head aside and slurped greedily.

The sun leaped into the sky and another day began with a vengeance. The pony blew and slobbered. Unable to rise, Gray Wolf rolled away from the pool to the scant shade of a small greasewood and a shelf of overhanging rock. He slept.

He was awakened by the strains of a weird chant. The dark figures of a ragged mustang and a wild rider were silhouetted against the glaring sky. His own mount nickered softly and stamped his feet with a show of some of his old cantankerousness.

Caution wiped the sleep from Gray Wolf's eyes. He rolled quickly back to the edge of the life-giving pool. He could not afford to miss the opportunity to drink his fill of the water he had only sipped before sleeping. Lying on his belly, with hands braced solidly ready to push his body erect, he drank deeply. He kept his eyes on the wild, unkempt figure that rode down the slope toward him.

He was Apache, and he rode up to pull his mustang to a stop and look down on Gray Wolf with cold, hostile eyes. Gray Wolf did not take his eyes away and he did not cease his drinking. He saw out of the side of his eyes the others who rode up from different directions to surround him. Leisurely he arose. He spoke, using the Cheyenne language, but knew before the words were uttered that they did not understand. He turned to the inadequate but universal sign language. He told them who he was and asked to be taken to their chief. None of the cold, intent faces relaxed, but the leader motioned him to his horse. He mounted and rode with them, up over the ridge from whence they had come. They rode, silent, withdrawn, with only their wild, black eyes to reveal that within them they carried some secret and terrible passion. Gray Wolf could feel it moving, boiling, like some great geyser stirred from inertia to awakening for eruption. They rode with bitter blood, oblivious to the beauty of the day or the beauty of the land around them. They did not ride in amity, even with themselves.

The sun turned to a dusky gold and moved behind towering mountains toward which they had ridden the whole day. All around them weird rocks and grotesque cacti were exquisitely magnified in the veil of gold. Gray Wolf took note of everything and the Apache noted that he noted.

The trail, if there was a trail that the Apache were following, was invisible to the Dakota. They rode a long, weaving climb, up and over curves and mounds and slopes of bare rock. But for the many deep cuts and chasms, it resembled a plain of irregular swells. Bits of green, other than the spiny cacti, sprouted here and there from the barren red and yellow sand.

To the west loomed a great mountain with a colossal face of colored crags and cliffs. With hawk eyes Gray Wolf scanned the region of ledges, benches, canyons and rock, and the trail always led up.

Finally they came to a place where a small, clear spring flowed from somewhere under the wall. The Apache drew rein and dismounted. They drank and watered their horses, indicating that he do the same.

The water was good, not bitter like that of the other seep miles back on the edge of the desert. It made Gray Wolf feel better even while it made him conscious of his acute hunger. He had not eaten for two days and his belly protested. But there was no food in his own parfleche, and the Apache made no move to camp or eat. They remounted and the ride was resumed.

Beyond the spring, brush, sage and a few flowers grew. At first they were few, but finally even grass sprouted here and there. The lofty rise of the mountain shut off the sun, and they rode on in the hot, fragrant shade.

Suddenly they rounded a jutting abutment and entered a deep rent in the rock. There was scarcely width for a horse and rider. Two of the warriors rode in. The others waited in haughty silence for Gray Wolf to follow. They rode a short distance and then the gorge opened up into a great amphitheater of rocks and purple sage and yellow flowers, with patches of green and gray cedar and black-pointed spruce thrusting up from out of the cracked rock and earth. There were aisles and lanes through the maze of sage and grass to a broad grassy meadow where wild roses and strange white lilies swayed to the drowsy melody of bees.

At the far western end, above a magnificent jumble of mounds, slopes and ridges, a thin waterfall fell like a long, silver strand to disappear in the luxuriant growth that seemed to choke the bottom. It was a place weathered out of solid rock by Wakan Tanka. It was a place to fulfill a warrior's dream. The peace and solitude appealed to Gray Wolf as no place he had ever seen. The hot sun shot through the branches of the trees, and jays and mockingbirds flitted from cedar to spruce to piñon. It was another world, haunting and sweet-scented. He felt as if he could live here always—until he died.

In the meadow there were hides pegged out in the sun. Farther on, a few lean, racy mustangs nickered and stomped their hobbles. Down the slope, where the grass was less luxuriant, a dozen or more strange, squalid lodges fashioned from the boughs of trees were grouped. Naked, bony children, with wild, tangled hair and dirty beyond definition, gaped at him with dull, haunted eyes. They looked starved. In such a retreat, in such a bountiful valley, this was a strange and awful thing. Gray Wolf knew at once that there was something here that did not belong.

A warrior, older than the others, dirtier and more ragged than the others, came out of one of the lodges. He was taller than his squat kinsmen, yet dwarfed by Gray Wolf's remarkable height. His hair was straggling around his wide, dark face and was unlike the coarse jet hair of his comrades. It was fine and soft and a rich, dark brown. There was something wildly fierce and searching in his gaunt, worn face.

When Gray Wolf dismounted and stood before him, the Apache's body stiffened as if he were scornful of the gigantic Dakota. His eyes raked rudely up and down the bigger man. His words, when they came, were a guttural staccato, and although they were meaningless to Gray Wolf, it was easy to discern that the Apache considered him a captive. To show his feelings about such an attitude Gray Wolf folded his arms across his chest, drew himself to his fullest height and stared down disdainfully at the Apache leader. The leathery face hardened and the bold eyes narrowed. He shot impatient questions at the warriors who had brought Gray Wolf in. They answered with eager tongues and the conversation went on for several minutes while fat, filthy women peeped from behind lodges and the children stared. Finally the leader raised a lean, dark hand, snapped sharp orders and pointed across the canyon. It seemed that the warriors accepted the order with some reluctance. They moved away, leading Gray Wolf's pony. The leader motioned Gray Wolf to follow and with a look of contempt stooped to enter the brush lodge.

Gray Wolf saw that the lodge had only just been raised. The grass of the floor was not yet trampled. The fire pit contained fresh sticks that lacked a flame and there were no ashes under them. There were no sleeping couches along the walls and no gear hung from any peg. He kept his eyes down, not wanting to insult his host by noticing the shabby quarters. He waited quietly and respectfully for an invitation to sit. Instead the Apache turned and spoke in the *Wasicun* tongue. Defiantly, he struck his breast sharply.

"I am Victorio," he said. "I am the chief of my band."

"I am Gray Wolf," Gray Wolf answered, "warrior of the Dakota."

The Apache's eyes widened. For a moment he appeared stunned and then without warning he threw back his head and laughed. It was a loud laugh without any real mirth. Gray Wolf's lips tightened. He had never before received rude treatment in any Indian camp. He had been told that the Apache were not over-friendly, but he had never expected discourtesy. Anger coiled inside his pride and the pressure of his knife concealed under the flap of his breechclout gave him a feeling of comfort and a small amusement of his own. Not one of these venomous little warriors had detected that weapon, and discourteous as it would be, if provoked beyond reason he would show them their neglect.

As abruptly as it began the Apache ceased his hilarity.

"Nantan Lupan!" he said and shook his head.

Gray Wolf did not understand the Apache words. He waited in silence.

"Well, Nantan Lupan"—Victorio's voice was heavy with sarcasm and insult—"tell me how it is that my warriors find you in Apache land."

The added discourtesy of starting a conversation before a proper welcome angered Gray Wolf even more. This Apache was more than discourteous. He was ignorant.

"How is it you have come here, warrior of the Dakota?" Victorio spoke as if addressing a wayward child.

"Are you chief of the Apache?" Gray Wolf asked the question very softly, letting his displeasure sound in his words. "If so then I will tell you. If not so then I would ask who is your chief?" Pointedly he looked about the poor brush hogan, and pointedly he looked at the ragged Victorio. The Apache stiffened under the scrutiny. He seemed to think for a moment, then his body relaxed and his discourtesy left him. He called loudly, and one of the fat, squat women came in answer. She fell heavily to her knees and put a flame to the sticks in the fire pit. After the flame started she heaved herself up and waddled out. Victorio motioned to a place beside the fire and sat down cross-legged. He took a pouch from his belt and took from it some strange brown paper and a pinch of tobacco. Carefully he rolled the tobacco in the paper and drew his tongue across it to seal it with wet lumpiness. He handed it to Gray Wolf.

It took all of his Dakota courtesy to accept the repulsive-looking thing, but Gray Wolf accepted it and waited until Victorio had rolled another for himself. After Victorio had put fire to his tobacco Gray Wolf followed the example. This was a poor people indeed, he thought, who did not even possess a pipe in which to place their tobacco. But he puffed at the smoke and gave no indication of his displeasure with this kind of smoking.

"I have been rude." Victorio said it slowly and sincerely. "It is because the Apache cannot often call a stranger brother and your name in my tongue is Nantan Lupan. This is a name which brings anger to the heart. In Apache lands this is the name of the white-eye soldier who stalks the Apache as one stalks the coyote with the madness sickness. I see now that you did not call yourself this name just to make an insult to Victorio."

"I meant no insult. It is my name," Gray Wolf answered. "And in my country it is a name to be honored."

"A name that is honored in one place may not be so honored in another," Victorio said. "In the white-eye world the name Nantan Lupan is probably an honored name also. But that does not make it the sound of wind on Apache ears. If my Dakota brother wishes to find welcome in Apache wickiups it would be wise to answer to another name."

"I shall be glad to answer to any name the Apache would give in honor," Gray Wolf said, "for I came with no quarrel to the Apache. I carry no peace in my heart or my hands, but it is not for the Apache but the *Wasicun* that my anger rises. I travel in Apache lands because for many turns of the seasons I have walked alone. I have walked alone because my own chief made a peace with the *Wasicun* which my heart would not accept. I have walked in the lands of the Cheyenne, the Arapaho and now the Apache. I carry anger in my heart for no man of any tribe unless he be the slave of the *Wasicun*."

"Then you are in heart an Apache." Victorio smiled sourly. "I am not chief in this land. This is not even my land. My land is far to the south, but we are here only just before you because this same Nantan Lupan was close on our trail and we could not shake him off without crossing the desert in this direction. The chief of this country is Cochise, who is my friend. Maybe this is the chief you seek?"

"I seek only a place to rest my body and my spirit," Gray Wolf said. "I have too long lived only for killing and revenge and it grows sour in my belly. When I came to the edge of this great place I saw nothing of life, and I came into it to find peace. I am tired of fighting. My fathers are gone and my brothers are gone and there is only the *Wasicun*. My heart is heavy with such living. I seek to find a place where I can live awhile in peace with the foxes and the birds as brothers."

"And you think to find this place in Apache land?" Victorio laughed bitterly. "My brother, long before the Dakota knew the white-eye existed the Apache was already old in warfare with him. This place you want—it is not in Apache country—not the land of Cochise nor my land or any other land I have seen. The white-eye is everywhere. He is like the air that blows over all places. He has taken the water holes and all of the places the Apache once held as their own. They are even in the middle of the sands where the sun dries the water out of a man's skin and blows him away. So if you find this place, you tell Victorio and he will go there with you."

Gray Wolf was silent. He was silent with the muteness of hopelessness.

"There is no place such as you seek, brother," Victorio said. "This place is only found by those who are gone from here. There is no life for us, neither Apache, nor Dakota, nor any other of our people anymore, but fighting, always fighting, and there is no rest from it. You have fought for many turns of the seasons? I have fought since I was tall enough to draw a bow. You talk of dying? I know of dying. Not since anyone can remember has an Apache died of old age."

The old woman came back into the wickiup and she brought with her two bowls of boiled meat. Victorio took one and handed the other to Gray Wolf.

"Here is food. What else is there for man? Eat it. It may not be the kind of food the Dakota eat, but it is good. It is the first we have had for many days, and by your looks it is probably the same for you. So even if it is different from what the Dakota eat, it will taste good to the ghost you now are.

"Ha!" he exclaimed. "That shall be your Apache name— Ghost!" He said it as if he relished the sound of it. "Yes, it is a good name if you will answer to it."

"I will answer, especially if in answering I will taste a thing as good as this meat tastes to my empty belly." Gray Wolf ate greedily, and it was not until the bowls were empty that either of them spoke again.

After they had satisfied their hunger they talked, and Victorio shared his small supply of tobacco. Gray Wolf smoked with more appreciation than he had had for his first cigarette, because of the sharing. The hours passed and the night came and again they shared meat and it was good. Finally Victorio addressed Gray Wolf in a voice warm with hospitality.

"I could take you to Cochise so you could ask his permission to walk in his country, but if you will join with my band and become a brother to Victorio, you already have that permission. You are without a home. No man is complete without a home, regardless of the country where he walks. Make my camp your home. We are few, but we hold out a welcome. Many of our women are without men of their own because of the killing and the dying, and there are many who would look upon you with favor. Apache women are well trained in the ways of giving a man comfort. Choose one of them and stay with us."

Gray Wolf suppressed a shudder. The vision of intimacy with any one of the fat, unclean creatures he had seen made him flinch.

"I am in no mood for a woman's comfort," he said.

"A man who is in no mood for a woman is a dangerous man—to himself and to others," Victorio said.

"My trail is the lonely trail," Gray Wolf answered. "I have had a woman. I have had a home. I have had a clan and all these things are gone. I do not want any other."

"A man who refuses to live because he has suffered has not suffered very much," Victorio answered. "A little suffering is like a little poison. It pains greatly and does not make you sick enough to vomit it out. One day when you have suffered as the Apache has suffered, then you will vomit out what galls your soul, and you will live each day for that day and deny yourself nothing because of it. The Apache learned long ago that this is so. He learned long ago to choose between hunger and honor, comfort and duty, life and death. He has also learned that with the choice of honor and duty and death there is little of eating, little of comfort, and little of life, but it is better to have a little than nothing. But no man must turn from that which he feels is right himself. No! He must not, not by gun nor wounded pride,

nor knife nor any weakness of heart or"—and he smiled gently—
"even the advice of a good friend."

"This is a truth," Gray Wolf agreed, "and I must find my own
path, but even if I do not feel the need of a woman I do feel the
need of brothers and I will gladly sleep in the warrior lodge of
Victorio's camp if I am welcome."

"You are welcome, Ghost." Victorio rose and Gray Wolf rose
with him. "There are but two warriors who are not with women
at the moment, and you may sleep with them. But who knows,
tomorrow you may have to sleep alone. Our men and women do
not have time for waiting these days and by tomorrow night you
may sleep in a lonely wickiup.

"We are no longer like the two fighting cocks who came into
my wickiup." Victorio smiled and laid his hand on Gray Wolf's
arm. "It is good. It is pleasant to find a brother and make him an
Apache."

Gray Wolf laughed, and returned the gesture of friendship.
Perhaps the Apache were not as crude and as uncultured as they
appeared to be. Their manners seemed crude, their tobacco unpleasant, their food strange, and their persons unclean, but the
welcome, now that it was given, was as warm as any he had
known. He went to his blanket feeling good within himself and
sleep came very quickly, even if the eyes of his sleeping compan-
ions did lack warmth as he lay down beside them.

Days passed into other days and the seasons changed. Gray
Wolf learned in that time that the uncleanliness of the Apache
was a forced condition of unwashed pride. And he learned that
their rudeness was acquired, and their rags were disdain for the
larceny of their lands and the constant plunder of their camps.
Everywhere soldiers and settlers gathered to take their water
holes, the rivers and any fertile spot of desert and mountain.
There were enemies behind them. There were enemies in front
of them and there were enemies all around them, all of the time,
riding ruthlessly, hunting them down to kill them or herd them
into pest-ridden agency camps. Like varmints, the Apache had a

bounty on his scalp. No man, no woman, no child was secure in his right to the breath of his living.

In the Powder River country, Gray Wolf had learned to distrust the *Wasicun*. In Cheyenne country he had learned the bitterness of hatred for them. In Apache country he learned virulent malice. The *Wasicun* had been a plague. The *veho* of Cheyenne country had been a menace, but the white-eye of Apache country goaded a vengeance that grew into a giant shadow that covered a man and blinded him to either honor or justice or compassion.

But Gray Wolf learned other things, too. He learned that while the Apache woman could never become lovely to his eye, her courage, her chastity and her pride made her lovely to his heart. One such woman was Lozen, warrior-woman and sister to Victorio. She was unlike most of her sisters in that she was slim of body and muscled like a man. She possessed a courage that more often than not put warriors of no mean mettle to shame. Lozen had long ago placed her womanhood on the altar of revenge, and since that day no Apache had shown her the distinction of being a maiden. Try as he might, Gray Wolf could not, in spite of her image, treat her as another warrior, and Lozen responded to his deference with an eloquence in her eyes that he could not meet.

With the same resignation that she had donned warrior's clothing, she accepted Gray Wolf's friendship and held her head high and proud under his serene and quiet gaze. But it was she who rode most often at his side. It was she who pointed out the guiding signs in the vast sweeps and rolling swells of desert, seas of bleached grass and seared sage. It was she who became his tutor and interpreted for him the pale mesas, domes and bluffs. It was she who taught him to prepare a water pouch and bury it deep in a marked place for emergency use in this land without water. It was she who taught him how to become invisible in a land that provided no cover, and it was she who acquainted him with all things edible in the barren land. And it was she who best demonstrated to him the dignity and the modesty of Apache womanhood. It was she who helped him overcome his intoler-

ance to being unwashed when there was water only for wetting
the tongue. It was she who taught him the comfort of a lodge
fashioned from the boughs of brush, and the joy that could be
known in possession of so small a thing as enough rawhide to
resole a moccasin.

And in return Gray Wolf was constantly by her side in every
encounter with an enemy or meeting with a friend. He was ever
quick to challenge those who were wont to sometimes refer to
her as "Victorio's dirty virgin." Although it was often a question
of who protected whom, they grew very close to one another in
the months that passed, and Lozen came to replace Crazy Horse
in Gray Wolf's heart. And if he sometimes suspected that Victorio hoped for something more intimate between them, he did
not dwell on it, for he liked the warrior-woman as a friend and
had no wish for any interjection that might spoil that friendship.
He was vaguely sorrowful that he could not fulfill those hopes,
but adoration was not a part of his admiration for Lozen, and he
had long ago determined never again to take a wife for whom he
did not feel the insatiable thirst of desire.

The wild, forested hills of his own home had never called to
him as did this lonely land of rocks and sand and sun. And the
hearts of his own kinsmen had never spoken to him as poign-
antly as did these wild, proud hearts of the Apache. Their very
ferociousness was appealing in its justification. Their utter disregard for the results of that ferocity was a magnificent declaration
of pride and dignity. And these things were good in Gray Wolf's
eyes.

The seasons passed and he lived with them. He hunted with
them. He fought side by side with them and raided with them.
And if he did remain immune to Apache women's charms, he did
not stint the full obligation of a warrior. He lived the life of an
Apache with all the passionate purpose of an Apache. He
learned to speak the language of the desert and to listen to the
winds that blew in constant movement across the sands. He
learned to hunger and to thirst. He learned to sleep without
sleeping, on the ground, unwashed, unfed, exhausted and
stripped of every worldly possession save the gun in his hand

and the knife in his belt. He learned to eat food that was raw, lest a hail of bullets deprive him of the only morsel available. And he learned more. He learned that the white-eye was everywhere and that he was an enemy, whether he be soldier or settler, traveler, God man, Mexican or *gringo*.

In his own home he had learned the horror of losing brothers to wanton killers. In Cheyenne land he had learned the desperateness of *Wasicun* raids on peaceful peoples. In this land he learned the vivid anguish of being hunted, relentlessly, ruthlessly —stalked day and night. He learned that the Indian, regardless of clan, tribe or nation, was a thing to be exterminated. He learned that the Indian, regardless of honor, dignity or intent, was entitled to neither respect, nor property, nor home, nor sustenance. He was entitled to neither comfort, nor family—no—not even the breath of life. He learned that he was regarded as an animal, to be hunted down and destroyed whenever and wherever he allowed himself to be caught. And these lessons washed away any reservations he might have had in his hatred of the *Wasicun*—the *veho*—the white-eye. For as long as he had been able to meet and fight as a man, he had struggled to hold to his honor and his code of ethics. But when he became as a varmint, he responded with a fiery vengeance worthy of the regard in which the *Wasicun* held him. And Victorio was well pleased with his Dakota brother even as he relinquished the dream of mingling Dakota and Apache blood.

It was a morning late in a summer season when he awoke to find that the impotence that had settled in his loins had faded. He was restless and turbulent. He wanted a woman. He wanted a woman of his own—a woman appealing and desirable and devoted; a woman who would fear for him when he rode into battle; a woman who would smile with happiness when he returned; a woman who would bear him sons and daughters to run to him and cling to his legs with the love of being his sons and daughters; a woman who would make his lodge sweet with the smell of cedar; a woman, who, if Wakan Tanka should call him to the Cloud Land, would weep with loneliness for him. This morning he wanted this woman. No creature knew the number of his own days, and every creature was entitled to a mate between his coming and his going. And there was no woman in this land of the Apache to tame the torrent of this desire.

He went alone away from the camp. He went until he was out of sight and sound of the others, and he raised his arms to the morning light.

"Wakan Tanka, hear me—"

He hoped that Wakan Tanka was not confused. He had prayed so many conflicting prayers of late that the Great One would have to be wise indeed to separate them all and grant those that were his real heart's desire. He hoped, too, that Victorio and Lozen would understand when he told them he was going away. He knew that it would be toward the north that he would find the woman he wanted, and to find her he would have to leave his Apache friends. He felt now that he had been indecisive in all of his desires, capricious in all of his emotions, wavering in all of his purposes. Living with the Apache had somehow brought these things straight in his mind. They lived each day to its fullest, knowing that tomorrow they died, and he felt a shame that he had denied himself this way of life. Each day was for the joy of living—not lamentation for useless dreams of what once was. A man should accept what life gives to him— even if it is death—and he should accept it with joy. And very suddenly, on this chill morning, Gray Wolf knew that he was not in the mood to deny himself all of the joy of life. He wanted a woman. He was going to find a woman.

Victorio listened in grave silence when Gray Wolf told him he was riding northward this morning. Lozen's eyes were not raised from her bowl, but she did not eat with her usual gusto as she listened. They were leaving for the southern wintering places and the camp was already prepared for the move. Lozen set her bowl down and smiled shyly at Gray Wolf as she rose.

"May you travel in peace," she said. "Maybe some day you will ride again into our land. It will make our hearts glad if you do." Gray Wolf saw the unhappiness in her eyes and tried to look around it.

"I will ride again with my Apache brothers and sisters," he said. And then she was gone, hurrying away to look after some detail she had already seen to.

"A man must do what he must do," Victorio said. "I had hoped that my Dakota brother had found a home among us. It seems that it is not so. I am sorry."

"It is so," Gray Wolf said, and wished he could find the words to tell why he had to go, but he could not. "It is so. I have found a home with my Apache brother."

"I think maybe you have not," Victorio said. "A man is never at home until he has a woman and children to greet him when he returns from battle. My Dakota brother does not have this with his Apache brothers. Maybe he will find this elsewhere, and if he does, I hope he remembers he is still a brother to Victorio and Victorio will always feel a happiness for his Dakota brother and any who belong to him."

Gray Wolf was silent. Wise Victorio had seen his heart and yet did not condemn him.

"I had hoped it would be my sister Lozen who would call to my brother," Victorio said, "but a heart that does not hear cannot be blamed. It has always been so. When you have found her, bring her to us, Ghost, and we will love her as we love you."

"It hurts my heart that it could not have been as you wished," Gray Wolf said.

"What a man wishes for another is foolish wishing." Victorio smiled sadly. "Think no more on it. Watch your trail, brother, both in front and behind you."

"I will watch," Gray Wolf said. "I hope that Lozen will not be hard in her heart against me."

"You do not yet know my sister," Victorio said. "Lozen is an Apache woman. She is an Apache warrior-woman. Her pride is greater than her heart."

"I am smiled upon by the Great One to have such friends," Gray Wolf said.

And then they were gone. They rode out of the draw and Gray Wolf watched them disappear from sight. He waited until he no longer heard the sounds of their going. He looked around, hating almost to leave this place where they had last slept. Then he went for his own pony and packed his few possessions together. He rode out and pulled the pony to a standstill to look down where the tiny caravan crawled southward. Out in front of the column two figures rode side by side. As he watched, one turned. He saw the uplifted arm and knew that Lozen was looking back, saying the thing she had not been able to voice. With a gentle sadness in his heart for her and for himself, he lifted his arm and answered her farewell.

10

The desert lay veiled in shadows of lilac and blue and gray, streaked through with the pink reflections of a scarlet sunset. Gray Wolf watched the sun sink into its own fire on the far horizon. The long reach of sand and desolation no longer held the aura of menace that it had had the first time his eyes had searched its unfathomable magnitude from this same spot so long ago.

Recrossing the wastes had posed no hardship on either him or his pony, which was now cropping contentedly in the haze-filled canyon where he had made his first camp on the edge of the desert.

He sat in the fast-fading light, as motionless as the wind-worn cliffs at his back. His thoughts drifted over the solemn silence, the bleak, waterless arroyos, the bold peaks and the windy wastes. This was a land that had charmed his soul. This was a land that could not be ignored—a land that abhorred ignorance, punished indifference and rewarded vigilance. The undulating sands, the arid expanse, the white heat of summer and the bone-chilling cold of winter decreed "Love me or hate me as you will, but do not take me for granted. Know me or die!" The golden air, the halcyon silence and the unravished panorama promised strength, wisdom and oneness with the universe. This was a good land. It had taken his petty weaknesses and held them up to pitiless scrutiny. It had taken his indecisions and mocked them. It had segregated his follies and rewarded his diligence. And when it had finally lifted him from the miserable mass of doubts and fears, it had christened his soul with peace and laid upon him the mantle of tranquillity.

The sun was gone. The scarlet fingers of dusk faded, and the purple night was softened by a full, round moon that rose swiftly to cast a mellow light over the world. Stars emerged to flicker and glitter, and far out where the land met the sky there was a hint of another hue.

He watched it for a long time. It was the flicker of fire. His eyes, still not finely focused to desert distances, were unable to tell him how far away it flared. His mind was sufficiently schooled to know that it signaled disaster—disaster for Victorio, for it was in the direction of the Apache chief's travel. And no Apache made such a fire. No white-eye, unless he was burning an Apache camp, would make such a fire in the night either, for this land did not harbor even a white man stupid enough to show such a signal in this limitless vista. Victorio was in trouble.

With a terrible urgency Gray Wolf ran to his grazing pony and pulled him away from his feast of grass. His eyes were hard, and they penetrated every shadow as he rode out toward the flame that already seared his own heart.

The sun was straight up before he reached the place. He had ridden all through the night. He had neither seen nor heard anything irregular, but he knew that something was very wrong. He approached, wary and suspicious.

He left the pony tied a long way off and wound his headband around its muzzle in case the animal had any inclination to nicker. He crept in a circle, peering from every angle at the place where the stink of charred skins marked the spot. He came upon boot prints leading to the place of the smell. He followed them. Scuff marks in the sand told of the struggle. Empty rifle cartridges told of the gunfire that distance had silenced. Blood on the sand reported the wounds; moccasin prints and unshod-hoofprints traced the flight. Anxiously he searched the sand. He searched every twig and every rock. He found nothing more. He went to the boot prints that led to the camp and followed them over their back trail. He found the place where the white-eye camp had been, down under the bank of an arroyo. The ashes showed that the fire they had made had been cold before Victorio had come up. On the far side the prints of shod hooves showed that the boot-wearers were not Pony Soldiers. The prints were irregular and wandering, not the even two-by-two of the cavalry. There was no blood spattered along the boot trail, nor any in the boot-wearers' camp. Gray Wolf's lips pulled back into a thin line. He went to where he had tethered his pony. Mounting, he sat and pierced the distance with searching looks before he turned the pony into the trail of the shod-hoofprints.

He followed them for the rest of the day, and he followed them after the moon came up to show where they had met and mingled with others that pressed the sands beside the ruts made by wagon wheels.

Diego de Francisco was nervous. He was an absolutely fearless young man, but responsibility made him apprehensive. Had he been making this trip for any reason other than to escort Carlotta safely to her parents, he would have welcomed the adventure. As it was, the delay and the episode that followed did not seem in keeping with his father's admonition for speed, care and sobriety. Neither was it in keeping with the warnings they had received at the fort. The young lieutenant had called De Vargas a fool, and De Vargas had not taken kindly to such a label. He had suspected, and Diego had agreed, that the lieutenant had taken too much pleasure in Carlotta's company. And yet, Diego worried.

De Vargas was an able man. He was a proud man. He showed the breeding of his Spanish ancestors in his every move, and no doubt he had been correct when he had scoffed at the warnings of the soldiers who were, as he had said, mere peons wearing uniforms. Still, Diego remembered the old man, dressed in filthy buckskins, who had watched them and listened with something akin to sorrowful amusement. He had spat a long brown stream of tobacco juice onto the ground.

"Looks ta me," he had remarked to Diego, "like ya fellers is agonna learn mighty quick about some things. Shore do feel fer the ladies an' them handsome hosses. Seems a pity to hand them over ta the 'Paches. 'Paches don't have no appreciation for thoroughbreds—hosses ner wimmin."

There had been something about that old man that had bothered Diego. He wished De Vargas had been a little less positive
in his statements and his actions. He did not have De Vargas's
thin temper nor De Vargas's arrogant unconcern for the opinions
of men he considered less than gentlemen. But De Vargas was in
charge, and rightly so. He had the years and the experience that
the rest of them lacked.

The first day out from the fort had not been momentous. They
had traveled slowly, making the journey as easy as possible for
Carlotta and her grumbling duenna. But even so it was a wearisome time, and the second day De Vargas surrendered to Carlotta's plea for respite from the bumping wagon. They had
camped soon after noon. And every day since they had stopped
with but a half day of travel. They should have been across the
desert and safely sleeping in the town ahead. But De Vargas had
laughed at Diego's apprehensions.

"You sound like those peon soldiers," he said. "Have we seen
even one Indian? Of course not!" De Vargas was disdainful and
he had ridden off with the others to chase some long-eared
jackrabbits.

Diego had stayed with the women and the wagon and the
drivers. He had tried to amuse Carlotta, and he had not been too
worried until darkness came and De Vargas and the others had
not yet returned. Then they had heard what sounded like distant
gunfire, and Diego had refused to allow Juan to light a fire.

It had been late before De Vargas came riding back. He was
full of high spirits and they had all crowded around to tell of
their adventure. They had been resting their horses in a dry arroyo when they had spotted a band of Apaches in the distance.
They had laid in wait, and when it had turned dark they had
jumped the camp the Indians had made.

"And do you know what they did?" De Vargas laughed glee-
fully. "These fearful and dangerous Apaches? They ran! They
ran faster than the old jackrabbits." He slapped his thigh and
was very pleased with himself. "This is what Apaches do when
real men go after them."

"They even left all their goods behind," young Sebastian chimed in.

"And we burned them," Alfredo added.

They all laughed and chided Diego because he had missed the fun. And Diego had felt for a little while that maybe his fears had been foolish. He really would have liked to have been in a small skirmish if the circumstances had been different. But he could not forget his father's orders that nothing should interfere with their duty toward Carlotta. Diego felt the responsibility of his task heavy on his shoulders, and all through this day, even while he had seen nothing to bring it about, he had fought an increasing feeling of dread. He had tried to voice it to De Vargas, but De Vargas had scoffed.

"You take things much too seriously, little cousin," the older man had said. "What is there to fear? If I did not know you from boyhood I would almost think you do not possess all the courage you should. But this I know is not true. You are over-conscientious, and it is to be understood."

And De Vargas had refused to quicken their pace. The savages had run off, and he was insistent that the ladies enjoy as much comfort as possible. Maybe, Diego thought, De Vargas was enjoying Carlotta's company himself. It was not inconceivable.

Carlotta de Francisco was a lovely girl, carefully schooled as a Spanish lady should be. She had enchanted every male in Southern California since she had come from Spain over a year ago. Scarcely seventeen, she had all the attributes so highly prized by strict Spanish ladies and gentlemen. Perhaps De Vargas was quite right in traveling so slowly. This was a rigorous journey for one so fragile. But Diego shuddered at the thought of exposing her to an Indian attack. He was confident that they could handle any danger that might threaten their dainty charge, but his worry was for what such an experience might do to her. He scanned the desert in all directions. There was nothing but clumps of brush and mounds of sand. He was glad they would be out of this place tomorrow. What a godforsaken country it was. He crossed himself reverently and muttered a hurried Hail Mary.

The sun was almost to the horizon and the sky had turned vermilion.

"What a perfectly beautiful sight." Carlotta opened the canvas at the back of the wagon. She stood waiting to be lifted down. Diego sprang to her side. He lifted her to the ground. Maria, the middle-aged, sober-faced duenna who lived among past associations that would never come again, grunted as Diego handed her down.

"How I hate this place," she said. "How much longer must we endure this terrible country?"

Carlotta took no note of the woman's complaints. She was used to them. She had listened to them since the day they had embarked to come to this new land. She well knew that Maria considered it a barbaric country full of uncivilized peoples. But Carlotta loved it. She had loved California, and now she loved this wild and beautiful land. She loved the experience of being on the trail with only Maria's authority to regulate her life.

"Such a terrible place to die!" Maria moaned.

"Oh, hush!" Carlotta spoke sharply. She did not intend to have the loveliness of the sunset or this moment of being complete mistress of herself spoiled. Had gentlemen not been present she would have slapped the woman soundly. She walked away lest her impulse become more powerful than her display of decorum. She stood, face raised to the sky, rapt in the glory of the evening and her freedom from supervision.

Directly in front of her, encircled by a halo of sunset, a giant, half-naked savage arose from out of the very sand. There were feathers caught in the heavy braids that hung down over his powerful chest. Even in the glare of the blinding sun behind him, she could feel the intensity of the dark, piercing eyes.

A long rifle hung almost carelessly over one arm. The other hung gracefully relaxed at his side. It was not fright that transfixed Carlotta. It was a curious thrill of response to the beauty of the majestic and barbaric figure standing in the aura of crimson sunset.

A GOOD DAY TO DIE 199

There was no sound. It was a moment of suspended awe, and then he was gone—gone as if he had melted into the earth. It had been like some strange apparition—some mirage—some trick of the mysterious land and the burning sunset. Behind her she heard a low moan. Maria had fainted.

A scene of confusion followed. Every eye had witnessed the specter, for every eye had been, slyly or openly, on the girl. The teamsters began to grab up pots and pans. They ran into each other in their confusion and panic. De Vargas cursed them profoundly to help allay his own startled anxiety. He looked at Carlotta, who still stood like some living statue. He ran to her side.

"Don't be frightened," he said, taking her arm. "Please don't faint."

"I am not going to faint," she answered, and was surprised to hear her voice speaking in a whisper. She was relieved that he attributed her behavior to fright. Carlotta de Francisco must never be suspected of having been thrilled by the sight of a savage. She had never before in all her sheltered life seen a man not properly clothed, but she felt certain that neither Diego nor De Vargas, no, nor any other man of her acquaintance, possessed such a magnificent body as that she had just seen. Her mind saw again the bronze chest and the great bronze arms. She wondered what it would be like to lay her head against such a massive shoulder and the thought horrified her.

Carlotta de Francisco, in spite of her careful rearing, often suspected that she possessed some unaccountable common streak. She had learned to conceal carefully what she felt were coarse and vulgar curiosities. And this inner excitement she had felt at the sight of a half-naked savage was more shocking than even some of her most inelegant flights of fancy. For the first time in her life she felt a real and genuine inclination to swoon. Faintly, she heard De Vargas shout. Hands clasped her roughly and she was swept off legs that had suddenly gone weak beneath her.

In a short time the wagon was lumbering at a cruel gait over hammocks of sand and brush. Juan beat the horses to make them run. Even De Vargas was urging haste. The strange apparition of the sunset had not been an apparition—unless a dozen pair of eyes had all been subjected to fantasy—and no one laughed now, or joked about the Apaches.

Night fell and it was difficult to see the faint trail they had been following. The wagon bumped and swayed. Maria moaned and wept. Carlotta clung to the side of the wagon, white-faced and already cleansed of her brief enchantment. She remembered now only the fierce and piercing intent of the burning eyes.

Hours passed, and the horses stumbled to a standstill. No amount of effort on the part of the frightened teamsters or the other anxious riders could force them to move. No amount of prodding or punishment could persuade them to pull the wagon another inch. They stood heads down, sides heaving, and ignored the whip and the lash. Further progress was impossible. De Vargas ordered them unhitched.

Diego wanted the women to mount two of the thoroughbreds and ride on with a smaller escort. De Vargas would not permit it. He insisted that they must all stay together. Only one Indian had been seen, and there had been nothing more to indicate that any trouble stalked their flight. It was folly, he insisted, to tire the thoroughbreds more in case they might be needed to make a last-minute dash for the town that was most certainly not far away by now. They would keep a constant watch for the rest of the night for the sake of the ladies, but they were, he argued, in no danger now. They were too close to civilization for any attack, and De Vargas was not the type of man who would subject himself or any of the rest of them to ridicule by riding hell-bent into a settlement like a cowardly greenhorn.

The men were divided in their opinions as to just how far pride should go, especially when it concerned the safety of the women, but De Vargas was firm. They braced themselves to sit and shiver and wait for dawn or death.

All sounds of the night became magnified by their fear, and no one slept. De Vargas and Diego walked up and down, grim and silent, staring out into the wavering moonlight. The swish of sand from the passing of a desert rat startled their nerves, and the sound of the wind kept them alert and ready. They moved away from the wagon and peered among the shadows that were nothing but shadows.

Carlotta sat close to Maria. She was wide awake and badly frightened. She expected to hear fiendish screams with every moment. The silence took the last vestige of her courage. She recalled, against her will, all the horrible tales of savage behavior that she had heard since she had come to this country. She recalled, too, the things that had been said about what savages did to women. She recalled the shushings and the warning gestures and the carefully guarded "you know what's" that she had heard the women use at times when she had interrupted their gossip. She had often wondered what the "you know what's" were, but had never had the courage to ask. She had known instinctively that they were things no unmarried lady was allowed to hear, and although she had tried many times, she had never been successful in eavesdropping. So her imagination ran rampant, and her mind, unable to picture real tortures, writhed in the agony of the unknown.

The moon sank behind the horizon and the black of predawn grew blacker. The men drew together to form a tight circle around the wagon, not speaking, straining their ears to catch any stealthy movement.

There was nothing but the soft sound of the wind.

"I've always been told this is the time they attack," one of the men whispered.

"Don't be a fool!" De Vargas's voice was sharp from the blackness. Then, in a softer tone, "Diego, I'm going to walk around and speak to the others. They are getting edgy. It will be light in another hour."

Diego answered in acknowledgment. He wished he could be as cool and confident as De Vargas. He heard the man move away, speaking now and then to one or the other of the tense, unhappy sentries.

The darkness lightened and turned to gray. Weary eyes squinted to pierce the gloom that held nothing but the vague silhouettes of brush and hummocks. The full light of day came gradually to reveal an empty expanse, and then they started talking a little, awkwardly at first, full of the embarrassment of their fear. Diego took a turn around the wagon. He looked for De Vargas. He did not see him.

"Where is De Vargas?" he asked one of the grinning boys. The grin died.

"Why—" He hesitated, and the fear came back into his eyes. "I don't know. He was here a couple of minutes ago."

Diego felt the shock of alarm in his vitals. He ran around the wagon. The sky was taking on a rosy hue.

"De Vargas!" he called sharply. There was no answer. The others came crowding around, looking at each other, their eyes telling each other that they knew the peace of the night had been too good to be true.

"De Vargas!" Diego called louder. Only the sound of the wind and the cheep of a desert sparrow answered. They stood, awed by the invisibility of a very present enemy.

"He's somewhere." Diego gave a half laugh that was so false it was more frightening than the silence. "He is playing a trick on us," he said, not believing his own hopes.

They found him, only a few feet away, behind one of the mounds where he had gone when nature had demanded a moment of privacy. He lay in the unnatural position of a body abandoned by the spirit. The hilt of his own knife stood stiffly up from the front of his red-stained shirt.

They buried him with Carlotta's rosary clutched in fingers curled in the form of grasping at something. And they left the wagon, riding away on horses that moved as fast as men could make them travel.

Diego determined to get to the settlement without any more delay. He was not concerned with what anyone thought as long as he could get Carlotta to safety. His heart mourned De Vargas, whom he had known and loved all of his life. He had deplored the necessity of burying him in such a desolate country with no box to hold his body, no padre to pray for his soul and no family to wet the earth with their sorrow. He hated leaving him, but he did it because there was nothing else to do. It was a dire necessity now to find aid and shelter from whatever it was that pursued them, and Diego was certain now that they were pursued by eyes that noted their every movement. If they rode fast, he reasoned, they would come to the settlement within a few hours at the most. But Diego was not sure. He had no idea where they were. Somehow in the night they had lost the faint trail that had been their guide, and now they had lost De Vargas, who had led them. But somewhere over one of the swells of sand around them there was a settlement, and Diego meant to find it.

The hours passed in awful suspense and punishing fatigue. They rode with no sound but that of the horses' hooves plodding in the sand, and their own anxious breathing. Even the sparrows seemed to have ceased their cheeping. A silence, more nerve-racking than the threat of sure death, closed in around them.

It was Juan who found the tracks, and with great relief Diego set his horse on the path. A wagon had traveled this route not long ago and it seemed a positive sign that assistance was near at hand. Cheered and refreshed by this inscription of civilization, the riders spurred forward.

It was just before sunset when Diego began to suspect the trail they were following. The tracks of the wagon weaved in and out between the mounds of sand with too little defined direction to suit him, and yet he refused to be disheartened. By the time the sun was down and they were all weak with hunger and thirst and exhaustion, he knew that they were following a false trail, and he did not have the heart to tell them. As the light grew more faint, he urged them on. Keep to the tracks and keep riding, he told them; before long they would see a light. And when it seemed as if they would drop of their own hopelessness, the light appeared. It was a long way away, but it was a light and Diego was glad he had not voiced his fears. Once again the flagging spirits rose, and with new energy they pushed the weary horses forward, stumbling again in their urgency. No matter, Diego thought, we can follow the light.

"Madre mía! Mother have mercy on us." Juan was the only one who could voice their despair. They sat, too numb to dismount, too dejected to feel more fright. Before them were the remains of their own wagon. The soft glow of the embers lit up the narrow mound of the grave they had dug in the hours of the sunrise.

There was a thud. Carlotta fell from her horse. The darling of Spanish aristocracy lay in a genuine faint with her face in the sand of the desert, and no son of a grandee jumped to assist her.

Gray Wolf flattened himself against the earth. An instinct developed from a lifetime of wariness signaled the approach of danger. He raised his head a little to scan as much as he could see of the surrounding area. His vision was blocked by the rolling swells and arroyos. He laid his cheek against the ground and listened. Faintly against his ear he felt the vibration. Occasional sharp tremors in the steady beat told him that shod hooves were striking against stones. The rhythmic pulse was the precise unison of trained cavalry. Pony Soldiers were converging upon his own private war. The tempo of the approach was prudent but constant. The soldiers were being led by the remains of his revenge, which lay for miles along his back trail. They were restrained by their uncertainty, but urged on by desire to cheat him of complete fulfillment. The thought sent a hot lust over his body, but swiftly as it came, the heat in his veins cooled. This was not a time for emotion.

One by one he had killed them. He had killed them in unhurried and casual silence, relishing the terror he had created in the arrogant monsters who had so enjoyed creating a terror of their own. And one by one he had, much as he had hated that part, slit the throats of the beautiful horses they had ridden to exhaustion and left abandoned to the wilderness when their use of them had ceased. The Old One had died of her own accord, and for that Gray Wolf was glad. His vengeance did not feed well on old women, and he was glad she had spared him the necessity of plunging his knife into her quaking throat. Only the young woman and one of the men still lived. He was not sure why it was that he had left her until this time. Perhaps it was because as long as she lived the men, to the very last of them, seemed to hope for her sake. Days ago he had decided that she must be the daughter of some great chief to be so carefully guarded. He had killed with every darkness since he had found Victorio's camp and the blood and the burned possessions. And except for the one time when he had stood before them to let them see him there, they had not caught a glimpse of their killer. Daylight had always been a respite for those still alive. They were unaware that the respite was now over. Soldiers were coming.

Gray Wolf snaked forward to where they rested. He sprang. He was swift and as silent as ever, but this time they saw the death that had hounded them these last awful days. Diego reached for the pistol he kept at hand, but he was dead before his fingers could curl around it.

She looked at him and her eyes were as deep as storm clouds. All fear was suddenly washed out of their depths and anger stormed up. She raised her small head defiantly, and she spat with all the fury of a vixen at bay. In spite of himself, an admiration for her started to grow.

"Savage!" She spat the word. "Come on, kill me. Kill a woman to show how big and brave you are."

He knew she said it without knowing that he could understand her. He was so moved by her magnificent fury that he thought of leaving her here to the soldiers, who would glory in her rescue. And then he knew he would do no such thing. She turned her back on him. Her hair had come down from the sleek knot she had worn at the nape of her neck and it spread over her back, black and glossy. He reached out to touch it. It was very beautiful. She stiffened under his hand and whirled to claw at him. Her mouth opened to scream and he clapped his hand over her lips to smother the sound. Her fingernails dug into the flesh of his arms. She arched her back and her little feet flayed against his legs. She made strange strangling noises under his hand and squirmed and fought furiously. She let go his arms and reached up to claw at his face and yank at his hair.

She was wrapped in layer after layer of clothing, and he nearly lost his grip on her. She jerked violently and the cloth of her dress parted to expose a strip of bare skin. She ceased her clawing to pull the cloth together, shrinking away, covering herself with her hands. He was shaken in spite of himself at the

sight of the soft ivory silkiness. It was the most beautiful skin he
had ever seen. It was neither dark nor white. He stared down at
her, and then remembered another time and another white
woman—another white woman who had pulled the cloth away
when his eyes had been on her. And the remembrance brought
dark clouds to his mind. He scowled angrily and grabbed at her.
She sank her teeth into the flesh of his arm. He shook her hard to
break her loose, but she only clamped harder. He dropped to
one knee and forced her to the ground. He held her and reached
with a free hand into the many skirts that enveloped her. She let
out a little yelp when she felt his hand on her leg. Her teeth
opened from their grip and her eyes took on a terrified look. She
grabbed at his hands and made little squealing sounds as she
tried to push her skirts down. He struggled with her, angry because he knew what she was thinking.

Wasicun women! he thought. They are always afraid a man is
going to rape them or else they are afraid a man is not going to
rape them!

His fingers singled out a layer of white cloth. He yanked at it
and it gave. She flopped over on her side as the cloth ripped,
drawing her knees up and locking her arms over her breasts. Her
eyes were wide and wild. She started shivering and shaking. He
tore the cloth into strips and gagged her. He used another piece
to tie her hands after he had pulled them behind her. He left her
there trussed up like some captive calf an Apache would sometimes carry into camp. He ran for his mustang. He knew that the
soldiers were dangerously close. The struggle with her had taken
more time than had been wise. He hurried back and set her on
the ornate sidesaddle of her own horse. He took the reins of the
dead man's horse as well and leaped to the mustang's back. He
rode in the direction opposite the sounds of the shod hooves. The
sun was resting on the western horizon. He smiled a little and
tugged at the reins of the captive horses, pulling them along to
a faster pace. Darkness would soon befriend him, and inside him
a heat that was not anger rushed to flow along the course of his
veins.

The early morning sun was pale and without heat. The mountains would soon be locked in ice and snow. The willows were already brown in the pockets. The wind shifted irritably and shook ripe seeds from their stalks. The clouds to the north were darkening, warning of the cold wind that was coming down from somewhere off the grass-covered plains.

Gray Wolf looked down at the girl. She was lying over the horse's neck, half senseless with fatigue. He had tied her to her mount after the second night of riding. He had stopped only long enough to remove the heavy saddle and hide it where he hoped the Pony Soldiers would not find it. They were flanked on both sides now by the determined bluecoats, and more kept to the trail behind them. The messages that flashed from every side kept him from the course he wanted to travel. He zigzagged from cover to cover, hunting a place where he could hide his trail. But the trail of three horses was not easy to cover in land like this. He had thought of killing the girl and turning the horses loose, but even as he had debated it he knew now that he would never do it. There was a keen and deep pleasure in what he was doing. The more they pressed him the more he determined to take her and the horses straight through the whole army if necessary. There was really no point to it all, except for the pleasure it gave him to defy them. And now there was something more than mere defiance. Gray Wolf recognized breeding— he recognized it in horses and people. And he knew that there was good breeding in the horses he led and the girl who lay almost senseless on the back of one of them. It seemed to him that she was neither white nor Indian, but perhaps the best of both. Her frailness was white. Her pride was Indian. Her coloring was a blend of both.

She had not uttered one word of protest or complaint since he had overpowered her back on the desert. She was brutally bruised from the torturous hours astride the horse, but her eyes still flashed defiance at any effort to ease her discomfort. Like those of the magnificent horse she rode, her delicate bones belied her pride and her courage and the strength of her spirit. She would mother some magnificent sons. He did not know why such a thought should have come to him, but it had, and he had looked upon her with different eyes since the thought.

He was no longer fooled into thinking that one day the *Wasi-cun* would be driven from this country. The day of the Indian was drawing to a close. Their blood staining the ground was the red flare of their setting sun, spreading over the hills and the plains—the signal of their dying. A new world was dawning, and although he knew that he could never accept this new world, he did mean to give of the genes of his loins to sons and daughters who would be of this new world. Already many men had taken white women to give them sons—a new people for a new world. He had not cared much for this when he had seen others do it. But now it seemed like a good idea. Children belonged to their mother. If he took this woman and she bore him sons those sons would be white and the whites would scarcely kill their own. It would be the only way the sons of Gray Wolf, the Dakota, would walk the lands of their father with any pride and dignity. There was no place in this world anymore for Gray Wolf. He knew that before long he would stop a bullet or worse—but he would never submit to surrender and the life of an agency Indian. But his sons could be the sons of a white mother, and no hand, neither white nor Indian, would be against them. As he arose, he pondered the future as if there was no question as to whether it would or would not be available to him.

The clouds rolled and threatened, and looking-glass messages caught the last glints from the sun, mocking his dreams as vain ones. He laughed a gleeful and savage laugh, and sought a way between the coming storm and his relentless trackers.

He heard the water before he saw it. Up in the mountains where the thunderclouds mottled the sky, they had emptied their burden and it rushed down over the rocks and crags, splitting the ground like a violent mud-colored giant, roaring, brawling, full-throated and wicked.

The mustang, wise to the ways of nature, balked and snorted his distrust. But there was no turning back. There was no time for seeking a narrower or safer crossing. There was no time for hesitation.

He tied the reins of her horse around his waist, took a firm grip on the halter of the other and forced his own pony into the greedy current.

It seemed as if some giant hand reached up to lay hold of them. It swept the pony off its feet. The mustang floundered and the water surged up over Gray Wolf's head. He fought to keep his legs clamped around the pony's body, which bunched and stretched more violently than if he was in a mad gallop. The current swept them along with branches, boulders and pieces of log that churned in the water. A terrible fear for the girl's safety welled up in him. The only thing that saved him from sheer panic was the evident fact that the thoroughbreds seemed more capable in the water than his own wiry mount. They swam powerfully, purposefully. On and on they swept, then the icy pressure on his chest seemed to lessen. His own pony was swimming. The rush of the water seemed a little less violent. Hooves hit bottom. The mustang plunged and heaved and then went down as his hooves slipped in the heavy silt. Gray Wolf was thrown aside and he found himself being rolled and tumbled in the murky, silt-clogged torrent.

He struggled up and released the air from his burning lungs. Before he could gasp another breath he was under again. He felt as if his head would burst. Sand filled his eyes and clogged his nose. It felt as if the skin was being scraped from his back and his chest. With what seemed to be the last of his strength, he rolled to claw at the shifting bottom. The girl's horse was plunging, maddened now with fright and the thing that dragged at his reins. Gray Wolf's hand found the reins which still held around his waist. He pulled at them and found a footing. His head was above the roaring water. It took all of his strength to stay erect against the pull of the stream and the jerking of the horse. He managed to get the reins from around his waist and, as he eased them as much as he could, he and the horse pulled themselves out of the clutching current. The horse stood, heaving and shaking and trembling. Gently he drew the frightened animal to him, speaking as softly and as soothingly as his winded voice would allow.

The girl hung, inert and sodden. Her hair streamed water down the animal's side. Farther down, the other horses were pulling themselves out of the water. They stood heads down, their sides heaving. Gray Wolf went to the girl. She was terribly pale when he turned her head so that he could see her face. There was a bluish lump on her forehead, but she was breathing. He tied the horse to a clump of brush and went to bring the others.

He had no idea where he might be, but it was growing colder and he knew they would have to have a fire this night if they were to survive. Wearily he mounted the mustang and, leading the other horses, he rode away from the banks of the roaring water. He did not press the weary animals to more than a slow walk.

The girl's continued inertness worried him. He did not want her to die now. He had allowed himself to dream of her as his own, and in so dreaming, she had become his own. He wanted to do something about her immediately, but the necessity of getting away from the soldiers was even more urgent. He did not think they would risk crossing the river in its present roaring state, but even if they did, the long sweep downstream had given him the distance he needed to lose them entirely if he could keep going long enough to find a place where they could safely build a fire. But she looked so helpless, so slim and so young in her sodden clothing. And then without wanting it and without the ability to push it away, he remembered another place and another time and the meaning of it when he had looked at another small and helpless figure, limp and senseless, and a terrible sick disgust pervaded his soul. His heart recoiled from the thoughts that had been in his mind. He pulled his pony to a halt. This was a *Wasicun* woman he had taken and dreamed of making the mother of his sons. In a rage of memory for that other woman he drew his knife and slid to the ground. He would finish this madness now. He strode back and stood for a moment looking at her limp figure. He raised the knife.

"Small Owl!" He whispered the forbidden name, and the agony of it reached his pain. He grabbed the sodden hair and

pushed the head back. It rolled with inertness, and for a moment
her face took on a strange resemblance to the woman long since
in Cloud Land. The moment passed, but the strangeness of it
had startled him. The pain inside him eased, and he felt an unwelcome compassion. He cut the bonds that held her to the
horse. He put his arm under her and lifted her down. He cradled her in one arm as one would hold a sleeping child. Then he
mounted, took up the reins of the two thoroughbreds, clucked to
the mustang and rode toward the deeper recesses of the mountains.

Gray Wolf divided his attention between the trail, to fix the
landmarks in his mind, and the girl he was carrying. Her body
was a dead weight and cold. Once she opened her eyes, but they
held the blank look of incomprehension.

He guided the pony onward and upward, over rugged rock
and along deep cuts until he came to an arroyo with brush-
covered sides. A swift stream flowed over smooth rock and he
rode along it to where it cascaded down from the sides of sheer
gray cliffs. He rode past the waterfall and found another opening. He turned into it and there a valley opened up to a sheltered, steep-walled haven. There was something about this
place that told him it was safe. There were trees growing and
patches of grass for the horses. He laid her down on the ground.
She did not regain consciousness. He left her to slip the bridles
from the horses and take his pack from the mustang. He gathered wood and built a fire. He hung the wet blanket to dry.
There was some pine and spruce a little farther in, and he went
to cut boughs for a wickiup. He hurried to complete it before it
should become dark. The cold was increasing with the advanc-
ing day. When it was done he moved the fire inside and watched
with satisfaction when the smoke rose perfectly up through the
smoke hole.

He made a pile of smaller boughs for a couch, then carried her
in and placed her on it. He wished fervently that there were another woman who could perform the next vital duties. But Gray
Wolf had never wasted his wishes on futile desires. Her clothes

had to be removed. They were sodden and cold. He pulled off the outside dress and then a skirt that was under that. There were more skirts. She must, he thought, be wearing everything she owned. Carefully he hung the garments from the wick-iup dome to catch the heat from the fire. After he had removed all of the skirts he was faced with a strange stiff garment that laced up the back and some strange-looking leggings that he thought must be a *Wasicun* chastity belt. He was glad to find that some *Wasicun* women wore such things. It suggested that perhaps not all of them were wanton women. He felt very guilty removing this garment. He had been taught since young boy-hood that to remove the chastity belt of a maiden was cause for the greatest dishonor possible. He pondered for a long time be-fore he could bring himself to commit such a grave offense, but the garment clung to her like a second skin and her flesh was so cold that he feared to leave it on. What a pity, he thought, that *Wasicun* women did not have the advantage of a proper belt made of soft doeskin and small enough not to hamper any move-ment. With doubtful resignation he sighed and reached for the ruffled pantaloons.

He fed the fire as much as he dared and rubbed her arms and legs to bring back warmth-giving circulation. She sat up sud-denly and her eyes were wild. At the sight of him she cowered back and half sobbed. He spoke to her gently as one would to a child. She stared at him for a moment and then fell back with a soft cry. She covered her eyes as if to shut out a terrible sight. She moaned and shuddered and lost consciousness again.

For two nights and two days he watched over her, keeping the blanket around her when she would toss it off as the fever burned. Often she tossed and moaned and then she would col-lapse again to lie like one already dead. For hours at a time he sat and held her hot, listless hand. And he talked to her, using the soft-sounding Dakota words reserved for very small children. He carved a comb and smoothed out her tangled hair, perform-ing that special duty of devotion that Dakota men reserved for beloved wives. He bathed her face and her hands and her body with cool water. He brewed hot broth from the deer meat he had brought in the only time he had left her. He brewed it in his cup, the only utensil he possessed, and he pressed it to her reluctant lips.

On the third day she awakened, weak and quiet. Her great dark eyes followed him suspiciously whenever he moved. Nor did the wary look lessen under his most tender ministrations. He still talked to her soothingly, and although she appeared to listen, her eyes did not change.

The following morning it was as if the past three days had never been. She grabbed at the clothes he held out to her, and she managed to put on all of them under the cover of the blanket while he watched her in bewilderment. Her actions confused him. She must know by now that he did not mean to harm her. He knew it himself for the first time. He knew he would never take her against her will. He wanted her for a wife. He had tried these past three days to show her this, but her eyes were again defiant and murderous. He had the nasty feeling that if he went over to her she would make every attempt to rip open his jugular vein. He suddenly felt very weary.

It had been days since he had slept. The exhilaration of his dreams as he had tended her had pushed his fatigue into the background. When she had been so helpless, he had allowed himself to think that consciousness would bring a different relationship between them; that she would know he had touched her only with respect; that she would know how he felt and would return that feeling; that she would see she was in the hands of an honorable man and be glad of it. But he could see now that he had been carried away with a nonsense that was unbecoming a warrior and a man. Because he had treated her as he would have treated a wife for the past three days did not make her a wife. Because he had treated her as he would treat any chaste Indian woman did not make her an Indian woman. She was still a *Wasicun* with the unfathomable *Wasicun* ways. Instead of the joy he had anticipated, he felt infuriated. He wanted to walk away now and keep on walking—walking until he would find another woman—a woman he could hope to understand.

And Carlotta de Francisco, watching the indifferent, incomprehensible face of the giant savage who held her captive, prayed passionately, "Mother of God, pray for me now," and she ignored the necessity of supplication for the hour of death.

Gray Wolf left the wickiup as full of gloom as the dreary day. The clouds were thickening and bearing down. It began to snow thick heavy flakes that melted as soon as they touched the ground. A bitter wind whirled down the canyon, and he knew it would not be long before the snow turned to sleet. The ground grew wet, and his worn moccasins soaked through. His feet turned numb, but he walked on, unmindful of the cold. He knew he should have been well on his way toward home and friends and family instead of being in this foreign canyon brooding over a foreign woman.

The horses were back in a protected recess. He went to them, feeling as always the wonder of their beauty and gratified by their response to his gentleness. They nuzzled at him with velvet noses, and some of his gloom lifted. He ran appreciative hands over their glistening coats and coiled his fingers in their manes. Wearily he laid his face against one of the proud necks and gave himself up to the pain of his loneliness and his confused existence. If only he knew the words to say to a *Wasicun* woman, but how could he know the words? He could keep her as a captive, force her to his will and hope that one day she would come to accept him. But he did not want that. She was too beautiful, too spirited and too proud to be a captive, and yet with her every look and every action she had shown that she would consent to nothing more. He did not understand this, but how could he? She was of one world and he was of another, even though both of the worlds were lost to each of them. He had hoped that they might create a world of their own, but now he was sure that one blanket would never stretch to warm them both. He stood, cold and weary, and tried to face the truth of it.

He left the horses and sought the protection of a jutting shelf where he could sleep. And when sleep came, dreams came with it.

Small Owl came to him to fold him in the warmth of her blanket, only to snatch it away and change her face into the face of the *Wasicun* girl, who mocked him. And he felt a cold that was colder than the wind and the snow. Then the *Wasicun* girl came to raise a knife over his heart and he was unable to raise his hand to stop her. When the knife was about to plunge into his heart her glittering eyes turned soft and her smile was the gentle smile of promise. The knife turned into a blanket and she covered him gently as a woman in love covers a beloved. And he was warm with the warmth of summer.

The sound of gunshots was distant, but it penetrated his dreams as sharply as if they had exploded in his ear. He was awake instantly. He did not move, but listened, fixing the direction and the distance.

A fight was being fought far away and yet much too near. With each moment the reports sounded nearer. It was a running fight and it was moving swiftly in his direction. He leaped from his sleeping place. The horses were cropping indifferently at the clumps of wet grass. The leaden sky gave no clue as to how long he had slept. He ran to the wickiup. It was empty. The fire had burned to embers. Two hours at the least, he calculated, since he had left her. She was gone and his blanket was gone with her. A quick inspection told him that she had gone alone and of her own accord.

The guns were speaking more distinctly. Very quickly he rolled the deer hide he had hung over the opening of the shelter. He stamped out the embers of the fire and scattered the ashes. He dismantled the wickiup and threw the limbs into a crack of rock. He stuffed the hide in a niche where he could find it later. He looked around. His clean-up job was not good enough to fool any Indian, especially an Apache, but a *Wasicun* would probably pass it by without note. Regretfully he left the horses where they were and took to the girl's trail.

For one so helpless, she had traveled fast and far, over washes, through brush and jumbles of rock. He found the blanket where she had dropped it. He found a place where she had fallen and finally he found her. Her face was scratched and dirty. Her clothing was torn and the palms of her hands were raw where the sand and gravel had scraped away the skin. Her hair was a tangled mass and perspiration stood on her forehead and stained the underarms of her dress in spite of the cold. She was crouched behind a boulder, weeping.

Below her he caught a glimpse of a darting figure.

Apache!

The girl had seen them too. Fright had wiped the defiance from her face, and she was pathetically glad to see him. She did not claw or fight as he gathered her up in his arms. Carrying her, he crouched low and ran, bounding over the rocks, seeking a place to hide her. He kept away from the canyon that had been their shelter. He dared not be caught in a box canyon where there was as much to be feared in discovery by strange Apache as by the soldiers pursuing them. Hunted Apache were blood brothers to cornered catamounts, and less patient.

For once the girl seemed to understand his actions. She clung to him, locking her arms around his neck, making her light weight even lighter. Her brief glimpse of a painted Apache face seemed to have enhanced her captor considerably.

He crossed the ridge. Below them, coming from the other direction, were more soldiers, sneaking into position behind the rocks and boulders.

Ambush.

The Apache were going to be caught in a cross fire. It was more than he could endure. Dropping the girl, he pressed his hand over her mouth in a warning. He crouched low. He raised his voice in the piercing battle scream of the Dakota. The scream brought Apache eyes around to look behind them. He had done all he could. Motioning her to follow, he started to crawl. He turned to see her sitting where he had put her. Her eyes were wide with fright as she stared at him. His scream had frozen her with its fierce paralyzing penetration. He hoped it had had as favorable an effect on the soldiers, but he doubted it. He crawled back to grab her arm. He pulled her along until they were over a small rise that hid them from both soldier and Apache eyes.

He picked her up again and ran. There was no place to go but into the mouth of a canyon. He did not like it, but there was no longer any choice. He rounded the projection of jutting rock and scanned the terrain. The walls of the canyon were dotted with caves, big and little. Far up on one side he saw the mouth of a small one that was above the line of eyes that would be taken with the larger openings that were easy to reach. He swung her to his back and locked her hands at his neck and started to climb. It was precarious footing, and he dared not think of what would happen if she started her clawing. He did not look down.

When it seemed as if he could not pull himself up another time the small aperture was there before him. He crawled up to the narrow ledge and lay on his belly, shrugging her off his back. He was panting with exertion.

There was scarcely room for them both, but it was high and small. In a matter of minutes they could see the fleeing figures of Apache women and children coming into the canyon below them. They were herded by old men, who took them to the refuge of a large cave that was scarcely more than a recess in the wall opposite the little cave where Gray Wolf and the girl watched. Gray Wolf groaned with dismay at the Apache choice. It had but one saving factor, the parapet of boulders along the front. Almost immediately it became evident why they had chosen that particular place. Retreating warriors backed into the area below and leaped to join the rest of their people. The men lay down behind rocks and brush and within seconds the canyon looked deserted.

When the soldiers came cautiously through the pass, there was no sign of life. Gray Wolf watched the soldier chief scan the walls with an experienced eye. It did not take long to see that this soldier was too wise in Apache warfare to be fooled for long. In only the time it took for him to scan the walls two times he motioned to the cave where the Apache huddled. But he did not order his men to attack. He was also too wise to assault a position where his men could be killed before they could reach the shelf. More soldiers came running in to surround their chief. They held a brief council and then some of the soldiers came across the canyon toward the place under their own hiding place. He turned, ready to clap a hand over the girl's mouth if she indicated any inclination to cry out. He need not have feared. She was hypnotized into silence by the grim drama of death that was being staged before her eyes.

From a point directly below them, the soldiers started climbing up the side of the canyon and Gray Wolf knew what they were going to do. They climbed until they were in a position to fire, aiming their shots at the roof of the cave where the Apache crowded together. From where they hid, Gray Wolf could see the effect of the bullets that ricocheted down into the massed cluster of people. The firing continued for a long time and then abruptly ceased.

The soldier chief went out into the center of the canyon.

"Surrender!" he shouted to the people. "Surrender and you will be spared. If you do not surrender we will kill you all."

A silence followed. Gray Wolf could see the warriors crawling back to join the people. He could see them as they renewed the paint on their faces. Then he heard the soft strains of the chant echo from the cave. Apache warriors were singing their death song.

Suddenly they came bursting out, shooting as they sprang. They fought like tigers, flinging themselves into the hand-to-hand struggle that came as soon as their first shots were expended. It was over quickly. The warriors were hopelessly outnumbered. Their freshly painted faces and their bodies were soon lying on the earth, riddled with volley after volley.

Again the soldier chief called out to the people in the cave.

"Surrender," he called to them.

Again a silence followed his shout. Then some of the soldiers climbed the rocks over the cave. They pushed at the boulders and started them rolling down. The rocks gathered speed and knocked loose even bigger ones that crashed and smashed down onto the rocks and rebounded into the cave. Men, women and children were smashed into a pulp beneath the great stones. Gray Wolf was sickened with the awful sight. All but a few were soon dead or dying. They were unable to resist. The soldiers climbed quickly up to the shelf and herded the living ones out. They pushed them into a bunch and marched them out of the canyon. A terrible silence hung over the ghastly scene.

The girl's face, when Gray Wolf finally turned to look at her, was whiter than ever, and her eyes were filled with horror. He felt a small guilt at being glad that she had seen with her own eyes the way her people treated his people. She whispered something which he did not understand, and her eyes seemed to be fixed down into the pit of blood and gore that had been women and children and small babies only moments before. He put his arm around her shoulders and she sank against him like a child grateful for protection.

He waited a long time before he attempted to climb down from the dizzy heights. He would have waited longer if he had not been afraid that he might miss his footing if he attempted the climb in the dark. A misstep with her in his arms caused him more concern than the possibility of soldiers lingering in the area. The *Wasicun* was wont to suffer his squeamishness of such dirty jobs after the deed was done, and it was reasonable to believe that they had put as many miles as possible between them and the scene of their butchery.

He led her out of the canyon, cautious of each step and every sound, trusting nothing, wanting to leave this place of horror as quickly as possible, but not so quickly as to make a false judgment. She followed, her fright and her horror subduing her.

Over the ridge, near the place where he had screamed out his warning, a small sound that should not have been there brought him to a rigid halt. Something ahead of him had moved. A small pebble rolled and the chattering sound was loud to his ears. He pushed the girl down behind the shelter of a boulder and touched his fingers to her lips. When she saw that he meant to leave her she clutched at his arm, her eyes showing the whites in the darkness that was now all around them. Tenderly he pried her fingers loose and shook his head. Giving her a look of his promise to return, he left her and wormed his way forward.

It was a woman, one of the doomed band, wounded here on the hillside and left behind when the rest had rushed on to their fatal haven. She saw him and raised her butcher knife, prepared even in her pain to sell her life only with a life.

"Tse! Tse!" He hissed the Apache warning. She watched him, uncertain and ready with the knife.

"Put down your knife, Grandmother." He spoke softly.

She leaned forward a little to look into his face. Then she saw him more clearly. The knife dropped wearily. This was the one who had screamed the warning. This was the Ghost—the Dakota who was Victorio's brother. She had heard about him and now she saw him.

"The soldiers are gone," she said. "Where are the rest of my people? Only a few went with the white-eyes."

"Dead," he answered shortly, not prolonging the painful thing. "Where are you hurt?"

"Here." She said it simply, and pulled back her hand to show the mass of bloody skirt she had wadded up to press against the place where her life's blood was flowing out onto the ground.

He spoke words of encouragement and left her to get the girl.

Reluctantly the white girl helped him to bandage the wound with strips torn from one of the many skirts she wore. Then he left them both and went to bring the horses. He ran, and even in the darkness he did not stumble. The Apache had taught him well.

He caught the horses and took the deer hide from the place where he had put it to make the travois they would need.

Before the first light of day they were back in the camping place. Before the sun was straight Gray Wolf had erected another wickiup of fresh, sweet-smelling cedar. All through the morning he sang softly to himself the song of thanksgiving that the Apache had taught him the art of providing shelter so quickly.

11

It was a cold winter, but Gray Wolf did not notice. They stayed in the canyon because there was nothing else they could do. The Apache woman took a long time to heal and he would not leave her. He hunted more meat than they could eat, to obtain the skins they needed to seal the brush lodge against the cold, and he never allowed the fire to die.

The white girl nursed the woman as well as any Indian could have done after Gray Wolf showed her how to do this, and the woman took much pleasure in being bathed with cloths provided by parts of the girl's very versatile raiment. The Apache woman brought peace to the isolated little wickiup. She talked with the girl in the language of the Mexicans, and the girl understood her well. Gray Wolf never indicated that he understood them both. He took great pleasure in listening to their voices and the words that were spoken freely because they believed he did not understand. Often "Grandmother," as he called her in the Apache tongue, repeated the things the girl had said. Often she omitted subjects she did not think would please him. Especially did she omit the subject of escape. The girl had begged the woman to help her get away as soon as she was well. And Grandmother had chided her for such a suggestion. Gray Wolf had been amused and angered and amused again at the girl's reasoning. He did not worry. He knew that Grandmother would never help with such a rash attempt, but he wished the girl would give up her thoughts of going back to her own people. He could see that his captive was not going to be a submissive one. But Grandmother did not mention these things to Gray Wolf, for Apache women gave gentleness for gentleness, and the woman would al-

ways be grateful for the way the girl soothed the pain and
cooled the fever that clung through the many moons of the cold
winds.

There was no real change in the weather, but Gray Wolf knew
that the time of the new green leaf was not far away. He knew
too that they would have to leave this canyon very soon. He had
hunted all the game the area would provide, and there was not
enough forage for the horses. They were already thin from the
winter of sparse grazing.

Grandmother was strong enough now to move about without
too much trouble, and she knew Gray Wolf's anxiety to seek
more sheltered quarters. The weather was still cold and there
was the promise of more snow the day he decided that the time
had come. The breath rolled from the lips like clouds, but there
was good jerky in the new parfleches and good skins to ward off
the bite of the cold when they packed and started south. Gray
Wolf had given up the idea of going home.

Nantan's entire army was between him and the trail northward. The massacre in the canyon before the fall of the big
snows had whetted the old Wolf's appetite, and he was sweeping
the mountains and the basins with company after company of
soldiers, and guides who had forgotten that they were Indian.
They were leveling Apache camps and taking prisoner all whom
they did not murder. And Gray Wolf had two women now
whom he did not intend to turn over to the *Wasicun* who dared
to carry the name of Wolf.

Somewhere to the south Victorio roamed. Grandmother's only
remaining relative was an uncle who lived with that band. It
seemed only prudent to try to join him. Grandmother knew this
country well. She knew the places of the rancherias that must be
avoided at all costs, and they traveled fast, taking a devious
route down through the rugged mountains toward the place that
was called Mexico.

The weather remained cold. Frequently they dismounted to
trot along, giving the horses a rest and warming their own blood.

Gray Wolf took every precaution to avoid detection. They
chewed strips of dry meat and lit no fires to give off a smoke that

would taint the frosty air and betray them to the keen noses of the traitor scouts. And they suffered.

Neither Grandmother nor the white girl uttered any complaint, but it was evident after only three days that they could not endure much more. Grandmother's wound became tender with the jolting of the horse, and the white girl was not used to riding astride. Neither of them seemed to be able to relax to the rocking motion of the horses, and they tired to exhaustion. It was a worrisome thing, for unexpected trouble could come upon them at any moment—in the time it took to look away and back again. And as if the thought brought the action, Gray Wolf caught the flash of brilliant color down on the mountainside. Then he saw the streak of racing ponies. At the same instant he heard the distant pop of gunfire. He pulled his mustang hard into a jumble of boulders and forced the animal into the narrow aperture. He glanced over his shoulder and satisfied himself that Grandmother was forcing the white girl's horse to follow. They squeezed into a place that was scarcely big enough for the horses to stand. He pulled the girl down and forced her to crouch almost under the animals' bellies.

The horses, sensing danger and fighting the confines of the small place, twitched and trod their feet. Quietly he spoke to them, laying his hands on them reassuringly. Grandmother stood with one hand ready to clamp the mustang's nose should he show signs of whistling.

The riders raced up the mountain, straight toward them. They fired back over the rumps of their ponies. When it seemed at the final moment as if the charging mass would plunge directly into their hiding place, the ponies swerved aside with the precision of a drill team. For one brief instant, the leader had looked straight down into Gray Wolf's eyes before he had pulled his pony aside. They rode on, riding like demons, their painted faces strained and their headbands wet with the sweat of their effort. They drummed past, firing as they swept by, filling the air with gun smoke that settled down into the rocks, stinging the throat and the eyes, but covering the three in the rocks like a mantle.

The troopers saw the sudden change of course and cut across

below to take advantage of the small gain, shooting and cursing and spurring their horses mercilessly. Gray Wolf chanted softly to the Power to protect the unknown warrior who had perhaps sacrificed his own life and the lives of his followers to lead the soldiers away from the jumble of rocks on the cold mountainside.

Then they were gone. The sound of the pounding hooves and then the sound of the firing faded. Gray Wolf was in a torment to get away from this place. He had to pull the nervous horses and force them into the open. The mustang took this particular time to show his perverseness. He bucked and pitched and balked.

A warning cry from Grandmother made him drop the reins of the stubborn animal and leap forward. The white girl had bolted her horse and was riding with all the ability of a Comanche, bent over, urging her horse over rock and brush and cuts. Gray Wolf leaped to the back of the other horse and raced after her. At first he did not gain, then, cutting across, he finally reached the rump of the animal. He urged his horse on. For a straining moment they ran side by side, at such speed that he feared the horses would go down with broken legs or worse. Reaching out, he grabbed at the reins. Her horse, thoroughly frightened now, fought the iron hand that pulled him back. Finally it slowed down and came to a standstill. Both animals were heaving from their effort. If it became necessary at any time during the rest of this day to make a run for it, they were lost. Gray Wolf was so angry that he did not trust himself even to look at the girl. She slipped to the ground and stood with pale face and compressed lips. They waited for Grandmother, who came riding up on a strangely subdued mustang that had a trickle of blood running down from behind one of his ears.

Without a word Gray Wolf put the girl back on her horse. Leading his own as well as hers, he strode off. Grandmother rode behind, equally silent.

There was, he decided, no use in trying to locate Victorio, risking their lives with a woman who could be relied upon to do crazy things. Instead of continuing south he turned sharply. He knew where he was going. He was going to the canyon where he had spent the summer when he had first met and known the Apache. That place was the closest thing in these angry hills to home, and no amount of weariness, feigned or real, in the white girl touched his heart or slackened his pace.

It was just as he had left it. He could see that no man had been here since the day he had left with Victorio's band. The water still fell, in a smaller but still lovely cascade. A few places where the sun could not penetrate were still covered with heavy snow, but aside from those places, the canyon was dry and free from the incessant winds that blew in unprotected places.

Grandmother's eyes sparkled. She set to work immediately raising a wickiup, and she did not work alone. A few sharp words and the white girl moved quickly to help. Gray Wolf felt a satisfaction settling inside him. Since the escapade on the mountainside, Grandmother was taking no more nonsense. She set about teaching "white one" things any sensible girl should know.

Gray Wolf turned the horses loose and took his bow to go in search of meat. He began to feel happy again. It would be a good thing to have a snug place again, and it was a good thing to have his woman and an Old One in the wickiup, even if one was white and the other Apache. Properly trained, the white one would make a good wife, and Grandmother was busy with the training. Cheerfully he chanted under his breath as he walked, calling on Wakan Tanka to take note of his need for meat and singing the deer song afterward.

"Brother, I need your coat to cover my woman. I need your flesh to feed my family. I will be quick and merciful. Come, my brother, and fill my needs."

The season passed all too quickly, and at no time during the coming of the warm sun and the long days did they see any sign of humans other than themselves. There were good hides on the drying racks, and there was a new shirt for him as well as new dresses for the women. Grandmother was an untiring worker and she saw to it that White Girl followed her example. There were strips of meat on the drying rack over the fire, and the wickiup was always sweet with the smell of fresh cedar. And White Girl came to look like an Indian girl.

They all ate, slept and lived within the small confines of the one wickiup, and in the days and moons that came and went White Girl never spoke to, or even looked directly at Gray Wolf. But since it was proper decorum for a maid to behave in exactly that manner, Gray Wolf never knew that she ignored his presence deliberately with the intent to insult him. And as the time went on he was content with life, for he knew that when the proper time arrived he would take her as his wife, but she became irritable, for her refusal to notice him did not seem to have any effect at all, and Carlotta de Francisco was not used to having no effect at all on any man.

Carlotta sat on the ground with her back against a tree. She fingered the fringe on her doeskin dress and pondered her predicament. Life, once she had become accustomed to the primitive existence, was not as bad as she had anticipated. Savages were different from what she had expected—and what had she expected, really? She did not know.

She had heard talk about the terrors of being in the hands of the savages. She had heard stories of cold-blooded murders, but they had been the murders of people she had never known, and she had not been interested. She had been much too busy enjoying life to bother with things that had no relation to her own existence.

When the journey across the wilderness toward a reunion with her parents traveling from Spain had become a reality, she had started out with a joy that had come from the first freedom she had ever known. For the first time, she had been alone—except for poor, dead Maria—with a group of young, desirable men, all courting her favor. It had been an intoxicating experience, leaving no room for thoughts of danger.

Then she had seen them murdered, and it had been a weird, unreal experience. It was still unreal, like some terrifying dream from which she must awaken. She longed now for Maria—Maria, so much more dear in death than she had ever been in life—who had died from sheer terror.

Carlotta had expected to die too, and she was not at all sure, even now, why she was not dead like all of the others. When she had found herself a captive, she herself had felt a terror that had seemed impossible to survive. But she had survived, and since then she had tried over and over to recall everything she had heard about savages and the fate of captives, but she could not recall anything that seemed to be of help. Ladies had always referred to such things as "you know what" and Carlotta did not know what "you know what" meant. Such discussions had always been accompanied with much fluttering of fans, signs of the cross, murmurings of "God have mercy," and the shaking of heads.

Carlotta had been raised in her parents' villa in Spain, schooled and molded by a harsh and ever-present duenna who had devoted her life to forcing her lively charge into accepting the fact that she was a girl—a girl who must, whether she liked it or not, mature into a lady.

Carlotta had been a resentful pupil, for she had had no sisters, and she had envied her brothers their freedom. She had been unable to see any difference between boys and girls except that girls were forced to wear cumbersome clothing and to keep their feet on the floor, their voices soft, their backs straight and their hands folded. Later she had come to realize that there was a difference. Boys, as they grew, developed muscles, wrestled with one another, and did as they pleased. Girls had to pretend to be fragile even when they were not, were expected to be charming even when they did not feel like it, and were supposed to find enjoyment in fine embroidery. Still later she saw that boys grew into men who grew beards, came and went without supervision, got roaringly drunk and were excused because of "high spirits." Girls grew busts, were expected to be shocked by anything that smacked of fun and were constantly watched day and night lest they ruin their reputations by some unseemly act.

Eventually Carlotta had lost her boisterous inclinations, more from the constant fear of chastisement than any desire, and had come to enjoy being a much-sought-after young lady who practiced all the arts of dissembling that made a lady socially successful.

She had expected that one day she would marry some eligible young man of her father's choice, but she had not anticipated the event with any pleasure. As far as she had been concerned, marriage was just another disadvantage of womanhood. It imposed more restrictions and brought to an end the only pleasure a girl was allowed—that of flirtation. Never, in all her otherwise detailed training, had the ultimate intimacy between men and women been mentioned, and Carlotta had always supposed that the mysterious incantations of the priest performing the marriage ceremony brought about the dull duties of motherhood. She had no notion of the actual physical difference between men and women, or the real function of either in the scheme of life. She had, however, been strictly trained in the proper attitude of personal modesty.

She had been badly shocked to awaken as she had, under a bower of boughs, to find her person completely nude within the folds of the rough blanket that could have been placed about her only by the hands of the giant savage who had sat and looked at her with such inexpressible intensity.

She had run in terror the moment she had been given the chance, only to run directly into the band of painted savages that had made her captor take on the appearance of a kindly padre. The sight of those creatures had filled her with a terror that had surpassed any she had yet experienced. Her captor was as barbaric as anyone she could have imagined, but he had not the ferocity of face that she had glimpsed on that mountainside.

When he had found her and had carried her off and up the frightening cliff, she had been almost grateful for a time. Then she had witnessed the terrible slaughter below and she had been physically ill. She could have been glad, she told herself, if it had not been for the babies, but the sight of them being clubbed to death and crushed beneath the rolling rocks had sickened her to the point of real faintness. As she had watched the brutality, she had come to feel that all men, white or savage, were truly bar-

barians, and with that feeling her captor had seemed less menacing.

When she had watched him care for the old woman, she had
come to feel that perhaps he was, after all, just another man, and
Carlotta knew how to handle men. It had given her courage to
attempt an escape. But the attempt had solved nothing except to
turn what fear she had left into a hatred that gave birth to an
avowed vengeance. Even the silent tears of loneliness and homesickness that she had shed in the dark of nights had dried. And
her hatred and her desire to see her captor killed, as he had
killed, gave her strength. The crude couch of pine boughs became softer to her body, which hardened under the ceaseless toil
that the old woman forced upon her. The nauseating food had
become more palatable and the cold had become less chill. She
had discovered a strong and vibrant strength under the pale skin
that had darkened in the hours of exercise in the open air and
brilliant sun. She had changed her defiance to apparent
meekness in following the old woman's instructions and had
begun to master the arts of an Indian woman's duties, and her
heart plotted constantly in ways to win the confidence of her
captor to the point where she could betray him. She had pretended to lose her desire for escape, and yet the giant savage
took no more notice of her than he had when she had defied
him. So she sat and pondered a way to bring him to his knees,
and decided that the only course left, regardless of the dis-
tastefulness of it, was woman's ultimate weapon—flirtation and
pretense of complete surrender—not of her person, but of her
heart. It had never failed among the men she had once known.
Why, then, should it fail now?

She heard the old woman call. She sighed. There was another
revolting task to be done. Reluctantly she rose and walked under
the trees toward the wickiup.

She forced a shy smile on her lips and cast a coy glance in his
direction. He was not looking. It was frustrating. It was infuriat-
ing. She had been making advances far beyond the necessities of
arousing the interest of any white man. She had tried making her

eyes show promises that would have had any white man groveling on the ground, and he had not even seen those promises. He simply did not look at her. She lay on her couch and watched him openly as he pulled on his moccasins, but he went outside into the early dawn without a glance in her direction.

She rose quickly and, with the pretense of getting water, followed him. He took the path to the waterfall and she followed. She did not know what she would do if she caught up with him, but her desperation lent her the courage to proceed without plan. He did not look back before he disappeared through the brush.

The sound of splashing water stopped her before she stepped out into the small clearing around the waterfall. She parted the branches and looked. He stood like a bronze statue with the water cascading down over his naked body and, aghast, she was unable to move. She was welded to the earth by the revelation of the very apparent difference between man and woman. Her breath caught in her throat and it was a long moment before the realization came that she, Carlotta de Francisco, was standing in a wilderness peeping through the bushes at a man who stood stark naked in his morning bath. A rush of crimson shame came up to choke her throat and hammer at her heart. Forgetful of the necessity of keeping her presence a secret, she turned and fled, flaying out at the branches that seemed determined to hold her back. She raced back to the wickiup and with breathless relief found the old woman still asleep. Quickly she tore off her dress and crept back under the blanket to lie with the fear of discovery clawing at her modesty.

For many days thereafter she watched him furtively, but he gave no indication that he had been aware of her presence at the waterfall. Still she was afraid, her guilt nagging her peace of mind. But when she was unable to catch him in even so much as a glance in her direction, she relaxed, convinced that he was indeed unaware that she had been a witness to his complete and naked self. And she pondered, with a strange excitement that filled her whenever she allowed herself to recall the picture he had made, as to whether or not there was a difference between savages and white men, or whether white men, civilized men, such as she had known all her life, were formed and fashioned in the manner of this giant who was not charmed by coy smiles or promising glances.

Wary of frightening her back to her former actions, Gray Wolf pretended not to see the shy glances the white girl cast in his direction. Since the episode at the waterfall she had started a fascinating thing. Every night as he had stood to strip his tunic off before getting into his blankets, a wave of crimson had come up into her pale cheeks. He had never seen such a thing happen in a woman's face and he was delighted by it.

He had been fully aware of her changing attitude toward him, and he had been suspicious of it even as he had delighted in it. The morning at the waterfall he had been ridiculously happy. He had felt his chest swell when he had felt her gaze upon him. He had preened like a cockerel currying admiration. But after she had fled with the proper modesty of any maiden, she had been so obviously frightened that he had felt somewhat ashamed of himself and his coquetry. He had waited, watching her as always from the sides of his eyes, and he had known when she finally became convinced that he knew nothing of her indiscretion. And now she was again casting the glances at him when she thought he was unaware. He wondered how he might take note of her interest without frightening her back into shunning him again. He was flattered and pleased to have her regarding him as something less than loathsome, and he wished he knew more of the ways of the white woman. And then his flirtation was interrupted. Victorio's band came back to the canyon.

The fawns were losing their spots, and the rocks were retaining their heat from the sun far into the night when Gray Wolf first saw the band. They were far out in the desert, but he knew the chief by the way he sat his pony, and he knew Lozen's figure beside him. He was at the pass to greet them as they rode in. The two men clasped each other like brothers, and Gray Wolf felt an uneasy pleasure at the glad light in Lozen's eyes. That light continued to dance until she saw the white girl, and then it faded quickly. It was the only indication Lozen gave of what was in her heart, but the white girl saw it as women always see such things in other women, whether they be civilized or savage. And between the two there was a hostility that gave Gray Wolf more encouragement than all the coy glances and all the shy smiles that had left him in doubt.

The coming of the band was a joyous thing for everyone except the white girl. Victorio's people were out of meat, and Grandmother entered eagerly into trading some of her abundant store for an iron pot and some bolts of bright calico that she immediately made into a great tentlike dress. Her offer to make one for the white girl was refused. She reveled in the gossip of the women of the band, and she played hostess with all the dignified abandon of pure delight. The white girl was left alone. Apache women were loyal to their own and they ignored the white girl as if she did not exist. And Gray Wolf left the wickiup early and returned late when he returned at all, and those nights Grandmother noticed that the white girl was restless in her blankets.

The days passed pleasantly, and the nights passed pleasantly, and Lozen, who had thought in the beginning that the white girl had already been wifed, came to realize that regardless of appearances there had been no union between the Dakota and the white woman. To test her suspicions she flaunted her companionship with Gray Wolf, and when he fell willingly into her scheme to keep him away from his wickiup all one night, she was convinced. But Lozen was a woman, and with the eagle eye of the rejected she soon saw that Gray Wolf's every attention to her was calculated to enhance himself in the eyes of the white-eye woman. Pride put a smile on her lips and a fragile hope returned joy for even his most meaningless gestures. And, womanlike in her frustration at being used as a weapon of his wooing of another, she directed her hostility toward, not him, but the woman she envied. All the rancor in her heart poured from her eyes when they came to rest upon the girl.

The pale two-horned moon changed to light the night like a great and shining ball. Under its light they sang, softly as one must with enemies all around, and danced and laughed. The young men relaxed their fierce warrior expressions and flirted a little with the girls. Gray Wolf flirted a little, too, with Lozen, and was happy that she knew he did not really mean it. But they rode together during the days, as they had ridden together before, and Gray Wolf raced the thoroughbreds against every horse in the band and laughingly turned down all offers to trade. And as time went on Lozen's eyes burned brighter and brighter and she looked more and more often in the direction of the white girl who slept in Gray Wolf's wickiup. And Victorio, who knew his sister so well, decided that they must leave the canyon before some act of Lozen's would cause a breach between himself and his brother-friend.

Grandmother's eyes filled with tears at the parting, but she would not leave the big Dakota who had saved her life and become her son. She stayed behind when they left and called her farewells and smiled with love of them. And they smiled back with love in their eyes, but no one smiled toward the white girl, who stood apart by herself. No one even cast a glance in her direction except Lozen, and her look was long and contemptuous. And it was only the white girl who was happy with their going.

The canyon seemed to be filled with an unreal silence after their departure. In the nights that followed, Gray Wolf found that he suffered from an aching loneliness. He missed the singing and the companionship that they had brought with them and taken away with them. But then the visitors started coming.

Victorio passed the word about the mountain haven, and they came. They came in small groups, in pairs, and alone. They came to rest from wounds of body and of spirit—refugees from terror and weariness. And as they rested they talked. They talked about running for their very lives. They talked of the starvation. They talked of the agencies where even buzzards could not live, and they talked of chains of iron and of humiliation and of death. And only the browning of her skin, her doeskin dress, and Grandmother's guardianship kept the white girl from harm, for the hearts of those who came were hard against all whites.

After Victorio's departure, Gray Wolf pondered hard and long on a way to bring about a proper union between himself and the white girl. He knew now that he loved this woman whom he did not understand. His heart ached as she struggled to perform tasks that her delicate hands found difficult and her delicate senses recoiled from accepting. But she was brave, and her bravery endeared her to him as no other quality could have moved him. He found he was unable to take her simply as a captive. He yearned to comfort her and to find the way to kindle the glow of happiness in her eyes. He wished he knew more about *Wasicun* men and how such a man would approach a *Wasicun* woman. He found himself mortally afraid of offending her.

He had brought her presents that would have revealed his heart to any Indian woman, but they had left her unmoved, and he knew his gifts had not spoken for him. He thought of enlisting the aid of Grandmother, but he was afraid she knew less of the girl's delicacy than he, and whereas Apache men held their women in high esteem, they lacked the delicacy of a Dakota, and he was more afraid of Grandmother's blunders than he was of his own.

Throughout the days and the nights he pondered, forming first one plan and then another, only to reject each in its turn.

Then one night as he turned on his couch to look toward where she lay, the light from the full moon came down through the smoke hole and caught the gleam of her eyes. It told him that she was watching him as he had been watching her, and in that instant his ponderings were done.

He slid from his blankets and went to her side. She jumped when he touched her and lay rigid. Silently he reached for her dress and held it out. She drew back, and for a moment the old, wild look came into her eyes, and then she relaxed. She took the dress from him and pulled it down over her head, pushing it down under the blanket that she held up under her chin. He picked up her moccasins and held them until she put her feet out. Very gently he put them on her.

He took her by the hand and led her out into the moonlit night. Meekly she followed and his heart began to pound. All the wild yearnings he had suppressed surged through his veins, and it took all of his powers to walk to the place he had long ago selected as the place of their union.

It was a lovely place. Ancient pines had dropped a carpet of needles thick and soft under branches that drooped down until their tips formed an arch that was a living wickiup. He hoped she was pleased with his choice, but he could not tell. Her small hand had turned cold in his, and when he motioned for her to sit, she dropped to the ground as if her legs were weak. And she sat bolt upright, nervous and frightened. He wondered why this should be and sat down beside her to place his cheek against hers in a caress. She jerked away as if she did not know what he was about to do. He thought of the things he had heard agency Indians tell about white girls who knew nothing of what was expected of them as women until their husbands taught them. But he could not really believe such stories. He pulled her gently to him, but she pulled away. Perhaps, he thought, these stories were true. If this was so, he would have to teach her her role in life, and Gray Wolf was annoyed with a people who would leave their girls in such ignorance. He was gentle but persistent. He took hard rein on his own emotions and was slow, deliberate and gentle. When she saw what he was really about to do, she fought and scratched and gave frightened little gasps. But she could not elude him. Carefully, gently he pressed her back, never allowing his body to keep pace with his desire. She seemed wild with fright when he pushed her skirt up, but her strength was small against his determination. She fought against him until the resistance of her virginity gave way under his insistence, then she went limp, shuddering a little with suppressed sobs. With all the tenderness he could maintain, it was finished.

He cradled her face in his hands and whispered soothing Dakota words of love and tenderness, but she turned her face away. He pulled her head up on his shoulder and ran his fingers through her hair, murmuring softly.

And Carlotta lay on his arm and swallowed her tears and shivered with the pain. She felt bruised and outraged.

This, she thought, is the "you know what."

He was all gentleness now, and somehow in the darkness of the shadows he did not look the savage he was. She turned her face just a little so that she could see his face by looking up. In the dim light he looked more like a man than he had ever looked before. Thoughts raced through her mind. He was so unlike his usual stern self that it seemed at this moment almost as if he was the captive and she the captor. If this was the way to keep him so, she would do it.

Very suddenly she knew, with the unerring instinct of all creatures in the ways of nature, that this was the real association between man and woman, and that this was the association of men and women when they married.

Mother of God, she thought, and I am not married. But, she reminded the recipient of her prayer, it is not my fault. I did not know this was going to happen. I did not even know about this at all.

And then she knew, too, that this was what women had talked about when they had spoken of the "sacrifice" and of "women's duty" in marriage. This, then, was the weapon used for manipulating men's will.

Later, she thought, when I have my freedom I will confess to a priest and gain absolution for my soul. But now I know how to make him do what I want.

And her tears ceased and a small smile hovered around the corners of her mouth and a gleam came to her eyes that was more like the gleam from the barrel of a dueling pistol than the gleam of love. But in the shadows Gray Wolf saw the gleam when she turned her face toward him and his heart was happy, and when he turned to her again she did not struggle against him. He still used all of the restraint that he had been taught in the lodge of Sparrow Woman and other women of her kind, but to his amazement and delight the girl, eager to enslave him entirely, lent her own efforts toward binding him to her. And to Carlotta's surprise the pain was gone and a very different sensation took its place.

Before the sun came to tip the top of the tree over their heads, Carlotta de Francisco had learned more of life than all her years of careful training had taught her. She learned, too, she believed, why it was that people had so often spoken of the "rewards of sacrifice."

The third time he had turned to her she had met him eagerly, and although she did not think of it then, it was no longer a question of captive and captor. Youth and high emotion, satisfied to complete fulfillment, betrayed her. And a passion such as he had never known existed in woman betrayed him. They lay under the green, sweet-smelling limbs of the pine, no longer savage and lady, but man and woman, each complete for the first time in either of their existences.

For Gray Wolf it was a time of matchless beauty. He walked, he talked, he breathed with an excited anticipation of living. He still did not understand this woman who brought him so much of the joy and wonder of life. She was fiercely opposed to any union between them within the confines of the wickiup where Grandmother slept peacefully in her blankets beside the door. She carried on a strange pretense in front of the old woman, and he learned quickly that to experience the sensuous satisfaction of her rampant ardor he must insure her of complete privacy. He was utterly baffled when, even after he replaced the small wickiup with a spacious Dakota lodge, she still withdrew in cold composure unless he led her away to the place under the pine. Within close proximity of others she would sit quietly and allow him to comb her hair in the age-old ritual of intimacy and she would sit beside him in the place of a beloved woman, but the moment he showed the hint of desire she would withdraw. And in their sleeping couch she lay limp and unresponsive even after he had hung a skin between them and Grandmother's bed. He longed desperately to understand her, but their worlds were too far apart to be bridged by anything less than the passion they shared—away from the place that was their home.

Sometimes in the long silences of the evenings he would watch her and try to evaluate her, but to measure her by Dakota standards was like trying to measure sunbeams in a water gourd. He was eager to be able to speak to her in fluent comprehension, but the words he knew were not adequate for probing thoughts. A restless hunger inspired him to seek the aid of knowledgeable Apache in learning the language she spoke best, and he was careful to keep his objective secret from her, hoping one day to surprise and please her with his understanding. And this hunger and this desire kept his eyes from turning homeward while his heart yearned for the sociability of his own.

And Carlotta spent her days doing the bidding of the old woman and struggling with emotions she had never before known existed. When she went with him to the pine tree she would forget for a while that he was a savage—the savage who had murdered her own. And she would forget that he was the savage who kept her from her home and her parents and the people she knew and understood. And even sometimes in the evenings when he would sit and tenderly brush her hair and look upon her with such apparent adoration she would almost forget. But then, in the glaring light of day, with its backbreaking toil that even her "sacrifice" did not lessen, she did not forget, and she hated him even more for having made her forget, and she hated herself.

Her heart hardened in the friction of her torment, and she became a master of deception, and she watched him. She waited, and she learned his every mood. She learned his every weakness —the greatest of which was herself.

12

The coming of the snows checked the constant flow of fugitives who had, all throughout the summer, sought out the canyon as a place of rest and recuperation from wounds and weariness.

Most of them who came stayed only long enough to gather strength to rejoin band or family. But some, those who no longer had a band or a family to return to, stayed, salvaging some joy of life by uniting into a family bound not by the blood that flowed in their veins, but by the blood that flowed in the ashes of their extinction. And they looked to Gray Wolf as their chief. And they raised their wickiups in a circle, that universal hoop of life, beginning and ending on either side of the Dakota lodge.

It was not a large band. Eight homes were raised and there were but two prime warriors beside himself, but Gray Wolf was content. The canyon was secluded and far from the trails usually traveled by the *Wasicun*, and it took but one pair of eyes to guard the pass against surprise.

Kicking Bird was a Kiowa. He had been the first to stay. Gray Wolf had first seen him staggering up the mountainside, carrying his Apache wife and baby, both pierced by the same Pony Soldier's bullet.

Gray Wolf had gone down and taken the precious burden from the Kiowa's exhausted arms and brought them into the canyon. The baby died after two days, and Kicking Bird had gone alone to bury the tiny body in a secret place. Pony Girl, his wife, had taken a long time to recover, and Kicking Bird, his gratitude eloquent in his eyes, had pledged his loyalty to Gray Wolf and asked to stay and share the Dakota's fate.

Kicking Bird's wickiup was built on the right side of Gray Wolf's new lodge, and the village was begun.

Chico and his mother, Bonita, had been next. Chico was an agency boy, taken from his mother's wickiup to be schooled by the Pinda-Lick-O-Yi.[1] As he had grown older, the boy had suffered a loneliness for his own that had driven him to run away from the God man, who was kindly but a white-eye. Chico had found his mother, and they had taken to the hills lest the agency people find them and return the boy to the schoolroom.

Chico swaggered extravagantly when Gray Wolf looked upon him as a man responsible for his mother and set him to regular guard duty and occasional hunts. Bonita sang softly and smiled often. She worked early and late, with the tireless energy of a happy woman.

After them came Lame Leg and his wife, Bead. They were both very old and nearly blind. They had been led by their granddaughter, Grass, a girl not yet in her puberty.

Grandmother and Bonita helped Grass raise a wickiup for the girl's grandparents, and both women busied themselves in teaching the girl the vital lessons of drying meat and making skins into soft and pliable material for clothing,

After that other people began to see that a village was in the making, and in rapid succession several more joined the band.

Cut Face, a barrel-chested, fierce-faced warrior who spoke not a word as to the fate of his own, came to them with a deep scalp wound. When it healed he stayed. Gray Wolf was glad to have him, for this was a warrior who, in spite of his sullen unsociability, was truly a warrior. And the women raised a wickiup for the lone man and furnished it with blankets and robes and made him a new shirt and moccasins.

The next wickiup was that of Knife and his two wives, sisters whose jealousy of each other had not mellowed since the long-ago time when the stalwart Knife had been unable to choose between them and so had taken them both to wife. Knife called them simply "The Girls" and did not distinguish between them.

[1] White-eye, hence white man.

White Horn, racked with the coughing sickness brought on by the sword wound in his chest, which would not heal, had brought with him a young wife, large with child.

And in the bright autumn days the women raised the last wickiup and prayed for a medicine man to come and complete their clan. But no medicine man came, and the wickiup stood empty and the snows started and the mountain passes were blocked with winter.

The snow came faster and faster and it piled up in the draws, and the cold wind blew and the game came down from the heights. Finding food for sixteen hungry mouths presented a constant claim on the talents and vigor of the three seasoned warriors. Only Gray Wolf, Kicking Bird and Cut Face could face the rigors of the winds and the hours of stalking necessary to bring home fresh meat. Lame Leg was too blind. White Horn was too sick. Knife was too old. Chico's arm lacked the steel of skill and his fingers still fumbled under stress. Arrows were too precious to wager, but the boy's pride was preserved by assigning him to be the number one home guard.

Gray Wolf would have preferred to have hunted by twos, but because Cut Face was not inclined to be companionable and because there were only three of them, he had to decide to allow Cut Face to hunt alone. And that unsmiling warrior seldom returned empty-handed. But other than to partake sparingly of food that he himself provided, Cut Face never joined in any of the small festivities the camp arranged on every possible occasion. He lived in the solitude of his own womanless wickiup and brooded in the retreat of his silence.

Knife's wives provided the camp with much of their amusement. They quarreled constantly and with such childish vehemence that it was a game to wager on the current winner. Only Knife paid them no attention. He had long ceased to be alarmed or even interested in their harmless battles.

Roberta, White Horn's wife, drew near her time, and Grass, in midwinter, became eligible for her puberty rites. Bead wrung her hands in distress and lamented the lack of a medicine man to sing the sacred songs of womanhood over her granddaughter.

She could not be comforted and everyone understood, for such
sacred times should not be neglected, neither for want of a medicine man nor even to guard the safety of those who had already
known the precious blessings of this very special confirmation of
womanhood. They who had faced starvation, tragedy and death
with dry and proud eyes wept bitterly that this girl must be denied the ceremonies of life. And Cut Face disappeared. He was
gone for six days. When he had not returned on the fourth day
Gray Wolf went to circle the hills and look for a sign, but there
was no sign. There had been an agreement that no man would
be gone from the camp more than three days, and by the fifth
day the woe of double tragedy filled them all. Gray Wolf and
Kicking Bird took turns circling far out on the ridges and down
into the canyons, but still they could find no trace of the sullen
warrior.

Then during the night of the sixth day he slipped into camp
and no one knew of it until the morning revealed smoke from the
smoke hole of his wickiup. Nor was he alone. With him was a
medicine man, ancient, toothless, crippled and bent, but a medicine man, burdened with all of the sacred bundles of his office.
And across the door of Bead's wickiup was a fine young deer,
fitting food for a feast to celebrate the birth of an Apache
woman.

It was a winter that Gray Wolf was always to remember with
pleasure. There were sorrows, but there were many happinesses.
The Hungry Moon came without dread. Food was not plentiful,
but there was enough. It was cold, but there were blankets and
fires burned warm. The camp was small, but it was complete.
There were the old ones to cherish and give of their wisdom and
tell the old stories of brave men and courageous women. There
were young ones to love and give of their laughter and their
fearlessness of life. There were weak ones to exact the discipline
of constant care, and there were strong ones and stalwart ones to
protect and provide for them all. There were dissensions, but
there was the medicine man to sing the sacred songs and bring

peace. There were the laughter and the tears that make life, and it was good.

As the snows began to melt under the warmth of longer days, Chico began to haunt the path where Grass walked to fetch water. And Grass tossed her shining braids and slopped water as she ran away from his bold eyes. Cut Face was seen once in a while with a look that was almost a smile as he went his own silent way. Roberta, White Horn's wife, brought forth a lusty-lunged boy baby, and Gray Wolf's woman, who was now known as White Lily, learned that she was with child.

With the revelation that her "sacrifice" with Gray Wolf had begat a baby within her, Carlotta was filled with the fear of eternal damnation. She tried to voice her fear to Gray Wolf, but he was unable to understand either damnation or the reason for such a thing. He did, however, understand and respect his woman's right to a marriage ceremony by one of her own medicine men, and when Carlotta learned that she used every opportunity to press her case. Even his attempt to have their own old medicine man sing over their marriage did not satisfy her. She followed, she said, the Jesus Trail, and no one but a God man could say the sacred words that made her marriage proper in her sight.

A God man meant a white settlement, and to Gray Wolf a white settlement meant danger of the gravest sort. But it was a woman's right to be married according to the traditions of her own tribe, even if that tribe was *Wasicun*, and he pondered how he would be able to make his woman happy with her union.

Grandmother was outright suspicious of White Lily's motives and said so. Roberta and Pony Girl stood with White Lily in her insistence that her rights be respected. It afforded a wonderful opportunity to break the monotony of their lives, and they discussed at length how this thing could be accomplished. When White Lily heard of this talk she became very agitated.

"No," she said. "Such a thing cannot be considered. The God man must be in his own special God house when he says these words." And Grandmother became more suspicious than ever.

"A God man is a God man," she said, "and what does it matter where he says the words? Is not the whole earth God's earth!" But White Lily was adamant. It had to be done in a God house or it was not right.

And Chico, who knew where such a God man lived, listened avidly and hoped Gray Wolf would soon decide that it must be done as White Lily said. If they did this rash thing it would have to be Chico himself who would guide them, and he spent many hours dreaming of the glory of such an honor.

Gray Wolf listened to all the arguments, for and against, with conflicting emotions. If he did do this thing it was not going to be for the sport it would bring to anyone. He would do it for one reason only—to give to his woman the right that was hers. But he had to be sure before he could decide that it was a thing White Lily wanted because she wished to be, before all her own people, the wife of Gray Wolf the Dakota. When a man made an error, it was not only himself who paid for the error. Everyone connected with him suffered in one way or another, and Gray Wolf was not a man to bring retribution upon innocent people. In spite of himself and his wish not to, he was still apprehensive over White Lily's actions. He could not understand her mind, and it made him nervous. He could not understand her many moods, and it made him alert. He could not see into her heart, and it made him fearful. But he loved her, and when her eyes would turn from warmth to cold calculation, he told himself that it was because her marriage was not yet a marriage and would not be a marriage until a God man made it so. Reluctantly he gave up trying to comprehend her words of eternal damnation and accepted her belief as something too complicated and foreign to grasp.

Spring blossomed and the long days started. White Horn grew weaker and one day he coughed the last of his life's blood upon the ground, and he died. Roberta stood, her baby clutched in her arms, her face graven in calm resignation as they took his body up the steep cliff to bury it in a secret place. Carlotta was horrified when, after the men had carried the body away, Roberta set fire to the wickiup that was her home, and burned it and everything in it. To burn those things that had taken so many months of backbreaking labor to produce was more than ruination, it was sacrilege. But everyone else understood and approved the action, and they looked upon the white girl with blank and distant eyes when she voiced a protest.

When in less than a month Cut Face moved his belongings into the new wickiup Roberta erected and asked the medicine man to come and sing, Carlotta was more than horrified. She could not understand how Roberta could possibly accept the sullen, ugly-faced warrior for a husband so shortly after the death of a man she had professed to love. She refused to go to the sing, and from beneath her own blankets she wept once again with longing for people she could understand, women who mourned their dead mates decently in black veils, with tears, and sought seclusion among possessions to which they clung to preserve memories. She could not, would not, understand this stoic acceptance of life and of death. And then the child within her moved and the movement brought, not the surge of beauty that comes from the miracle of motherhood, but a swelling wave of terror and aching loneliness for her own mother. And her tears gave birth to racking sobs that no one heard.

From the beginning of her pregnancy, Carlotta had faced a new and unexplained attitude in Gray Wolf. No more, not even when she openly urged him, did he lead her to the place under the pines. He was, if he possibly could be, more gentle than ever with her, but he was unmoved when she offered him her body. His calm withdrawal from those occasions that had always been approached with such eagerness on his part had frightened her. She had wondered if she had lost her hold over him. It was true that he still touched her with an almost reverent gentleness, but the passion that had been her chains about him was gone. And she, who had never known the true meaning of love, and who felt not love, but hatred, for this man who had fathered the life within her, did not understand him, who now felt nothing but love for her. She did not know the effort it cost him to turn away from her when she would offer herself, and she did not know of the reverence for life that made him subdue his passions while she carried the new life within her. He did not know that she had never discussed these things with the other women and was still totally unaware of any phase of life other than that which she had experienced with him. And he did not know that his discontinuance in their passion frightened her and filled her with misgiving and made her eyes turn cold with bitter calculation toward a growing urgency of which he had no knowledge.

She was more than half her time toward motherhood when he decided that the time had come to make things right between them. It was in the dark of the moon when he awakened her one night and led her quietly from the lodge. It was so dark that Carlotta could barely distinguish the darker shapes of the wickiups. He led her away from the village and through the narrow pass. Chico was waiting with the horses.

"Lead the way," Gray Wolf said.

"Huh!" Chico's voice sounded the excitement he felt at being such an important part of this event that would be told around the campfires for as long as stories were told.

It was a long and silent journey. There was no sound except the clop of hooves over rough ground and the chirp of night insects. Carlotta wondered how the boy could find his way in the blackness that came just before the dawn, but she did not care as long as he did find it. She was at last—she knew without the words voicing it—on the way to a priest and—she was almost afraid to think it lest her emotion would betray her—freedom.

The trail led downward, sometimes so steep that she had to hang on the horse's mane to keep from going over the animal's head. At other times they brushed so close to towering rocks that her leg was scraped by the stone. Dawn came to show the desert still below them. It was a deep, wide gulf of gray that turned pink with the rising sun. The horses stopped and Gray Wolf and Chico dismounted. They stood and looked long and searchingly over the vast area below them. Satisfied that nothing moved, they mounted and rode on.

Carlotta suffered. Her body ached from the unaccustomed seat on the horse, and she ached with the emotion within her. She dared not voice any protest lest she discourage the already reluctant warrior. The sun was directly overhead before they stopped again.

Gray Wolf chose a spot where a sandy bench was formed between two overhanging shelves of rock. He and Chico set about making a shaded camp. Gray Wolf took a blanket and stretched it out. He urged Carlotta to lie down, and against her will she was touched by his concern for her. She watched him as he walked to the edge of the rim. He stood like a statue, gazing out into the nothingness of the desert floor. The child within her moved again and this time the experience struck the maternal fiber in her being. Without her wanting it or expecting it, a wild tenderness for the child and for the man who had fathered it filled her. The movement ceased and the feeling drained away, and with its going the elation that had filled her from the start of the journey went also. She turned her face toward the wall of rock so that she could not see the man on the ledge.

In spite of herself her mind went back to review all of the things that had happened to her since she had left the secure existence she had known in the sprawling and luxurious house in California. Her mind spared nothing, remembering everything— the tenderness as well as the hardship, the freedom as well as the captivity, the beauty as well as the horror. And for the first time she realized that at no time during all the many months that she had been a prisoner had she been ill-treated. The life had been hard. It had been hard almost beyond endurance, but it had been no different for her than for the other women. But they are Indian women, her heart insisted. Her mind, however, refused to be swayed by the comparison. In spite of her desire to dismiss them as animals, she was seeing with an acute perception the conceit of her own cultural perspective. The turmoil churned up the tears that seemed to come too easily these past days.

Instantly he was beside her. Forcefully and despite her resistance, he drew her into his arms and held her. He did not speak, but cradled her as if she were a child, and in spite of herself the strain and the tumult within her calmed. She did not know when she slept.

It was late in the day when she was awakened by the smell of meat roasting. A rabbit was spitted over the fire, and she ate with relish. She was rested and all the doubts that had stirred her were gone. She was again resolved that once within a civilized community she would rid herself of this wild and primitive life.

For three days they rode, and then they changed to ride only under the cover of darkness. By this change she knew that they must be near the trails that white people traveled. Her heart throbbed with something that she was unable to distinguish as either hope or dread.

It was very dark the night they left their horses and crept silently into a small village where adobe houses were clustered around a small plaza.

"Tish!" Chico gave the warning. He flattened himself against a wall, and Gray Wolf pressed Carlotta back. Across the plaza a door opened and a flood of light outlined the figures of a man and a woman as they stepped out into the street. Their voices were indistinct as they spoke to someone within. Then the door closed. The lantern they carried cast long, grotesque shadows as they walked away. They rounded a corner and were lost to sight. After they had been gone for a long time, Chico spoke in tones that were softer than a whisper.

"This is the place," he said, patting the wall behind him. "The padre lives over there." He indicated a small house next to the church. Gray Wolf drew a long, deep breath.

"Go," he said, and Chico crept forward to tap gently on the door. They waited. Chico tapped again.

Somewhere in the back a light was struck. Gray Wolf drew back. He reached out and gripped Carlotta's hand. Her fingers were icy cold. For the first time the warrior allowed himself to think of Grandmother's warning.

"Don't trust that one," the old one had warned. "She will get you killed. It is what she wants and it is all she wants."

He wished he had not thought of the old woman's words, especially here in this place. In the darkness he turned to look down at her. Her face was only a blur. He wished he could see her eyes, but it was too dark. Carefully he let go her hand and shifted the knife in his belt.

I trust her, he thought. We have known love and she carries my child. I trust her. If she wanted me dead she would not have become my woman. I trust her. And he wished he could make his mind believe the words his heart was saying.

Chico moved back from the shaft of light that fell from the doorway that opened beside him.

"Padre," he said, breathless with his excitement. "I am in need of you in the church."

"Who is it?" The man raised his lamp and his voice was loud and without caution.

"For the love of Our Lady, Padre, do not shine that light upon us and do not speak so loud," Chico pleaded.

The man seemed undecided. Gray Wolf could feel his doubt.

"Father." It was Carlotta who spoke. "Father, please come to the church."

"Is that a woman?" The priest raised the lamp higher.

"Sí, Padre." Chico moved farther back. "It is a woman—a lady who is in need of you. Do not awaken anyone, Padre."

The man hesitated but a moment longer.

"I'll only be a moment," he said. The door closed.

"In here." Chico's voice was thick with importance. He moved toward the heavy doors of the church.

"No!" Gray Wolf pulled the boy back. "You stay and watch." He did not like this at all. He did not want to go inside a *Wasicun* building. Chico had said over and over on their way to this place that a God house was as safe as a mountain. Yet he did not like it. It made no sense at all that a God man could not say sacred words under God's sky, but maybe the *Wasicun* did not have the same God. It certainly did not seem so. They were too different to be the same one, and yet how could there be a different one for different people? There were different chiefs for different people, so perhaps it was reasonable. It was not for Gray Wolf to say. But he did not like this God of the *Wasicun* who had to hide in a place made of wood and stone. He wished he could have made White Lily see that the Wakan Tanka was a much better and a more sensible deity than this God. But it had not been possible and, much as he did not trust any of this and much as he disliked it all, it was a thing that had to be. A thing that must be, must be. With his heart thudding with misgiving, Gray Wolf felt his way up the steps.

Carlotta opened the door and a musty, sweet smell rushed out into the night air. It was a strange sight that met his eyes. The blackness was softened by a dull red glow that came from a small fire flickering from a blood-red cup hanging from the roof. It was far down at the end of the room, which was crowded with benches. Only a narrow path opened between those benches.

Another light appeared and the voice of the God man spoke.

"Are you there?" he called. "What is it I can do for you?"

Carlotta went forward. Gray Wolf followed, alert to the shadows, fighting the smell that deadened his nostrils to betraying odors. At the end of the path was a low fence. Carlotta dropped to one knee and Gray Wolf saw her make a sign in front of her. The God man saw it too and his face softened just before the rays of his lamp fell on the half-naked giant behind her. The man fell back a step, but Carlotta's words rushed out.

"Father, help me—"

The bewildered man motioned for them to follow him. He went back into a small room. He set his lamp on a table and sat down as if his legs would no longer support him. He motioned to other chairs and Carlotta took one. Gray Wolf slid into the room to stand with his back flat against the wall near to the door.

"Father, help me," Carlotta said again, and then in rapid Spanish she continued with words Gray Wolf could not follow. Only now and then did he catch a word. Her voice rose to almost hysteria, and the God man kept looking from her to Gray Wolf, the bewilderment in his eyes changing to a grave and troubled look.

He spoke, and although his words were too rapid for understanding, it was clear to Gray Wolf that this God man was not eager to say any sacred words that would make the marriage between him and White Lily. They talked back and forth, and Gray Wolf grew more and more nervous. This was taking altogether too long for his peace of mind. His hand fell automatically to the hilt of his knife. He spoke for the first time.

"Come," he said to Carlotta. "He does not wish to say the words."

"Wait!" The God man jumped to his feet, and Gray Wolf fell into a half crouch at the sudden movement. The God man sat back onto the chair.

"No," he said and raised his hand as if to protect himself. "No. You do not understand. I mean you no harm. Do you understand me?" He had spoken slowly and formed the words carefully.

"I understand your words." Gray Wolf was wary.

"Then listen to me." The God man leaned forward in his eagerness. "You have done wrong. This child is not of your people. You took her without her consent. You must go away and leave her with me. I will take care of her."

"She is my woman," Gray Wolf said. "I do not need you to take care of her. I need only for you to say the words of marriage."

"No. No." The God man shook his head and spoke as if he was speaking to a wayward child. "You do not understand. She is not your woman. You took her from her people and you took her against her will."

"She carries my child." Gray Wolf was stubborn. "Say the words that will make her happy to carry my child."

"I cannot do that." The God man was just as stubborn. "You took her against her will."

"I did not make the child against her will." Gray Wolf was haughty in his anger against this man. He wanted very much to speak with respect to him because he was a God man, but it was becoming more and more difficult.

"What is this?" The God man looked at Carlotta. A crimson color rose in her face, so vivid that even the lamplight reflected the blush. She spoke again, so rapidly that Gray Wolf could not understand her. The God man looked bewildered again.

"Father. Father. It is no use," Carlotta said. "Give me your blessing and give me absolution, for I have sinned. But I had no choice. I had no choice."

She broke off to run and kneel before the God man. The man looked at her, and he looked at Gray Wolf. He placed his hands on the head bowed before him. He said something Gray Wolf did not understand, but the sound of it made him draw his knife. The man closed his eyes and Gray Wolf knew then that he was saying words of magic. From outside there came a soft "who-o-o," a warning. Gray Wolf sprang to Carlotta. He pulled her to her feet. The God man made the same secret sign Carlotta had made in the other room. Gray Wolf sprang to the door, pulling her after him.

"No," the God man called after them. "Do not go. No harm will come to you here. I must talk with you more."

There had been enough talk. Gray Wolf knew that Chico had not warned without cause, and what good were more words. If the *Wasicun* God could not hear a few words he could not hear many. That was a reasonable thing. He pulled White Lily after him and pushed at the big doors to peer outside. There was a shout somewhere across the opening in front of the building. There was a sound of feet running and then another shout. Doors opened and people came out with lamps held high. Gray Wolf saw Chico run away from the place where he held Carlotta peering through the slight crack. The boy was drawing attention away from the church. He shouted and Gray Wolf saw some men run after him. Everyone was looking that way. Gray Wolf swung the girl up into his arms and slid out of the door and ran back the way they had come. They were drawing away from the sounds of excitement where Chico was keeping the attention concentrated. He ran as fast as he could with her in his arms and the unfamiliar darkness and the houses all around. Ahead of him he could see open country. In a moment they would be away from here. Already he began to feel better. Then the girl in his arms opened her mouth and screamed. She screamed again before he could drop her to her feet and place his hand to stifle the sound. Almost beside him a door was swung open. There was a flash and a roar. Gray Wolf felt the impact of the lead as it struck him full in the chest. With one sweep he grabbed her up again and ran toward the open country. There was a roaring in his head that grew louder and louder. Behind him he could hear the pounding of feet. His own feet seemed to have left the ground. In front of him, out of the darkness, darker figures rose. He used all his strength to fight them off, but his arms refused to obey. His body seemed to grow lighter and lighter, until like a bird he was flying up and over the earth in a glorious release from the bondage of life.

There was an eruption of pain, an explosion of fierce heat within his chest that spread out to his fingertips and down his legs to weight his feet so heavily that he was brought back down to the earth with a jar that wrenched his back. He had fallen. Beneath him he could feel White Lily writhe under his weight. Faintly he heard her sobbing like a frightened child. He covered her body with his. In the dark, he was afraid, they would mistake her for an Indian and kill her before they saw their mistake. He flattened his body to take the blows that he felt were coming.

He was dying. His murderers were shadows clawing at him with hands that had no substance. His thoughts drifted. He had wanted no part of the violence that had been his whole life, but he had endured it. He had wanted nothing but honor and the feel of the sun upon him, the sound of the wind in his ears, and the love of a woman. It had all been for nothing, save the seed that was now inside her, growing into a life, the culmination of all those who had lived before him. He could not allow that seed to die before its birth, and the enormity of his own dying angered him.

Desperately he slashed at the shadows that threatened him and the precious being beneath him. The warmth of his body faded, yielding to an eternal cold, and the clamor grew more distant. It spun out into a long, thin thread of sound that finally snapped into silence and emptiness.

13

It was night. There was a nauseating stench of enclosure and sounds that were insufferable. There was a dim square of pale light high above him in the blackness. He felt numb and unreal except for the searing pain in his chest. He lay, trying to master his agony. His whole body was stiff and bruised. He was thirsty, and his hands and feet were icy cold. He lay very still for a long time, trying to determine where he was. The smell was the smell of the *Wasicun* and a *Wasicun* lodge. He was a prisoner. He was shut up inside walls that he could not see but could feel pressing down around him. He tried to raise his hand to touch the fiery place in his chest, but his hands would not move. It took him a long time to realize that they were tied. Painfully he tried to move his feet, but they too were tied. He was flat on his back, lying on a thing that sagged in the middle, bending his back torturously.

Somewhere in the distance someone spoke in gruff, guttural tones. There was a scraping sound and the clank of metal. Then everything was quiet again.

He must have lain for hours before the pale square of light grew brighter. He tried to think, but his thoughts would not stay in a line. They flitted back and forth with scenes from his childhood mingling with scenes of gray shapes reaching out for him. He tried to think of White Lily, but she eluded him. There was a painful throbbing in his head and something bound his temples tight against the throb. All he could be sure about was that he was not dead, and that he was shut up in a *Wasicun* place where there was no air to breathe. His senses told him what he could not see. He was alone in this place between these walls, but outside and all around him was the *Wasicun*.

The square of light brightened. He could see the room. It was small and made of squares of mud, one stacked on the other. The light came from a hole in the door beyond which were the sounds of a camp awakening. There was nothing in the room except the thing on which he lay. There were heavy bandages around his chest and his head. The light hurt his eyes and he closed them against it. He must have slept, for it was brighter when he heard them coming. There were two of them, one following the other. He kept his eyes closed as they came in. They brought with them a wave of the pungent *Wasicun* smell that was sweat and wool and something else that he had never been able to define.

"He's still out cold," a voice said, "an' if you ask me he ain't never gonna come around. Good thing too. He's as mean a one as I ever seen an' I seen a lot of 'em."

"I didn't ask you." Gray Wolf recognized the voice of the God man. "This man has an immortal soul as much as any other man."

"He's a murderin' savage!"

"Must you keep him tied like that?"

"Can't take no chances. Might come to and then there'd be hell to pay. Colonel's order, Padre, and you best be glad of it. This here's a wild one. He'd jest as soon rip out yer guts as look at you. Would, too, given the chance."

Gray Wolf heard more footsteps. They stopped and turned into the room.

"Good morning, Father." The new one spoke. "How is he?"

"He seems the same," God man answered.

Someone came close to Gray Wolf and took his wrist in strong, firm fingers.

"Untie him, Luther. Let me take a look."

Gray Wolf felt the hands pull away the bandages. Callous fingers probed the burning hole in his chest and the pain of it made him catch his breath.

"He's coming around." The prober sounded alarmed. Gray

Wolf heard the click that was the unmistakable sound of a gun hammer. He opened his eyes and looked at them.

At the foot of his bed a slovenly bluecoat stood looking down with the dispassionate gaze of a man watching an insect. He chewed laboriously on a great wad of something that pouched out the side of one cheek.

"One move, laddie," he said, "and I'll hafta spoil all Doc's work."

He shifted the cud to the other cheek.

"How do you feel?" The God man was peering over the medicine man's shoulder. "He understands some Spanish," he explained to the others.

"Does—does he?" Cud Chewer sneered. "Well, he hain't no 'Pache, lessen I don't know my Injuns."

The medicine man worked at the wound and the pain was so terrible that Gray Wolf closed his eyes to conceal his torment from their sight. He forced his muscles to relax and the strain to leave his body.

"He's out again," the medicine man said. "I don't know if he's going to make it or not. It isn't likely unless his fever breaks. Hard to really tell. These people are sturdy."

They walked away from him and Gray Wolf lay in exhaustion.

"I'll stay for a while," he heard the God man say. "If I can have some water I'll bathe him. It might help cool that fever."

"It'll help all right." Cud Chewer snorted.

"All right, Luther." The medicine man spoke sternly. "Never mind the remarks. See that Father has the water."

The cool water on his face and body felt like a deliverance. The open door let wafts of clean, fresh air into the stifling atmosphere. He breathed as deeply as his pain would allow. God man worked gently, his hands as light as a woman's. Gray Wolf wondered why he was doing this thing. He opened his eyes. God man smiled at him.

"Don't be afraid," he said, and Gray Wolf was too exhausted to feel anger at the suggestion that he, a Dakota warrior, would be frightened by a *Wasicun*. "I am only trying to help you."

God man brought a cup of water and held it to Gray Wolf's

lips. As much as he wanted the cool liquid, he kept his lips closed. For a long moment he looked deep into the eyes above him. They were quiet eyes. They were serene eyes. They looked back without hatred, without contempt. Gray Wolf drank.

The suns came and went and Gray Wolf did not know the count of them. But gradually the pain lessened and the fever burned out. Every day the God man came and brought with him food and water, and Gray Wolf ate and drank as a child dependent upon its mother. He did not talk when the God man talked to him, but he listened with growing respect for this *Wasicun* who treated him as one man treats another.

As he healed he wished for the relief of movement, but he could not move. The soldiers kept him tied to the torturous cot that bent his back painfully. When he was alone, which was most of the time, he worked his muscles, one against the other, trying to renew his strength, for he determined to be ready when the time came—the time when they would free his bonds long enough for him to make an escape. But when the time came he was not ready. He had laid so long that the joints of his legs would not hold his weight.

They came, a young officer and Cud Chewer. They untied him and made signs for him to get up. He tried to stand and for a moment he almost succeeded. But as the circulation returned to his legs they weakened under the needling pressure and he fell heavily. They stood over him and watched him coldly as if none of it was any concern of theirs—as if it was of little consequence whether he stood like a man or crawled like a snake.

A fierce heat of anger filled him at his own weakness, displayed before *Wasicun* eyes. He crawled to the side of the bunk to draw himself up. He was partway up, with one arm over the edge of the cot, when Cud Chewer shifted his position. Gray Wolf knew before the movement started that the man was going to kick him.

As the boot came up he summoned all of his strength to draw himself up and, at the same time, to lunge forward. The kick landed deep in his groin, but his head smashed into the soldier's midsection. They went back down—together. The pain in his

head from the smashing blow and the pain in his chest was maddening. Through a red haze of agony he grappled for the man's
throat. His prey rolled away from him and shook him off. A
wave of black nausea engulfed him and he was unable to find
the man again. A wild throbbing started in his head and the
room danced fiercely around him. He heard voices shouting and
the heavy tramp of booted feet. He heard a voice that he
vaguely recognized as his own, screaming the Dakota battle cry.
He struggled to get up, to stop the dancing in his head. He
wanted only one thing in this world—to get at the throat of Cud
Chewer, who had kicked him. His fury refused to lend him
strength. He felt himself being picked up by the head and the
heels. There was a terrible jolt as he was thrown back onto the
cot. Blackness washed over him and he sank back down into the
limitless pit of emptiness.

When he woke again the God man was standing over him.

"How do you feel?"

Gray Wolf said nothing. Stupid *Wasicun,* he thought. How
should a man feel when he has been kicked when he was already
unable to stand, when he has been mauled when he was too
weak to defend himself. A bitter hatred filled him, even for the
God man, who had never been anything but kind. He closed his
eyes and turned his head away in disgust. The God man moved
around to where he could look into his face.

"That was a stupid thing to ask," he said. "Often we white
men say stupid things. But not all of us are brutes. I have
brought you water."

Gray Wolf sighed. Maybe the man could not help being a fool.
He was a *Wasicun.* Certainly no other hand had offered him
water. No other hand had offered him comfort. Wearily he nodded. The God man brought the cup to his burning lips.

"I am only trying to help you," God man said. "You do not
make it easy for me. The soldiers have come to live without sympathy. They do some terrible things, but it is the life they must
lead that makes them do it. It is the fear in them and their terrible responsibility of making it safe for people to sleep in their
beds."

Gray Wolf wanted to hoot with derision. He said nothing.

Making it safe for people! What people? Not Dakota people! Not Apache people! Not the people whose land this was! Only *Wasicun!* Those were the only people *Wasicun* recognized. Yes, even this God man, who was by nature a just man, thought of people as *Wasicun*, not Indian.

Gray Wolf kept his face straight and his eyes from showing the bitterness he felt. And then an appalling thought came, uninvited and unwanted. His own son—the one that was even now in the making if White Lily was still alive—he would be a *Wasicun.* And Gray Wolf felt a sickness that did not come from the throb of his head or the burning in his chest.

Gray Wolf stared straight ahead. He would not show any signs of friendliness in front of the bluecoats, who might, after they had disposed of him, take revenge upon the little God man. The priest looked perplexed. He let his hand fall away from Gray Wolf's arm in uncertainty. Gray Wolf was sorry that he did not understand.

They came and motioned for him to sit down on a crude bench. He watched them dully as they placed the heavy chains on his legs and then his wrists. He stumbled when they led him toward the wagon, and they crowded around to watch. He looked into their faces as he passed, memorizing each one. He would remember. Perhaps one day he would see one of them again at another place. He hoped it would be so. The God man walked beside him.

"Do as they tell you," the God man said. "It cannot be forever. One day you will be free again."

Gray Wolf still did not answer. He did not turn his head, but he would remember this too. Maybe one day he would see this God man again, too, and in another place. He hoped that this too would be so. Then he would be able to make the little man know that he valued his friendship. It was always good to remember things so that all debts—good and bad—were paid in full. But this was not the time to pay debts.

He climbed with much difficulty into the wagon. It started

with a jolt and soon the place where he had been was left behind and the hostile eyes of the bluecoats who stayed there and
the concerned eyes of the God man were no longer upon him.

They jolted and bumped along. It was unmercifully hot. The
heavy chains rubbed the flesh of his legs and his arms raw. Flies
found the bleeding places and tormented him. He was thirsty,
but no one offered him water except when they stopped for the
night. His chest ached and throbbed, but even so he was glad to
be out under the sky where the air was clean and fresh and free
of the stink of man. At dawn they were on the way again. He
was so weak that he fell from the seat to the bed of the wagon
and he lay there for a long time before he gained the strength to
drag himself into a sitting position. The soldiers took no note of
him except to fall back now and then to look at the chains as if
they feared that he might break them when they were not
looking.

They grumbled a great deal about the heat and their discomfort, and they blamed him for their misery. He was glad they
did. He even wished he was to blame for it.

His fever came back and burned in his blood. For many hours
he was barely conscious of the passage of time. And another day
passed. They gave him water again, and much as he hated it he
drank, for he knew he must or surely die. He did not mind
dying, but he did not want to die in a *Wasicun* wagon with iron
chains binding his hands and his feet. They offered no food, but
he did not care. He could not have eaten anyway. He fell back
in the sand and gave himself up to the luxury of the softness of
the earth under him. He slept and did not awaken until the first
gray light of dawn.

There was another day of torture, and then he noticed that
they had come to a place where wickiups were built close to the
trail that led to a cluster of squat buildings like the ones back
where they had come from. His heart leaped at the sight of
Apache who stood watching the wagon as it passed. Dogs
barked and children stared wide-eyed as they pulled him out of
the wagon. He was hurried past the stoic faces of the Indians
and taken to a room so small that he knew he could not lie down

in a straight line. It was completely bare, with a hard-packed earth floor. Only a small square was cut from the door, and it was barred with strips of iron.

"I've got trouble with the one I already got," he heard one man say after they had locked the door, leaving him. "We won't be able to transfer them for weeks and I don't feel any too good having them here."

"Them's my orders," he heard the driver say, and then they were out of hearing.

An Apache wearing a soldier's coat opened the door. He brought a plate of sour beans and placed them on the floor. He did not look at Gray Wolf nor did he say a word of any kind.

White Indian! Gray Wolf thought and spat after the man. He did not touch the mess on the plate, nor did he indicate that he heard when they came and took it away again. He did not sleep during the night. He was alert to the new sounds of this new place, and he was suffering with the chains that still held him.

He was taken out the next morning by the same Apache, who held a rifle on him as he shuffled to line up with other Indians who were in chains as heavy and burdensome as his own. They were all herded like tethered cattle to a place where a ditch was being dug. A shovel was given to each one and they were told to dig. Gray Wolf watched as the others took the things like stupid slaves, and when the handle of one was shoved at him he ignored it and stared off into space.

"Take this shovel, ya damned son of a bitch, if ya don't want it over yer head!" The soldier jabbed the handle into Gray Wolf's midsection.

"Take it." One of the chained Indians spoke softly. "If you don't we all suffer."

Gray Wolf hesitated, but only for a moment. There was little point to making others suffer at a moment like this. Patience was the thing to remember. He took the shovel.

The labor and the intense sun made him sick and dizzy. The earth tipped crazily and he was barely aware of the voice that spoke seldom but encouragingly. Whenever he felt darkness growing more powerful than his will, he heard a voice, soft but insistent.

"Stay on your feet. Do not fall. Stay on your feet."

He did not know who it was who spoke to him. Perhaps it was the man who was in back of him. Perhaps it was the man who was in front of him. He did not know. But he stayed on his feet and scarcely knew when they led him back with the others and pushed him into the cell. Vaguely he wondered where the others were, but he was too sick and weary to dwell upon it.

Soon the same Apache who had brought the beans the night before and who had held the gun over them all through the day came with another plate of sour beans. He set the plate down and, glancing quickly over his shoulder, he spoke.

"Eat. Under the beans. Get your strength."

It was the same voice Gray Wolf had heard all through the day. He looked up at the Apache. The flash of the black eyes spoke more than the words the lips had voiced. They told Gray Wolf that life was not yet hopeless. He pawed aside the beans and there under the mess was a small bundle of herbs, tainted by the glob that had covered them, but fresh on the tongue. He chewed them carefully and knew by their bite that he would sleep soundly this night in spite of the chains. And he did. The next morning he felt refreshed, but it did not last long. The sun, the heat, the galling chains and the labor that pulled at his chest left him in a daze of weakness. But again that night the herbs were there, and there was a bit of meat that he could eat without gagging.

The days passed in a long agonizing line of suffering. His only hope lay in the stoic friendliness of the Apache, who gave no indication of that friendliness except in the plate, where healing herbs and bits of palatable food appeared with regularity. And strange as it was to believe, the pain in his chest grew less, and although he grew even more gaunt and his eyes sunk into their sockets, he grew stronger. He became so thin that one night, quite by accident, he found that he could work the bracelets off over his hands. After that, as soon as it grew dark he slipped them off and massaged the places where the skin had thickened and grown rough. He tried to get the leg irons off, but it was impossible. They would not slip over his feet.

There were times when the guards talked within earshot, and from their conversations Gray Wolf learned about such places as Ojo Caliente and Fort Stanton and Fort Apache. He learned about Indians who "broke out" and returned to freedom. He learned about battles and about massacres and about the death struggle between the Indians and the whites. And always there was the name of Nantan Lupan—the gray wolf of the desert who was relentless and from whom there was no escape. And then one day he heard them talk about how Nantan Lupan was being sent to the north by the Great White Father because the Cheyenne and the Dakota were on the warpath.

Gray Wolf shook with agitation. He had endured long enough in this place. The summer was dying and so was his endurance. He knew that someone was expected to come for the Indians who wore the chains, to take them to a place that was far away, where they would be prisoners to do only the *Wasicun* bidding for the rest of their lives. He knew he must escape before this could happen. He grew edgy. He was no nearer to freedom than he had been the day he had been put in chains. There were those who actually did awaken to the day when their chains were removed, but they were the ones whose spirit had been broken; they were chained in bonds stronger than the iron ones from which they were free at last. Others found freedom when they fell dead, their chains still binding their lifeless limbs.

Despair began to dominate Gray Wolf's emotions and he found himself on the brink of flinging himself at one of the guards, forcing them to shoot him, so that he could find his freedom in death. But always there was the vision of his body, still chained, being flung into a hole in the ground, and his fellow prisoners being forced to shovel the dirt over him. And there, too, was the vision of his son—already born—somewhere in a world that was torn with strife between the people who were grandparents to him. These things stayed the impulse that came back day after day, and he would hope again for a little while.

One night when he was almost without any of that hope he

saw Chico. They had brought them back and lined them up to count them as they did each night before sending them to their cells. The boy was lounging lazily against a post in the compound. He was smoking a cigarette, letting it hang from the corner of his mouth, Mexican style. He was dressed in the baggy pants of the Mexican and there was a big hat stuck on the back of his shorn locks. He was laughing and joking with the soldiers who lounged around him. The sight sickened Gray Wolf and he stared at the boy, but Chico let his eyes pass over the men in chains with no interest or recognition. Then Gray Wolf knew. Help was near. Chico was playing a game.

He could not eat even the bit of meat in the bottom of his plate. His heart pounded with the excitement inside him. He waited.

Tomorrow, he thought, I will be free. Softly he began to sing. He sang the Dakota song of thanksgiving.

The Apache guard came. There was a bluecoat with him. The Apache looked down at the untouched supper. The bluecoat shrugged with disinterest. The Apache picked up the plate. He hesitated only for the second it took for him to tell Gray Wolf with his eyes to pay attention.

"So," he yelled loudly, "the food is not good enough. Eat it anyway." And with that he flung the contents of the plate directly into Gray Wolf's face. Something hard hit between his eyes. It fell with the mess into his lap. Quickly, as if he would throw a handful back, he closed his fist over the mess. Feigning fear at the sight of the gun the bluecoat raised, he drew his hand back. Carefully he wiped his hand on the floor, pressing the hard object down into the beans.

The Apache threw back his head and laughed. The soldier joined in as they looked at Gray Wolf with beans dripping down his face and sticking in his hair. The soldier clapped the Apache on the back and they laughed together as the door swung shut. The soldier turned the key in the lock outside and they left as the soldier told the Apache that he was a real card.

Gray Wolf waited until the sound of their voices said that they were far away from the opening in his door. He felt among the beans. The hard object was a key. Carefully he cleaned it off. He put it into the lock of the chains on his feet. It turned. He turned it back and lay back to wait for darkness, when the soldiers gathered in the place where they drank and played games with small pieces of cardboard painted red and black.

He slipped the chains off his hands. He fitted the key in the chains at his feet and for the first time in many suns his legs were free.

He heard laughter from across the compound and the boisterousness grew louder. He relocked the leg irons and stood. He worked his legs up and down, getting accustomed once again to the feel of freedom. He heard the soft grate of metal against metal and he stepped to the small square of light. It was Chico. The boy motioned for silence and opened the door. Gray Wolf slipped out. Chico pressed him back to the side and then closed the door. He locked it again and, motioning for Gray Wolf to wait where he was, the boy sauntered back across the yard and went into the building where the soldiers were busy with their games and their drinking. He was gone for a long time and it was hard for Gray Wolf to stand and wait when freedom called so loudly. Here and there soldiers walked, and once one of them came so close that Gray Wolf was afraid to breathe for fear of turning the man's eyes his way. But the soldier was more interested in what was going on in the place where his comrades were enjoying themselves, and Gray Wolf relaxed as he walked on. After a while Chico came outside. He turned and walked away from where Gray Wolf waited. It was another long time before he slipped in beside Gray Wolf and beckoned. Gray Wolf followed, glad to be moving at last. They slipped between the buildings and out among the wickiups. Here and there Apaches sitting beside their fires raised a hand in a silent salute as they went by. Soon they were in open country. Behind a clump of brush they came to where Chico had tied two horses. Gray Wolf's heart leaped. They were the thoroughbreds.

They mounted and for a long way they walked the horses in total silence. Then Chico turned. He grinned wildly.

"Pretty good, huh?"

Gray Wolf grinned back. "Pretty damned good!" he said, and the horses broke into a swift canter.

It was a strange night, a silent night, except for the low growl of thunder far off in the distance, where a weird moon hung just over the horizon. No wind stirred, although it was cold. No coyote or wolf called. It seemed as if nature held its breath in conspiracy with their escape. They rode without speaking again, pressing the horses into a fast pace wherever it was possible.

Gray Wolf was conscious of a mounting excitement. He saw the strange shafts of rock and stretches of valley with intensified appreciation. Quite suddenly, with all the defiance of his nature, he felt the urge to voice his feelings for freedom and his hatred for the *Wasicun* with his irons and his bars and his stinking cells. He turned to look back the way they had come. Far away below them he saw the faint flicker of the lights. Raising his clenched fist skyward, he screamed with all the power of his lungs. It was a foolish gesture and he knew it. But he felt better for it. And, as if approving his brother's act, a wolf howled a long, wailing challenge as he stood outlined boldly against the dim skyline. The wind began to blow and the low rumble of thunder grew louder. Lightning flashed. And before the light of a new day, rain fell in torrents to wash out all signs of their passing, and in the amber ranges many miles to the north, Gray Wolf felt the first rays of the morning sun and laughed with a wild and glorious joy.

They made camp late that day where a spring gave them relief from thirst and a few tufts of grass provided a little food for the horses. Over a meager meal of roasted rabbit that was a feast for Gray Wolf, Chico told him all that had happened. The boy had difficulty in keeping back his tears as he confessed that it had been his curiosity that had kept him from seeing the white man who had discovered him that bad night and who had shouted and awakened the whole village. He had run, he told Gray Wolf, fast, but not too fast, to attempt to draw the white men away from Gray Wolf and White Lily. He had circled back after he had lost them, only to find Cut Face and Kicking Bird, who had White Lily and the story of Gray Wolf having been killed. It had been, Chico told him, his own warriors, who had followed them to the God man's place, that he had tried to fight off in the darkness of his fading senses. But the shot that had felled him had called others and the warriors had not been able to do anything except save White Lily. All that night the white men had stayed awake and alert and it had been impossible for anyone to find where they had taken Gray Wolf. Chico had stayed behind when the others had returned to the canyon, trying to find out what had happened to his chief. He had cut his hair and stolen some Mexican boy's clothes so that he could stay near when he had learned that Gray Wolf lived. He had come to this last place ahead of Gray Wolf, and he had planned and plotted to free the chief he had betrayed with his weakness. He had stolen the key from the soldier's pocket after he had drank a great deal of the firewater, and after he had freed Gray Wolf he had relocked the door and put the key back in the same pocket from which he had taken it. The Apache guard who had provided the key for the chains would get it back in the morning when he made believe he was searching the cell. It was all a pretty good joke on the soldiers, wasn't it? And who was there to be blamed for the escape from leg and arm chains and from a locked cell? He, Chico, had thought of the whole plan himself. After all, Gray Wolf was known as Ghost to all of the Apache, wasn't he? And who could expect anything else from a ghost?

The boy was pathetically eager to find forgiveness for his one act of laxity, which he believed had brought about the whole terrible time. And Gray Wolf, who sat and heard the boy out, gave his forgiveness. It was an easy thing to forgive while feeling freedom that had more meaning than before he had known prison. He laughed loudly at the boy's cleverness.

"One day," he said, "you will surely be a great chief. But I do not know if it will be in this life or the next, the way you do things."

Chico grinned broadly and then promptly fell asleep, his exhaustion erasing none of the joy of his redemption.

Gray Wolf did not sleep. In his mind he saw White Lily, and as his heart would jump gladly at her image his ears would hear again the scream that had come from her lips. He had kept himself from thinking about it during the terrible time of the chains, but no longer would his mind turn it away. Had she screamed in fright or had she screamed in betrayal? He knew the answer, but he did not want it to be so. Quite suddenly he was almost afraid of seeing her again, and if it was not that somewhere a child of his own seed was now suckling at her breast he would have turned toward the path to the north and Dakota country.

Moving on the next day, they kept a sharp watch, but there was no sign of any rider behind them. They took a winding way to avoid contact with either *Wasicun* or Indian. They reached the mountains days later. It seemed a very long time since they had ridden away from the canyon, and they did not know if they would find anyone there. But just before dark they came up and saw Knife, who was standing guard, rise until he was silhouetted against the sky. He waved down to them, pleasure in the very stance of his aged body.

The trail down into the canyon and the camp seemed long. He dreaded the end and at the same time had to keep a stern command over his impulse to rush forward. Outward coolness came with an effort. He dismounted leisurely. They came running, arms raised to clasp him, and Chico strutted back and forth under the eyes of Grass. White Lily was not among them. After the glad cries of happiness and wonder over his safe return and after Grandmother had wept her tears of joy, Gray Wolf turned at last toward his lodge. He was conscious of the studied lack of interest that came over them as he walked toward the home he had built with such loving hands. The flap was back. Inside, her back was toward him. He stood for a moment, but she did not turn.

"I am home," he said.

She stiffened, her posture strained and doubtful. Then she turned toward him. She turned slowly and her eyes were wide with fear. A cold shadow passed over his heart, which could no longer deny the fact that she had meant to betray him. She had meant to have him killed. It was a sickening moment, and the echo of that scream bored into him, begging for cold revenge. Angrily he denied it.

He turned his gaze to the familiar lodge. Everything was the same except for the cradleboard hanging from one of the poles. In the dim light he could not see the face of the sleeping child. He approached it slowly. The anger was draining from him. He placed a finger against the small cheek. The baby stirred at his touch and opened vague little eyes to stare blankly for a moment. Then the tiny mouth puckered and opened in a yawn. Promptly the eyes closed again in sleep. Gray Wolf was enchanted. It was a moment beyond all moments. He had to strive for self-control. Here before him was the product of his own seed, shaped into the form of a small man. All anger was washed away and he turned away with blurred eyes. He was conscious only of an unutterable gratitude to life, which had allowed him this moment. Rapture and agony twisted inside him when he turned again to face the woman who had betrayed and blessed him all in the same time. He moved toward her and the rapture of the miracle in the cradleboard overpowered the agony of the betrayal. His heart leaped. He stepped close to her and his arms folded around her. She shivered, and then her head fell forward. He bent his face to her fragrant hair. He was shaken to his depths. She put up her hands and pushed away from him. Her eyes were tragic. She was about to speak. He placed his fingers over her lips.

Would she never learn that there were times when there was no need for words? Did she not already know that regardless of her treachery he loved her? He would always love her. He would love her even if there came a time when he must kill her. It was but a tragic trick of life that she was a *Wasicun*. She had meant harm to no one but him, and she had meant that harm only because of the conflict between her heritage and his heritage. This he could forgive. This he had forgiven the moment he had touched his son. For that son was the link that was stronger than any conflict, stronger than any difference between them, stronger than the misunderstanding of each other. He knew she was afraid that he would not, perhaps could not, forgive what she had done. She was afraid even after his touch had told her that he had forgiven. But she did not understand. How shallow she was—a mere reflection of the beauty of life, without substance, without the heart to understand the true depth of love. But then she was *Wasicun*. She was concerned with words more than deeds. He smiled gently, feeling toward her some of the tolerant gentleness one reserves for a child. He drew her back and held her close.

"Is this a small warrior or a little maid who sleeps now in our lodge?" he asked as if nothing but the time of the separation lay between them. She made no reply except to cover her face with shaking hands. He pushed away the impatience he felt toward her for clinging to this thing that was better forgotten. He saw that he was going to speak the words he did not want to speak. He composed himself so that he could lend composure to her.

"This thing—" he said, scarcely knowing how to speak without saying the words he could not bring himself to say aloud, "—it is forgotten. It is not a thing ever to think on again. It must be as if it did not happen."

"You know what I did?" Her voice quavered like a small child's. His impatience roused again. How could she imagine that he did not know? Had he not been there? Were not the marks of the chains still livid on his wrists? Did he not still feel a strange twinge inside his chest when the cold morning air filled his lungs? Had he not retained his senses even under the kicks, the whip and the prod of the rifle butts when he had been too weak to resist? How was it that she reasoned? But it was of no use to try to comprehend.

"You speak words as foolish as your acts," he said, and prayed that she would be satisfied. She looked up at him for a long time and her eyes were the eyes of a child who has been discovered in a bad thing. He looked back down at her, the impatience disappearing before the love he could not help. She finally lowered her eyes and her shame was plain when she went to kindle the fire against the cold of the evening.

Gray Wolf watched her when she nursed the boy. He watched with all his feelings in his eyes. She had never looked more beautiful. She had grown strong and full-bodied and browned. She had ceased her weeping, but her face was still full of the strife of her soul. She had been through a difficult time. The people in the camp had let her know very plainly that they had been aware of her treachery. They had let her know, too, that only because she was the beloved of the chief did she walk among them. She had lived in terror during a time when she should have been most loved and protected. After the child had been born she had lived in even greater terror lest they take her child from her arms. She did not, even after all the time she had lived among them, understand them or know them. She had lived with fears of revenge that she had shaped by the *Wasicun* standards of justice, and she had had visions of torture made vivid by the false tales of self-glorified frontiersmen and sycophantic fighting men. And when that revenge and that torture had not come, she had been sure that it was a thing delayed to increase its impact. She had been sure that Gray Wolf was dead. She had been sure, too, that Chico was dead. And the disapproval of her had been evident and no one had tried to ease her pain. And now she was bewildered, for here in this lodge, where she had tried to keep herself away from the cold eyes of the others, sat the very man she had tricked—and he sat watching her with eyes that were calm and serene and free of guile.

And Gray Wolf's greeting of his woman quelled the resentment that had lived with them all during the long days of his absence. If he was willing to forget the thing she had done to him then they were more than willing to forget it as well. With simple directness they came to the lodge and talked with her as if there had never been any darkness between them. Grandmother bustled about the lodge as she had not done since the start of it, and White Lily was filled with turmoil that was plain in her unguarded eyes.

14

Gray Wolf did not realize the passing of time. He was too filled with the joy of watching his son awaken from the detached existence of infancy to awareness of the world. And Gray Wolf was eager to show the boy that world. His delight in each new display of the child's inquisitiveness was absolute. He spent every moment possible with the child. He called him "Boy," for he wanted no name that would haunt the young man as his own cradle name had once haunted him. He came to resent all tasks that forced him to be away from Boy. Even hunting trips, which had once held such joy, lost their charm. He was always the first back to camp after each trip, and the people took delight in his delight and the winter went swiftly.

He had known even back in the prison camp where he had first heard of the gathering of the Cheyenne and the Dakota that with the melting of the snows he would be taking the trail northward, but it came all too quickly.

The people were dismayed when he told them that he must go. But they understood. They understood, except for Chico. Chico followed Gray Wolf wherever he went and the hurt was deep in his eyes. When he would not give up, Gray Wolf took him hunting and under the open sky he talked to the boy. He spoke sternly of duty and honor and of how he himself had too long neglected such things.

"You must know, Little Brother," he said to Chico, "that we fight a war we cannot win. We have nothing but our honor and a little time. We made this camp in this place to make that little time a little longer. You can stay in this place. The others can stay in this place, but I am not Apache. I am Dakota and my brothers are even now fighting to their death and I must be with them. Stay here and help take care of my Apache people. Going is my duty. Staying is your duty."

They talked for a long time, and Chico's eyes lost their pleading look and grew bright with pride and purpose. And everyone smiled a little and treated him like an honored warrior.

Everyone conspired to make the time of the snow a happy time. Even The Girls ceased their constant bickering and combined their efforts to make the clan a harmonious family. Grandmother put aside her tears and no one spoke the words that said, "Once we part we never see each other again."

The sun was almost warm and the days were longer and the snows were gone from all but the darkest places when Gray Wolf lifted White Lily to the back of her horse. Boy was grinning from his saddle basket, and the people sang the brave-heart song. And before the wind shut out the sound of their singing, Gray Wolf was lonely for them. But he did not look back.

It was a long and tedious journey even from the first. They traveled many miles and many days away from the trail to avoid homesteads and herds of cattle, settlements and talking wires, forts and wagon trains that had come to cover the land. Gray Wolf was dismayed. Remorse filled his heart. He had gone, after Washita, to find a place for himself, and he had neglected home and duty, and when he had not been looking a new and foreign people had taken all the lands.

He cut across mountains and valleys and wild and rugged places where he was sure the *Wasicun* had not penetrated. And in those places he found them. He swung out into the vast and empty plains to avoid them and in the plains he found them. He turned and he dodged and a terrible urgency began to goad him. He passed up the hospitality of lodges where he would find a welcome, because he could not now waste time. Dreams came to him in the nights, showing him the things that had happened to his people while his duty had been sleeping in the arms of his own comfort. And as he traveled northward the new green leaves rode before him—and so did Nantan Lupan.

In the rolling lands of Dakota country the concentrated fury of a thousand wrongs drew the people from the far corners of their chaotic world. Only blood—*Wasicun* blood—could atone for those wrongs, and the gentle boy who had become Crazy Horse swooped like a hawk over the land seeking that atonement. The once shy voice had become as thunder and such men as Sitting Bull, Gall and American Horse listened. Two Moons, Dull Knife and White Bull heard, and they came. And no warrior ever rode before Crazy Horse as he threw himself into the battle that was now a war to the death, without mercy for the vanquished.

And Gray Wolf saw the flashes that winked from the tops of the cliffs and knew before he came that a great battle was being fought. He pressed the horses hard and his urgency made him deaf to all but the sound of gunfire too distant to be heard by anything but the heart. But as fast as he rode it was over when he came to the place where the great camp stretched along the river in the grassy meadow.

He left White Lily and Boy with an Old One and called for a fresh horse. He rode like the wind to where a small creek ran down a deep gulch. The water there was red and he felt a great satisfaction, because he knew the river was red with *Wasicun* blood.

In a dry coulee that ran close by a hill, he found the place where the tumult of sound had led him. He galloped up and wheeled his horse into line beside Crazy Horse, who sat, grim-faced, watching the face of the bluff. The warrior turned as Gray Wolf pulled to a standstill. For a moment the two brother-friends looked at each other in a frozen tableau of emotion. A glow started in the melancholy eyes and brightened to black intensity.

"Beauty comes at strange moments," Crazy Horse said.

"And burns brighter because of it," Gray Wolf answered.

"It is a good day to live." Crazy Horse almost smiled.

"It is done then?" Gray Wolf scanned the bluffs and the warriors scattered about the base, their rifles pointed upward.

"It is done." Crazy Horse nodded. "I am sorry you missed it. It has been salve for a sore heart. But it will fill your heart to know that the Long Hair lies this day with his face turned up."

Gray Wolf felt the race of his pulse as his heart pounded with joy.

"I would see this," he said. "It is the only sight that will fill my eyes enough to take away that which has been in them for too long."

"Come then"—Crazy Horse turned his pony—"and let your eyes feast."

Together they rode through the thick dust of the hot, cloudless day. They rode to the river and crossed to the hill on the far side. There, where the land was scarred with deep, bushy gullies, white blotches that were the naked bodies of Long Hair's Pony Soldiers lay. The women had already stripped them of all the things they had possessed and they had taken their revenge for the bones of tribesmen who lay buried in a thousand unknown graves up and down the mountains and over vast stretches of the plains. The ugly sight did not stir Gray Wolf's heart. He looked upon the grotesque forms with dispassionate calculation. In the midst of the mutilated bodies lay one, untouched, and yet somehow more graceless than the others in its unsevered completeness.

Crazy Horse pointed. "Look upon Long Hair," he said, "and let your heart know peace."

Gray Wolf raised himself high on the pony's neck to look closer. It was indeed Long Hair, but the flowing mane that had given him his name was cropped short.

"Who took his hair without taking his scalp?" he asked.

"No one," Crazy Horse said. "His hair was like that when he came to this place."

"Who was the warrior who closed the eyes that looked so lovingly on Dakota country?"

Crazy Horse shrugged his shoulders.

"Who can say? White Bull found him, but he did not kill him. No Dakota killed him. No Cheyenne killed him. Who can say? Some say it was one of his own soldiers. Others say it was his own hand. I say it was Wakan Tanka. But whoever it was, he leaves his body here and now faces those he sent before him. The hearts of our people can be glad again."

"My heart is glad," Gray Wolf said, and he smiled a smile of bitter satisfaction.

They turned their horses away and rode back to the camp, where the sun was warm and the water of the river sparkled a smile of its own. The sounds of a few distant shots told the story of snipers who kept the last of the *Wasicun* pinned to the bluffs.

There was good fry bread and a little meat and much laughing among the women, who were already making supper for the warriors who were coming in from the battlefield. They sat down in Crazy Horse's lodge to rest and talk of the things that had happened while they had been away from each other. And Morning Dew came to help with their food and hover near the son whom she had not seen for so many summers. And Gray Wolf smiled into her eyes and felt a happiness that was free from shadows.

For a long time Gray Wolf sat and listened to the things that had happened this day here on the Greasy Grass. And then for a long time he sat and listened to the things that had happened while he had been away in the land of the Apache.

Old friends came by and stayed to join the talk. Iron Hail, grown now to full manhood, came to sit close by Gray Wolf and brag of his fine sons and of the battles he had fought with honor. Lame Deer came to speak his joy at seeing his old apprentice again. American Horse came and spoke little and displayed his jealousy because a boyhood brother-friend now sat in the place of honor beside Crazy Horse, the place American Horse had come to claim as his own.

And they talked. And they talked. And when the name of Red Hawk was not spoken Gray Wolf's spirit mourned the father he had abandoned for edens that did not exist. And when they spoke of Red Cloud, broken and beaten, a slave now to *Wasicun* whiskey and agency handouts, his heart broke with the burden of his shame for having deserted an honorable chief. And the talk went on and Gray Wolf was sometimes lifted from the depths of despondency to the heights of hilarity, only to be flung back into dejection as he heard all that had happened to his people during the time of his going and coming. And the hours passed and always in the back of his mind was White Lily and Boy, who awaited him in the lodge of the Old One on the outskirts of the camp. He waited for the time when they would pause and wait to hear his story of the many summers they had not seen him. And finally they did. Slowly, with pain and with pride, he told them of the places he had seen, the people he had met and the battles he had fought. And finally he told them of the son he had sired and that even now that son and his woman awaited his bringing them here to the place that was home.

And Morning Dew's eyes glistened and Crazy Horse saw the gleam.

"I would like to see my brother's son," he said.

Gray Wolf went and when he had brought them back Morning Dew clasped Boy to her aging breast with eager arms and tears of joy ran down her furrowed cheeks. She took no note that her daughter-in-law was *Wasicun*. She put her arm around the girl and led her away to rest in the warmth of her own empty lodge.

And because he had cast the incident forever from his mind, Gray Wolf spoke no word of his wife's treachery, but Crazy Horse had developed an insight he had lacked in boyhood.

"Your woman," he said, "has the face of a flower, but there is the sting of the wasp in her eyes."

"She comes from a hard country," Gray Wolf explained. "It is a country that gives a sting to men as well as women."

"I think my brother is blind." Crazy Horse smiled a little. "I think the sting is there because of my brother and not because of her country. I think my brother has no more luck with love than Crazy Horse. See this scar?" He touched his forehead.

"I see it."

"This I wear because of love." He said no more, but Gray Wolf knew that Crazy Horse knew the meaning of the scars on his wrists and ankles.

They sat silent for a while. Gray Wolf dreamed of a more gentle White Lily and Crazy Horse dreamed of a doe-eyed girl named Dawn, and the anger of Dawn's outraged husband. And all around the people were preparing for the burial of the warriors who had this day ridden their last ride.

Cheyenne passed, the bodies of their fallen on pony drags, going to search for caves off the main trails where they could bury their dead according to Cheyenne tradition. And here and there Dakota brought the bodies of their dead to lay on the scaffolds that had been built inside some of the larger lodges. Old men rode around the camp, dressed in their finery, and sang the brave-heart song as widows and mourning families laid torches to the death lodges.

Groups gathered here and there for fight-kill talks, but their voices were low in respect for those who mourned. And the night was far gone. One warrior made a new kill song and the words came to them softly from near a fire a little way from them.

> *"Long Hair! Where he lies no one knows.*
> *His woman is crying*
> *They seek him everywhere.*
> *Look this way! He lies over here."*

It began to rain and they went inside their lodges, but no one slept.

At sunup, as soon as the morning prayers had been sung, the women began to break camp. Food was scarce. Too many people had camped too long in this place. They would move southward.

Gray Wolf left White Lily and Boy with Morning Dew and went with Crazy Horse to talk with other chiefs. A few soldiers still held out in the high bluffs, and Sitting Bull said that they should be left alive to spread the word of what had happened on Greasy Grass.

"If we kill them all," he said, "more will come against us."

And Gray Wolf remembered where he had heard these same words before. Red Cloud. A shadow passed over his heart. How many, he wondered, of those who sat here today would become too old and too tired and too discouraged to continue fighting for their homes, their families and their freedom? Maybe even you,

Sitting Bull, he thought. Maybe you and maybe Gall, who stands so proud and so satisfied. And maybe even Dull Knife, who still has the Washita in his veins. Maybe any one of them. But never me! Never Gray Wolf! He studied the austere features of his brother-friend—and never Crazy Horse! We will die, he thought, yes, even after this great victory we do not have a chance, so we will die. Crazy Horse and Gray Wolf will never be agency Indians. They will die men.

He heard the "Henala! Henala!" as one after another the chiefs saw the wisdom of Sitting Bull's words. Crazy Horse was silent. He looked over at Gray Wolf. He sighed and shook his head. He too was remembering Red Cloud's brave and futile words of wisdom. And he too was seeing Red Cloud as he was today, old, broken, dependent on *Wasicun* mood for the meat in his mouth. Angrily the little warrior turned on his heel. He strode away and Gray Wolf followed. They had gone a long way before Gray Wolf could figure out what seemed to be wrong here. Then suddenly he realized it. Crazy Horse was leading. Gray Wolf was following. After the surprise of it, Gray Wolf smiled. It was a small smile with a touch of bitterness. But he walked on, seeing the justice in his following. Crazy Horse was a Dakota warrior with honors gained in defense of Dakota people. He was married to a Dakota woman and had lived his life on Dakota lands. Gray Wolf was a warrior with honors gained in the lands of the Cheyenne, the Apache, the Arapaho. He was chief of a scraggly band of refugees, married to a *Wasicun* and a vagabond at heart. Crazy Horse was revered by his people. Gray Wolf was scarcely remembered.

They rode, following the trail of the camp, and Gray Wolf kept his pony's head back even with the withers of Crazy Horse's mount. The warrior rode for a time, deep in thought, and then he turned.

"Why do you ride behind your brother?" Crazy Horse asked.

"Because my brother is a Dakota chief," Gray Wolf answered.

Crazy Horse pulled his pony up. He sat and looked long and sadly into Gray Wolf's eyes.

"I am no chief," he said. "I will not ride behind Gray Wolf as in the old days, but neither will I ride ahead of him."

Gray Wolf did not answer. Side by side, their legs touching, they rode on. And behind them American Horse's face darkened.

Late in the day they came upon the camp the people had made close by the foot of a mountain. Cook fires were burning and there was fry bread and meat, and far into that night the camp celebrated the victory dance. They danced in wild jubilation and told over and over the feats of bravery that had been done in the big battle. They made honor songs for warriors who had counted coup. They sang and they laughed and they told each other how the soldiers would leave their country now and they could go back to the old ways of life and of living. And Crazy Horse sat inside his lodge, moody and morose. And Gray Wolf sat with him.

"Hear them," Crazy Horse said. "Listen to the children. Already they have decided that they will drive us to the agencies or they will kill us."

Gray Wolf wished there was some argument against this logic, but he knew there was none. Crazy Horse was not a fool. He knew. He knew, too, as Gray Wolf knew, that it had been thus from the very beginning. In spite of patience, in spite of persistence; in spite of tenacity or treaties; in spite of valor or victories, the people had never had but one alternative—live the *Wasicun* way or die!

"It is a good day to die!" he said, and his voice rang with the timbre of his unswerving resolution.

Crazy Horse raised his head. Very suddenly, like the sun coming from behind a black cloud, a smile spread over his face. He leaned forward and his arms clasped Gray Wolf's arms. It was like the old days of their boyhood and the pact was made between them. No! Neither Crazy Horse nor Gray Wolf would ever be agency Indians.

"It is a good day to die!" Crazy Horse said and he laughed. It was a loud, free, ringing laugh.

Black Shawl raised her eyes to stare in startled wonder at her husband, whom she had never before seen so much as smile.

15

It was not a good summer. The buffalo were scarce and the soldiers many. Winter was approaching and with it starvation seemed almost certain.

The rifles the men carried were to make an impression rather than for use. Their ammunition was gone and it was impossible to replace it. The *Wasicun* was guarding his supply more carefully than he guarded his life. Gunrunners and nefarious traders could no longer be relied upon. They had come to fear the Army more than their former customers and the soldiers were even more inexorable in weeding them out of the territory than in hunting down fugitive bands.

The rifle had so successfully replaced the bow that many of the younger men were woefully unskilled in the use of the only weapon that was now available. They were unable to bring down a man with an arrow, much less a buffalo.

Disgusted and discouraged and fearing the hunger that their women and children faced, clan after clan surrendered and in numb bewilderment submitted themselves to *Wasicun* dictation.

And Gray Wolf found himself the center of dissension. American Horse did not like losing his place to a man who had been elsewhere during the difficult years that had passed, and he was loud in his criticism of Gray Wolf. He suggested more than once that Gray Wolf's absence had been prompted by fear. Gray Wolf, and Crazy Horse, too, closed their ears, knowing the cause of the attacks, and excused them as symptoms of the jealousy sickness. Everyone hoped that American Horse would recover and gain back his dignity, but he did not. The more his remarks were ignored the more vindictive he became, and late in the summer he called for followers to go with him and set up a separate camp. People were torn by the necessity of making such a decision. A split of this kind made them all vulnerable to both attack and the hunger that was sure to come. Crazy Horse did his best to dissuade American Horse from such folly, but the unhappy warrior was firm. Gray Wolf argued to no avail.

"You have said I was afraid," he said to American Horse. "Then stay and see my fear."

But jealousy had closed American Horse's ears to wisdom or reason, and he took his family and four warriors who, out of loyalty, would not see him unprotected. They went a few miles away and set up another village. Almost immediately the proof of his folly came. A company of more than two hundred soldiers discovered the little camp. The old chief and the four warriors scrambled into the bluffs. They held the soldiers off as long as they could, but American Horse was shot through the belly and surrendered before Crazy Horse could come to his aid. That night American Horse died, and two of the other warriors were dead as well as some of the women and children. The rest were prisoners, and Crazy Horse and Gray Wolf and Sitting Bull watched from the cover of the hills as the bluecoats herded the wretched survivors away.

Their own camp was too close to risk encounter or any attempt at rescue. They rode back to break the camp and move farther back into the hills. But the disaster to American Horse's village lay heavy on the hearts of the people. There were those who looked darkly toward Gray Wolf and his white wife. There were others who blamed the presence of the *Wasicun* woman for the scarcity of game and the clumsy marksmanship of the younger warriors.

"She has witched them," they said. "That is what makes their arrows go astray. And she tells the bluecoats where to find our camps."

And again there was dissension. Gray Wolf would have taken his wife and his son and left, but Crazy Horse argued against it, and Morning Dew wept bitterly and defended White Lily savagely.

"It is discouragement that twists their minds," Crazy Horse said. "Be patient with them. Your place is here with us. We are your people." And Gray Wolf tried to be patient, but the open distrust and hostility they showed White Lily did not improve her tolerance toward the life he had chosen for her and she began to speak of surrender and to bemoan the fact that Boy would surely starve unless Gray Wolf took the *Wasicun* trail. And Gray Wolf was glad that Morning Dew could not understand the words his woman spoke, and more and more he stayed at Crazy Horse's side and away from his lodge.

Then Sitting Bull announced that he too would separate his forces and, on the pretext of easier hunting, he took his clan and moved northward. And the Cheyenne went, too—south, to the Powder River country. And winter came and with it an intense cold.

But the icy temperatures did not stop the soldiers. Dressed in heavy woolens and furs, with wagons filled with food, they kept to the trail and pressed the band from one shelter to another.

One freezing day a few Cheyenne staggered into their hidden camp to report that the soldiers had destroyed their village and killed most of their people. They were hungry and they were almost naked. There was little food, but it was shared, and it was necessary to move the camp that very night to get away from the bloody trail their bare feet had made in the snow. The soldiers were close behind. For days they ran. They ran from one place to another, but it was impossible to shake the well-fed soldiers from their trail. The people were tired. They were hungry, and many were frostbitten.

One cold day the soldiers caught up with some of the women and children who had fallen behind and Crazy Horse turned back. They fought hard that morning and for a while it looked as if they might be able to rescue the prisoners. Then the soldiers pulled the canvas from one of their wagons and there was the deadly wagon gun.

The shells screamed up into the places where the warriors held their positions. It was intolerable, and warrior after warrior was torn to bits. The snow began to fall in heavy, thick drifts. It hid their retreat. They moved back into a precipitous canyon where some fallen trees formed some shelter from the storm. The encounter had been disastrous and their situation was desperate. There was no food at all. There were a few thin pieces of blankets, no lodges and only a few half-starved ponies. They dared not build a fire lest the smell of the smoke reveal their hiding place. They huddled together all through the night, using the warmth of each other to try to keep from freezing to death. The morning light proved that they had not been successful. Many of the old ones were sleeping the long sleep and many of the babies were dead.

White Lily was reduced to almost complete collapse. She wept openly and uncontrollably.

"Give up," she said to Gray Wolf. "How can you be so brutal? Have you no love in your heart for your son? Look at him. Maybe tomorrow morning it will be him that is dead. Look at your mother. Don't you love them?"

"I love them too much," he answered, "to make them slaves." He was glad that no one else could understand her words. From no one else were there any tears. There was no mourning now for those who had departed. There was only a little envy for those who now knew peace.

The following days and weeks were fought with despair and hope and new despair. It took all the combined efforts of every male, young and old, to find enough food to keep them from actual starvation. And only White Lily said the word "surrender."

She talked all of the time to Gray Wolf and she talked of nothing else but surrender to the *Wasicun*. She pleaded. She begged, and then when desperation erased all caution, she threatened. She threatened deliberately to fall back so that she would be taken prisoner with Boy. She threatened to find a way to betray the whole camp to the soldiers. And Gray Wolf did not dare leave her side. She talked about *Wasicun* ways and talked of the good food the *Wasicun* always had in abundance. She talked about the warm lodges the *Wasicun* built and she even talked about the sweet aroma of new-made bread and the warm comfort of a soft bed and doors closed against the cold wind and snow. She tormented Gray Wolf in a thousand ways and he bore the torment to save her face before his people.

Then the weather turned warmer and they moved to a new place, more sheltered, and there was hope again. And he showed them how to make lodges as the Apache made them and they were happy for the slight protection their brush houses gave them. And the hope came easier. The Hungry Moon was past and the streams and ponds shrugged off their icy covers to glitter in a warmer sun. And then the snows began to melt and soon there were only patches left here and there. The children sought the sunshine and their thin little faces turned to it with delight. And it seemed as if they could live again. But the game did not return and food was a precious thing that had to be divided very carefully. And the green grass began to show here and there and the buds swelled, but still the game did not come. So they left the camp reluctantly and moved southward hoping to find the buffalo. But there were no buffalo. There were only bones with rotting flesh or already bleached white and bare. And they were hungry. And Crazy Horse could endure it no longer. An Indian, gone *Wasicun* and fat at the agency, came with a paper telling Crazy Horse to surrender and come and live in peace under the *Wasicun* rule. And Crazy Horse went alone for a while to talk with Wakan Tanka. When he came back he called the people to him. He spoke, the sorrow wringing the words slowly from his mouth.

"I have tried to keep you free. I have tried to keep you Dakota as you were born. But the only freedom for Dakota is in the long sleep. For myself I would choose this long sleep. But for our children we must surrender. The *Wasicun* have not beaten us. Hunger has. In the agency there is food for our children's mouths. And because I will not desert you even in this, I will not seek my freedom in the death I prefer. I will endure the humiliation of my manhood. I will go with you."

"No! No!" The cries came from all around. "We do not mind death. We will stay free until that time."

Gray Wolf stood in utter disbelief. He could not believe he had heard these words from his brother-friend.

"It is better to die here," he cried. "You made an oath that you would never surrender."

"To see my children fill their bellies once again I even break my oath," Crazy Horse said to him. He lowered his head, but everyone could see the water that fell from his eyes.

And again the people cried "No! No!" but their voices were not so loud. Already they were seeing the children eating and their courage was thin.

"There is no more to say," Crazy Horse said. "Get ready. We go."

He turned away and would not even look at Gray Wolf. White Lily came running.

"What is it?" she asked, knowing that something was happening.

"Crazy Horse surrenders," Gray Wolf said, his bewilderment bringing out the words before he thought.

"Surrenders?" Her voice was eager.

"Crazy Horse surrenders!" he said sternly. "Not Gray Wolf!"

"But if he surrenders—? I thought—" Her chin was starting to quiver in the fashion he had come to dread.

"Go to Morning Dew and do not anger me!" His voice was loud and hard and he did not care at this moment that he had spoken to her as he had never spoken before. She gave him a startled look and her chin stopped quivering. Her eyes turned bright with an anger of her own. She turned and if a small creature like her could stalk, she stalked away, fury in every movement of her body.

Crazy Horse stood apart. He had turned once as if he would come to speak with Gray Wolf and then when White Lily had run up he had hesitated. He stood now without pursuing his first intention. He raised his head and looked at Gray Wolf. Gray Wolf looked back. They said nothing. They stood, not touching each other, their eyes saying the farewells their tongues could not voice.

Women and children gathered and started down the trail. They were wasting no time. The decision had been made and they limped and staggered on their way to the Red Cloud

agency with the hope for food and the despair of the vanquished.

Crazy Horse turned away. Gray Wolf stood and watched him
go. There was no word that could be said. He knew the cost of
this decision to his brother-friend, and he knew too that they
would never see each other again. Words would only make this
terrible thing more terrible. Crazy Horse was already gone. In
his place a man, older than his years, without even the dream of
the old life left to him, turned his feet to walk the *Wasicun* trail.

Crazy Horse walked rapidly, leading his scraggly pony, to the
head of the column. He mounted and turned to look back over
the gaunt and ragged line. Their faces, old and lined with the
hardships and the hungers, looked up at him, earnest and trusting. Even the faces of the little ones were drawn and hollow
with their misery. Crazy Horse winced at the look in their eyes.
His lips drew down thin and hard and his eyelids dropped over
the glitter of his stare. He took a deep, shuddering breath. He
squared his pinched shoulders and lifted his chin so high that
the knot in his throat protruded comically from the front of his
fleshless neck.

He waited, watching them, until the majestic poise of his pride
caught them and drew their own emaciated bones up and out of
their unspeakable weariness. Only then did he turn his tottering
mount and stagger out, ragged and regal, at the head of his people, who followed him, their backs straight and their heads high,
even as their feet left bloody blotches on the grass behind them.

Gray Wolf watched them go, clutching to the last moment of
their nearness. They crossed the marshy meadow to the high
ground beyond and disappeared from sight. The sound of their
passing grew dim and was finally gone. The magic of the morning was gone with them. A silence settled over the land. Even
the happy music of the birds seemed shocked into silence.

He stood and stared at the empty hill for a long time. He felt
again the awful aloneness that had haunted him for most of his
life. And he felt more. He felt the grief of futility and the sting
of submission as acutely as if he had surrendered.

"They surrender," he said, and the words were bitter on his tongue.

"They surrender because Crazy Horse is wise." White Lily stood beside him. "Crazy Horse knows it is futile to starve and freeze. It proves nothing."

"It proves much!" His retort was more explosive than he would have wished it. He had not, in fact, meant to bicker with her again.

"It is better than starving," she insisted.

"It is not better." He was angry and he strained to keep his voice from revealing the anger. This was not a time when he felt inclined to match words with her.

"It is better," she said. "It is better than all this killing. It is better than freezing."

"It is not better than freedom." He could not keep the sharpness from his voice. "Freedom is better than food. It is better than fire. It is better even than the love of a woman."

"Maybe it is better for a man"—her voice lost some of its sharpness—"but it is not better for a woman nor a child."

He knew that she was not going to stop this kind of talking. He wondered how he had ever longed for her to talk to him. She had taken a long time to do it, but now it seemed as if she would never stop her words. There was no way to reason with her. She refused to understand anything except what she thought and what she felt. She had become a nagging woman. Gray Wolf had often laughed at men who had found themselves in the same lodge with a nagging woman. In fact such women were a source of amusement to everyone. But there had been few of them. This woman of his was such a one, and like the other men he had seen so afflicted, he was at a loss as to how to quiet her.

When they had started for the Dakota lands he had started with such hopes and such dreams. He had been sure that here in his own land they would find contentment together. He had explained to her all along the way how comfortable Dakota lodges were and how happy Dakota life was. And she had seemed glad and she had even laughed sometimes and taken delight in Boy as a mother should do. She had begun to act like a wife instead of like a captive. And then they had come and the soldiers had driven them without mercy. Game had disappeared. Hunger had stalked along with the biting winds. It had been a winter almost beyond the endurance of Dakota women, who were blood sisters to cold and hunger. For her it had been torture and she had blamed him for the misery instead of placing the blame where it belonged—on the *Wasicun* who had driven them from cover to exposure, from haven to privation, from weariness to exhaustion.

She had, even during the worst of the time, tried to prevent him from sharing his small catches with others. She had turned her face away from honor as if it was a thing that should be cast aside because she was hungry. Boy's hunger and her misery had brought him a misery of his own that had nothing to do with an empty belly or a frozen body, but it had not brought shame, for the shame of it was not his. But she had brought him shame. She had brought it by her lack of grace in sharing with others whose hunger and misery were as acute as her own. But she had not even known that her actions had been cause for shame. The only thing she had known was that she and her child were hungry and that she and her child were cold and she had felt that they suffered only because he was too stubborn to bow to *Wasicun* will.

That this land was not *Wasicun* land did not matter to her. She saw no reason for fighting over land. That this was Dakota country and not the *Wasicun*'s to allot and govern was of no concern to her. That this had been the land of his fathers for as long as anyone could remember was as nothing. That it was *Wasicun* who were at fault was of no importance in her eyes. Nor was the fact that the rest of the people felt as he felt of any concern. She did not care about the rest of the people. She cared only for food and shelter for herself and her son.

He had tried, in the beginning, to make her understand honor, integrity and justice. She had scoffed at his principles and had criticized his concern for anyone other than herself and Boy, as if only concern for them was the thing that made honor. And he had come to learn that it was *Wasicun* reasoning that made her so, and he saw, too, the folly of his heart in loving her and wanting her. But even as he saw the folly, his heart refused to relin-quish its desire and he had come to agree that both he and Crazy Horse had never been lucky with women.

"I would rather die than live as a *Wasicun*," he said.

"You do not know what you say." Her tongue was sharp again. "You do not know what it is like to live as the *Wasicun* lives. What is so terrible about having enough food to eat? What is so bad about a warm house? What is so terrible about a soft bed with clean sheets instead of a pile of skins? And what is wrong with living like a human being instead of an animal?"

He was really angry now and she saw it. "I live like an animal only because *Wasicun* forces me to it. *Wasicun* ways are not my ways."

"And Indian ways are not my ways," she cried. "You say it is better to die than to be a prisoner. Am I not your prisoner? Should I die instead of living your ways?"

His anger turned to uneasiness. There was logic in her words that he did not like to admit.

"You want my son to grow up like a *Wasicun*," he accused.

"My son is a *Wasicun*," she flared.

And the very words he had once thought would bring him comfort stung his chest with more fire than the charge of lead it had once taken. She had bested him in verbal combat. She had an uncanny ability to take his own beliefs and turn them into deadly ammunition against him. For one awful moment he had the nauseating desire to be a *Wasicun* so that he might have no aversion to beating her soundly.

Gray Wolf stood beside the stream and contemplated the dancing ripples. The music of its babble sounded rude and ill-mannered in buoyant unconcern for the fate of mortal man.

Two suns had come and gone since Crazy Horse had led the people into submission, and Gray Wolf had been unable to pro-vide even a mouthful of meat for his woman, his son, and his mother. All nature seemed to have recoiled in rebuke for the faithlessness of her favored earthlings and there was no life to be

seen in all of the countryside, save their own and the foolish
frolic of these meandering waters.

In his grief and his need, Gray Wolf had sung the *hanblea-
klake*,[1] but the winds had died to mute quiescence and there was
no sound but the inane chatter of the water, which did not even
nurture a minnow. He had called aloud to Wakan Tanka for sustenance, but the rolling hills had hidden their bounty. Not even
a rabbit had scampered across his trail. He had sung the song of
Thunder, but the sky stood in distant denial.

His head felt dull and heavy after the tempest of uncontrollable loneliness, which had abated before the stress of necessity.
His heart was deaf to his own want, but the need of his family
was a clawing beggar, plucking at his distracted mind. He was
agonizingly aware of White Lily and Boy and Morning Dew,
who followed his frantic footsteps in silent and aching hunger.
He did not know that White Lily's sufferance was imposed by
fright. He had, in fact, no knowledge of the burning intensity in
his face, which had become eroded into a fleshless frame of desperation as he wrestled with his double anguish, nor was he
aware that his famished and gutted features posed a sinister as-
pect to her frightened heart and that she attributed his fierce
and frenzied expression to the brash, abusive taunt she had flung
at him in her frustration. She knew nothing of the writhing humiliation he was feeling as he walked in the darkness of inadequacy.

So engrossed was he in his misery that he failed to note the
approach of the dispirited group of people who stumbled to the
opposite bank of the stream. He was stupefied at having been so
insensible to his surroundings and then he was vaulted out of his
numbness.

Lame Deer stood looking at him with a surprise that matched
his own. They plunged into the water and stumbled toward each
other.

"How is it I see you here?" Gray Wolf's voice was gruff with
emotion.

[1] A vision song.

"I have said I would never eat if I must eat of *Wasicun* meat." Lame Deer's ironic smile was grotesque. "And," he added, "I have not eaten. I do not care for my own belly, but"—he turned to glance back at the spent figures of his little clan—"I care for them. Do you have food?"

"I have no food." Gray Wolf's elation died in compassion. "My own family starve. I have found no meat."

Lame Deer clasped Gray Wolf's arms and they stood for a moment, each taking strength from the other. Gray Wolf's elation began to return. He felt the inadequacy flow out in a flood of thanksgiving for this reunion. And with the thanksgiving came some of the old confidence that was as much a brother as the man who stood clasping his arms.

"I have no food," he said, "but now that I am once again with a brother we will all eat of meat before the day closes its eye."

Lame Deer nodded and this time his smile was soft with hope.

"Come over here," he called to his people. "Come and camp with our brother Gray Wolf and start the supper fires."

With little cries of gratitude the women struggled to their feet. With some of their old energy the half dozen warriors jumped into the water. They came wading noisily, pushing back the pangs that increased with the very thought of meat.

White Lily and Morning Dew saw the gladness in the faces of the women and took heart. They, in turn, saw the expectancy in the eyes of the two women who awaited them and felt confident. They all made happy noises as they gathered sticks and put them in a' place for a fire.

Gray Wolf called the warriors aside.

"There is no food in my camp," he told them. "But we must not think of this. We must remember what we were taught by our fathers. We have food. All we have to do is find it. Let us remember to think this way and go and bring it back from wherever it is."

And they did find it, in less time than it took the sun to lengthen its shadows by the breadth of a man's hand.

It was a lone buffalo, cut off from his kind by the same hand that had isolated them. And even in their weakened state they had no difficulty in bringing down the great beast, who stood as if welcoming the death that would free him from his desolation.

He was old and he was tough. He was a bull—something any one of them would have refused to touch in the days of plenty. But he was meat. He was nectar. He was life.

In the late night hours Gray Wolf and Lame Deer talked. They agreed that to resist longer was madness. But being men of nerve and courage and endowed with complete assurance of the invincible divinity within the fabric of their mortality, it was to them a magnificent madness that neither of them could quell.

The odds against them were stupendous. The *Wasicun* had denuded their lands. The buffalo herds were no more. Smaller game animals that had not yet disappeared under the deadly accuracy of the ever-increasing number of rifles were so shy that it was almost humanly impossible to get within an arrow's flight. Finding food ceased to be a pleasant pastime. It was a constant commission, plagued by the proximity of *Wasicun* hunters, *Wasicun* settlers, *Wasicun* soldiers—all convinced that the Dakota was another product of a wilderness to be conquered.

Gray Wolf and Lame Deer talked of these things in the night, and they talked of the alternatives. They spoke of Red Cloud, the greatest of great chiefs, surrendering to a life that was but a sodden shadow of the once great man, selling honor and the lands of his fathers for whiskey, to which he had become a slave. His fate could not, must not be their fate. They talked of Little Wolf and Dull Knife, surrendering only to be sent far away to a place that was not their home—a place where they would surely face starvation. They talked of Kill Eagle, who had surrendered only to find himself living out his days in a filthy hovel with iron bars between him and air to breathe; of Gall, denouncing his own for a few rations; of Crow King, turning liar and cheat to curry favor and meat; of Bobtail Horse, slave to the soldiers he had once fought so bravely.

These were fates neither Gray Wolf nor Lame Deer could accept. These were the fates that accompanied surrender.

They talked of Sitting Bull, grieving with homesickness, far away in the Grandmother's Land, accepting hospitality from cousins too distant to radiate the warmth of family and too destitute to share with gladness.

That too was a fate that could not, must not, be their fate. Neither surrender nor departure was the answer—and who else was there now left free in their own land, to hold together the sacred hoop of universe that bound the sky and the people into one?

And they thought, each in his own mind, of all the brave ones who no longer walked the paths of earth, who had deserted life rather than honor. Although neither of them spoke their thoughts, they agreed that this was the fate they must choose for themselves—and for those who looked into their faces for wisdom.

And the pact was made. As the gray mists of morning pushed back the night, they lit their pipes and the smoke of their prayers mingled with the silver luster of another day.

The meat was strong in flavor and tough of fiber, but starvation imparted appreciation for every morsel. They ate, slowly at first, of the broth, seasoned with wild onions and green herbs. And when their stomachs bulged with the fragrant pottage, they chewed on ribs braised and turned into tenderness.

White Lily, Gray Wolf's woman, ate with a savage relish that Carlotta de Francisco would never have dreamed possible. Since they had arrived in Dakota Territory she had come to value the importance of basic needs. No longer did she indulge in vain yearnings for the comfort of a featherbed, the feel of silk or the taste of wine. Her desires had modified to an avid appreciation for the warmth of fire, food for the body, and shelter from the elements. She had learned, during this past winter, of the latent endurance within her own being, and had found hidden depths of self-sufficiency. That awakening had brought about a subtle change in all of her values, and it made her conscious of the man in the savage who had claimed her and fathered her son. She had come to recognize in him something so sincere, so honest and strong that she understood how it was that he was beyond submission, beyond compromise, even beyond vacillation. She had come to see that within him ran a fiber of dauntless courage that no army, no hardship, no hunger nor even death could shatter. And she resented this new awareness, for it brought with it a compassion, an understanding and a regard that she did not cherish.

She had seen his people cruelly pressed under the heel of progress. She had suffered that pressure herself. And there were times when she almost wished that she had been born a primitive savage capable of keeping pace with his magnificent defiance. But she had not been born primitive. She could not hate civilization. And this past terrible winter had brought her resolution to return to civilization into an even finer focus.

She tried with wiles and words to sway him from his dogged tenacity, but she failed. He turned deaf ears to her tirades. He swept away her resolutions with his response to her wiles and once again they lived in excited enchantment with each other. And with food for her child and herself, summer warming the air, and the ardor she found so desirable, she almost forgot her mission. But it did not last.

16

They moved, as soon as the buffalo meat was prepared to carry, back into a world of wild cliffs, rocks and canyons. It was a place as weird as a bad dream. It was filled with caverns and hollows and cracked and stained walls. It was a place that even the Dakota themselves called the "Badlands." There was no food to be found within its confines. No roots or greens that made meat palatable grew here. No game roamed the peaks and depressions except lean, hungry wolves that howled in the nights. The warriors were forced to leave its formidable protection to hunt. The place was wilder than any place they had yet been, and White Lily's only consolation was that she no longer was constantly under the guard of one of the women. She could, for the first time, enjoy some solitude. Time became as nothing, and she spent long hours sitting on the edge of some high ledge, pondering schemes that might soften Gray Wolf's hatred and suspicion of civilized man's ways.

She no longer wished death for him. It was not possible for her even to believe that she had once seriously wanted him dead. He had, in fact, become dear to her when she recalled the many times when he had been thoughtful of her comfort. But she did want him to relinquish this wild and primitive existence.

Boy was growing. He was no longer a baby, and when he playfully imitated the warriors she was horrified. She began to have horrible dreams of soldiers running the little fellow down, shooting him before her eyes, heedless of her screams that he was the son of a white woman. She had other dreams that there were feathers growing from his head in the place of hair and that regardless of her frantic plucking of them they remained, and she was unable to keep his savage heritage a secret. She dreamed, too, that he used his tiny carved ax to scalp his own mother. Too many nights she awoke, wet with desperate perspiration and cold with fear. Then she would lie awake and envision Gray Wolf himself cold and inert in some lonely canyon, unable to protect her from the eyes of a people who hated her because of her heritage.

One bright day when she sat by Gray Wolf's side and watched Boy at play with the other children, the game became rough. Boy was pushed off his uncertain feet and he pulled himself up to display a face distorted with fury. He raised his head and screamed the chilling Dakota war cry in a high childish treble. White Lily jumped to her feet. She ran to the child and chastised him severely. Immediately the delighted light in Gray Wolf's eyes died. He looked at her with an almost fierce expression before he turned and walked away. She knew that nothing she had ever said had stung him more bitterly than this impulsive restraint she had placed on his son. She was sorry—she was sorry and she was not sorry. She was torn with love and fear, with understanding and doubts—that were more terrible than her hate had been.

And more and more she took to the high ledges to sit alone and plead with her God to save them all—knowing that only God could do it.

Gray Wolf rode beside Lame Deer, deep in thought. This hunt had been less than successful. He was weary to the bone and there was very little to show for it. All the game that they had caught these past suns had been small game, and the people were in dire need of clothing and lodges. There had been barely enough to keep their stomachs from aching with hunger, and there had been few herbs and greens to supplement the constant fare of meat. Without greens the children would not be healthy during the cold moons. Without clothing and lodges they would surely freeze when the cold winds blew again. Gray Wolf knew he had been deceiving himself and he had been deceiving the people who trusted him. There was little hope that he could keep up this deception much longer. They were safe now in their camp in the Badlands. They would be found only by chance, and that possibility was very remote. Even brash Pony Soldiers turned back from its forbidding crags. But safe as it was, the food was scarce, and when the cold winds came it would be a place where neither man nor beast could survive without the proper shelter. He was ready to stay and play a waiting game with starvation and there was good and just reason for his doing so, but there was no excuse, no reason, no justification for the awful punishment of such a thing for White Lily and Boy. She was not of Dakota blood and Boy was her son. It was bad enough for the other women and children, for it was they who suffered most in this struggle between the *Wasicun* and The People. But they were The People and it was their fate to endure. Not so White Lily. Not so Boy.

Gray Wolf knew that instead of allowing his woman and his son to suffer again as they had suffered this past winter, he must lead them to a place where they could join their *Wasicun* relatives. He knew this and he dreaded it. He had known it for a long time now. He had known it as he had watched Boy play warrior games. And his heart broke. He had known it when he had held White Lily in his arms and his agony had been supreme. He knew that once he had taken them to the *Wasicun* he would never see them again and his torment was infernal. How often his heart had wept at the loss which he already felt. How terribly it wept even now.

Big Ankle saw it first.

"Look!" he cried and pulled his pony up between Gray Wolf's and his father's. High up on the ridge over their hidden camp rose a spiral of smoke. With sick dismay they reined in to watch. They waited, but no break came in the shaft of gray against the sky.

"What is it?" Big Ankle looked at his father and when he saw nothing but bewilderment in Lame Deer's face he turned to Gray Wolf. "What is it?" he asked again, the anxiety deep in his voice. Gray Wolf shook his head like a man who shakes a bad dream from his awakening.

"It does not come from the camp," Gray Wolf said, and his

words were flat and weary. Cold sweat broke out on his body and the bile of bitterness came up to fill his throat. "It is a signal," he said. "It is a *Wasicun* signal. I think now we must ride fast. Soldiers may already be before us."

They all looked down at the ground, hating to look upon their leader's shame, for they pitied him. They knew of his love for his *Wasicun* wife, and they knew, too, her aversion to them.

"You ride to the fire." Lame Deer took command in his compassion. "We will ride to the camp."

Gray Wolf took the order with gratitude in his heart for such a brother. He struck his heels hard and raced his pony over the ground.

"Wakan Tanka, hear me," he chanted as he rode, "let not my people die because of my weakness. Let Lame Deer ride before the soldiers." But Wakan Tanka heard the chant too late.

He came to the fire, which still smoldered. He scattered the embers with frantic feet. From deep down in the split came the sharp, staccato sound of shots. He knew that his prayer and his intention had all come too late. He sat down in the ashes and bowed his head. He sat for a long time and gradually the burning inside him turned as cold as the dust of the fire. He rose and walked as one already dead, down the trail she had used to bring him to this. Down near the end, where it led to what remained of the camp, he found her. She lay where she had fallen, but he saw that no wound had closed her eyes. She lay in a faint. He raised his eyes and there before him lay Boy, small and forever silent, in a pool of his own blood. His small carved ax was clutched tight in his outstretched hand. Close beside him lay Morning Dew and Big Ankle's grandmother. All around were the others and farther away, down where the trail led from the camp, lay Lame Deer and Big Ankle and the warriors who had ridden beside him such a short time ago.

It was deathly quiet and Gray Wolf stood, holding back the flood of despair that knocked at his heart. He heard her cry out and turned to watch her. She pulled herself up and screamed. He made no move to stop her, not caring if the soldiers heard or not. She screamed again and ran to the place where Boy lay in the blood that was turning black on the ground.

"They killed him," she cried and raised her arms as if pleading with him to undo what she had done. And somewhere in the back of his heart a small compassion stirred and died. He wished he could comfort her, but she seemed like a stranger. The link that had bound them was forever gone and there was no path across the angry waters between their worlds.

"Come," he said. "I will take you back to your people."

"No!" she cried. "I have no people. They have killed my son."

He almost smiled and from the abyss of his desolation the compassion stirred once again, but the door of his heart would not open.

"Come," he said and walked away. He did not look back. His weariness was too great. He led the way down to the plains and out toward the place that had swallowed up a nation of people.

For a long time he walked, slowly, deliberately, keeping his emotions locked inside rigid stoicism. The love he felt for her struggled to be acknowledged, but this last stunning blow had crippled it and made it an unwelcome thing. Yet even as he denied her his feet lagged in their purpose, reluctant to do the duty he assigned them. His step slowed until he came to a standstill, waiting for her to catch up. He waited for a long time and when she did not come he turned to look back over the trail. It was empty. He stood awhile longer in weary uncertainty before he began to retrace his steps. As he went anxiety began to stimulate the cold emotion inside him and his mind began to formulate pictures of waylays, *Wasicun* scorn and hungry appetites. He walked faster and faster until he was running.

He did not find her until he came back to the place of the awful day. She was there on her knees, digging into the ground with her hands. She was not crying. Her face was grim and bleak. She did not seem to see him until he took her arm. He tried to pull her up.

"Come," he said.

She pulled away sharply. "No!" she said, and there was something in her voice that was different from the tone he had come to know.

"No!" she said again. "I will not. I will not leave him like this. I will bury him."

And he knew she would not go until it was done. He felt a harsh pity for her torment and knew he would not tell her that the task was useless—that the lobos would reach the small body before another sun could shine. He envied her the ignorance and knelt beside her to help with hands that knew this labor so well.

The night was far gone before it was done and the wolves were skulking in the deeper shadows. She fell on her knees beside the mound and pressed her torn hands against the ground. She did not cry out or moan. She knelt as if in some terrible dream. He stood and watched and waited, vaguely annoyed at his patience with her. He knew her pain and could only envy her the newness of it. Finally he pulled her away and guided her stumbling steps up the trail. She did not protest.

For many days they walked, slowly because their strength was small. And they walked in silence because this thing was now between them. There was little food, but their bellies did not crave nourishment. They walked toward the place where he intended to leave her near to her *Wasicun* people—where he could leave her to start the forgetting that he knew his heart would never permit. But he was determined to be where he would not see her face and feel his heart twist away from that which was right. When they came to the place he saw that someone was coming from the agency.

It was Yellow Bird, old now with more than years, and her husband, and behind the pony they dragged a travois covered over and carefully wrapped. Even before he drew back the blanket Gray Wolf knew that it was Crazy Horse, his brother-friend —who had surrendered The People, and now his life.

"They feared him to the last," Yellow Bird's husband said, and his voice was hollow with his grief. "The soldiers cut into his heart because they feared Crazy Horse, my son, even when they no longer had cause to fear him. And they murdered him."

Gray Wolf raised his face toward the sky. A hard, aching knot in his throat twisted his voice mute.

"We go to bury him where none can ever find him," Yellow Bird said. "Do not surrender yourself, my other son, for nothing but death awaits you there. Keep every sun that can be yours, for they kill all who would lead the others."

Gray Wolf nodded. The old woman clasped him close for a moment and then turned away. Gray Wolf watched them go as she and the old man plodded wearily over the empty, empty land. When they had gone he spoke with a voice that was deep with bitterness.

"Go!" he said. "From this place you can find your own kind."

"I will not go," she answered. "I have no kind except the Dakota. My son is dead. The *Wasicun* killed him. I will go with you from this time on."

"Your son is dead because of a *Wasicun* woman," he said, "and my son is dead because of a *Wasicun* woman. Such a woman does not belong with the Dakota. This I have known from the first, but I would not deny my heart. I deny it now. There is no link between us from this time on. The link is broken. Go back to your people that you brought to kill my son."

She did not flinch before the words he had meant to make her flinch. She stood straight and determined.

"I will not go," she said again. "The link between us is not broken. It is there in a son that was and it is here"—she pressed her hands against her belly—"in the son that is to be."

He looked at her and saw that she spoke the truth and he wondered how it was that he had not known that another life was already in the making. Gladness leaped up before caution could suppress it and for a moment it showed in his eyes before remembrance blotted it out.

"I will not be father to a *Wasicun*," he said, and this time she understood his words.

"You will not be father to a *Wasicun*," she said. "You will be father to a Dakota."

She spoke the words like a Dakota woman. She stood before him like a Dakota woman. She even looked like a Dakota woman, but doubt wrestled with the gladness and meddled with his determination.

"I go to death," he said. "Maybe even before this sun shall set. Maybe not. But I go to death. I will not surrender. I am a Dakota. I was born a Dakota. I will die a Dakota."

"And I go with you," she said.

He looked at her for a long time, struggling against the longing inside him. He turned away, unable to speak, powerless to heed the protest of warning inside him. His ears closed to all sounds except the sound of her footsteps following.

And the gladness inside him blinded his eyes to the glint of the glass that was held to *Wasicun* eyes. And the winds were still and said nothing of the words that were spoken behind him, and his ears did not hear the sound of hooves that struck sparks from the rock that covered the land.

EPILOGUE

In December of 1949, as near as I can determine, Del received this letter from Derabus (Gray Wolf), her great-grandfather, who was living on a Seneca reservation in New York State where he had been since his capture shortly after the story ends. He had relinquished death for captivity to protect his wife.

Dear Del,

I'm writing this for your grandfather. He has never written a letter before but he wanted to send this to you this year. He dictated it to Frank and I'm writing it as Frank translates it. Here it is.

On the day which you will read this I will dwell in my mind of 26 snows ago. The dawn looked upon a barren earth that had been covered with a blanket of white during the sleeping of the sun. As the Great Spirit laid his fleece upon the earth to warm it, so that night he laid in my grandson's lodge a child, a woman child—to warm the heart of her father. He made this child fair of skin liken to her grandmother to warm the lonely heart of an old man, her father's father.

As is the custom of our people, I took the woman child in my arms and prayed to the sun to make her of gentle heart and compassionate spirit, as becomes an Indian maiden.

I was unmindful of these new times when a maiden may make her voice heard in deciding of important matters, and so I did not pray a prayer for a brave—that she should keep forever in the ways of her fathers. This I forgot, and for this I am an old man unfavored by the sweetness of a gentle smile from the maiden I named Milissa. Taken by her grandmother's people, she turned away from her own and forgot the teachings of her fathers. She claimed herself a white woman and lived their ways and among them. She thought the Indian ignorant and cruel and uncultured. But this was because of her guidance; that taught her shame of her people.

Was the Indian who fought for his lands, his home, his women and his children more cruel than the greedy white man who crosses the waters and fights for power and for plunder? He speaks of equality and democracy but did he, or has he, made practise of this in this land? Where then is the white man more than his Indian brother?

These tired eyes have looked on more than a hundred snows and summers. And they starve for a look upon the countenance of Milissa. This tired voice would speak to her of her fathers and teach her of her noble forebears.

Her very name is Milissa, which means Pure, like a blanket of snow, and warm, and comforting, and protecting. Yet she carries the name of a white woman, denying the love of her people. I would speak to this maiden Milissa, granddaughter of my son, daughter of my son's son, and sister of Canawaba, pride of the Seneca nation.

Derabus

Del did visit her great-grandfather, and stayed for six months. For the next twenty years her main commitment in life was the writing of this story, which she finished less than two years before her death in 1971.

—Robert H. Barton